Consequences

Cynthia Victor

Consequences

WHEELER
PUBLISHING, INC.
ROCKLAND, MA

★ AN AMERICAN COMPANY ★

Published in Large Print by arrangement with New American Library, a division of Penguin Putnam Inc., in the United States and Canada.

Wheeler Large Print Book Series.

Set in 16 pt Plantin.

Library of Congress Cataloging-in-Publication Data

Victor, Cynthia.
    Consequences / Cynthia Victor.
        p. (large print) cm.(Wheeler large print book series)
    ISBN 1-56895-904-4 (hardcover)
    1. Sisters—Fiction. 2. Sibling rivalry—Fiction. 3. Parent and child—Fiction. 4. Large type books. I. Title. II. Series

[PS3572.I263 C6   2000]
813'.54—dc21
                                                                    00-032505
                                                                    CIP

*For Dale Mandelman, Diana Revson,
and Ellen Seely—beloved friends.*

ACKNOWLEDGMENTS

For their very valuable help and support, a heartfelt thank you to the following people: Harriet Astor, Carole Baron, Richard Baron, Elizabeth Beier, Dr. Gregory Berk, Barry Berkman, Amy Berkower, Carolyn Clarke, Robert Counts, Robin Desser, William Dioguardi, Susan Ginsburg, David Klein, Glen Lewy, Susanna Margolis, Sarah Marks, Karen Mender, Susan Moldow, Diana Revson, Constance Sayre, Lorraine Shanley, Michael Skurnick, Dr. Joph Steckel, and Dr. Mark Steckel. Special thanks to three wonderful editors, Linda Marow, Audrey LaFehr, and Carolyn Nichols.

Prologue

Madison, Wisconsin

Claire Carlisle sat in her car, paralyzed with fright. She couldn't do it. She wasn't capable of it. Even if she could, she would never get away with it.

But she had no other choice.

And the time was now. Across the street, the heavy wooden doors of the Albert Leonard Preschool were being pushed open by what sounded like hundreds of tiny boys and girls. Claire watched as the children spilled out into the crisp, bright winter day. It was the early morning break, and the youngsters were spending their half-hour recess in the sunny school playground. Scanning a sea of colorful parkas, Claire felt another spasm of fear as she spotted Meredith, her two-and-a-half-year-old, heading for the swings, her bulky pink snowsuit impeding her progress. Despite everything, Claire couldn't suppress a smile as she watched the child awkwardly make her way, toddling with great determination across the yard. Only seconds later, Claire's older daughter, Liza, came tearing out of the building and ran straight to the jungle gym. With a rush of tenderness Claire observed her four-year-old, so lovely and agile, as she

1

swung herself up effortlessly to the highest row of bars.

They were both there. Now. *Now.*

Taking a deep breath, Claire got out of the car and crossed the street. The swings were closer, so she headed in that direction first, stopping just at the edge of the playground.

"Meredith," she called out to her daughter as softly as she could.

The little girl looked over. Her face lit up with joy when she saw who it was.

"Mommy, Mommy," Meredith yelled, running as fast as her little legs could take her toward Claire.

Across the schoolyard, Liza was in her favorite climbing position, hanging upside down by the knees, her arms swinging loose. As the older one, she had long been taught to look after her baby sister, so from high on the jungle gym, Liza quickly recognized Meredith's voice above the din of children playing. She looked over to see Claire gathering Meredith up in her arms, and began shouting out, waving wildly to attract her mother's attention.

Still holding Meredith, Claire took a few steps toward her older daughter. Even upside down, Liza could tell something was wrong. Why wasn't her mother smiling, happy to see her?

Claire tried to keep her voice calm. "Come down quickly, sweetheart. Can you do that for Mommy? I need you to come with me."

Claire looked over to the school building and froze. Liza followed her gaze. At the far end of the playground, through the school's first-floor window, she could see one of the teachers pointing to Claire and talking rapidly to someone. The principal's face appeared in the window as well.

Claire looked back to her daughter. "Hurry, Liza, hurry!" God, Bennett had actually done it. She only had a few seconds.

Liza was seized with fear. She started to grab for the bars, trying to right herself to see what was going on. "Mommy, wait," she cried. The school doors opened wide again, and Liza could see the principal rush out. Her mother looked strange, angry and scared at the same time. Something awful was happening. Meredith could feel it too and she began to cry, clinging tightly to her mother.

It may have been a matter of seconds, but they equaled an eternity Claire would replay in her mind again and again. Liza moving too quickly, losing her grip on the bars and slipping. The scream, that long fall, as if in slow motion, until she hit the ground seven feet below with a loud, dull thud. For a moment, silence gripped the playground with Claire, the principal, and all the children stunned as they watched Liza lying motionless on the ground. The spell was broken as blood began to ooze out across the cement from beneath her head, and the children started to scream.

Everyone in the yard rushed toward Liza, and Claire was momentarily forgotten. Meredith wailed in her arms. She desperately tried to focus her thoughts. If she stayed, they would never let her near either one of her girls again. Even if she could get physically close to Liza before they stopped her, she couldn't risk moving the injured child. I can't take her now, Claire thought. She has to get to a hospital. Some force began carrying her back, away from the schoolyard. Her mind shrieked out in protest: No, no. God help me, I can't leave her behind. *Somebody help me.*

But there was no one to help. Claire turned, and, clutching Meredith, ran blindly back across the street to her car. The school principal looked up from Liza's limp form just in time to see Claire drive off, Meredith beside her in the front seat. From where he was, he couldn't see the tears streaming down Claire's face or hear her wracking sobs as she sped away.

He looked back down to Liza Carlisle. She was stirring slightly.

"There, there. Don't try to move," he told her, stroking her forehead. He had to lean forward to catch her faint words.

"Mommy, is that you?" she whispered.

Chapter One

London, England

The little girl was all alone in the room. She sat completely still on the piano bench, an array of stuffed animals and toys piled high around her, as if to form a protective wall. She heard her mother walk through the foyer, listened as the telephone was lifted and a long series of numbers dialed. Unaccountably afraid at these sounds, not quite sure what was happening, she somehow knew that to hear, to really understand, would be dangerous. Safety lay in staying exactly where she was, shutting out everything else. Lifting her hand, she reached out toward the piano keys and began to strike a note, one single note, very loudly. She struck the key over and over until she couldn't hear another thing.

From where she stood in the drawing room, Claire listened to the piano echoing through the house. She wished John were here with her, but he had left for an early appointment. Before they had left America, she had admired her younger daughter's ability to be by herself. Even as an infant, she would lie alone in her crib, fully awake and contented, smiling at the mobile over her head or gurgling at the moving shadows playing across the walls of her nursery. When she wanted company, she would cry her baby request and then be glad to see the faces around her. Claire had been proud of her girl, private and friendly in just the right amounts.

Now the child's self-possession had turned into isolation and it was terrifying to Claire. Meredith was lost in her own world, unreachable. No, Claire reminded herself yet again. Not Meredith. Page. She must get used to calling her that. She sighed. Taking her to a new country, changing her name; how much more could her child tolerate? Already it seemed as if the pain of an entire family had made its home in one little girl. The sins of the mother, Claire thought guiltily. The sins of the father, she couldn't help adding bitterly.

She put the telephone down. Busy. Again. Was it Liza talking on the other end? Was she happy? Lonely? The sound of the piano in the next room was an ominous accompaniment to Claire's thoughts. She knew that Page would go on and on, harshly repeating the same tone, the A below middle C. Claire had been hearing it for months. How did she know exactly which note to play every time?

Oh God, what had she done to her? Forcing herself to stay calm, Claire walked across the drawing room. She loved to look out the broad windows, finding comfort in the luxurious green of London's Hyde Park, right across the street. If only the beauty of the park and the tranquility of the house could comfort her daughter as well. Claire turned her head, taking in the play of late afternoon light that dappled the well-appointed room, its glowing fireplace welcome in the chill of early spring. All of it was testimony to the peace this house could offer if the wounds could be healed.

But the child's silence was a constant reminder of how deep those wounds were, her sounds at the piano her only means of communication. She had begun talking at a very early age. Yet, since they'd arrived in London, she had refused to speak. Not one word. The only comfort she seemed to allow came from the toys and animals she crowded around her. Carefully, she would stack them up, adding an actual physical barrier to the ever-present barrier of silence.

And Liza. Her first child. How was she managing? Would she ever forgive her mother for leaving? Claire missed her oldest daughter so painfully she sometimes thought she would die. She never imagined that four months would go by without being able to reach her. Countless times every day, Claire would go to the phone and dial the number in Madison. But Liza never answered. Either the line would be busy or a cold, unfamiliar voice would tell her that Liza wasn't home. Claire wanted desperately to get on a plane and fly back there, but she didn't dare.

The two people I love most in the world, Claire thought sadly. I can't talk to Liza. Page can't talk to me.

She shook her head slowly. She'd made a choice. She'd give anything if she could have been the only one affected by it, but that wasn't the way life worked. If she'd known what she would have to give up, would she have said no? Claire forced herself to answer: I would do it again.

Chilled by her admission, Claire continued to stare out the window, the silence of the house punctuated by the disturbing noise at the piano. She looked at her watch, measuring how much time had gone by since she had last dialed, then walked back to the phone and tried one more time.

Good. At least the busy signal had been replaced by ringing. Someone was answering. She held her breath as she recognized her husband's voice on the other end of the connection. Don't say anything, she told herself. Don't even breathe. Bennett paused, then repeated his "Hello."

Claire put her hand over the mouthpiece. She was too afraid to speak, too afraid even to hang up.

"Claire, I know this is you." His voice was cold, terrifying in its quiet power. "I know you've been calling. I know everything that happens here. Save your money. Don't call again. Do you hear me? *Do not ever call again.* I know exactly where you are, exactly where to find you...and *Page.*" His voice was jeering. "Exactly how to go about taking *my daughter* back to her home. Did you think your feeble efforts to hide from me would work? It may interest you to know that I'm now sole legal custodian of both my daughters. The case has already cleared the Wisconsin court system. You'd be amazed at how they frown on a woman who steals one child and leaves her other bleeding on the ground. If you ever, ever call again or attempt to contact Liza in any way, I'll come to London and collect my younger daughter as well, and you'll never see either one of them again. Is that understood?" The sound as he slammed down the phone echoed through Claire's mind as she stood, motionless, unable to replace the receiver.

Finally, she hung up, battling to clear her thoughts. She would call Brenda Frakes, her next-door neighbor back in Madison. She'd been afraid to talk to anyone back home. What if she let their location slip out? But she had to find out if Liza was all right. Claire picked up the phone once more and dialed.

"Hello." Brenda's friendly American voice was immediately soothing to Claire. Her shaking began to subside as she prepared to speak.

"Oh, Brenda, thank God you're home." Claire was breathless with emotion. "This is Claire. I just spoke to Bennett. Please tell me, have you seen Liza? How is she?"

Brenda made her feelings more than clear. "How could you do it!" She practically spat the words out.

"You don't understand..." Claire said, her voice trembling.

"Where are you?" Brenda asked angrily.

Claire faltered. "I can't tell you that."

9

"My God," Brenda said furiously, "what kind of mother are you?"

"Brenda, please—"

She heard the connection being severed.

From her place at the piano, Page heard her mother's cry as she ran out of the drawing room and bolted upstairs. Later that night, the child saw the look of sadness on her mother's face as she sat down to dinner. Confused and frightened, Page was certain of only one thing. Her mother had to be all right or everything was lost.

The little girl looked across the table. "Mommy, did I do something wrong?"

Claire stared at her daughter, flooded with relief at finally hearing her speak. She grasped Page's hand.

"Oh no, baby. You haven't done anything," she said, her voice breaking.

How could she ever make her understand?

Chapter Two

New York City

Liza leaned forward, took a deep breath, and blew out the candles. There were fifteen children sitting around the dining room table, clapping and cheering, clamoring for a piece of the enormous birthday cake with the bright pink roses on top. Liza turned to Ellen, nanny and head housekeeper, who stepped forward to hand out the portions of cake and vanilla ice cream.

As the birthday girl, Liza was served first. She reached up to hug Ellen, burying her face in the woman's neck and mumbling "I love you" as they embraced.

"I love you too, lambie," answered Ellen softly, brushing Liza's long dark hair away from her face before going on to serve the other children. The older woman then stepped back to her place beside Marie, the maid Bennett had hired when he moved to New York eight months before. In crisp, fresh uniforms, the two stood behind Liza, ready to attend to the children's needs.

Despite all the noise in the room, Liza could hear Ellen talking to Marie. "The poor little thing. All those months while Mr. Carlisle was here in New York and we were home in Wisconsin. I thought my heart would break, seeing her so afraid and sad. She would cry herself sick unless I sat with her every single night until she fell asleep."

Marie said nothing. She took little interest in Liza or in the household beyond her immediate chores. At the moment, she was thinking about the work these children were making for her, messing up the beautiful dining room. This was no place for a bunch of screaming five-year-olds. If Ellen hadn't insisted on arranging the party, Marie thought with irritation, she could be spending this Saturday afternoon relaxing in her room.

Oblivious to Marie's indifference, Ellen continued. "I'm sure Mr. Carlisle had his reasons, don't get me wrong." Her disapproving expression belied her words. "But I certainly do wonder what they were."

Liza didn't want to listen anymore. She jumped up from the table and ran down the long hallway to the den where all her presents were now stacked in a corner. Her guests, classmates at the private school she attended in New York, followed her, laughing, fighting, sliding along the hallway's waxed wooden floor. Sitting cross-legged, Liza greedily tore open one present after another, ripping the brightly colored wrapping paper and bows as quickly as she could, only glancing at what was inside before moving on to the next one.

The magician Ellen had hired had gotten started late, and the party was behind schedule, so Liza was only halfway through opening her gifts when a stream of mothers began arriving to pick up their children. Liza remained seated on the floor, ignoring Ellen, who was calling out to her to come see her guests off at the door as a polite hostess should. Liza could hear the mothers talking to their daughters, kissing them, gathering their party favors. She was silent, rocking back and forth ever so slightly.

The last two children were playing with balloons, their mothers chatting in the hallway, when Liza heard her father arrive home. As Bennett greeted the women, Liza jumped up and ran to him. She threw her arms around his legs and held on tightly.

"What's this?" he asked, smiling broadly at their guests to indicate his amusement at Liza's sudden clinging. He knelt down to hug her. Liza pressed her face against his cheek, cool despite the heat of the August day. "Did you have a good birthday, angel?" he asked. She didn't reply.

Bennett looked up. "Thank you so much for bringing your lovely children to help us celebrate Liza's birthday. I'm only sorry that an emergency at the office kept me away. I hope we'll be seeing a lot more of you."

The women thanked him warmly and left with their children. Ellen stepped forward to lock the door behind them as Marie went to begin cleaning up the kitchen.

Bennett stood, prying Liza's arms from him. "What's the matter with you?" he demanded angrily. "Don't hang on me like that, ever."

Liza stepped back. The sudden changes in her father's mood were so frightening. It was just like when her mother first disappeared, before they'd come to New York. Bennett had spent so much time with her then, tender and loving as he had been only a moment before. They were always going out, ice skating, sharing popcorn at the movies, walking in the park. But as thrilling as it was to have so much attention from him, she didn't want to do any of those things. She was desperate for her mother and had to be dragged crying from her bedroom before each activity. Besides, she could tell something about the way her father acted wasn't quite right. If they were going to do all this, how come her father appeared to enjoy himself only when other people were around? When the two of them were by themselves, he was silent, seemingly unaware of her presence, or worse yet, annoyed at her, snapping, criticizing, once even striking her.

Then, there had come a day when all of that stopped. She never knew why, but they no longer did anything together. Bennett went his own way and Liza spent her time at home with Ellen. Soon after, Bennett left. Liza thought she would never see him again. But Ellen was there, taking care of her. A very long time later, the two of them had come here to this big apartment in New York to live with Bennett.

Having just had the special treat of her father's hug, Bennett's harsh words hurt Liza all the more today. Tears welled up in her eyes. She had tried so hard to be good all day, and not talk about the bad things again. But she just couldn't keep it in.

"Daddy...where's Mommy?" She blurted out. "Why isn't Meredith here anymore?"

"I've told you a hundred times. She's gone away," Bennett responded sharply.

"But why? I want her. I want Mommy." Liza began to cry in earnest.

"Stop it, Liza." Her father's annoyance was obvious.

Liza couldn't control herself any longer. Her sobs grew even louder. "I want Mommy. I want my mmmmommmmyyyyy!!!!"

It was as if Liza released all her anguish in that one word. Her vision blurred by tears, she felt rather than saw Bennett grab her roughly by one arm.

"You little monster. Didn't you just have a party with magic and cake and who knows what else? What do you want me to do? Your mommy left you, Liza. She took your sister and they went away." Bennett's face was red with fury. *"She didn't want you anymore, do you understand? She left you behind and she's never coming back!"*

Releasing his grip, Bennett turned and walked away in the direction of his study. Liza stood where she was, frozen to the spot, too stunned even to cry. She couldn't see him struggling to control his anger, fighting to restrain his urge to hit her.

Liza had no way of knowing that her father had difficulty even looking at her, so closely did she resemble Claire. For Bennett, Liza was a continual reminder of the greatest humiliation he had ever known, an unbearable embarrassment he couldn't erase no matter how much power or wealth he had. Claire's selfishness in running off was unspeakable. He had felt himself subject to curiosity and pity, an unacceptable situation for him. Not to mention the spiteful glee with which the news spread around town. Everyone seemed to take delight in this sordid story of how the mighty Bennett Carlisle had fallen. The scandal was only enhanced by Claire's stealing one child and abandoning the other. Claire had dug her own grave in Madison with that one, he thought. Everyone was shocked that she could do such a thing.

Bennett had made sure to look devastated by the loss of his little girl, Meredith, clinging to the rejected Liza in his grief. In truth, he found it difficult to summon up any feelings beyond his fury at his wife. The main reason he'd tried to hold onto them in the first place was to punish Claire when she told him she wanted a divorce. Privately, Bennett was surprised that Claire had left Liza behind, although if he had been the one to run away, he wouldn't have wanted to be saddled with either of his children. He sincerely hoped Claire didn't call his bluff by contacting Liza. He would be forced to back up his threat and take custody of Meredith as well. He had neither time nor patience for that right now. Things were going so very well for him.

Bennett had to compliment himself on his quick recovery from Claire's betrayal. After she left, he had immediately formulated his plans. He waited several months for appearance's sake before putting them into action. It was easy to turn over his daily responsibilities at the bank to others; as the owner, it wasn't necessary for him to be an active participant in the bank's everyday business. He flew to New York to select a suitable apartment. The duplex on Fifth Avenue and Sixty-seventh

Street had just come on the market, with an asking price of a million dollars. His offer of five hundred thousand, cash up front, easily secured it for him. Next, he hired an interior designer whose name appeared regularly in *Architectural Digest.* Bennett considered the man's fee outright robbery, but he knew the value of having the correct imprimatur behind his elegantly furnished rooms. He set down a deadline for the completion of the apartment—a demand that nearly doubled the already exorbitant decorating budget—during which time he took a suite at the Plaza Hotel. Once the duplex was finished and he was completely settled in, he sent for Liza and the housekeeper, Ellen.

The apartment, with its lavish furnishings, was only a building block in his larger plan. Bennett intended to secure a spot in New York society comparable to the position he had enjoyed in Madison. He knew, though, that his illustrious ancestors and Midwestern bank weren't going to help him here. By New York standards, he was small potatoes. He needed far more money, far more power, if he was going to be taken seriously by the people who counted.

He purchased a seat on the New York Stock Exchange and devoted all his concentration to increasing his considerable fortune. He wondered how he could ever have been content to be a Wisconsin banker, finding he was addicted to the market, with its frantic pace and constant risks. Financial disaster waited only one wrong step away, and Bennett exulted in his abilities to beat the odds. His steel nerves and razor-sharp instincts served him well, and he was already moving into a different class of wealth.

Bennett wanted to hear no more of Claire. Let her go, let her rot, let her die. She had brought him the ugliness of public humiliation, and he hoped that she was suffering every possible misery in her new life. He knew that being without Liza would tear Claire apart. If she wanted to make it even worse for herself by tempting him to take away her other daughter, he would be only too happy to accommodate her.

What was important was that he get on with his own life. And that didn't prove difficult for him. He knew how to make money, and he knew how to spend it well. Bennett had no problem enjoying the material fruits of his labors. And there were more than enough women who were delighted to satisfy him in every other way. The "right" kind of woman was always available to accompany a powerful man like Bennett to dinners, parties, and weekends. His hard good looks made him especially attractive as a partner and they found his voracious sexual appetite an unexpected bonus. Not often, but occasionally, he lost his usual control in bed, and a few women caught a glimpse of something far darker; his intensity turned to roughness, his sexual energy to force. Not that they would ever see more than a hint of this; he had other women for those nights.

Hearing the door to her father's study slam, Liza could barely breathe, so shocked was she by his words. Ellen ran to her, swooping her up in sturdy arms and hurrying upstairs to the girl's bedroom. Liza's tears were beginning to flow again as Ellen gently sat down with her on the large canopied bed and rocked her.

"Picture..." Liza wept. "Picture, please."

Ellen rose and went to the white bureau in the corner, pulling out a framed photograph from the top drawer. It was a portrait of Claire, Liza, and Meredith, taken on the grounds behind the house in Madison on a sunny afternoon. Claire was sitting on the grass, holding a sleeping one-year-old Meredith in her arms. Liza, two and a half at the time, was seated behind her mother, absorbed in the process of setting up a tea party; an array of miniature teacups and saucers was spread out in front of her. Claire was smiling straight into the camera.

There were no other traces of Claire or Meredith in the house. None was permitted. But Ellen was only too happy to keep Liza's secret in this case.

She brought over the picture, and Liza gazed at it quietly, careful not to let any of her tears spill on it. Several minutes passed before she looked up. Her face red and still wet, she managed a smile for Ellen.

"Daddy didn't mean that," she told her. "He made a mistake. Mommy's coming back. I know it."

Ellen could only return Liza's smile in silence. After a moment, she held out her hand. "How about a nice warm bubble bath for the birthday girl?" she asked cheerfully.

Chapter Three

Rome, Italy

Claire lay quietly in the darkened room, not wanting to disturb John, who seemed to have adopted the city's rhythm overnight. Amazing, she thought, watching him sleep, two-thirty in the afternoon and the only sounds seemed to be an occasional flurry of birds scurrying across the sky. They had arrived the previous afternoon, and she'd been surprised by the shops closed in the middle of the day, the tightly shuttered windows, the sunny quiet of the streets. John had explained that in Italy, most everything stopped from noon to four, and always had. There was satisfaction in the way he'd said it, the pleasure of coming back to a place he loved and finding it unchanged.

Her eyes roamed over his body as he lay on his side facing her. The gray hairs on his chest only emphasized the sinewy strength of his torso. When he was dressed, wearing his impeccable Savile Row suits, John looked like the wealthy, elegant businessman he was. Tall and slender, his molded features always set in a pleasant expression, he approached life unhurried, with a strength that supported rather than bullied those around him. But naked, bathed in the brilliance of the afternoon sun, he looked sensual and earthy. Rather like one of the statues they'd seen that morning in the Vatican Museum, Claire thought, tempted to run her hand over his well muscled shoulder.

"I dare you to." John's voice startled her.

"Reading my mind again?" she asked, smiling as she reached over, giving in to her urge to touch. "I thought you were sleeping."

"Why don't you close your eyes and take a rest, darling?" John said fondly, putting his arms around her and cradling her head against his chest.

She ran her fingers lightly over his back. "You're one to talk," she answered. "At home, I have to beg you to take it easy. It's that British industriousness. That's what brought us here, after all."

His only sign of assent was a gentle kiss on top of her head, making her feel like a sheltered girl. John had been modest in telling her about the efforts that were now being formally recognized by the Italian government. But judging from the grand reception at the airport, and the enormous apartment just across from Villa Borghese that they'd been given for the week of their stay, she knew that, true to form, his explanation had been unnecessarily humble.

He had been in Italy for several years after graduating from Oxford, happily studying architecture among the ancient structures. One afternoon, he received an odd telephone call. A man who identified himself only as Italo asked John to meet him the next day to discuss some important piece of business. Both mystified and amused by the drama, John agreed to go to a small café in the Piazza Navona for the rendezvous. When Italo Forzina, an ordinary looking man in a brown suit, sat down, he spoke for a long while about the joys of gelato and the fine spring weather and the beauty of the women strolling up and down the piazza. Patiently, John waited. Finally, Forzina made the reason for the meeting clear. At a time when the terrorist groups that were to plague Italy for the next twenty years were forming, they needed an unknown young man, a person who traveled easily from one city to another, to find out what groups like the Red Brigade were up to.

John had been stunned. As they continued to talk, he was reluctant. Why him, he'd asked. Couldn't they find someone with some experience in these matters? But Forzina had explained how they'd located John, and why he was so perfect for the task. It seemed that he'd been recommended by people back in England who'd known him since childhood, who understood his strength and courage as even he himself did not. And over the next couple of years, he had reason to find out a lot about his courage. And his nerve.

Not only did he infiltrate one of the most dangerous groups in Milan, but he managed to circumvent the kidnapping and murder of one of Italy's most beloved politicians, a man who'd endeared himself to his countrymen during World War II, and continued as the symbol of Italian democracy.

It was for these efforts that the Italian government was rewarding him so many years later.

"Recipient of the Prize of Rome," Claire murmured proudly, the vision of a brave young John so alive to her it was as if she had been with him to see it. No, she reminded herself, there had been another woman at his side.

"Do you think you'd have stayed forever if Anna hadn't died?"

John pulled away and looked at Claire. Could she be jealous of the young woman he'd married that fine spring day in Venice? Beautiful, brave Anna. She'd been with him every step of the way as he'd solidified his knowledge of architecture and design, the fruits of which would enable him to become one of England's leading hotel builders. He'd adored her, mourned her when she died, and yes, had left Italy when she was no longer there with him. But he hardly ever thought of her anymore. When he met Claire, his mourning was over.

Although he was taken aback by Claire's question, John was hardly surprised that Anna was on her mind. Later that afternoon, he was meeting Anna's father for a drink. Antonio Spirelli had called him in England when John's award had been announced, fiercely proud of his former son-in-law. Claire had been invited to go along that evening, but had begged off. She insisted the two men would have an easier time without her, that she'd prefer to see Rome on her own for a couple of hours. After all, she'd said, John was practically an adopted citizen, while she was a curious tourist. He hoped that was the real reason she chose not to come. Was it possible that she could doubt how strongly he felt about her?

He slid his leg between her thighs, pushing her satiny slip up until it was bunched around her hips. His hands began to wander over her breasts and down to her belly, her skin coming alive as he caressed her through the fabric.

The pleasure he was evoking coursed through her, but at the same time made her feel suddenly guilty. "Wait, John. Perhaps we should call Page." Claire's voice was breathless. "She's only seven, and she's never been alone before."

"She's hardly alone," John laughed in response, thinking of the large house in London and the staff who were undoubtedly monitoring her every move. "We'll call her later, I promise."

Claire couldn't stop her legs from widening as the excitement his hands were causing began to spread throughout her. The pressure of his knee was firm, and she held tightly to it, rocking slightly and feeling wave after wave of pleasure. Wearing her lacy underpants, only the flimsiest barrier to his touch, made it somehow even more exciting to her, promising yet a deeper layer of intensity.

John slid his hands underneath her filmy slip and played lovingly over her breasts. She felt his touch as if it were an ecstatic electrical charge, stunning her with the longing for more. After long moments, he pulled the slip over her head, impatiently dropping the garment on the softly carpeted floor. She felt her breath stop, heard a sound she never meant to make escape from her throat, as he moved his leg, pulling off the underpants that separated him from her. Suddenly, he paused.

"Surely you know how much I love you." He searched her eyes.

Claire looked up at him, her face lit with joy. She had never believed this kind of happiness existed. Never known that wanting someone, having someone, could feel this way. "Oh, surely I do," she said, holding him close as she urged him inside her.

Claire was happy to wander by herself, but John had insisted she use the chauffeured car that their Italian hosts had provided. As the over-sized Alfa Romeo rushed through the narrow, crowded streets, she was glad he had. She'd never seen traffic behave the way it did in Rome. Driving seemed to be a death-defying sport. Cars routinely ignored red lights, double lines, pedestrians. After a few minutes of sheer terror, she had sat back and begun to enjoy the freewheeling spirit of it.

Rome was extraordinary, she realized, savoring the particular cast of light that splashed even the most dilapidated buildings with a kind of magic. She was dazzled by the beauty of Bernini's fountain in the Piazza Navona, delighted by the dish of *gelato cioccolato con panna* she bought in the *gelateria* across the way. The men and women strolling the walkway were a stylish crowd, dressed in chic clothing that was beautifully cut, yet bore no resemblance to the equivalently expensive fashion of London.

She felt almost indulgent in her pleasure and decided it was time for more serious sightseeing. Asking her driver for a suggestion of someplace interesting, she was taken to the Basilica of San Clemente, located in the hills above the Coliseum. He explained that what seemed an ordinary, if ornately beautiful Catholic Church on its street level, was actually four levels deep.

Claire made her way to the very bottom level, the Temple of Mithras, where ancient cultists had gathered to worship centuries before. The space was dark and airless. She shivered in the small, shadowy rooms, her earlier pleasure evaporating. Suddenly, she found herself thinking about life before John. About Bennett. She wondered why. But even as she asked herself, she knew the answer. The beautiful layers of the temple masked a cold, dark structure within. Of course it would remind her of Bennett, of the living death John had saved her from.

All of it had been a surprise from the moment she'd met John in Madison. Her name at the time had been Carlisle, and she was well known as the wife of Bennett Carlisle, president of the Madison National Trust Bank, the fourth generation of Carlisles to wear that title. She was twenty-seven, a pretty young mother of two, a capable wife, an adornment to her prominent husband. Back then, if she suspected there was turbulence behind her impassive exterior, certainly no one else did. The only surprising things about her in those days were the streaks of silver in her lovely, black hair, unusual in such a young woman. To her daughters, Meredith and Liza, she was just Mommy—kind, smart, and always accommodating. When she met John Warren, this picture of Claire shattered forever.

She had been taking a graduate class in art history at the state university, keeping her hand in while the children were still small. At four and two, the girls really needed her at home, she felt, so she took just two mornings for herself each week, trudging up the enormously steep climb of Bascom Hill every Tuesday and Thursday. At the top, she would enter Van Vleck Hall, where slides of Rembrandt and Botticelli were displayed in a huge, unlit classroom. Other students would be lulled to sleep by the dim light and the intense heat of the room meant to offset the harsh Wisconsin winters, but Claire was fascinated by every moment of these lectures. The rest of her life may have been devoted to her husband and daughters, but these days were for her. She couldn't wait until Meredith and Liza were a little older so she could pursue her doctoral degree full time. Then she would teach, or better still, work in a museum. The possibilities were endless—that is, if she could convince her husband of her plans. But the more she loved her classes, the more resistance he offered.

"You should be at home with the girls," he'd say every Tuesday and Thursday morning like clockwork as she prepared to leave with him to go downtown. Tight-lipped, he would drop her on campus before proceeding to the bank, relieving her of the frigid walk from the university parking area.

Bennett was a cold man, his character aptly reflected by the abruptness with which the sleek, navy-blue Mercedes would take off just after she got out of the car. When they met while still in college, he had seemed terrific, a little formal maybe, but obviously well raised and so good-looking. At eighteen, Claire was much too naïve to see the hidden cruelty beneath his shetland sweaters and preppie chinos. She had observed that he was somewhat selfish, but his air of stability offset whatever fears she might have had.

When she considered the possibility of a life with Bennett, Claire responded almost desperately to its unspoken promise of safety. It was a feeling she longed for, one that had completely eluded her in the past. Joan McCloud, Claire's mother, had been from a fairly well-off Baltimore family. Her father, Stephen, was a responsible if not terribly successful insurance salesman. He was only thirty-seven when he died of a sudden heart attack. With the help of her family, Claire's mother was able to carry on financially, but emotionally she was never the same. Before her husband's death she had been a vibrant, attractive woman. After he died, she seemed to fade, not going out, not dressing up, an old woman overnight. She asked no more from life. Except one thing: the total attention of her only daughter.

Claire felt invaded by her mother's obsessive interest in her, and perfected ways to avoid the constant emotional demands. Inevitably, Claire had to battle her mother for the right to apply to a college out of town. When Joan died of an aneurism during Claire's senior year of high school, the battle was over, yet a small voice within her questioned whether she had the right to go to college, to enjoy herself on dates, in classes, dressed in the cashmere sweater sets her grandparents were more than happy to provide.

Marrying Bennett made her feel she had found a place for herself. The day that the twenty-year-old Harvard man chose her, only a freshman at nearby Simmons College, Claire felt so special, so lucky. He was handsome and tall, incredibly smart and worldly in ways she never would have expected from a Wisconsin boy. But, as she soon learned, Bennett wasn't just another kid from the Midwest. His family was wealthy, Madison's pre-eminent citizens. The first time he brought her to meet them, she was awestruck by their immense home and their formal manner. The Carlisle mansion made her grandparents' house look tiny by comparison.

Claire told herself she would get used to his family and they to her. They might seem standoffish, but that was just at first. After the wedding, they would warm up to her. She knew it would all be fine; love made everything easy.

But she had been too eager for the security she wanted, rushing into Bennett's arms without ever really seeing him. After their marriage, she saw him quite clearly. She remembered the day she had brought home the painting that had caught her eye in a gallery on State Street. She had been so sure Bennett would love the image of the two women strolling down a garden path; it had reminded her of Manet. Certain he would be thrilled, she had had it framed and hung in the dining room. When he got home that night, she saw how wrong she had been.

"What's this piece of crap?" he demanded, staring at the painting with disgust.

"I thought you'd like it," Claire stammered, startled by his tone of voice.

"Your job isn't to *think*," he retorted contemptuously. "This is a pedestrian picture by some nobody. It doesn't belong in my house." He glared at her. "When I want your opinion, I'll ask for it. This house belongs to a Carlisle. I trust you'll remember that in the future."

He acted like royalty, in his city and in his home. His love depended on her acquiescence to his every wish. He told her how to look, how to act, and, after their children were born, how to handle every detail of their upbringing. Whenever Claire showed any inclination to do something her own way, Bennett would punish her, first by withdrawing, then by outright insults. As she struggled desperately to think for herself, resisting his efforts to curb her independence, Bennett's insults finally turned into occasional bouts of violence. When she had shed the last vestige of innocence, she realized she had married a bully, a man incapable of love. Yet leaving him was unthinkable. She was a woman who honored her commitments, who put her children's welfare above any other consideration. She would stick it out. She had to.

At their first meeting, Claire Carlisle and John Warren had literally fallen on top of one another. It was a Tuesday morning, and Claire was on her way from class to the library. Bascom Hill was in its customary December condition of powdery snow over large patches of ice. John wasn't accustomed to dealing with the icy steepness. When he fell, he

31

brought the woman in front of him right down with him.

"I'm so sorry," he said. It wasn't until he had assisted his hapless victim to gather her scattered books and papers that he actually looked at her. Expecting a college girl, he was startled to see a lovely young woman gazing back at him. He admired the white streaks in her hair and her snow-white complexion, but there was a look in her light blue eyes that told him not to come too close. John sensed that she wasn't really a cold woman. The spark of warmth was there, hidden, but somewhere very much alive. He had seen enough people in trouble to know that this woman was afraid of something and was hiding behind an invisible wall.

Claire was surprised that the man she faced wore no gloves in the frigid Wisconsin air. She looked at his feet and saw the expensive leather shoes already ruined by snow.

"I'm afraid you haven't paid enough attention to the dress code," she said.

He smiled pleasantly, startled by her teasing. In England, his well-cut overcoat and costly loafers were entirely correct, but in this icy wilderness, compared to her sheepskin jacket and fur-lined boots, they looked silly even to him.

"My apologies," he said, his eyes twinkling. "I'm afraid no one warned me about your weather. I promise you, I'm most assiduous about the dress code at home, but Wisconsin apparently has some unusual rules."

Claire admired his British accent. "Are you from London?"

"Yes," he answered. "I arrived only this morning. May I buy you a cup of coffee to make up for being so clumsy?"

How friendly he is, thought Claire. She'd always imagined Englishmen were stuffy, but this man certainly didn't fit that description. Still, friendly or not, she had no intention of going anywhere but the library.

"Thank you, I'm perfectly fine. Nothing to apologize for." She gave a small wave, clearly meaning good-bye, and started to go.

"You know, I truly do need some advice," he persisted, his voice holding her.

She turned back and saw his imploring look.

"England is never this cold, and I'm not sure what I'll be needing here. Please come and share a coffee, and tell me what to buy." He smiled, adding mischievously, "Otherwise, I might freeze to death in your city. Of course, it wouldn't be your fault. Almost no one would blame you, really." He hung his head in mock sorrow at his own demise.

Claire began to laugh. Whoever his man was, he certainly was charming. "Okay," she said. "I give up. I have no intention of single-hand-edly destroying the Madison tourist business."

He extended his hand toward her. "I'm John Warren. How do you do?"

The two began to walk. Claire couldn't help noticing how attractive he was, how comfortable he seemed as he escorted her through the streets, asking questions about the various buildings and shops, commenting on the differences between America and England. Claire judged him to be about forty, although his athletic stride and easy smile made him seem younger. This was a man at ease with himself, she thought.

She led them to a coffee shop. Opening the door for her, John reflected aloud, "I should learn something about Madison if I'm to be of help here."

"Of help to whom?"

"I'll explain it to you if you don't think you'll be too bored," he said. Claire couldn't imagine this man ever being boring. He was so filled with vitality. And so warm. A wonderful combination, she thought. What a contrast to Bennett. Claire quickly caught herself. How terrible to compare her husband to a stranger.

"Now, you were going to tell me why you've come here," she said taking a sip of steaming coffee the waitress placed in front of her.

"And so I shall." John wondered what was going on in her mind. He'd noted a variety of expressions cross her face, but he was unable to interpret them. Suddenly, he felt an intense urge to know this beautiful, sad woman. An image of Anna came into his mind. There was no resemblance between the two women, but he remembered feeling the same way the first time he'd met her. He hated to admit this to himself. After all, as soon as he and Claire had been seated, she had removed her gloves, exposing the gold wedding band on her left hand. John was an ethical man, and pursuing a married woman was against everything he believed in. Why was he so drawn to her?

"You were saying..." Claire gently prodded him from his thoughts.

He kept his voice neutral as he explained that he'd come to Wisconsin to help out his old friend Max Holmes, the eccentric American he'd roomed with in public school, which in England meant private school, as he explained to Claire. Max was building a new hotel on Lake Mendota, and John himself had been in the hotel business for a number of years. He said this matter-of-factly, but Claire had the feeling that he was extremely successful. His assurance, his manners, the elegance of his clothing— it all bespoke a man who no longer had to prove his worth to anyone. How different from Bennett. No amount of success would ever bring her husband that air of confidence with grace. Oh, no, she thought. I'm doing it again. She nervously shifted the conversation.

"Let's talk about what clothing you'll need and where to buy it. Then I'll no longer be responsible for your freezing to death." And then I can leave you here and stop thinking those awful things, she added to herself.

John offered his pen, and Claire made up a list on a paper napkin: fur-lined gloves, fur-lined boots, a warm hat, and assorted other Wisconsin necessities. Returning his pen along with the list, she pushed her chair back and began to rise. John instinctively put a hand on her arm to stop her. The touch was friendly, not intimate, yet it made her feel intensely lonely. He saw her freeze. What was she afraid of? Had it been so long since she'd been touched? he wondered. And what kind of man could be married to such a lovely woman and make her so sad, so guarded?

"I really have to get to the library." Claire stood up.

If she's so uncomfortable, John thought, perhaps he should let her leave. No. Regardless of the consequences, he just couldn't watch her walk away.

"I do wish you would shop with me. I haven't had a woman's help since my wife died." He saw sympathy spring into her eyes and was embarrassed by his shamelessness. "It was many years ago. I'm sorry. I shouldn't have brought it up."

Claire couldn't help but respond to how much he wanted her to stay. When was the last time any man had looked at her with such open admiration? She'd make one stop with him, she decided. Besides, the university bookstore was on the way to the library.

"I'll take you across the street for gloves," she said, "then I'll go. I'm sure you can carry on by yourself after that."

But he didn't have to carry on by himself. They got caught up in talking about books, pointing out their favorites on the store's shelves. John was amused by the school's fascination for football, and by the time he'd finished quizzing the salesman about Badger sweatsuits and Badger underwear, he had Claire finding it funny as well. They were laughing so hard as they left the store, she found it impossible to leave him. It seemed natural to go on across the way to the student union and share a pitcher of the watery, school-approved 3.2 percent alcohol beer. The cavernous room they were in was noisy, filled with chattering young students, all of whom seemed to be dressed in black tights and loden green sweaters, de rigueur Madison fashion then.

Simply sitting there with John, so removed from her everyday life, Claire felt like a rebel. She found she wanted to know more about him. As he began to answer her questions, she realized just how special he was. Although he made only passing reference to his years in Italy, and was modest about his hotels in England, she saw that he was a man of substance, of strong character.

She knew she should have said no, but Claire was unable to resist when John asked if he might have a telephone number where he could reach her. It's not as if he couldn't find her anyway, she rationalized. The Carlisle name was hardly a secret around Madison.

It was just after nine the next morning when John called to invite her to lunch. Elated and frightened by what she was doing, Claire put on a silk blouse she'd bought specially for a dinner she and Bennett were invited to given by the governor of Wisconsin the following Wednesday night, so she would look just right. They met at the Edgewater, a restaurant overlooking the lake a few blocks from campus, and talked until late in the afternoon, way after the last of the lunch crowd was gone.

Every word Claire said seemed to have significance to this wonderful man. He didn't merely listen to her, he looked as if he felt what she felt, as if he were sharing her experiences. Perhaps, she thought, other women were used to this kind of attention from a man, but she couldn't remember a sensation like it. Being able to express her thoughts without fear of criticism, she found herself giving voice to the feelings that had so shamed her in childhood. She felt intoxicated. After seven years of marriage to Bennett, she had found a man who made her aware of parts of herself she had forgotten about, who infused her with his extraordinary vitality.

Never throughout her marriage had Claire even considered sleeping with another man. Until now. And worse, she knew it wouldn't stop there; a relationship with someone like John would never remain a simple affair. She told herself that she couldn't risk it. Her children. Her husband. Her responsibilities. John was careful never to touch her, never even to hold her hand when they were together. But he let her know with every glance, every caressing word, how much he desired her. Bit by bit, Claire felt her resolve slipping. Bennett's outbursts now seemed impossible to bear, a grim contrast to her happy hours with

John. Seeing her husband at the end of each day filled her with dread. Was he so much more brutal because he sensed her slipping away, or had he always been that way; had she been too beaten down to notice?

Less than a week after she met him, Claire knew she was in love with John. Still, it was a month before they touched. Sitting on a bench one day, a freezing wind blowing off the lake, Claire haltingly talked about her marriage, what a mistake it had been, how she felt compelled to make the best of it. John held her, finally, first in comfort, then in passion.

"We're meant to be together, Claire," he said gently. "We both know it."

The weeks that followed were the most difficult of Claire's life. John never pressured her, and, for her sake, he made sure that no one ever saw them together. In the mornings, he would go off with Max, who could hardly believe his good luck in having John to consult with week after week. In the afternoons, John and Claire would meet in an apartment he'd rented, spending long hours making love and talking under the eiderdown quilt.

Claire felt tortured by her double life, but the stolen time was magical. John was an experienced man. He knew how to please her, how to evoke her passion, then raise it higher still. Under his tutelage, she learned for the first time what pleasure meant.

John had been operating his London business mostly by telephone, only going back to England for two quick weekend trips, but after a couple of months, he told Claire he would have to return home for at least a few weeks. She was left alone with Bennett, with his bitter criticism, his obvious indifference to her and their children, and now, hardest of all for her to bear, his occasional lovemaking, which had always been hurried, self-serving, almost brutal.

For the first few years of their marriage, she had blamed herself. If only I knew how to please him, she had thought night after night. I'm too inexperienced. As time passed, she began to wonder. The men in the books she read and the movies she saw were nothing like Bennett. Then, with John, she saw what lovemaking was supposed to be. It was as if a door had opened and light was flooding a dark room. She was changed forever.

By the time John came back, she had arrived at the decision they both knew was inevitable. Although she believed that what she was about to do was wrong, she couldn't continue to live with Bennett. And she couldn't live without John.

On the Sunday night after John returned from England, nearly three months after they'd first met, Claire knocked on the door of her husband's study and went in to ask for a divorce. She didn't tell him there was someone else, she had no wish to humiliate him. Instead, she spoke of her sense of isolation, the emotional and physical scars he'd inflicted on her. She wanted no money. She only hoped he could accept the situation so they could part

40

with as little damage as possible to the children and to each other.

Bennett stared at her in silence. When she finally responded, Claire realized how blind she'd been to think an amicable parting was possible. He spoke to her with the contempt that only generations of money and power can breed. Completely calm, apparently unfazed, he ordered her to leave the house at once. The children were now his, and only his. Claire would soon understand what her wilfulness would bring; she'd never lay eyes on Liza and Meredith again. He would see to it. Madison was his city.

As Claire listened, she realized with a shock that he meant every word. And, in a moment of terrible clarity, she knew he could make it all come true. She ran out of the house, driving straight to John's apartment. Hysterical, she poured out the story. When she'd quieted down, he spoke.

"If your husband is as influential here as you say he is, there's only one way to hold on to them."

Claire looked up at him, her eyes filled with hope.

"You're going to have to take your daughters away from here. And you'd better do it quickly, first thing tomorrow morning, before Bennett has a chance to arrange court orders and the like."

Claire covered her face with her hands. Could she deprive even a cold, loveless man like Bennett of his daughters that way? There must be some alternative. Uncomfortably, she thought of her own years without a father. How could she do the same thing to her children? But she already knew there were no choices left. If she stayed, if she hesitated for as much as a day, she would lose her girls forever. This was the only way.

Friday morning, John, Meredith, and Claire—heartsick at having to leave her older daughter behind—arrived in London. Under assumed names, the three had first flown to New York, where John called in every business favor owed him until he came up with passports for Claire and her child to use on the flight across the Atlantic.

Claire hated to confuse Meredith by changing her name in the middle of so much upheaval, but she felt it was imperative they hide their real identities in order to keep Bennett from finding them; they became Mr. and Mrs. John Warren and their daughter, Page Warren. As she was to learn later, their efforts were wasted. Bennett's influence must have been even more widespread than she'd imagined. Despite the fact that he hadn't even known of John's existence, her husband had located them within months.

Bennett had made it clear he would never give Claire a divorce. But having begun her new life in England as Mrs. John Warren, she and John had to continue the charade that they were married. And so they had gone on that way, pretending to the world that they were husband and wife.

And Page, only two and a half when it all happened, wiped her life in Wisconsin out of her mind. As far as she was concerned, her father really *was* John Warren. London really *was* her home.

"Signora, please, they are closing up the church for the night."

The sight of her Italian driver shocked Claire back to the present. She allowed herself to be led up the narrow steps and around the dark, winding paths, until they emerged into the top layer, the ornate church with its modern information desk and comforting fresh air.

Claire was thoroughly shaken. As she once again took her place in the backseat of the car, she couldn't get the image of Bennett out of her mind. She ached for Liza, still dreamed of her other daughter almost every night. She only wished she could board a plane for America, disguising herself, somehow find the means to steal Liza away. But she was terrified to act. Bennett's threats were more effective than he could ever have imagined. She looked blankly out at the streets that had seemed so beautiful just an hour before. She was paralyzed with fear. If she disobeyed Bennett, she was certain she would lose it all. She'd already lost Liza. She didn't dare take the chance of losing Page and John as well.

God help me, she thought. *God forgive me.*

Chapter Four

"Break a leg, Patricia! Good luck, Francis!" Page watched her friends walk nervously onto the stage, their violins tucked carefully under their arms. From where she stood in the wings, she could see all the familiar faces, mostly parents of her fellow students at the Corcoran Music Studio, with a few sisters and brothers already twitching in their seats before the children's orchestra had even begun to play. Her own parents were right in the middle of the front row, John carefully taking in every aspect of the recital, Claire wearing a slightly nervous expression, primed for her daughter's performance, which was next on the program. With the opening bars of Mussorgsky's "Picture at an Exhibition," arranged especially for young players, Page too was anticipating what she was about to do.

She'd been so excited that she was surprised by the sudden butterflies she was feeling at the prospect of performing in front of an audience. As the orchestra neared "The Great Gate of Kiev," the closing section of the Mussorgsky, Page grew almost frantic. She approached the school's director, who was intently monitoring the orchestra's performance.

"Miss Corcoran," Page entreated, her voice a scared whisper. "Please, Miss Corcoran." She finally seemed to have the woman's attention. "I don't think I can do it. Please. I just can't go out there."

Deborah Corcoran looked at the girl, one of her favorite students. Ordinarily poised and outgoing, Page Warren looked frightened to death. "Page, dear, you're going to do just fine. Your piece is splendid." She put a reassuring arm around Page's shoulders. "Performing in public is difficult, but you'll be wonderful, you'll see. And right after your solo, you get to play the Mozart duet with Cecily. Then you can share the worry."

Page didn't look convinced, but Deborah Corcoran turned back to watch the performance. She knew her young student well enough to know that nervous or not, Page would go on and do just fine.

Sure enough, after the orchestra had finished and all the children had left the stage, relief marked on their faces, Page strode to the piano looking perfectly calm despite the feelings inside.

"She has nerves of steel, our girl, doesn't she?" Claire whispered to John. "I would never have had the courage at her age, let alone the talent." Claire's pride in her daughter was evident in her tone.

"She almost certainly is talented." John's admiration was as obvious as Claire's, but his voice sounded a bit doubtful as he added, "I'm not so sure of the nerves of steel, however. I'm afraid we may be confusing *poised* with *frozen solid.*"

John often wondered what Page was really

feeling. The girl's creative endeavors often seemed to be followed by self-doubt. She would withdraw at the first sign of trouble, sometimes appearing to question praise even as it was voiced. So filled with contrasts. Outbursts of energy, then that strange holding back. Claire seemed less aware of this. Of course, he thought, Page was always at her most outgoing with her mother. With John, she was more cautious, her natural affection more closely guarded. Was there still a ghost of her real father in those moments when she seemed to keep John at a slight distance? He often pondered this. There was no doubt that Page had forgotten her life in America, had blocked out the frenzied scene at the school, the confusing trip to England. He and Claire hadn't meant to keep it from her; they just never found the right moment to tell her the truth. Now, as he noted the child's emotional swings between darkness and light, John didn't dare push Claire to open up the subject. Besides, as far as Claire was concerned, Page had forgotten everything, and here she was, clever and happy and sweet as could be. Perhaps Claire was right. He certainly hoped so.

Just as John suspected, Page felt almost paralyzed until her fingers touched the keys. Then, as her hands played the short, stacatto notes of Bach's Two-Part Invention, followed by the fluid downward scale, she began to relax into the music, her enthusiasm taking hold. When she finished, the audience applauded loudly.

"Well done, Page," Miss Corcoran called out from the wings.

As the audience quieted down, Cecily Smythe, an eleven-year-old student at the school, joined Page at the piano. She carried a book containing several Mozart sonatas, arranged for four hands, and placed it so each girl could see her part. Careful to let no one overhear what she was about to say, Cecily whispered into Page's ear as she held her fingers over the keyboard.

"Just too talented for words, aren't we, Page?" Cecily's comment was so quiet, the object of her attack could barely hear it.

Page turned to respond, and Cecily struck the first chord of the Mozart, as if she hadn't noticed that Page's eyes weren't on the music. Aware that she had missed her entrance, Page turned back to the notes, picking up where she could, her face reddening as she made several small mistakes in a row. They're all angry with me, she thought, crushed. I never should have pushed myself forward this way. Everyone's probably laughing at me.

As the two girls finished playing, Cecily looked at Page, whose flushed face and brimming eyes told her everything she needed to know. Page didn't dare to look at Cecily. She couldn't fight back. She couldn't say a word.

John and Claire brought a single red rose backstage when the concert was over. "You were wonderful, darling." Claire hugged her daughter tightly as she congratulated her.

"Super!" added John, putting his arm

around both Page and Claire. "Now, let's go home and celebrate."

Page was quiet as they made their way to the car waiting outside and remained so while Claire and John ran through the evening's triumphs over and over.

"What was it Cecily was saying to you just before the Mozart?" Claire asked. "You looked so serious."

Page looked at her mother. Obviously Claire had no idea of what had transpired just a few feet in front of her. And there was no way Page was going to tell her about it now. She hated to upset her mother. It was so important for Claire to know everything was all right. Besides, what could her mother possibly do about it?

"It was nothing, Mummy. She was just wishing me luck."

As the three of them walked into the house, the telephone began to ring. John walked into the drawing room and picked up the receiver.

"Yes. Oh, hello, Jean-Paul. How are you?" He listened as the caller spoke for a few moments. "Yes, I see. Well, no, that's fine. No trouble at this end. Besides, I wanted Claire's advice on this anyway."

John looked apologetic as Page and Claire entered the room. "I'm sorry, but I'm afraid we'll have an extra person at our celebration. Is that okay?" The question was asked of Page.

"Of course, Daddy."

John understood Page's quiet acceptance to be polite disappointment at having a stranger interrupt the festivities.

"Who is it, John?" Claire asked.

"Jean-Paul Laplage. He was supposed to come into the office tomorrow, but he has to return to Paris early in the evening, so I agreed to see him here. I'd especially like to get your input on this, Claire. Jean-Paul is the architect I think I'm going to use for the Paris Warren, and I want him to hear your ideas." John had been preparing to expand the Warren Hotel chain for months. The Paris hotel would be the first outside England to bear the Warren name.

"Your suggestions are invaluable. You're the one who made the Brighton Warren work. Frankly, darling, I intend you to be my secret weapon in the expansion of the empire." Despite his playful tone, the look in John's eyes underscored his serious intent.

She looked at him skeptically.

"Come on," he said, "you've been working with me unofficially all along. It's time to acknowledge what everyone already knows. Just take a look at Jean-Paul's sketches. Ask any questions you want and, please, make any suggestions."

John walked to Claire's side and took her in his arms. "Darling, I want you with me on this. I need you with me. You're going to be wonderful at it, and I swear, you're going to love it."

From the expression on her mother's face, Page could see that her father was right. Claire's porcelain skin was flushed with excitement, her passion for her husband as obvious as her enthusiasm for the opportunity he was offering. Page was forgotten as her parents continued to talk. "Jean-Paul...Paris building codes...number of stories...height restrictions...." The words tumbled out. None of it had anything to do with Page.

They're so in love with each other, she thought, observing their animated conversation. So perfectly matched. And now they can be together all day long, not just at night.

John and Claire never noticed Page leaving the room and making her way upstairs.

Chapter Five

"Liza, I really don't think this is a good idea," Ellen said sternly. "How are you going to get home?"

"It's no big deal. I'll catch a cab."

Liza turned away from the housekeeper and continued brushing her hair. Sometimes Ellen's worrying could be a real drag.

"Where are you going to find a taxi that late at night way down there?" Ellen asked, picking up the robe Liza had dropped on the floor and hanging it in the closet.

"There are millions of cabs out at night."

"Not on Thanksgiving night in the East Village, there aren't. I don't think a fourteen-year-old should be out wandering around by herself at two in the morning. As a matter of fact, I don't think your father would even want you to go to this party. I can't believe all the other parents are letting their children go to a party on a family holiday."

Liza regarded Ellen skeptically. "Daddy doesn't give a damn where I go, and you know it. Besides, *everybody's* going."

"Let's talk about this later," the older woman said, shaking her head as she left the room.

Regardless of Ellen's reservation, Liza had every intention of going to the party that night. This was her first day back in New York in two months and all her friends from her old school would be there. She couldn't wait to tell them about Beaumatin. A fancy Swiss boarding school sounded pretty glamorous—as long as you weren't the one who had to go there.

Black pants, a big white shirt, and cowboy boots. She wanted to look perfect. Mentally reviewing her choice of outfit, she had a sudden inspiration. All the girls were wearing their boyfriends' ties, knotted loosely. She didn't have a boyfriend, but she certainly had access to a man's tie. As long as she put it back in the right place her father would never notice one was missing. Wearing only her white lace bra and matching bikini underpants, Liza entered her father's room and stepped inside his walk-in closet.

He has so many beautiful things, she thought, running her hands across the rows of neatly hung silk ties. The closet smelled wonderful, masculine like him, with the faint fragrance of his cologne. She looked over the dark suits hanging in a precise line. His shoes, each pair in its proper place, gleamed brightly on the floor. The white custom-made shirts hung along one wall, starched and ready.

It was rare for Bennett to return home from the office before seven o'clock, and then it would usually be just to change for some black-tie event. Liza took a startled step back when he opened the closet door now and found her there. The two stared at one another, Liza frozen with embarrassment. She watched as his eyes traveled up and down her body. A strange look crossed his face. Liza knew she was unusually well developed for her age; she could see that her own breasts were bigger and fuller than the other girls' and her hips seemed wider, more like those of a woman. As her father's eyes bore into her, Liza felt an indescribable sensation, a horrible, sickening feeling. Too late, she tried to cover herself everywhere at once with her hands.

"You look just like your slutty mother." Bennett's tone was charged with emotion. Then, abruptly, he whirled around and walked out.

Not until her father left an hour later did Liza emerge from her bedroom, this time dressed in jeans and a workshirt. She came downstairs to find Ellen ironing in the kitchen. As close as the two were, Liza couldn't bring herself to tell the housekeeper what had just happened. She didn't know why she felt so reluctant to talk about it. Ellen would be understanding. She was her friend, her ally. She was there for Liza. It was Ellen who enrolled her in art and ballet lessons, who got her ready for school each fall, who sat and talked with her about the things she was learning in class. That was, she had, before Bennett decided to send Liza away to Europe this year. Ellen was the one who took her to the hospital emergency room when she was eleven and broke her arm climbing over that wall with Timmy Peterson. Liza suspected that Ellen somehow knew she and Timmy were making out in the parking lot when those boys began chasing them. But Ellen never asked. Instead, she told Bennett Liza had an accident playing in the park. It was Ellen who had come for her when she got caught shoplifting in a record store the following year. This time it was Liza's turn not to ask what transpired after Ellen had talked privately with the store owner.

Try as she might, there wasn't much Ellen could do to improve things between Liza and her father. Bennett had even fired the housekeeper once when she attempted to intercede on Liza's behalf. Liza, seven at the time, had defied the rule against playing in the living room and accidentally spilled a glass of red punch on the sofa, permanently staining the white silk. So great was Liza's terror of Bennett that she began to sob the minute Ellen brought her into his study that evening. Ellen had understood that Bennett would spank Liza, but the duration of the spanking seemed excessive to her. When she could no longer stand the child's screaming, she stepped forward and tentatively touched Bennett's arm. Enraged, he told her to pack up and leave at once. He would find someone who knew how to take proper care of a child instead of letting her run wild like an animal. Hearing this, Liza was consumed with fury. She broke away from her father and ran through the apartment, pulling and pushing at the furniture, smashing everything in her path, crying hysterically at the top of her lungs. After that, the issue of Ellen's leaving was dropped, and Bennett had never again threatened the housekeeper with dismissal.

Liza slung one leg over a chair and picked up an apple from the bowl of fruit Ellen kept filled on the table. "What time is dinner?" she asked, taking a large bite.

"Your father said he'd be back by seven. I'll serve the turkey around eight. What time is this party you're supposedly going to?"

The telephone rang before Liza could reply. Ellen saw the girl's face fall as the caller delivered what must have been bad news.

"Is something wrong?" Ellen asked as Liza hung up the phone, scowling.

"Well, you win. That was Tracy. There's not going to be any party tonight. Are you happy now?"

Liza stormed out of the kitchen. Ellen smiled and rolled her eyes heavenward.

Thanksgiving dinner was a grim affair. Liza sulked, pushing the food around on her plate, while Bennett barely said a word. As soon as he finished his pumpkin pie and coffee, he retreated to his study. Liza spent the rest of the evening reading in her room.

By the time she got up the next day, her father had already left for the office. She and Ellen were alone in the house. Perched on a stool in the kitchen, Liza watched Ellen fold an omelette into a perfect half-circle, then took her plate into the dining room to eat. Liza knew the housekeeper would join her as soon as she was finished cleaning up so they could finish their conversation about the clothes she needed for the winter months in Switzerland.

Other than the comforting sounds of Ellen moving about in the next room, the apartment was quiet. Liza flipped through a magazine as she ate. Her head jerked up at the crashing noise that came suddenly from the kitchen.

"Ellen?" Liza called out tentatively. There was silence. The housekeeper had had a mild heart attack the previous year, and Liza continually worried about her having another one. She tried not to let Ellen know how frightened she was by the prospect, but those two weeks when Ellen had been in the hospital after her heart attack had been unbearably lonely for Liza. She didn't know what she would do if anything happened to her friend. Louder, she cried out, "Ellen, are you okay?"

No response. Liza's stomach heaved with fright as she jumped up, knocking the chair backward. She ran into the kitchen.

Ellen lay on the floor, her eyes open but unseeing. She must have tried to grab onto something for support, for she was surrounded by the broken pieces of a large porcelain plant pot that had always stood on the countertop. Liza rushed over and knelt down, trembling. The housekeeper's breathing was shallow and faint.

"Ellen, please." Liza grabbed her by the shoulders, calling her name over and over. She knew she had to get control of herself and do something. Think. A doctor, an ambulance. She rushed to the white telephone on the table across the room. She didn't know whom to call, how to do this. Precious time was slipping by. She dialed 911. Three rings. Liza was shaking all over, nearly engulfed by panic, when an operator answered. She blurted out the emergency and their address.

Hurrying back to Ellen, Liza found that the housekeeper had stopped breathing altogether. She had seen mouth-to-mouth resuscitation somewhere on television; desperately, she tried to remember what to do. She put her own mouth over Ellen's, pinching the older woman's nostrils together at the same time, trying to push air into her lungs. Nothing.

Liza felt the stillness of death all around her.

Not knowing what else to do, she continued her efforts. In the silence that enveloped the house, the only sounds she heard were her own rhythmical inhaling and exhaling. Finally, she stopped, and, after a moment, gently reached up to close Ellen's eyes. Her panic had passed. She lay down on the floor next to Ellen, wrapping her arms around her in a tight embrace, and waited quietly.

The ambulance drivers arrived nearly twenty minutes later. Liza opened the door and led them to the kitchen. As they lifted Ellen onto a stretcher, Liza put on her coat calmly. She locked the front door behind them as she had so often been reminded by the housekeeper to do.

Liza rode in the ambulance, holding Ellen's hand tightly. From the hospital lobby, she called her father's office. Jane, his secretary, told her that Bennett was out, and she didn't know where to reach him. She asked Liza where she was, and, ignoring the girl's insistence that she was fine, arrived at the hospital herself within fifteen minutes. Jane spoke with the doctors and must have made whatever arrangements were necessary; Liza simply sat outside the emergency room until Jane took her home in a taxi.

Ellen's funeral was held on Monday morning at ten o'clock. Liza was relieved but a little surprised that Bennett allowed her to stay, particularly given how strained he was around her since the incident in his closet. Other than agreeing to the delay in Liza's return to boarding school, he made no reference to Ellen's death until he passed Liza in the hallway Monday as he was leaving for the office. It was only seven o'clock, but she was already dressed for the service, wearing black from head to toe. Her father looked at her clothes disapprovingly.

"You are far more caught up in this than you should be, Liza," he said, gently tugging at one of his shirt cuffs to adjust it beneath his suit jacket. "It's not a good policy to be close to the help, you know. That will just lead to trouble in the end."

Liza regarded Bennett. She could see that he believed he was giving her sound advice. She didn't reply.

"Arretez-vous ici, s'il vous plait."

"Oui, mademoiselle."

Gravel crunching beneath its tires, the taxi swung into the driveway and stopped before the main entrance to the dormitory. Liza stepped out.

"Merci bien," she said as she paid her fare.

It was a bitterly cold day. She ran into the building and hurried up the stairs to her room on the second floor. She saw with relief that her roommates—one the daughter of an Austrian diplomat, the other a pilot's daughter from Nice—were out. She didn't particularly care for them under the best of circumstances; right now they were the last people she felt like seeing. Closing the door behind her, she dropped her coat and gloves on a chair and lay down on her bed, not bothering to take off her boots. She hadn't stopped to change before going to the airport, and was wearing the same plain black dress she'd put on the morning before.

Liza bit her nails and stared at the ceiling. Despite having had little sleep in the past twenty-four hours, she now felt restless. It was a little early for dinner, but she wanted to get out of the room. She decided to look for Allison and Melanie.

Liza had kept her end of the deal. She had brought back an ounce of marijuana, purchased on Wednesday night when she'd first gotten home. She wondered if Allison had delivered on her promise of two bottles of vodka. Probably. Allison had told her over and over how easy it was to get anything she wanted from her parents. A politician and his wife live in a world of guilt when it comes to their children, she'd explained to Liza and Melanie with great authority; they're never around, so they try to make it up any way they can. If they even noticed the missing vodka—which Allison was certain they wouldn't—she would come up with some excuse and they would be only too glad to accept it.

Her friend Melanie, on the other hand, had worried endlessly about how she was going to get two cartons of cigarettes. Liza could already anticipate how they would have to hear the whole story of Melanie's terrors in carrying out her part of the agreement, assuming of course she had even gotten them. Sometimes, Melanie could be a real drag.

Heading down the hallway, Liza tossed out a greeting here and there to a few girls she knew as she passed their open doors. At the bottom of the stairs she came upon a student sitting down and holding her ankle, her head bowed. She appeared to be in pain.

"Are you okay?" Liza asked.

The girl looked up. Although there were over three hundred students at Beaumatin, Liza recognized her. They lived in the same dorm. Fair-skinned with long, dark blond hair and big eyes, she was a year or two younger than Liza. Classes at the school were determined by level of ability rather than age, but so far she hadn't been assigned to any of the same classes as this girl.

"You're somebody-or-other Warren, a Brit, right?" she asked. "What's the matter with your ankle?"

"I'm Page. Hi," the girl answered. She was clearly struggling to maintain her composure. "I just fell down half a flight of steps and I can't walk on this leg now. Would you mind very much getting somebody?"

Liza moved closer and extended her hands. "Maybe I can help you get over to the infirmary so you don't waste time sitting here. Do you think you can lean on me, and kind of hobble along?"

She pulled Page to her feet and hunched down slightly so the younger girl could put one arm around her shoulder. The building that housed the infirmary was nearby. Watching Page wince in pain as they made their way in the cold, Liza searched for some way to distract her.

"Aren't you the one who plays tennis all the time? I thought you were this great athlete. Pretty dumb, falling down stairs," she said.

"Yes, absolutely dumb," Page managed, smiling weakly.

"Your accent kills me, you know. Do you stand around and practice talking like that?" Liza tightened her grip around Page's waist.

"I—ohhh, this bloody ankle. I hope it's only twisted."

Liza left Page at the infirmary, hurrying back to the dining room to sneak out some of the biscuits and fruit that had been set up for dinner, then returning to help Page maneuver on crutches to their dorm. The ankle wasn't broken, but it was badly sprained, and Page was grateful to have Liza's help in making it up the three flights of steps to her own room. Both ravenous by this point, they shared Liza's food, along with two candy bars she brought up from her secret stash of food.

As they ate, they talked. This was Page's second year at Beaumatin, so she was able to answer Liza's questions about what she could expect during the rest of the school year. Page was taken aback by Liza's curiosity about the rules, as it was obvious she was only interested in how she might break them. Liza was in turn amused by Page's naïveté. What do you expect from a thirteen-year-old? She asked herself.

"Time to run, chickadee," Liza said finally, standing up. "See you around."

"Don't go," Page blurted out. Embarrassed, she collected herself. "I mean, well, thank you ever so much for everything you did for me tonight. You were great."

"Hey, it was nothing. So long." Liza gave a little wave and left. It was too late to look for her friends now. She set off to get some studying done before lights out.

The next day, Liza didn't meet up with Allison and Melanie until after lunch. All the girls had assigned seats in the dining room, which were rotated every week. Melanie was at the headmistress's table this week, the most dreaded position, while Allison and Liza were at the back of the room. The three met each other outside once the meal was over and headed for the lounge in the library, where they sat huddled together at a table in the corner. Allison and Melanie listened with morbid fascination to the story of Ellen's death. Melanie's pale face grew even paler as Liza explained how she had held Ellen in her arms while she waited for the ambulance. Liza's description was high on drama, but made no mention of her own feelings. Allison fiddled nervously with her long, straight blond hair. They were silent for a while until Liza changed the subject.

She turned to Allison. "Did you get it?" she whispered.

"Of course. No problem. I *told* you it wouldn't be," Allison whispered back, relieved to be talking about something else. "And you?"

"It's in my laundry bag."

Melanie leaned forward. "You wouldn't believe how hard it was to get the cigarettes. And then I swear I thought my mother found them when I came home on Saturday and she—"

"Hello, Liza."

The three girls looked up, startled. Page was standing before them, leaning on crutches and smiling.

"Oh, hi," Liza answered, off-handedly. She was embarrassed at having this younger girl act so familiar in front of her friends. There was a pause.

"Well, see you around," Page said brightly. The American expression sounded awkward spoken in a British accent, as Liza recognized her own words from the night before. She watched Page make her way on the crutches, hurrying a bit to catch up with her own friends. Liza knew this crowd of girls. They were the popular ones, the girls who were good at everything. They got the best grades, they did well in every sport. So Page was one of them, one of the perfect ones. She no doubt had this incredibly great mom and dad, too. Liza felt a momentary pang. She turned back to the two girls who sat waiting for an explanation of this encounter.

"Gotta go. What do you say to Lausanne tomorrow afternoon? A little trip to town, a little fun. I say, yes, let's do it!" Liza stood and picked up her books. "Meet you at one outside French History."

It was nearly two o'clock the next afternoon by the time the three girls had gathered what they needed and hitched a ride into downtown Lausanne. They knew they only had another couple of hours if they were going to make it back to school without detection. At their request, their ride let them off near the train station, and they headed straight for the ladies' room. There, they changed their blouses and put on the stockings, short skirts, and heels they had brought along. It took another half hour to fix their hair and apply makeup.

They walked up and down the streets, stopping to look in the shop windows as they tried to ignore the biting winter wind. With only sheer stockings on their legs, they were feeling chilled through and through by the time they came upon the Baron, a small but elegant old hotel.

"Let's go in and have a drink," suggested Allison. She and Liza looked at each other, their eyes lighting up.

"Are you serious? We'll get thrown out," Melanie said.

"Don't be such a baby, Melanie," Allison retorted. Liza stepped into the hushed lobby, confidently leading the way through the crowded bar to a small table surrounded by three deep wing chairs. They sat down as a waiter, a man in his sixties, approached.

"Bonjour, mesdemoiselles," he greeted them in a bored voice. *"Vous desirez?"*

"Trois Sept-et-Sept, s'il vous plait," responded Liza, wondering if the French term was actually something different.

He took a long look at the three of them. *"Pardon?"* he said flatly.

Liza wasn't sure they would have Seagram's Seven in Europe. Maybe they didn't even have 7-Up in Switzerland. Liza had never ordered a drink in a bar here before. She tried to remain composed.

"Oui, alors, vodka et tonic, trois."

"Excusez-moi, mademoiselle, mais quel age avez-vous?"

Melanie was beginning to fidget in her seat. Allison jumped into the conversation.

"We're eighteen. *Nous avons dix-huit ans,*" she snapped, trying to appear irritated.

The waiter stood there for a moment, considering them. Then, with a slight shrug of his shoulders, he turned away. *"D'accord, trois vodka tonic."*

The three girls looked at each other. Melanie clapped a hand over her mouth to prevent her giggle from escaping.

"I can't believe it. He's just going to bring them," breathed Allison.

Melanie sat back and smoothed her skirt. "Actually, you know, they're much more casual about drinking in Europe," she informed them in her most grown-up voice. "They give watered wine to little children at dinner."

"There were places we could go back in

New York to drink," Liza said. "All the kids went to the same ones, and they never bothered us. My friends and I would go to this bar every Saturday night and drink as many Seven-and-Sevens as we wanted."

Melanie was shocked. "What did you tell your parents? I mean, your father."

Their drinks arrived. Taking several quick sips from hers, Liza responded. "Oh, he never asked, and if he had, I would have just said I was going to somebody's house."

"Boy, are you lucky," Allison said, clearly impressed.

Liza smiled and took another sip of her drink. She scanned the room and pointed out two men deep in conversation a few tables away. They looked to be in their late twenties. "What do you say, girls?" she asked her friends with a wink. "Want a date with them?"

The three whispered and laughed about all the other patrons in the bar until they were ready to leave. Slightly drunk, they paid their check and made their way out of the hotel. It was getting dark.

Suddenly Allison called out, "Hey, it's Madame Rousseau's car."

They ran back into the hotel and looked out through the glass door. All three recognized the green Mercedes driven by the school's math teacher as it passed in front of the hotel. They could see the woman talking as she drove, animatedly gesturing with one hand to the student seated by her side. The girl was obviously one of the younger students, and it was a rare treat for any of them to get off campus. Only the oldest girls at school were permitted to go downtown, and that was limited to one afternoon a week. Passing through the administration building one day, Liza had seen them preparing for their outings, lining up in the building's entranceway for inspection by Madame Lenotre. All the girls would have to parade past the headmistress, who would determine that they were dressed as ladies should be. Liza had been fascinated to see Mme. Lenotre bend down and pull a chunk of skin on each girl's calf between her thumb and forefinger. Then she would pinch the girl's leg, *hard*, to ascertain that she was indeed wearing stockings. Some of the girls winced or bit their lip, but none made a sound.

Melanie turned to Liza. "Hey, isn't that the one who said hello to you yesterday at the library?"

"Yes, that's her," Liza answered. That Page girl again. So now she was a teacher's pet as well. Loved and adored by one and all.

Liza wasn't used to wearing high heels, and her feet were beginning to hurt. She was also getting a headache from the drink. "Let's go home," she said tiredly.

In the next couple of weeks, Liza came across Page Warren often. She wondered why she had never really noticed her before. Page always seemed to have people around her, was always in the center of things, looking so calm, so in control. She invariably acted happy to see Liza and hurried over to speak to her when she could. Her ankle was healing quickly, and she told Liza repeatedly how much she had appreciated her help that night.

Liza's feelings toward Page were mixed. She couldn't help but like her, as it was obvious everyone else already did. Page was so friendly, so eager to show she was interested in you and whatever you were doing. Judging by the girls who hung around with her, she was able to get along with just about anybody; it wasn't easy to win acceptance from that crowd.

At the same time, Liza resented this girl, a thirteen-year-old who seemed so on top of it all, when everything was such a struggle for her. Not the classwork—that was a breeze. But everything else. You could just tell that Page had a wonderful life both in and out of school. Humiliated by her own jealousy, Liza found it easier to keep the younger girl at a distance.

Both Page and Liza were among the girls permitted to attend the school's annual Christmas dance. This occasion was the one time Beaumatin's students were officially allowed to socialize with the boys from Le Mont d'Or, a boarding school nearby. Only those students who had maintained a certain grade-point average could go, and it was the major social event of the year. The girls spent weeks beforehand talking about what they planned to wear, how they would do their hair, and if they could get away with wearing more makeup than the school's limit of lipstick and mascara.

The dance was on a Friday night. In a raspberry-colored dress, her long hair flowing softly about her shoulders, Liza wasn't entirely aware of the sensual aura she created. She knew she looked pretty. But she didn't yet understand the power she held, the sexual vitality that flashed in her eyes and signaled from her figure. Tonight, she stood off to one side of the large, gaily decorated hall, talking with Allison and swaying her hips in time to the music. Many of the boys were watching her every move. But they hung back, afraid to approach her.

As she and Allison talked, Liza surveyed the scene. It was crowded and hot. Those professors who had drawn chaperone duty were either keeping watch by the exits or making their way through the couples on the dance floor, checking to be sure everyone was behaving according to the rules. On the other side of the room, she spotted a tall, dark-haired boy who looked about sixteen. He sure is sexy, she thought.

Allison followed Liza's gaze. "He's too old for us, Liza," she whispered. "He only goes for girls over sixteen. I'm surprised he's even here. Besides, everybody's madly in love with him."

Well, if someone's going to have him, why shouldn't it be me? Liza thought defiantly. "God, isn't he incredible? What's his name?" she asked aloud.

"Gerard. He's from Paris."

Liza wanted to study him further. "Could you get us some more punch, Ali?" she said, holding out her empty glass. "I don't want to leave this spot."

Allison, annoyed, took Liza's glass and walked toward the punch bowl at the far end of the room. Without the distraction of her friend, Liza was able to focus more intently on Gerard. Unconsciously tapping her foot, she contemplated what her next step should be. The direct approach was probably her best shot, she decided, and braced herself to cross the room.

Seeing Gerard start to move away from where he stood, Liza hesitated. Slowly, casually, he walked toward a group of girls. Liza recognized them: Page and her friends. Page wore a simple powder-blue knit dress, and had pulled her hair up in a loose bun. She was smiling as one of the girls whispered something into her ear.

Liza couldn't hear any of what was being said from so far away, but she could see Gerard speak to Page and then walk with her out onto the dance floor. She watched as Gerard put his arms around Page and held her close, far closer than the rules permitted. Page looked nervous. Having stepped onto the floor in the middle of a song, they had only a minute or so before it ended. Gerard put his hand on Page's cheek and looked into her eyes. He spoke to her, their faces so close, their lips were almost touching. Liza stood transfixed. Then, he took Page's hand and led her toward the exit, weaving in and out of the other couples still on the dance floor. Although they were in full view of all the chaperones, it seemed to Liza that she was the only one who had seen them go.

She turned her head away to find Melanie standing next to her.

"Don't sneak up on me like that," Liza snapped.

"He took her *outside*." Obviously having witnessed the same scene Liza had, Melanie was gleefully scandalized. Leaving the dance with a boy was strictly forbidden, punishable by expulsion.

"Oh, who cares?" retorted Liza. She ran her hands through her hair. "Come on, when are we going to start having some fun here? This dance is boring."

The blond one in the tweed jacket over there. He looked pretty good. Liza walked over and gave him a radiant smile. "It's my turn to dance with you," she said sweetly, noting the disapproving glare of Madame Werthe. Liza guessed she would hear about her behavior the next day. The school unequivocally disapproved of such forwardness on the part of their girls.

The boy turned out to be a seventeen-year-old from Texas, the son of some oil tycoon. Shy and a little overwhelmed by Liza, he was nontheless delighted by her attention. They danced for a while, then retreated to a corner. Donald was from a very strict family, and he was enthralled by Liza's stories of the freedom she had had back in New York.

She felt very much in control of the situation. Leaning her head lightly against Donald's shoulder, she smiled up at him. This was going to be a night to remember. "Do you want to come back with me to my room?" she asked him.

Donald was stunned by the offer, but he quickly regained his composure. Surreptitiously, hoping the chaperones wouldn't see, he put his arm around Liza's waist.

"You are one very pretty girl." His deep southern drawl struck Liza as humorous, and she had to suppress a giggle. But her request seemed to have freed him from his faltering shyness. "Let's go," he said eagerly.

Liza told him she would go on ahead so they wouldn't be seen leaving the gym together, and hurried back to her dorm. Few girls were around. Those who weren't at the dance were either studying or sleeping, avoiding one another's disappointment at not being part of it. Liza knew she was safe bringing Donald back with her; one of the roommates was at the library tonight, the other at the dance. She had barely gotten inside her room when Donald knocked on the door.

Awkwardly, they sat on the edge of Liza's bed.

"I really like you, Liza," Donald offered in a husky voice.

She turned to face him. He was three years older than she, but he looked young and a little scared. Tentatively, he leaned forward and kissed her. Closing her eyes and not taking her mouth away from his, she shifted closer to him. He eased her down on the bed, their feet still touching the floor. Liza put both arms around him. She wanted to seem passionate, to be passionate. She parted her lips and ran her tongue gently along his still-closed mouth. He pulled back slightly for a second, then responded by opening his mouth to her.

Slowly, he brought one hand up to touch her breast. Meeting no resistance, he reached around to feel for her zipper. Liza obliged by raising herself up a bit, enabling him to open the back of the dress. He tugged at her bra, obviously anxious to undo it before she changed her mind. Liza opened her eyes and saw that his own were closed while he continued fumbling with the clasp, rhythmically thrusting his tongue inside her mouth the whole time. An unpleasant feeling, almost nausea, hit Liza suddenly as he reached around and unsnapped the bra to expose the soft white skin and pale nipple of Liza's breast. He looked down at her as he cupped its fullness with his hand. He was trembling. Liza shut her eyes as she heard him groan with pleasure. They kissed for another few minutes as Donald continued to stroke her breast. Then he pulled his lips from hers and started to move them downward. Liza sat up. Suddenly, she found him revolting.

"You have to go now. I want you to go," she said, adjusting her bra.

Donald was flushed. He swallowed and took a deep breath. "Okay, sure. Can I see you again?"

"I don't know, you'll have to wait and find out," she replied as airily as she could. She rose and reached around to zip up her dress.

Donald's eyes shone. "You're wonderful. I'll write to you and you could write to me. What do you say?"

Liza didn't want him in the room for another second.

"Yes, definitely. But you really have to leave or we could both get in a lot of trouble."

She endured a few more kisses as she ushered him toward the door. Well, she had brought a boy back to the dorm and made out with him. The other girls would die of envy. All in all, it had been a pretty successful night, she told herself, kicking off her shoes.

The gym looked quite different the next time Liza was there, all the decorations from the dance removed and the cavernous room back to its echoing emptiness. On Thursday mornings, Liza and the other American students played volleyball. The game was unsupervised, just a weekly get-together that had become traditional a few years back. The European girls regarded the game as beneath them, a vulgar sport brought to Beaumatin by the Americans. Their attitude made the American students all the more determined that nothing interfere with their weekly game.

Liza enjoyed playing volleyball and looked forward to these workouts. After that day's game, she stopped to help put away the net before going to the locker room. As they dressed, most of the girls were discussing their plans for Christmas vacation, only two days away. Liza was spending hers at home. On those school breaks when she had gone away, it had always been with friends and their families. Ellen would always take care of the arrangements. Bennett never left New York if he could help it, and she knew he hadn't planned any kind of excursion for her this Christmas. It seemed as if the majority of Beaumatin's students were going to some exotic spot, but Liza didn't mind not being part of the competitive chatter. She would go home and sort through Ellen's belongings. Her father had reluctantly agreed to leave everything just as it was until she came back to attend to it. She was looking forward to the task, as if it meant spending some more time with Ellen.

Liza knew that Melanie was going on a Caribbean cruise with her family and was so excited she could hardly wait for the next two days to pass. She'd told Liza and Allison that she had the whole thing planned out. Her first day at home would be spent shopping for great clothes to take along. Then she would meet the members of the ship's crew and have a romantic adventure she could remember for the rest of her life. Allison was sick with jealousy. Her parents were taking her and her little brother to Disneyland for a week. The day she found out, she had greeted Liza with the words, "Shall I kill myself now or later? I'm so embarrassed I want to die."

Neither Melanie nor Allison were at the

volleyball game this morning. Liza wondered what had happened to them. She knew they didn't particularly love the sport, but they usually showed up anyway to be part of things. The locker room was emptying out, and noticing she had only ten minutes to get to World Literature class, Liza began to hurry. She was reaching for her coat when Page Warren came around the far corner into the row of lockers where Liza stood. She instantly recalled the image of Page and that Gerard boy together at the dance. A strange feeling swept over her, a combination of anger and shame at her own actions with Donald that night. There was no one else in the gym now, and standing so far down the row, Page didn't see Liza right away. The younger girl stamped the snow off her boots and put her books down on the long bench.

As Liza moved to slip on her coat, Page turned, her face lighting up with a smile when she recognized who was standing there.

"Hello. I haven't seen you anywhere this week," she called out.

"I've been around," Liza answered quietly.

Page began to walk down the row toward her. Liza reached into her locker for her muffler. She resolved not to let Page see she was upset in any way.

"So what are you doing here now?" Liza asked her.

"Tennis. My practice is always on Wednesday mornings, but we had to switch some things around this week because Madame Mignon was sick."

"Did you enjoy the dance?" There was a faint touch of sarcasm in Liza's voice. As soon as she said the words, she regretted them. Why was she torturing herself, she wondered.

Page suddenly turned pale. "Oh, the dance," she said. "Well, I...well..." She was clearly growing more unsettled with every word.

Liza was completely taken aback by Page's reaction. Something must be very wrong. "What's the matter?" she asked, feeling a surge of both sympathy and outright curiosity.

"I don't know who to talk to. Maybe you can help me. I just have to tell somebody." Page's agitation was increasing. "I feel really bad."

Liza was amazed. She had never seen Page act as if everything weren't absolutely wonderful, much less be so completely rattled.

"It's been bothering me all week, even though I keep telling myself I'm being silly. But, well, at the dance there was this boy. His name was Gerard."

Liza stiffened but said nothing as Page continued.

"He was very cute and very nice. We danced and then we went outside. I know you're not supposed to do that and it was wrong. He was just so wonderful, and he was older. I wanted him to think I was, you know, sophisticated like the older girls...like you."

Page paused. Slowly, she began to pull her gloves off, one finger at a time. "When we got outside, it was freezing. He gave me his jacket to wear and we ran behind the Science building where there's that little area. You know the one? Anyway, we were there and he began to kiss me. And I liked it." Page's face was red. "So we kissed some more. And then...he put his hand..."

Watching Page's eyes fill up with tears, Liza was getting frightened. "Page, what happened?"

"He put his hand under my dress, in my underpants. I kept pushing him away."

"Did you do it?" Liza tried to sound nonchalant. She nearly held her breath, waiting for the answer.

Page looked at her, shocked. "No, of course not. But I guess he thought I was going to. I should have stopped him long before all this. I should never have left the dance. I really thought he was going to *make* me do it. He got mad when I said I wouldn't. Then it seemed like he was going to do it anyway, and I got *so* scared. He ripped my dress in the back and everything."

Page sat down.

"Well," Liza demanded, "is that the end? What else happened?"

"That's all. But it was so terrible." Page stared at the floor. "He yelled at me, then he grabbed his jacket and walked off. He told me I was a tease—but he said a much worse word than that—and a child and he couldn't imagine why he'd wasted his time with me. It was all my fault."

Liza regarded the dejected girl. She couldn't

help smiling a little inwardly, even though she was instantly ashamed of herself. And her blond Texan had been so grateful when she let him feel under her bra. She was glad she wasn't the one in Page's shoes that night. Well, she wasn't going to admit that. Besides, it hadn't worked out too well for her either, since she'd gotten into so much trouble afterward.

"Page, you're being silly. Forget it. Nothing happened," she said impatiently. "And you didn't get caught, did you?"

Page shook her head.

"Well, be happy about that," Liza told her. "I had a boy in my room during the dance and they found out. Mademoiselle Garibaldi saw him leaving and told Madame Lenotre about it. I'm on probation right now."

The younger girl looked up. "Oh, Liza, how awful."

"Hey, it's no big thing. But, see, you shouldn't be all upset over what happened with that guy. No one knows, and he didn't actually do anything, did he?"

"But he did."

"You know what I mean. He didn't *do* anything."

Page sighed. "I suppose not."

The two girls were interrupted by Mademoiselle Dupont, the headmistress's assistant. A stern French woman in her forties, Mademoiselle Dupont was called "the hatchet lady" by the girls, since she was dispatched to do all of Madame Lenotre's unpleasant tasks.

"Liza, I've been searching everywhere for you," she said angrily. "You were supposed to be in class fifteen minutes ago. We're going to have to put an end to this volleyball business if you girls can't fulfill your regular responsibilities."

"I'm sorry, Mademoiselle," Liza intoned dutifully.

"Madame Lenotre wants to see you at once. I will escort you back to her office now. And as for you, Page, I suggest you get to wherever it is you're supposed to be."

"Yes, of course. I was getting ready for my practice—"

"I'm not interested in the details," Mademoiselle Dupont interrupted. "Just do it."

Liza followed the older woman out of the room, glancing back to roll her eyes at Page and flash her a broad smile. Liza didn't feel as confident as she appeared. She knew she had to be careful; she was already on probation.

They crossed the snowy grounds in silence to reach the administration building. The headmistress's office was on the second floor. Mademoiselle Dupont led Liza up the stairs and into the anteroom. There, seated on two hard-backed chairs, were Allison and Melanie. Liza brightened upon seeing them until she realized that they were avoiding her gaze. Melanie was sniffling and red-faced. The assistant's firm hand on Liza's shoulder indicated that she should proceed directly into Madame Lenotre's office. Liza knocked on the heavy oak door.

"Entrez-vous," came the reply.

Shutting the door after her, Liza approached the enormous desk, behind which Madame Lenotre sat, her glasses perched atop her head, her hands folded on the desk.

"Bonjour, Madame Lenotre. Comment allez-vous?" Liza offered in as friendly and polite a voice as she could manage.

The headmistress ignored her question. "You are on probation for a gross transgression of the rules concerning proper behavior during our dance," she said with controlled anger. "You know full well that you should have been expelled from this school for such an infraction. Beaumatin is one of the best and most highly regarded schools in all of Europe. It was only due to the fact that you are a top student and that we have a great admiration for your father's commitment to your education that we decided to keep you on here. You knew all this, did you not?"

Liza had no idea what this was leading up to, but she could tell it was something very bad. Her stomach tensed and she could barely reply. "Yes, of course, Madame. I am grateful to be here."

Madame Lenotre's eyes blazed. "I think not. If you had been, you might have thought twice before bringing in illegal drugs, endangering not only yourself, but the other students and the entire school's standing as well."

The marijuana, Liza thought. Of course. But how did Lenotre find out?

"I am learning about this only four days, *four*

81

days, Liza, after you were placed on probation for another serious offense. And it was not bad enough that you smuggled these drugs through customs into school, but you distributed them to the other girls as well. For your information, we have retrieved the marijuana from your laundry bag and disposed of it."

The only people who knew about the grass were Allison and Melanie. Before she could stop herself, she cried out, "Why did they tell on me?"

The headmistress regarded her coldly. "I do not believe that the parties involved would have participated in this criminal activity if not for you."

Liza closed her eyes. So she would take the blame all alone.

"It is the administration's decision to expel you from Beaumatin. You will leave along with everyone else the day after tomorrow. But you will not return." Madame Lenotre pulled her glasses down from her head and put them on. She regarded Liza closely.

"You are a singularly bright young lady. This is a great disappointment to the school and to me personally. But you are undisciplined and you show a streak of willfulness that is unacceptable here. Now you have crossed over the line to illegal behavior. This is the end of our association. Good-bye, Mademoiselle Carlisle."

The headmistress stepped on a buzzer hidden beneath the Oriental carpet that signaled Mademoiselle Dupont to enter. The door behind Liza opened and she was escorted out. Melanie and Allison were no longer in the anteroom. She went downstairs and out into the cold December morning.

Liza was able to complete most of her packing on the following day. She avoided the other students, and didn't see Allison or Melanie at all, which was just the way she wanted it. Her roommates, never especially friendly to her before, were suddenly full of sympathy, fascinated to know all the details. Liza declined to explain. For the next two days, she stayed in her room, emerging only for meals. As luck would have it, this was her week to sit at Madame Lenotre's table. But, in fact, it made matters simpler for Liza, as the normally strained atmosphere there made it easy to eat in silence without anyone encouraging her to speak. Still, Liza knew she was the object of extreme curiosity among the girls. The story of her expulsion had spread throughout the school in what seemed like only a few hours.

On Saturday, the day she was to leave, Liza was alone in her room. Her suitcase lay packed and open on the bed, awaiting any last-minute items she might have forgotten. Both her roommates had been picked up earlier that morning. A car would be coming for her shortly. Liza refused to think about what would happen when she got home to New York, to her father. She tried to keep her mind a blank as she stood looking out the window and smoking a cigarette. Smoking was strictly forbidden at the school, but she figured it didn't matter how many more rules she broke. The expulsion was final.

It was freezing outside, and even though the window was tightly shut, Liza could feel the frigid air seeping in through the cracks. She idly watched as a limousine pulled into the dormitory's driveway, and a chauffeur opened the door for his passenger to emerge. Blowing a few wobbly smoke rings, Liza regarded the woman who got out and stood alongside the car. She was rich, that was obvious right away. It wasn't just the fur coat and the flashes of jewelry. There was something about her that *looked* rich, well cared for. She had silvery hair, but Liza could see she was far from old. The woman pushed her black leather glove back from her wrist so she could glance at a gleaming gold watch. Then she looked up, as if she might find the person she was waiting for by scanning the windows.

Liza's heart stopped. Hastily, she dropped her cigarette and stamped it out with her foot. I must be going crazy, she thought. She strained her eyes, mentally comparing the woman's face to one in the picture. The same picture that was now hidden in her suitcase, treasured all these years.

The woman turned to look in the direction of the dorm's entrance. Smiling, she held her arms out. A girl came running into Liza's view, rushing to be hugged. It was Page. The woman's arms came around her, and something about the motion, about the way her head looked bowed over the girl, the way she held Page, brought forth a loud cry from deep inside Liza. She moved to open the window. It was stuck! Pounding on it frantically, she watched as the chauffeur opened the car door for them.

"Mother!" she cried out. "Mother!" She banged on the thick glass and tried again to pull it open. "Wait, Mommy, wait!"

Page entered the car first, followed by the woman. The chauffeur slammed the door behind them and took his seat in the front.

"Don't go, I'm here!" Liza was screaming at the top of her lungs. "Mommy, Mommy, come *back*!"

The car pulled out of the driveway slowly. Liza pounded on the window with both fists, tears pouring down her cheeks. She watched as the car picked up speed. "Come back, please don't go," she sobbed. When the limousine was out of sight, Liza pressed her face against the cold window, trying to catch her breath.

Little by little, the panicked feeling drained away as the realization of it all began to sink in. Her mother! She had found her mother! There she was—beautiful, rich, alive, her very own mother. It doesn't matter that she left without me now, thought Liza. I know she's here and I can find her again easily.

What a reunion they would have. The long, wonderful talks that lay ahead. For a few minutes, Liza basked in the warmth of having rediscovered the person who had been only a fantasy of love and comfort for so many years.

But the questions began, slowly at first, then flooding her brain. Why didn't she come for me before, if she was alive and perfectly all right? Maybe she doesn't want me. What if she *knows I'm here* and deliberately made sure I'd see that she doesn't want me? Maybe she doesn't care whether I know it or not. And who's Page? A daughter by another marriage?

A chill came over Liza. Page must be her sister, Meredith. Her baby sister. She must have known all about it. Of course she knew. How could she not know? And she knew their mother had chosen *her*. She'd probably gotten a kick out of acting friendly to Liza. It was just a big joke to her the whole time. Liza dropped down into a chair. They knew she was here and they didn't want her.

Liza had never told anyone, but for years she'd had a secret fantasy that her mother watched over her like a fairy godmother. At the very least, she'd always been certain that something prevented her mother from coming for her. She sometimes imagined that her mother had amnesia, or didn't know where Liza was and had detectives frantically looking for her all over the world. Despite what her father had said, Liza couldn't stop believing that her mother would never have abandoned her, would have had to be dead or hurt or kidnapped—*something* that made it absolutely impossible for her to contact Liza. She had thought of so many possibilities, so many reasons.

And yet there her mother was, dressed in furs, riding around in a limousine, happy as could be. Not a phone call, nothing in all these years. No, she was laughing away at how she'd taken Meredith and left poor stupid Liza behind. Bennett had been telling the truth. Her mother couldn't care less about her! The pain of it shot through Liza. She sat very still for a long time. Then, abruptly, she stood up and snapped her suitcase shut.

I'll get her for this, she promised herself. I'll get both of them.

Chapter Six

Page Warren sat by herself in the coffee shop on Sixty-fifth Street, pen in her right hand, half a tuna sandwich in her left. She reread the letter she was writing to her parents...wonderful classes, New York frantic but exciting, kids are great, geology professor's terrific...sounds like an ideal freshman year, she thought, finishing off the sandwich. Too bad so little of it was true.

Columbia was not at all what she expected. Going to college in America, attending an Ivy League university—it had sounded fantastic. Her advisor at Beaumatin was so enthusiastic. And her mother practically died of pride when she got in. But *being* at Columbia was another matter. The competition for entrance had been fierce, but it didn't end once she was there. The kids weren't scholars, they were killers.

When she met other students at school parties, they never asked questions like "What's your name?" or "Where are you from?" No, the official greeting at Columbia was, "What did you get on your SAT's?" If your answer was impressive, they would respond with something like "Well, I got a sixteen hundred, but I was totally drunk the night before." They'd say it as if they were revealing a dark secret, but that it was actually bragging was perfectly obvious.

With her long, dark blond hair self-consciously pulled back at the neck, and her pale, delicately featured face devoid of any make-up, Page was certain that others could tell how insecure she felt. But looking around the room—filled to the brim with college students—she was smart enough to know she wasn't the only one feeling intimidated. She had eaten in enough school hangouts to appreciate how unusual it was for so many kids to be sitting alone, just as she was. Most of the kids at Columbia had been the smartest in their high schools. What a rude shock for the smartest eighteen-year-old from Cleveland, Ohio, to arrive at Columbia and find out that every other student had done as well or better.

Page understood this, but the sheer aggressiveness of these kids made it hard to feel sorry for them. She was spared some of the pain. She'd never felt competitive intellectually.

She'd done well at Beaumatin, but so had most of her class. A boarding school with Beaumatin's reputation didn't keep you there if you didn't do well. An uncomfortable thought passed through her mind: if she really wasn't out to prove how damn smart she was, why had she ended up at a place like Columbia? Not that she had known that much about it from a continent away, but she wondered if she had chosen Columbia more to impress her parents than to please herself.

No, not being the best of the best wasn't unbearable to Page. What *was* hard was the coldness, the extraordinary assertiveness of everyone else at the university. Boarding school had been fun. The girls were nice to each other, classes were engaging, and there was always time for some tennis. But here, making it as a student was the only thing on earth. Camaraderie didn't seem to exist. Maybe it was just her, but it seemed as if everyone was involved in the deadly game of coming in first.

She knew that in some ways she had it easier than other freshmen. She didn't have to struggle for money and she could afford her own place. Maybe, she sometimes thought, living in a dormitory would have been a way to make friends, but she doubted it. It was sheer bliss to come back to the apartment her parents had rented for her on Sixty-eighth Street, right around the corner from Juilliard. In some ways, she acknowledged, she might have been better off if she weren't so privileged.

American students always seemed to be fighting for an advantage, a way to put another person in his place. The backbiting had been a shock; by now she was used to it.

And not only from her fellow students at Columbia. She often ate dinner at a friendly little restaurant across the street from Lincoln Center, where the Juilliard students hung out. Two students, obviously piano players from the music they often practiced fingering on the tabletop, had already singled her out. They quickly discovered a perfect technique to use on the elegantly understated Page, whose clothing never called attention to itself, but obviously was of the finest quality.

Muriel and Randy. The bad seeds, Page secretly called them. She'd see them there whenever she walked in. In fact, she'd only gone there two or three times before they had chosen her as a target. All she knew was how paralyzed with humiliation they made her feel. Today the two were right behind her, sitting with their boyfriends, Bob and Chris, from the acting department. She had occasionally watched the two guys, reading scenes together, seemingly oblivious to the young women they were with. Bob looked as if he believed himself to be the handsomest man in New York City. Chris was the arrogant one, quiet most of the time, insulting and rude when he bothered to speak. About five-eight, olive-skinned with black hair and surprisingly light green eyes, he seemed perpetually coiled to spring, suddenly, to meanness.

What a foursome, Page thought, aware that the two girls were looking at her.

"Check that out, Randy. Calvin or Ralph today, what do you think?" Muriel's voice could have been heard across the room.

"Oh, no, too terribly American. Too nouveau, *n'est-ce pas?*"

I don't even go to your stupid school, she wanted to scream. But she couldn't bring herself to do it. Instead, she picked up her books and walked out of the restaurant. She might as well go home until it was time for her five o'clock psychology lecture. But walking into her apartment didn't make her feel any better. As she opened the door and turned on the light, several cockroaches marched along the floor in front of her. They don't even bother to hurry, she thought, amazed at their boldness. She played back the messages on her answering machine. One call from Paul Zorrow, the sophomore from St. Louis who sat next to her in American Literature. She had gone out with him once and turned down his next two invitations. No, today would probably make it three. There was nothing really wrong with Paul. He was perfectly nice and not unattractive, but somehow she shied away from romantic involvements. She refused to think about her reluctance to date, although she honestly couldn't remember ever being as lonely as she was in this city. Impulsively, she decided to call her mother at the Warren headquarters in London.

"Sorry, Mr. and Mrs. Warren are out of the country. Is there a message?"

Page hung up the phone and lay dejectedly across her bed. That's right, she thought. Her mother had said something about their going to France. So there was no one to talk to. The usual. She gave up and napped until four.

As she boarded the subway for her class, she began to feel better. The exit for Columbia was at 116th Street, but if she got out three stops earlier and walked the rest of the way, she could stop in at her bank. There had been an error on her statement; she might as well get that taken care of as long as she had the time. She took a quick look at her watch. If she hurried, she'd have time.

It was nearly dark on the December afternoon as Page scurried along the walkway at the end of the Ninty-sixth Street platform. Soon, the rush-hour crowds would begin returning from their offices downtown. Now the area was deserted. She had no warning as a gloved hand appeared, pulling her back against the wall. A skinny teenager, wearing a long, dark coat and running shoes, turned her around and grabbed at her handbag.

Page knew that she was supposed to turn over the bag and the mugger would leave her unhurt, the gentleman's agreement of New York life. But Page just couldn't do it. Not today. Fury at Muriel and Randy, at the guy who'd interrupted her mid-sentence in her early-morning economics class, at the nameless fears that had controlled so much of her life— all of it rushed into her thoughts. She was damned if she was just going to *give* her belongings to this guy. Page was completely enraged as she clawed and kicked at her attacker.

"No, no, no!" she shouted over and over. Her assailant was stunned at her vehemence and for a moment looked uncertain about what he should do. Before he had a chance to decide, a man stepped in between them.

"Get your hands off her."

The voice was familiar. Disheveled and confused, the mugger ran up the stairs. Page was furious as her savior turned to face her.

"Why did you let him get away?" she cried, surprised to find Muriel's boyfriend Chris holding her arms. Her eyes were blazing.

"Listen, courage and smarts aren't exactly the same. You've got guts, but that kid could have really hurt you."

Page was still shaking with anger. "Damn it. I don't have to put up with this. I'm a person!" Tears of fury and helplessness started pouring down her face.

Chris's voice softened, his usual sneer replaced by a comforting quality she would never have imagined he could display. "Let's get up to the street and sit down. This dark tunnel is no place for you right now."

Page allowed Chris to guide her up the steps. Together they stepped across the northbound lanes of traffic to the island of benches that divided Broadway and sat down.

"I have to get to my class," Page said.

"You're not in any shape to go anywhere.

Just sit here for a few minutes and calm down. What's your name, anyway?"

"Page. Page Warren."

"So, Page, what was with you anyway?" Chris looked genuinely puzzled.

"It's been a bad day," Page replied. "New York is tough, Columbia is tough, and God knows your girlfriend and the rest of you don't make it one bit better." The extraordinary circumstances made Page more outspoken than she would have been under normal conditions.

Chris wasn't thrown by her words. "Muriel's okay. You just make her feel threatened."

"*I* make *her* feel threatened!" Page was practically sputtering. "All she ever does is insult me. She never even bothered to meet me before she started in."

"Hey—" Again Chris's tone was friendly, betraying no offense. "Muriel knows just enough about you to make her crazy. You're a student, just about her age. You've got money. You're at Columbia, which means you're smart as hell."

"Smart as hell!" Page almost laughed out loud. "I haven't had a moment of feeling smart or secure or happy since I got to this country. I've barely even had a conversation with anyone, let alone any positive feedback of any kind. Outside of the super in my building, you're the first person to even be civil." She stopped and looked at him. "What are you doing here, anyway?"

"I live here, above the McDonald's." Chris

pointed to the west side of Broadway, two stories up in a dingy brown building. "Frankly, it's hard not to be jealous, for Muriel—or even for me." He eyed her expensive cashmere coat. "I have nothing and neither does Muriel."

"What do you mean, you have nothing?"

"I'm at Juilliard on scholarship. In my neighborhood in Detroit, people don't go to college, and they certainly don't study acting. This is the biggest break of my life. If you think things here are tough, try it in my house for a while." Chris's scowl underscored the truth of his words. "This is it for me. I get through four years here and become a star. I make it or I'm on the street. I have nowhere to lick my wounds if I fail. The same for Muriel. One chance for the brass ring, that's it."

"But what if you don't make it? Succeeding as an actor is almost impossible. Neither of you may get where you want."

"We're good." The arrogance Page had heard in Chris's voice was back, but at least it wasn't directed at her.

Chris stood up and pulled her to her feet. "Come on, Rocky, I'll walk you to your class. Maybe I'll even arrange a match between you and Muriel." He smiled suddenly as he held up her hands, curling her fingers into fists. "But I guess that wouldn't be fair. After all, you've had sparring practice today."

Chapter Seven

"**I** said gin and *tonic*!" Liza was shouting to make herself heard. The bartender acknowledged her order with a nod. She watched him pour the smallest dash of gin into a frosted glass, then fill it to the rim with ice and tonic.

He pushed the drink across the bar. "Five dollars," he yelled.

"How much would it be with gin?" she muttered sarcastically, knowing he couldn't hear her anyway. She looked around the dark room, making out the faces she recognized. The same crowd, every night. This was getting to be a drag, she thought. When it opened six weeks before, The Corridor was the hottest club in town. Already it was tired.

She saw Justin Yates standing off to one side with Adam and Tony, the bass player and drummer from his band. Maybe she'd go home with Justin again, she thought. There didn't seem to be any better action here tonight.

Without appearing to have any particular destination, Liza ambled over to where he held court. As usual, Adam and Tony were listening while Justin did all the talking.

"I'm telling you, it's the only way to go," he was saying emphatically as Liza came within earshot. "You can't just have a video. It's got to be a great video."

Liza sidled up behind Justin, slipping her hand into the back pocket of his jeans. He whirled around. A smile broke across his face as he saw who it was.

"Hey, baby, what's shaking?" he said, pulling her close to him and resuming his conversation. "Adam, you know we need more money than that."

"Yeah, but where are we going to get that kind of cash?" Tony asked, taking a swig from his bottle of Rolling Rock.

"Shit, I don't know," Adam said. "Let's be creative. We just need someone with a camera and a place where there's enough room to set up our stuff."

"I think there's a little more to it than that," Liza said.

"Like what?" Adam demanded.

"Like lighting, like a decent set, like a concept."

"What do you know about it?" Adam was annoyed by her interference.

"Well, it's obvious *you* don't know *anything* about it."

Justin broke in. "If we had the money, we could do it. Good old U.S. currency. That's the only thing holding us back."

Liza looked at the three men appraisingly. She'd heard them play at a few downtown clubs and liked their hard, driving sound. Making a video would be fun. More fun than spending every night with the same people dancing to the same music. It seemed as if that was all she'd done in the seven months since she'd graduated from Vassar. Maybe it was time to try something new.

"What if I could get you the money?" Liza smiled.

Justin knew that Liza's father was rich, but it had never occurred to him that she might be willing to back the band. "And what would you want, Liza?"

"To be involved. I could put it all together. I guess I would be the producer."

The three men looked at one another. "We'd have to clear this with Sam and Brian," Tony said. "They have some say in this too."

"It'll be fine," Justin said peremptorily. "When do we start?"

It was 2:30 in the afternoon, and they had yet to do a single shot. Liza had gotten to the location, a huge mansion out on Long Island, by 7:00 A.M., ready to meet the video crew so they could get in to set up their equipment. Producing had turned out to be far more work than she'd ever anticipated. Justin's artistic vision included all five band members performing in a magnificent house; intercut throughout would be scenes of each one of them playing alone in a uniquely furnished room. He had definite notions of what he wanted them to be doing, from jumping on a trampoline in the kitchen, to wheeling through the living room on a skateboard. It was left to Liza to make it happen.

It took her weeks to find a house that met with Justin's approval, and countless calls to locate the props. She interviewed dozens of people until she put together a crew of four technicians whom she felt the band would like. The project had already cost much more than it was supposed to—and it was nowhere near over.

Despite her hard work, the day was turning into a disaster. It had taken all her powers of persuasion to get the band to show up by nine o'clock, earlier than any of them were usually awake. What a mistake that was, she thought. All they'd done was get in her way. Everything had taken so long, and now there was something wrong with one of the cameras. The owner of the house, conveniently absent that day, had neglected to mention that there wouldn't be any heat. Having to wear gloves along with their coats and scarves slowed the crew down even more. The guys from the band kept wandering off, their illicit activity clear from their continual sniffing. And if Justin didn't stop talking, she thought she was going to kill him.

Liza was getting fed up. Cables were strewn everywhere. Two of the enormous three-legged light stands set up throughout the house had already been knocked over by Sam's four-year-old son, whom the keyboard player had brought along uninvited. Individual lights hung precariously from the corners of armoires and bookcases, threatening either to burn the expensive furniture or fall on someone's head. Props and guitars were scattered about, and Liza had to pick her way through the mess as she answered questions and gave instructions.

"What's this?"

Liza was horrified to see Sam's son alone by the video recorders, randomly turning knobs and dials. Where was everybody? Why wasn't the idiot engineer with his equipment? She ran over, grabbing the child roughly by the arm and yanking him away. "Goddammit!" she snapped. "Get out of here!"

The boy started to wail. She pulled him with her into the next room, where Justin and Adam were bent over an antique mirrored table, chopping up lines of cocaine with a razor blade. Immediately, her eyes took in the cigarette butts ground into the Oriental carpet, and the dozen or so wet beer bottles resting on fine wood tables.

"Jesus Christ, Justin," she exploded. "I'm responsible for this house. Get that razor off the table."

"Hey, relax, everything's cool," Justin answered her calmly.

"No, everything's *not* cool," Liza shot back. "I don't expect you to help me, but at least you can keep the kid out of the way. And stop trashing the place—I have to pay for any damages."

Tony and Brian walked in from the terrace, wet snow covering their boots. "Are we ready yet? This is boring," Brian said to Liza accusingly, as he plopped down on the overstuffed couch and put his feet up on a hassock.

The cameraman stuck his head in. "Let's try it. We should be ready now."

Liza looked around. "Where's Sam?"

"I don't know, upstairs maybe," Tony said, reaching for a beer.

Liza hurried up the steps to the second floor, opening doors and calling out Sam's name. In the master suite, she found him, passed out on the king-sized bed, clutching a bottle of Scotch that was slowly dripping onto the silk coverlet.

I must have been nuts thinking this would be fun, she said to herself as she tried to shake Sam awake. He didn't respond, and she stepped back, looking down at him disgustedly. Forget this shit, she thought. I've had enough. They're all so smart, let them do it themselves.

She went back downstairs. The crew was in the living room, waiting. "Go home," she said to them.

They looked at her, bewildered. Overhearing, Justin came running in from the next room. "What are you telling them to go home for? Are you out of your mind?"

"It's over. I'm sick of all of you."

"But everything's finally working. What's your problem?"

"I don't have any problem."

"Listen, Liza," Justin was getting angry, "you wanted to be the producer. What did you think that meant? It's your job to deal with all of this."

"It's my money and I don't give a damn whether it gets dealt with or not."

"I can't believe you're pulling this after we've gotten so far. It's nice that you have so much money to throw away, you can just walk off and leave us hanging."

Liza strode to the door, pulling her coat tightly around her. "Get everything and everyone out of here right now. From this moment on, I'm no longer responsible."

She left the house and got into her car. Let's see, she thought, glancing at her watch. Three-thirty. With any luck, she could be in the sauna by five.

Chapter Eight

"Mother, the car is waiting."

Page threw open the door to her mother's office, her delicately etched face flushed with excitement.

Seated behind her desk, Claire Warren looked up from the papers she was working on, taking her usual pleasure in her daughter's appearance. Even when Page was a child, people had been fascinated by her finely drawn features. Now she drew attention away from her beauty, pulling her long, dark blond hair back from her face, and wearing only a hint of gloss on her lips and mascara to frame her large eyes. But her high cheekbones and defined features made her loveliness impossible to hide. Five foot six, slightly shorter than her mother, she had the body of a young ballerina, with apparent delicacy cloaking tremendous strength and physical agility. At twenty-three, Page had become more sure of herself, and it showed.

Slender and elegant, Claire seemed less approachable than her daughter. Her cool demeanor and upswept, prematurely silver hair gave her an air of correctness. Always dressed expensively but conventionally, Claire's pearl-white velvety skin, unlined even now that she was in her late forties, was her own special mark of beauty.

"I'm coming, honey. Just give me a moment."

Claire closed her fountain pen and put it neatly into the top drawer of the leather partner's desk. Together, she and John Warren had purchased the antique piece at which the two of them had worked face to face. It was her most prized possession—not because of its considerable value, but because they had shared it through such happy years.

Her own coat already on and belted, Page hurried across the room to pull Claire's Burberry from the closet, obviously hoping to hasten their departure. She held up the trench-coat and turned to look at her mother, who was already distracted by some papers on her desk. Observing Claire bathed in the September sun as it streaked through the ornate, leaded windows, Page couldn't help thinking that the magnificent office was a suitable frame for this successful and special woman. The room, like its owner, looked cool and sleek, but it was marked by unexpected touches of color and richness. Highly polished parquet floors and gleaming ivory walls were offset by the bold blues and deep reds of the Shiraz rug. The signed and numbered copy of Jasper Johns' *American Flag* that hung above the navy velvet sofa was a bittersweet reminder of home for Claire in this historic London building. Off to one side of the room, the collection of miniature old cars that had been John Warren's passion stood arrayed on a shining maple table, the tiny Model T's and Rolls-Royces a tribute to the humor and playfulness Claire still missed every day, even five years after his death.

"Mother, please, come on. You're hopeless."

Page laughed. Startled, Claire looked up. Page had inherited her mother's drive and energy, but her directness and sense of fun were new, so unlike the almost diffident child she had been. She has truly come into her own, Claire mused, pleased at the thought.

"Sorry, darling," she said, rising from her seat. "but I do wish you would give me some idea of what this trip is about. You're being so mysterious. At least tell me whom we're going to see."

Page answered with inscrutable silence until her excitement about the trip overshadowed her need for secrecy. "You'll be visiting Guy and Emma Rycroft. Lord and Lady Rycroft, actually. After you meet them, I promise I'll explain everything."

Few people other than Page would have dared to treat the busy and powerful Claire Warren in so highhanded a manner. But

Claire felt she could hardly be angry with her daughter for taking her on what might just turn out to be a wild goose chase. After all, Claire thought, frowning. Page has sacrificed so much for me.

"I see that look again, and you couldn't be more wrong," said Page quietly.

"You can't possibly know what I was thinking," Claire said, both amused and a little irritated by how transparent she was to her daughter.

"When I first got back to England, you had that look on your face every time I walked into the room. I *am* happy here. Actually, coming home from Columbia after Dad died was one of the best things I ever did. When I was studying so seriously, I had no room for anything else in my life. Besides, as much as I loved my classes, New York wasn't always a dream come true."

Page had never shared her darkest moments at Columbia with Claire, so there was little chance that her mother would have any idea how sincerely she meant this. Page wished she could communicate how happy she was to be working with her mother. Only after she started at Warren International did Page realize how much she loved the business, loved being an essential part of her mother's daily life as John had been before her. If her competitive instincts had not been aroused by striving for a four-point-oh, they were certainly in full force now.

"Mom, really, I loved college, but I love being

part of the real world even more." Page grinned as she held up her mother's coat once again. "Besides, I read books all the time. For my own pleasure."

Claire smiled in spite of her doubts, slipping into her coat and carefully arranging the collar, the sleeves, the belt as she spoke. "Okay, darling, you win." Noting her daughter's general air of vibrancy, Claire hoped it meant that Page was really happy.

Claire began pulling on her black gloves, gently easing on the soft leather. Page usually admired her mother's dignified appearance, but right now she had to resist the urge to tug on Claire's arm to hurry this process along. "We're going to be terribly late," she cried.

Claire raised her eyebrows. "I can hardly be held responsible for being late when I don't even know where it is I'm going, can I, dear?" she murmured.

"Mom, Chris is going to give up on us." Page was totally exasperated.

"How could he? After all, it would leave him no one to glare at," Claire responded archly.

Will they ever get used to each other, Page wondered as she and her mother left the building and found Chris Layton leaning against the door of the Bentley. He nodded silently at Claire, then grinned at Page. At twenty-four, Chris unleashed his engaging side a bit more often, although around Claire he was apt to retreat behind his old surliness.

Chris knew how fortunate he was to be driving for the Warrens. He and Page had become unlikely friends after she was mugged in New York. Chris got to see beyond the vulnerable scared girl. In turn, she basked in the warmth of protectiveness and kindness that lay just under the defensive rudeness Chris used as his emotional armor. He hungered for the London stage, and every sentence Page uttered evoked the sounds of Olivier and Gielgud. For her part, Page came to admire his outspokenness, his aggressive approach to life, so different from the ever-so-polite English boys back home. The two shared a respect for each other's privacy and a completely mutual affection, no romantic strings attached. From the start, they had been pals. And that was just how both of them wanted it to stay.

Chris and Page had kept up with each other after she left New York, exchanging letters and Christmas cards. In their correspondence, Page entertained Chris with British anecdotes, while Chris only vaguely alluded to his breakup with Muriel and her subsequent marriage to a much older—much richer—man in Westchester. True to the unwritten rule of their friendship, Page never asked for more information than he offered, though privately she felt relieved that the dreadful Muriel was gone.

Despite their ongoing communication, they didn't see each other again until Chris came to London after graduation, determined to follow in the footsteps of those actors he so admired. Although most of his Juilliard cohorts were off to Hollywood, he knew he would never be satisfied if he didn't try to succeed in the London theater. But he learned a hard lesson almost immediately. It was tough to make it as an actor in London if you were British; as an American, with his street-kid exterior, he had trouble even getting accepted into a professional acting class. To make matters worse, finding a paying job turned out to be nearly impossible under the strict policies of the British government. He never complained to Page about his problems, but she soon realized how difficult the situation was and moved to intercede. Claire's offer of a job driving the Bentley saved him from having to give up on his dream.

Despite the coldness between them, even Claire was content to have Chris around. The Warrens' chauffeur had recently retired after nearly twenty years with the family, so Page's request that they find a way to help her friend came at a perfect moment. Claire put up with his need for flexible hours, since most of her work these days took place either in her office or away in other parts of the continent, where a local driver would be hired. If there was an audition or special rehearsal that Chris wanted to attend, he could take off without having to worry about his job. In fact, Chris's career hadn't gone far enough for him to be unavailable very often.

The drive from the Warren building just off Grosvenor Square to the small village in the Cotswolds was not especially pretty to begin with. But as they left London and its suburbs farther and farther behind, the scene came alive. With trees ablaze in the reds and golds of autumn, and the ancient stone walls and tiny cottages dotting the landscape, it would have been easy to pretend they had traveled back hundreds of years, so little had changed in the small towns that formed one of England's most beautiful and ageless areas. Driving the Bentley past the picturesque village squares along winding old roads made Chris feel as if he were in the middle of an English legend, with King Arthur and Guinevere, Robin Hood, and Maid Marian.

They had turned onto the High Street in Chipping Camden, and it seemed as if the Bard himself might walk out of the pub on their left. In front of them was a sign proclaiming the services of a silversmith and, to their right, a row of limestone houses, behind which fields of green were visible for miles.

"It's incredible," Page exclaimed. "I feel as if London doesn't even exist. Look up there." Shading her eyes from the afternoon sun, she gestured toward a hill. "That church must be over five hundred years old. And those gravestones!"

"Are you interested in sightseeing or are you trying to sell me some real estate?" Claire admired the surroundings, but was annoyed by the sense that she was being manipulated. "Perhaps if you'd tell me why we're here, I could better appreciate my daughter's talents as a tour guide."

Page was momentarily discomfited by her mother's sarcasm, but recovered quickly. "Chris, go to the end of this road and turn left. Another kilometer or so and the mystery will be over."

Within five minutes the Bentley was pulling into a long driveway, richly bordered by wildflowers in every shade of blue and purple. At the end stood a massive stone house, surrounded by greenery. A large, tranquil pond adjoined one wing of the stately old structure. The other side of the house was framed by what looked like hundreds of willow trees stretching out and around to the back.

"This is absolutely spectacular," Claire caught her breath. Even after all these years in England, she couldn't get over the elegance and grace of these homes that had lasted for centuries, and the extraordinary landscapes, which, thanks to the damp English climate, seemed to accompany even the most modest cottages.

"Wait until you see the inside," Page said, as Chris hurried around to open the door for the two women.

"Page, what on earth does this have to do with us?" Claire's tone marked the end of her amusement at the game her daughter was playing, but Page was kept from answering by the sudden appearance of a middle-aged couple who walked out of the willow grove.

"Hello, Page. Welcome back to Camden Manor." The woman looked rather plain in her gray pullover and sensible walking shoes, but her voice carried the commanding tone of the British upper class.

"Emma, it's so lovely of you to have invited us," Page said. "This is my mother, Claire Warren. Lord and Lady Rycroft."

Claire extended her hand. "How do you do, Lady Rycroft? It's a pleasure to meet you."

The older woman cut short the formalities with a warm smile. "Please, dear, we're simply Emma and Guy. My forebears were grand enough to enjoy all of that, but now I'm afraid we cannot honestly afford it. We generally drag out the lord and lady nonsense when we need an extension on the heating bills."

Both Rycrofts laughed at this. Perhaps they really did have financial problems, Claire thought, but it certainly didn't seem to interfere with their good humor.

Guy Rycroft spoke for the first time. "Come inside and we'll have some tea," he suggested, offering his arm to Claire. His quiet voice possessed a gentle quality that made his guests feel at home right away.

They left Chris in the Bentley studying his lines for a scene, and headed up the walk. "Your home is so lovely," Claire commented as they entered the house. She was astonished by its grandeur. From the outside, it seemed to be a good-sized building, but as she walked through the hallway toward the library, the vast elegance was overwhelming. Even the furniture bore the stamp of substance, signs of age apparent, but unmistakable in its original quality. Despite the ravages of time and the

111

limited resources, this was one of the most imposing places Claire had ever seen. The house exuded a sense of history, of roots. She had lived in this country for over twenty years, but in this house Claire suddenly felt like the Baltimore schoolgirl she had once been.

"Isn't it terrific?" Page was thrilled to see her mother's reaction. It would make the plan so much easier.

"Well, of course we love it." Emma Rycroft passed her hand over the glossy hardwood top of the late-eighteenth-century chair in front of her. "It is a shame to be giving it all up."

Claire said nothing, but Emma Rycroft noted the confusion on her face. "You see, Mrs. Warren, Guy and I have tried everything we can think of. There's simply no way to keep up with the costs. So many of us are in this position now. Of course, it's selfish to complain. We have been privileged for so long. But it is awfully sad, nonetheless. I'm sure millions are cheering to see it all end, and I cannot say I really blame them, but...well there's little use in burdening you with our troubles."

Claire could not have been more sympathetic to the dignified couple standing before her. She was growing angry at Page, however, for exposing the Rycrofts in front of a total stranger. Page noticed the turn in her mother's expression. As close as the two were, even Page could feel intimidated by Claire's cool, appraising manner.

She hurried to explain. "Can we all sit down, please?" Page motioned Guy and Emma to the couch, her mother to a chair. Then she sat down, positioning herself so she faced all three of them. "Guy, Emma, I haven't really been fair today. You see, Mother, the Rycrofts and I met two Sundays ago when I was cycling through the countryside here. I had stopped to admire the house. Emma was outside working in the garden and we got to talking. We ended up having tea and chatting for an hour or two. I asked if I might bring you out here, and Guy and Emma kindly agreed. But, I haven't told any of you why I was so eager for you to meet. I have an idea. It could be awfully good for all of us. If it works, it might enable Guy and Emma to stay right here."

Page's speech was momentarily interrupted by the entrance of a young, uniformed maid carrying a carefully arranged tea tray. Emma poured the tea and offered her guests a selection of small sandwiches and sweet pastries.

With everyone settled back in their seats, Page continued, her attention firmly on the Rycrofts. "The Warren hotels are respected for their efficiency, but what makes them unique is their taste and sophistication. This has been my mother's contribution. She took a well-run enterprise and turned it into a work of art." Taking a deep breath, she finally brought her plan into the open.

"What if we could incorporate my mother's talents with the beauty of this house and your own charm? Camden Manor would be a wonderful vacation spot. Not just a glorified bed-and-breakfast, but a place where your guests

113

would be made to feel as if they were actually staying with you, living the lives your ancestors experienced a hundred years ago."

Claire and the Rycrofts all looked cool, definitely reserved. The young woman plunged on, even managing to add a chuckle to her voice. "Of course, the plumbing would be much more pleasant than anything the nineteenth century had to offer, but the basic amenities would be those of a more gracious time, a time just about everybody would love to return to if they could afford it and had the place to do it. Well, in England, almost no one can live this way anymore, with the possible exception of the queen. But we could give people that feeling, even if only for a few days." Page summoned the Rycrofts with her eyes. "You two would be the perfect hosts for the kind of weekends your ancestors had as a matter of course. With the Warren behind you, you could hire a staff that would make a tired businessman feel like a baron!"

Guy Rycroft looked both suspicious and confused. "What exactly are you suggesting?"

"Camden Manor would still be your home, Guy. But it would be more than that as well. On weekends and during the summer, paying guests would stay in your rooms, hunt in your fields, ride your horses. It would be as if you had invited them here. You and Emma would be their personal guides to a world they've never known. The idea may be slightly horrifying to you, but it could mean holding on to what you have. I know it would be something of an invasion into your life, but the two of you would have little to do, except, of course, be warm and gracious, and I can't imagine either of you ever being any other way. And remember, the house would be yours alone from Monday to Thursday."

The Rycrofts were the picture of astonishment as Page went on. "Warren International could afford to do whatever refurbishing is necessary and provide you with a large staff to handle the chores. All the housework and cooking. In no time, this would start to pay for itself. The old guard may be going broke in this country, but there are millionaires being created every time another movie opens or a new rock group releases a CD. There are so many people who can splurge on whatever they want, and here they can find something they can't buy anywhere else. Not for all the money on earth. Not the kind of authenticity you represent. The kind of life you come from has never been available to anyone who wasn't born to it." Page finished her presentation with a pleading look at the Rycrofts, followed by an uneasy glance at Claire.

Emma was the first to respond. "I don't know. This is completely unexpected. What do you think, Guy? Does it sound so very terrible?"

Guy noted the hope in his wife's voice. "I suspect I could get used to just about anything. Rock and roll singers, eh?"

A twinkle was beginning to show in his eyes. "Judging from the look on Emma's face, it seems as if I'm going to be getting used to this, doesn't it? Actually, I would do almost anything to stay in my home." The depth of this sentiment was readily apparent. Suddenly he turned to Claire, taking in her expression. "But this is all new to you, isn't it?" He shifted his focus back to Page. "It appears you have put your mother on the spot today. Perhaps we should discuss this at another time—if there is to be another time, that is."

Claire appreciated his tact. She also realized that this very quality was one of the most intelligent aspects of Page's grand scheme. Guy and Emma were absolutely charming. Being well-bred was simply a part of them. Indeed, anyone would be grateful to spend a few days in their company. Especially in such extraordinary surroundings. Yes, an infusion of capital into restoring the house to its former splendor would make it tremendously attractive to visitors. And those visitors would probably be willing to pay dearly for the opportunity to feel like a nineteenth-century lord, even just for a few days. Very dearly, in fact. Page had acted impetuously, but her idea might well be brilliant.

Claire kept these thoughts to herself as the Rycrofts showed them to the door. She was still angry at Page for her handling of the situation and had been cool for the remainder of the visit. She didn't want to build up the Rycrofts' hopes before finding out everything she could about the feasibility of the plan.

As the two women walked toward the waiting

car, Claire turned to her daughter. In a cold tone of voice, she said, "Never do that to me again. Those people deserve better than to have to debase themselves in front of someone who, for all you know, might be totally unsympathetic to your idea. It was unfair to me and could have been quite horrible for them."

Page acknowledged her mother's words silently. Whatever else Claire was thinking, she was not about to discuss it on this trip. Aware of the anger in the air, Chris said nothing as they drove toward London. Actually, Claire's thoughts would have been very surprising to Page, had she known them. While Claire was displeased with her daughter's impulsiveness, she was proud of Page's imagination and business sense. If Page could become this excited about extending the Warren empire, perhaps her leaving Columbia hadn't been such a tragedy after all.

As they drove by the stone walls and wildflower paths of the Cotswolds, Claire thought how proud John Warren would be of Page if he were still alive. God, how she missed him. What a team they had turned out to be. When she first came to England with him, she was a frightened young woman, uncertain of her place in the world. Warren International had been composed of six hotels, all in the United Kingdom. In the years since she became a full partner, the chain had expanded tremendously. Now there were eleven hotels, with properties in Switzerland, France, and Italy. Combining her talents with John's had made the Warren name among the most highly respected in all of Europe. And a timid, inexperienced young woman had grown to be the self-confident, knowledgeable head of a major company. The relationship with the tragic and complicated beginning had bloomed into the most exciting experience Claire had ever known. Even five years after his death, Claire could feel the heat rising up within her as she thought about John, so passionate and intense had been their union.

But she couldn't keep the price she had paid for that happiness out of her mind. Liza. What kind of girl was she now? No, she was a grown woman. Did she ever think about her mother? Claire wondered as the Cotswold countryside gave way to the grimier London suburbs. She found herself musing about Liza more and more. Could she ever forget the pain of her only communication with her daughter since she had left Madison so long ago? So frightened of Bennett, she had carefully waited until Liza's eighteenth birthday before contacting her, when no further legal action could be taken. With information she'd gathered over the years, Claire had traced Liza to Vassar, and written to her at once. The response was immediate: *You are no mother to me. I don't want to hear from you ever again. Liza.* Claire could still see the telegram in her mind. It was an image she couldn't erase. So many times since, she'd wished she could just fly to the United States, show up in front of Liza's dormitory room, explain away everything that had happened, everything she'd done. But each time she considered it, she saw those words again—*You are no mother to me. You are no mother to me.* There was no explaining it away. It was the worst punishment a mother could receive, and she deserved every syllable.

Page watched Claire's face. So sad. So far away. Her mother was in that world Page had never been invited to enter. She wished she could believe Claire was so angry with her that she wouldn't even speak, Page thought. But she knew this wasn't so. It reminded her of how excluded she had sometimes felt when her father was alive. She'd loved John very much, yet she always felt a little reserved in his presence. And her parents' extraordinary closeness had engendered even more painful feelings, feelings she didn't like to admit even to herself. Claire and John were such an amazing couple. There was little room for a third person, even their daughter. Page always knew they loved her, they made that abundantly clear. But there was just a little piece missing. How can I be so disloyal? Page thought, ashamed. But she couldn't help herself. As grief-stricken as she had been when John died, in a strange way she had also been excited. She was glad to leave Columbia, glad finally to be welcomed into her mother's world, to feel necessary, as if she were really a part of things. Still, she thought once again, looking at Claire, still there was some corner of her mother's life that was closed to her. Whatever it was, she hated it. And she hated herself even more for feeling this way.

When Chris stopped the car in front of the Warren headquarters, the looks on both women's faces kept him from saying a word. Page and Claire rode up to the sixth floor in silence. Just before they reached the door to Claire's office, they turned toward each other. Claire noticed her daughter's sad, guarded expression. Her own face softened.

"I intend to look into your idea carefully. Then we can discuss it." Claire reached out to touch Page's arm. "You know, dear, I think you may really have something here. I'm awfully proud of you."

A flush of joy, touched by relief, spread across Page's face. Claire put out her arms, and the two held each other. Both women were smiling as they walked into their offices.

The Warren board of directors reluctantly approved the idea for Warren Manor in Chipping Camden. Page worked eighteen hours a day to ready the Rycrofts' estate by the opening on December first. Despite her best efforts, the house wasn't even ready by Christmas. Plumbing fixtures took weeks to arrive, and then they didn't fit. The old wooden floors were more damaged than was first apparent and new matching boards proved almost impossible to find. After a serious rainfall, part of the roof caved in, destroying two of the upstairs bedrooms.

By the time the manor opened, Page had lost hope and decided she had drawn her mother into a losing proposition. When the first guests arrived, it was all she could do to smile, waiting for the next disaster to happen. Yet, by the third month of operation, the house was filled to capacity every weekend.

It was a cold morning in March when Chris drove her to Upper Slaughter, the potential site for Warren Manor number two. Page was alone with him, so she was sitting in the front seat of the Bentley. She'd been so busy over the past few months, they'd barely had time to talk. Now, she could see that Chris was bursting to tell her something.

"Okay. Out with it. What's going on?"

"Nothing. Nothing at all." He replied as if the question bored him.

"My dear," Page's tone was acid, "your line reading was better when you were a sophomore at Juilliard."

Chris was dying to tell her, but superstition demanded that he keep it to himself, or at the very least, not make a big deal of it. "Listen, it's really nothing. Not much of anything, anyway."

"Chris," she said, slowly and evenly, "your willingness to tell me what's going on hasn't resulted in even one actual piece of information. Now, take a deep breath. Let it out. Repeat after me. "What I'm so excited about is..."

"I give up. What I'm so excited about is a job. An acting job. A *paying* acting job. It's small, which is why I didn't intend to make a huge thing about it."

"That's absolutely wonderful! What is it?"

"Well, you know how much time I've been spending at the National Theatre." The theater company had become the hub of British theatrical activity and the gathering place for young, hopeful actors. Page knew that Chris could be found there practically every evening now. "Martin Purcell is doing an experimental version of *Julius Caesar* with modern dress and colloquial speech," Chris continued. "I've been bugging him for months and it finally paid off. I'm going to be playing one of the soldiers. And I don't have to do phony British. He wants an American sound and an American look. It opens two weeks from today. I only have a couple of lines, but I would love you to come, even if I'm a spear carrier." Chris heard the humility in his tone and quickly assumed the cockiness he found more appropriate. "After all, it's my London debut."

Page answered at once. "I wouldn't miss it. And you're too talented to be carrying a spear for long."

"Really, Page, make up your mind. A minute ago, you said that my talent as an actor had diminished since I was a sophomore." His hurt look made both of them laugh.

The day the play was opening, however, Chris wasn't finding anything particularly funny. Friday, March 20th, was the coldest day of the year. He hoped it wasn't an omen. He paced around his bedroom, pulling on a thick, Irish wool sweater. He felt as if he would never again be warm enough, never speak without hearing his teeth chatter. His nervousness was making it worse. Jesus, how could anyone be this panicked over two damn lines, he brooded. What if he were playing Julius Caesar? He'd probably have a nervous breakdown.

You're not the first performer in history to feel this way. Get it under control. Chris kept saying these words over and over to himself as if they were a mantra, but it did little to calm him. Shit. Nothing was working. The ring of the phone interrupted his torture.

"Yeah." It was all he could do to get out the word.

"Chris, it's me. Page. You sound funny."

"If you think I sound funny over the phone, wait until you see me onstage. I should keep all of England in stitches for months."

"Christopher, I'm coming over. Right now." Page was alarmed. She had expected to hear excitement in his voice, not terror.

"Listen, I always get nervous before a show. I'll be fine. I'll see you backstage afterward."

"I'm on my way over and we're going to the theater together."

"But what are you going to do with yourself? If you come with me, you'll be there an hour early."

"Let me worry about that."

Within a half hour, Chris and Page were seated side by side in the Bentley, riding across the Waterloo Bridge toward the National

Theatre. Chris was driving as skillfully as usual, but his hands were clenched on the steering wheel, his lips drawn into a tight, silent line. He looked withdrawn and angry, just as he used to all the time when Page first met him.

She reached over and lightly massaged the back of his neck. He could see the concern marked on her face. "Don't worry," he reassured her. "I'm always this way."

She was amazed. "You mean, you feel this way every time and you keep on doing it?"

"All actors feel this way and go on doing it. I almost threw up every time I went onstage at Juilliard. You just left New York too soon to see it."

Page was shocked by how cavalier he sounded. How could someone be so petrified and so casual about it at the same time?

Chris honked the horn impatiently at the car in front of him. "Hey, just as long as it disappears once I go on, I can live with it."

"But why would you want to?"

"I can't really explain it. Acting is what I want more than anything else I've ever done. This is just part of the package." Chris's voice became strangely mechanical. "I'll get it under control. I'm not the first performer in history to feel this way."

Page didn't doubt that Chris would get himself together for this performance. After all, he had very few lines. But she was shaken by what this was doing to him. Could fame possibly be worth it?

As if reading her mind, Chris said, "You

know, I don't need to be a household name or an international star. I just love being in front of an audience for a couple of hours."

When they arrived, Chris went to the dressing rooms, while Page wandered around the picture galleries, then listened to a string quartet play the music of Bach and Vivaldi until curtain time. But her worry about Chris lingered. Only when the curtain rose did she begin to relax. Chris was fine, just as he said he'd be. Whatever he may have been feeling inside, he looked calm and collected.

What strange creatures actors are, she thought, finally allowing herself to be swept into the action unfolding before her. As happy as she was for Chris, her eyes kept turning to the actor playing Cassius. Overhearing the conversations around her at intermission, she realized she was far from the only one whose attention had been focused on the tall young actor. What was his name? She flipped through her program. Simon Roberts. His Cassius was electrifying, not merely lean and hungry, but tensile, starving for power. The director's choice of modern dress and colloquial speech brought the character to light in a way Page had never thought about before. This was a man whose longings were palpable, whose actions were inevitable.

Returning to her seat after the intermission, Page thoroughly enjoyed the rest of Shakespeare's play. She was so thrilled for Chris. After the curtain calls, she made her way backstage as he had invited her. She found him surrounded by a group of actors, all congratulating each other with shrieks of joy. Chris saw her, and quickly broke from the others, rushing to her side.

"You were terrific!" Page's praise was welcomed by an ebullient Chris, who lifted her up and began to dance around the room. When he finally put her down, Page asked, laughing, "Is this the same man who was imitating a ghost about three hours ago?"

"I was a little nervous, wasn't I? See, I told you. It was nothing."

"Actors!" The way she said this made them both laugh. She had hung around Juilliard enough with Chris to have heard music majors often use the word in this same tone of voice to refer to the drama students. Sometimes it meant "idiots." Sometimes, it meant "lunatics." Occasionally, it implied moral degeneracy. The only time musicians found themselves in agreement with actors was when young, skinny, long-haired girls walked by in packs, and both future Glenn Goulds and potential Robert De Niros would turn to each other and say in unison, "Dancers!"

Chris brought Page over to a group of cast members. "Jill, Eric, Charles, Anna, this is my friend, Page Warren."

Page extended a hand to each as she congratulated them on their performances. All four of the actors responded politely, but Page felt out of place and decided it would be more fun for Chris if she made her way home alone. "I'll see you tomorrow, okay?"

"Oh, no, Page. Come with us. We're going for something to eat."

She smiled, and shook her head, starting to move off toward the exit, but was interrupted by Chris's protests.

"You can't leave. You've got to come with us."

"Why don't you, Page?" Eric joined in. "We'd be happy to have you."

"Okay, I'd love to," she finally agreed.

Page was comfortable walking with the five actors as they headed toward a quiet pub on Cornwall Road. They reminded her of the acting students she'd met in New York after she and Chris had become friends. Only when the actor who played Cassius joined them inside the pub did Page feel out of place once again. Simon Roberts sat down with the group ten minutes after they had ordered. Judging by his reception, she realized what an honor this constituted for the young actors at the table. Evidently, like those people she'd overheard in the audience, they too thought he was something special. Somehow their adulation annoyed Page. Sure, he was talented, but was he so full of himself that he would encourage his peers to be awkward in his presence?

And awkward was just what they were. Eric and Charles seemed filled with a false heartiness whenever they spoke to him. And Anna and Jill acted coy and flirtatious. The four of them seemed to be making no impression at all on Simon Roberts. Arrogant, Page thought, noting his lack of response. When he had first joined them, Chris introduced her and she had complimented him on his fine performance. His response was a curt "Thank you," and his eyes had moved immediately off her face. He was no warmer to the rest.

Only with Chris did Simon seem to come out of his hostile corner. At the moment, the two were sparring about how the Americans butchered the English language, with Simon imitating a flat-toned Midwesterner and Chris sounding like the queen of England. Suddenly, artfully, Simon changed his voice to the harsh sounds of an exaggerated New York accent. Page had loved and hated the city, but despite her own ambivalence, his caricature made her furious.

"That's not how New Yorkers speak, you know." Her tone was sharper than she intended it to be.

"Well, Miss Warren, we know it is certainly not the way *you* speak." His eyes took in her perfectly cut black velvet suit and simple but obviously expensive pearls as his voice adopted the upper-class quality that sounded so pleasing on Page, but embarrassing nonetheless when imitated.

Page had no intention of letting this irritating jerk have the last word. "I believe it's not so much a question of how you speak as whether you have anything to say when you don't have lines written for you." Her voice was quiet but she looked the actor straight in the eye.

Simon seemed momentarily stricken by the remark, but he recovered quickly. "So the young woman has wit in addition to beauty and wealth." His tone was somewhat admiring, but all Page heard was condescension.

She refused to prolong the exchange one more minute. "The young woman has work to do tomorrow morning." She rose and picked up her coat.

Chris was mystified. This marked the first time he had seen Page engage someone in subtle warfare like that. And Simon. He rarely even came out of himself long enough to look at other people when he wasn't onstage, let alone allow himself to be drawn into such a personal power struggle. Chris stood up, as much amused as baffled.

"I'll come with you, Page," he said.

She put a hand on his shoulder, signaling him to remain.

"Please, stay and celebrate. I'll see you tomorrow."

Simon Roberts watched her with suspicion. So she was the kind of woman who left her date in the middle of the evening. Chris Layton was much too nice for her.

Chris walked Page to the door, where even Simon noticed that they hugged with tremendous affection. Had he somehow gotten the situation wrong?

When Chris returned to the table, he saw the disapproval on Simon's face.

"What's that look about?" Chris asked him.

"It's none of my business, but if my girlfriend left in the middle of a conversation, I'd be annoyed, especially a girl that pretty."

Chris was beginning to enjoy this. "Oh, so you think she's pretty, do you?"

Simon was sorry he'd said anything. He hated to admit that he found such an ice princess attractive. "Well, I suppose..."

Chris smiled. "She's beautiful, and you know it. Why don't you call her up? She's the first woman I've seen make this much of an impression on you."

"Don't be ridiculous. She's your girlfriend, Chris."

Chris's voice grew serious. "She's my best friend, not my girlfriend. She also happens to be my employer. And I'm not kidding, maybe you really should call her."

Simon's expression was one of pure horror. "Call that woman? She would chew me up and spit me out."

Eric, always quick to spot a set-up, interrupted in his best Mae West imitation. "Maybe so—but only if you're very, very lucky."

Chapter Nine

The leopard tights were Liza's trademark. Not everyone could get away with sporting leopard tights under any imaginable kind of skirt, dress, or pants. But Liza wasn't everyone.

She had the body, she had the face, but most important, she had the attitude that made everything look exactly right.

At the moment, those brightly spotted tights were crumpled up on a chair, buried beneath the rest of the clothing Liza had worn the night before. The layered heap of silk and leather was the first sight to greet Liza as she woke. Coming out of a deep sleep, she found it almost impossible to raise her cheek from the pillow. Her mouth was so parched she suspected it might just be easier never to open it again. Moving her arm from beneath the sheet, she slowly reached out to retrieve her black top from the tangle of clothing.

As she silently raised herself up to slip the lacy camisole over her head, Liza considered her surroundings. High above the Hudson River, the bedroom was flooded with sunlight so bright she wanted to cover her eyes. On mornings like these, she would usually go straight for a Bloody Mary, but the only liquor in this room was the dregs of last night's bottle of Dom Perignon.

Liza didn't particularly like starting out the day with alcohol. Generally she preferred to keep her wits about her. What the hell, she figured, she had a bad day ahead of her. Or, what was left of it, she reflected, noting on the bedside clock that it was already past noon. Shit. She had less than an hour to get going. Fully alert now, she downed the last few drops of champagne straight out of the bottle, shuddering slightly at its warm flatness.

The sound of Tom's gentle snoring made her look over at his sleeping form. He lay with one arm thrown across his face. Having kicked off the sheet entirely, his suntanned body was exposed for her objective inspection. He was more than handsome enough, mid-thirties, sandy blond hair. He didn't seem too intelligent, but he had a pleasing way about him. The sculpted muscles showed he was a devotee of the gym. She'd seen him at a dozen parties before going home with him last night in a fit of boredom at an after-hours club downtown. She couldn't help thinking with a smile that investment bankers certainly had changed since her father's early days. As the image of her father crossed her mind, the smile thinned.

Liza put down the champagne bottle and strode back across the room toward Tom. Another fifteen minutes, then a shower, into a cab by quarter to one. No, better make that ten to one; there would undoubtedly be a little discussion when old Tom found out she wasn't giving him her telephone number. Too much trouble—just go with a phony number; okay, a quarter to one.

On the bed again, she eased Tom's arm away from his face as she slung one leg over his chest, straddling him. He began to mumble, gradually coming to consciousness. Naked except for the camisole. Liza rose up on her knees and moved forward to position herself on top of him.

It took him a few seconds to wake entirely and find Liza looking down at him. She had the most hypnotic eyes he'd ever seen. Both her irises and pupils were the same deep brown, creating the effect of the darkest, wettest ink or the shiniest marbles. He couldn't understand how her eyes always managed to catch the light when she smiled so they glinted brightly with pinpoints of white, matching the gleaming white of her teeth. Liza with a smile could appear seductive or sinister, depending on who was looking at her. Men invariably found her seductive.

Liza smiled now as she slowly began to lower herself over Tom's face.

"Care for some breakfast?" she asked.

The cabdriver was a maniac, apparently thrilled with the idea of beating the midday Broadway traffic by weaving in and out of any space he spied. Not that it would help, Liza realized, as she tried to hold her compact mirror steady in one hand while brushing on mascara with the other. It was already one-fifteen. Tom had shown some unexpected expertise that made it worth her while to linger, and Liza was late once again for her monthly one o'clock lunch with Bennett. There was no air conditioning in this taxi, and the open windows brought in only stifling air and soot. Perhaps she had underestimated just how bad this day would turn out to be.

Pulling out a cherry-red lipstick, she got some small pleasure imagining her father's annoyance when he saw her. The bright lips alone would have done it, but he hated her long hair loose and uncombed—a dark, inviting jungle—as it was today. The outfit, her camisole tucked into a belted black leather miniskirt, was going to elicit one of his famous looks of cold fury. Usually, her father controlled the talent for intimidation that had served him so well in business; Liza enjoyed being one of the few people who could bring that look to his face spontaneously. Maybe he would be too embarrassed to take her to one of his stuffy haunts for their date. Actually, *appointment* was more like it. This was the only time the two sat down together and spoke more than a few words, despite the fact that she still lived with him in the Fifth Avenue duplex.

Liza was well aware that she was past the age when she should have been out of the house. It was true that she'd been away for most of her teen years and early twenties, first at three different European boarding schools, then for her four years at Vassar. But after graduating from college, she quickly realized how convenient this arrangement was for her, her father's apartment so far superior to any she could afford. Liza found it simpler to stay on. And it didn't seem to make much difference; she and Bennett barely saw each other. He left the house early in the morning and was out most evenings at one of his countless black-tie dinners. Every so often his picture would appear in the newspaper after one of these galas, some lean and sequined socialite on his arm. On the rare nights he didn't go out, he immediately retired to his study to do God-only-knew-what. Liza preferred to sleep until early afternoon, work out in the specially equipped gym, make a few phone calls and begin the evening by meeting friends for drinks. Out by dusk and home at dawn was her favorite kind of day. Even when both of them happened to be in the apartment at the same time, the twelve-room duplex provided ample space for avoiding confrontation. Which was fine with Liza.

Bennett, however, obviously wanted to preserve a public image, the illusion that he cared about her. Hence the lunches—their unspoken bargain. They'd been having these get-togethers for years. The two of them usually went to some expensive restaurant, on view for all the right people. As they drank their coffee, Bennett would hand over the envelope, her $3,000 monthly allowance enclosed. He used the money as bait to ensure that Liza show up. Liza understood there had to be some kind of business advantage in playing the dutiful father. Business, money, and power were all he cared about, all he'd ever cared about. She often felt that he would be completely unmoved—more likely, relieved—if she vanished one day, never to reappear.

Except for his damned money, the feeling was mutual. What made it even worse was that with all he had, he gave her a lousy three thou and required these annoying command performances. Perhaps she should regard the lunches as a family ritual, she thought with a bitter smile, the way other families sang Christmas carols or painted Easter eggs together. Well, this was one little family ritual she could happily live without. On the other hand, there was no alternative right now.

Liza decided she wasn't in the mood to give Bennett the satisfaction of disapproving. She dug around in her oversized leather bag for what she needed. A few minutes later, the lipstick was completely gone—her wide, full mouth innocently bare—and the thick dark hair was pulled back tightly in a demure ponytail. Last night she had brought along a buttery soft, black suede oversized blouse to wear as a jacket in case the September evening turned cool. Now she slipped it over the camisole, leaving it untucked as she rolled down the sleeves and buttoned the front all the way up. The belt went over it, and she bloused the top, instantly eliminating the silhouette of her firm, full breasts and slender waist. By unzipping the skirt, she was able to pull it down over her hips and add a couple of inches to the hem length.

It had to be a full twenty degrees hotter than normal for this time of year, much too warm to be bundled up in suede. Drops of perspiration formed on her forehead to remind her just how much she hated playing the virginal daughter role. It seemed like forever before the cab pulled up in front of the building on Wall Street and she could escape into the air-conditioning. Businessmen hurrying through the cavernous marbled lobby didn't

136

fail to notice Liza as she walked with her usual determined pace toward the elevator bank that would take her to the twenty-third floor. She was still wearing the leopard tights, but that wasn't what made the heads turn. It was Liza herself, sleek, beautiful, and charged with some inexhaustible supply of sexual electricity. Despite her efforts in the taxi, she still looked as if she'd just left one man's bed and wanted nothing more than to fall into another's. Which, at the moment, was absolutely true.

The elevator doors opened to the hush of Carlisle and Poole. Silent, carpeted corridors, painstakingly tended plants, subtle and flattering lighting—every detail was a whisper, but the effect was an overwhelming tribute to money and the power it brings. This was Bennett Carlisle's world. Liza breezed past the receptionist without a word on her way down the long hall to her father's office.

Some years before, Bennett had decided to shift his focus from trading on the stock exchange to investment banking. Once he had made the change, as far as he was concerned, the business day seemed much too short. There were always bigger and better deals to be made, new challenges to get his adrenalin going. The high of arranging a merger between two major corporations was greater than any sexual pleasure he had ever experienced. When he and Alexander Poole opened the doors to their own firm, they marked their debut with an expensive but tasteful gathering. Two hundred of New York's most powerful drank champagne from crystal stem glasses, as they helped themselves to the caviar heaped into sterling tureens and surrounded by toast points, chopped egg, and onion. No speeches, no music, just quiet conversation. The party was brief, and perfectly appointed down to the last detail, just like Bennett himself. That the firm would succeed had never been in doubt by anyone in the financial community, but even its two founders couldn't have anticipated the enormity of its success. Now, over a decade later, the money just kept coming.

Bennett's secretary, Jane, had remained with him through the years. Seeing Liza now, she smiled broadly and gave her a warm hug. Liza returned the gesture with great affection.

"How are you, sweetie?" Jane inquired.

"I'm fine, really great," Liza responded.

Jane took Liza's hands. "Now I can thank you in person for that gorgeous birthday present. It was waiting back at my apartment when I got home last night. You really shouldn't have. I've never owned a necklace as beautiful as that one. I hope I have an occasion soon to show it off."

Liza smiled. "You've earned it, if not for what you've done for me all these years, then for all you've put up with from him. Why do you stick around with the son of a bitch?"

Jane only laughed. "I'll tell him you're here for lunch."

Speaking into an intercom, she informed Bennett that Liza had arrived. By the time he finally appeared ten minutes later, Liza was fuming. Barely brushing his cool lips against her cheek, he offered his hello into the air primarily for Jane's benefit. So polished and handsome, he seemed larger than life. Of course, her father was perfect as always, thought Liza as they rode down the elevator. Perfectly trim and fit, his thick silvery hair perfectly in place, his pin-striped suit perfectly tailored, his white shirt perfectly white. A perfect iceberg.

Bennett's limousine waited in front of the building. They rode in silence until they reached the Harvard Club. Liza groaned inwardly when she saw his selection. Not again. It was so boring and stuffy. From the instant they entered, Bennett was all charm and warmth to the maitre d', the waiter, even the busboy. As much as she loathed him, Liza had to admire her father's acting skill, his ability to win over practically anyone.

She wasn't prepared for the speed with which his mood changed as soon as their food was served and the waiter moved out of earshot. His face showed no expression, but displeasure and sarcasm were evident in every clipped word.

"I am not in the habit of paying four-thousand-dollar bar bills signed in my name at the hangouts you and your delightful friends enjoy frequenting," he said in a low tone. "Since you appear to be walking upright, I can only imagine that you did not personally consume four thousand dollars' worth of liquor in the past thirty days, but have been buying drinks for every man, woman, and child in the United States."

"Oh, for God's sake, is it a federal offense to be a gracious host? You're the one who taught me how important image is, you know," Liza retorted. Four thousand dollars meant nothing to him and it was ridiculous to reprimand her like a child. Lunch wasn't going to be easy to endure today.

Bennett spoke very slowly, his voice dropping almost to a whisper as his anger mounted. "I'll be goddamned if I'm going to waste my energy lecturing you. You have been told repeatedly that you are expected to live on what you are given each month. It may surprise you, but this particular gravy train does not run forever. I want to know, *right now*, what you expect to do about your so-called work."

Bennett's luncheon conversation with her was usually restricted to the smallest of small talk, so she was completely unprepared for this attack. Before she could help herself, she was on the defensive.

"There's no reason I can't be a good, no great, producer if I want to," she snapped. "I did a sensational job on that music video, and another group wants me to do one for them next month. You have no idea how this industry works. You can't make money before you invest some time and effort. That's a concept you should understand."

Bennett stifled an impulse to reach across

the table and smack his daughter. He forced himself to cut another piece of salmon very slowly while he regained his composure. She's a spoiled bitch, just like her mother and it's too late to do anything about it. But enough was enough. He'd carried Liza far too long. Twenty-four years old and still sponging off him. It was disgusting. Producer, his ass.

"I just need some time, just a little bit more, please," she wheedled.

Their eyes locked, and Liza knew she was in trouble. Her father was the one man she found difficult to handle. She mentally reviewed her other alternatives. There was no real money to be made in the near future. Her friends were full of ideas. At least, it seemed that way. But very little actually ever *happened*.

Of course, there was that music video a while back. Despite the problems with it, she unquestionably had a flair for the job. She knew how to get people to do what she wanted, and she quickly understood that this was what producing was all about. But the tedium of detail work in no way appealed to her.

For now, though, it suited Liza just fine to call herself a producer. "Idle rich girl" was no kind of title to sport in this decade. Film and video producer sounded glamorous, interesting. It kept plenty of doors open. But suddenly, her father seemed to be changing the rules. How much longer would Bennett support her?

The answer came right away.

"Here's what you're waiting for," Bennett said, pulling the envelope with Liza's check from his inside breast pocket and sliding it over to her side of the table. "You have three months to make whatever arrangements you feel are necessary. During that time you will continue to receive your monthly allowance. Then my financial support stops."

Liza was thinking fast, but she never got the chance to respond. Whatever she might have said was interrupted by a short, overweight man who chose that moment to stop at their table.

"Bennett, you son of a bitch. How the hell are you?" he boomed, pumping Bennett's hand vigorously.

Liza recognized his face; she'd seen his photograph in the paper. Ed somebody, a slimy little man who happened to have made a fortune in the stock market. Bennett adopted his polite, elder-statesman pose, immediately responsive to another man of wealth. Their visitor pulled up a chair and the two men became engrossed in conversation about some oil deal falling through. Liza stifled a yawn. Ed wasn't so caught up in the discussion that he couldn't eye her the whole time, she noted. He was undoubtedly trying to guess her relationship to Bennett. Finally he went fishing. "Bennett, old man, you go out with the most beautiful women in New York," he said. Ho, ho, very sly, thought Liza contemptuously.

"C'mon, Ed, I know you're joking. Haven't you met my lovely daughter, Liza?" answered Bennett.

Liza bit her lip to keep silent. Now wasn't the time to embarrass Bennett, considering the ultimatum he'd just delivered. Ed picked up their wine bottle and filled Bennett's empty water glass. With an openly admiring look at Liza he raised the glass high and offered a toast.

"May there always be lovely ladies like this one to bring sunshine into the lives of us poor helpless men."

Bennett raised his wineglass and smiled as sincerely as if these words had warmed him to the very foundation of his being. Liza was not to be outdone. She lifted her glass as well, opening her eyes in an expression of innocence. A modest tilt of the head and a demure smile followed. "Aren't you just the nicest man?" she purred to Ed. He practically licked his lips. Liza glanced over at Bennett, whose face remained impassive.

When the toast was completed, Ed and Bennett continued their seemingly endless conversation. A few minutes later, Liza was on her way out the door, having claimed a suddenly remembered appointment. Tuning out his table partner for a moment, Bennett, like most of the other men in the room, watched her exit. His thoughts, however, were far different from those entertained by the other male diners.

If only she didn't look so much like Claire, with those high cheekbones and the flawless white skin. The resemblance had gotten stronger as the years went on. He hoped it was just his imagination, but he thought he'd actually noticed some of that damned silvery hair today, just like her mother's. And despite the expensive boarding schools, summer camps, and European trips—appropriate for the daughter of the wealthy Bennett Carlisle, and, not incidentally, a convenient way of removing her from the house—she'd turned out completely selfish. As spoiled as rotten fruit. He was repulsed by her public revels, out all night every night. No matter what he did with his nights, Bennett maintained discretion at all costs. Liza on the other hand didn't know the meaning of the word. She flaunted her body shamelessly, he thought, as if to invite every man who still had a pulse to give her a try. She'd always been that way. Well, he wasn't going to foot the bill any longer.

But, actually, he thought, she was a small price to pay for his revenge against Claire. He had derived tremendous satisfaction through the years imagining his wife's misery over the loss of her older daughter. Claire hadn't given up easily, but when she had fully understood that he had every intention of carrying out his threats, she'd retreated into silence in order to hold onto her other child. Bennett had anticipated that Claire would come back for Liza when both girls were older, and custody no longer an issue. He smiled, remembering. Claire had waited until Liza turned eighteen before attempting to contact her, no doubt to be sure Bennett couldn't pull some legal maneuver at the last minute. But she had misjudged him, the depth of his hatred for her. He was waiting.

Liza had been at Vassar then, in her freshman year. He had simply explained to the school administrators that a man in his position had many enemies; he had even received a number of threats from abroad. He was concerned about his daughter's welfare and security. Please, he had entreated them, if anything out of the ordinary happened, they were to let him know right away. Naturally, when someone turned up to confirm that a Liza Carlisle attended college there, the school officials called Bennett immediately. His thanks were effusive. He knew immediately this was Claire's doing. It was simple to have the letter he knew would eventually come redirected to him.

Sitting alone in his study, Bennett had read the letter Claire had written to Liza. In it, Claire had poured forth the whole story. She took full blame for what happened and begged her child to forgive her. The letter ended with the request that Liza tell Claire if and when she would be willing to meet face to face, and a standing offer of a home with Claire and her younger daughter—whom she referred to as Page—in London. He had laughed, marveling at her tenacity. The next day, knowing that his secretary's fondness for Liza made her untrustworthy in this matter, he waited until Jane left for lunch before calling Western Union himself to send a telegram. There had been no further communication from Claire after that.

"More coffee, Mr. Carlisle?"

Bennett was startled to find the waiter standing at his side, holding a steaming silver pot. "No, thank you."

"So, what do you think of that?" asked Ed, flushed with excitement.

Bennett realized that his companion had been so busy talking, he hadn't even noticed Bennett's total lack of attention.

Bennett paused, looking thoughtful, before replying. "Interesting. Very interesting."

Liza stood on the sidewalk outside the Harvard Club, considering Bennett's ultimatum. She decided to take a walk and think things over, heading south on Fifth Avenue. Why, after all this time, was he cutting her off? she wondered. He knew perfectly well she was not in any position to take care of her own expenses. Without pausing in her stride, Liza removed the suede overblouse and released her hair from the constraining rubber band, not even noticing the interested stares she was getting from several men walking by. She was much too busy wondering if a bigger bastard than her father had ever existed on this planet.

The post office was only a few blocks west. Liza realized she'd had a destination without being conscious of it. She hurried now, reaching into her bag to find the post-office box key, veering to avoid an old man sprawled out drunk in her path. Taking the steps two at a time, she headed to the public mailboxes.

Liza had rented Box 2P27 under a fictitious name nearly seven years before. Periodically she would stop by to see if there was anything new waiting there. It wasn't that she received her letters here or used it for business purposes. This was her secret mail drop, devoted solely to the subject of Claire Warren and her daughter Page.

After Liza's expulsion from Beaumatin, Bennett had lost no time in getting her enrolled in another Swiss school. It was simple enough to write to her old friend Allison that she bore her no ill will for the marijuana incident. This way, Liza was able to follow the comings and goings of Page Warren. Allison knew that Liza and Page had some kind of relationship, so she saw nothing out of the ordinary about Liza's occasional questions on how the younger girl was doing. With Allison's unwitting help, Liza was able to find out where Page lived, and some of the details of her life away from school with Claire.

Liza kept track of their every move. Once she realized that the Warrens were well known in England, she subscribed to a wide variety of British magazines, searching for anything about them. It was an inefficient system, but every so often, she came up with something. By the time she was ready to start Vassar, her technique had grown more sophisticated; she hired a British clipping service and rented the post office box.

At first, the clippings came sporadically. As their business continued to grow, the Warrens became the subject of more and more articles, all of which eventually made their way to Post Office Box 2P27. Every month or so, Liza would grit her teeth over the newspaper and magazine accounts waiting there for her—news of Warren hotel openings, features on the enlightened Warren management style, flattering personal profiles.

From the stories, Liza gathered enough nuggets of information to piece the entire picture together. Page was being passed off as the legitimate child of Claire and John Warren. With a few changes in the dates, Claire had established a fictitious family history for the three of them, a history featuring the blatant lie that she and John Warren were married. Among the few things Liza knew for sure about her parents' situation was that Bennett had never been divorced from Claire. She had watched her father keep other women at bay for years with this excuse. Technically, Claire was still married to him. Yet the clippings made it seem as if Bennett and Liza never existed. The so-called Warrens were known for their elegant parties and charity work, as well as the magnificent townhouse where they lived. They were sought after and admired. Page obviously wasn't resisting the charade. Why should she, thought Liza cynically. After all, the lovely "Page Warren" stood to inherit the Warren fortune plus a dandy position in London society.

It didn't take long before an article turned up with a photograph of her mother and John

Warren together. They were on their way to the ballet. Claire as swathed in mink, jewels glittering, while John Warren sported a belted cashmere overcoat. It was just another night on the town for London's favorite duo, noted the reporter. In the picture, Warren was holding Claire's hand and had his other arm around her, helping her into their vintage Rolls-Royce. With one foot on the car's running board, she had paused to look up at him. Claire seemed to radiate happiness as the camera snapped the two smiling at each other. Nearly a head taller than Claire, John Warren was slim, with broad shoulders. His build was very similar to Bennett's, Liza observed. However, the resemblance between the two men stopped there. Warren was also handsome, but in a completely different way. Beneath wavy dark hair, his brown eyes were warm and friendly. The mouth was a generous one, full and giving—a powerful contrast to her father's, with his thin lips so often pursued tightly together. He held Claire protectively, his large hands gently embracing her as if she were made of the most fragile crystal. It wasn't the display of wealth that disturbed Liza. It was the almost palpable sense of warmth, of a happy family, so obvious in the pictures, that underscored the cold emptiness of her own life.

John Warren was fifty-seven when he died, two years after Liza first saw his photograph. He had been coming home from a business meeting and was killed instantly when a drunk driver smashed head-on into the Rolls. It was in his obituary that Liza first learned Page had actually been living in Manhattan for a year, studying at Columbia. A brief follow-up story several weeks later covered a press conference in which Claire confirmed that she was taking over the Warren hotel business completely, and her daughter Page was returning to England to join her. There were no pictures this time.

Though she pored over every detail, Liza never shared her discovery with anyone. There was no point in telling Bennett, who had long ago forbidden her to discuss Claire or Meredith and didn't even seem to care whether they were alive or dead. No, this was going to be among the three of them: Liza, her mother, and her sister.

How simple they must have found it, how convenient for both of them. They'd just slipped off, assuming stupid little Liza would never find them. Why not let the whole world know that Liza was so unworthy, so unlovable, her own mother couldn't be bothered to keep her? Well, it wasn't going to be that easy. That day back at Beaumatin, Liza had made a promise to herself to make them pay for everything they'd put her through. It was a promise she intended to keep. Only two questions remained. When? And how? No rush. Liza could bide her time. She enjoyed thinking of herself as an invisible eye, watching them silently. She went on collecting the clippings, studying them, waiting, waiting. When the time was right, she would know.

Liza walked through the ugly institutional

doorway, past the long lines, right to Box 2P27. It had been nearly three months since she'd last looked for news from abroad. How lovely, there was something in the box right now. Bless the little old Fulbridge Clipping Agency, they hadn't fallen down on the job. Liza slipped the oversized envelope into her bag, left the post office, and grabbed a taxi home.

It wasn't until she had undressed, bathed, and was relaxing naked on her king-sized bed that she permitted herself the pleasure of reading what was in the familiar gray envelope. She propped up several pillows against the black lacquer headboard and lay back, slicing open the envelope with a mother-of-pearl letter opener.

The contents took her by surprise. Over a year before Liza had read about Claire's grand scheme to restore the graciousness of old England in renovated castles and country estates. The idea of reviving former British glory immediately caught the fancy of the press, and they wrote about her plans in glowing terms. But after the initial flurry of publicity, Liza hadn't seen any other references to this end of the Warren business. She assumed the project had failed or been abandoned. As it turned out, either Claire had kept it under wraps or the Fulbridge Agency was getting lazy, because these clippings told her the whole thing was very much alive.

According to an article from the feature page of the *Daily Express* dated three weeks earlier, it had been "a very happy birthday for Warren Manor." The first Manor, a farmhouse in the Cotswolds, had been a big success, and had been photographed by a magazine in London. The writer gushed that "Here one can only truly find escape from the modern world, cared for by maids and butlers so attentive and silently efficient, one can only imagine they have somehow been transported from another century. No detail has been overlooked in creating the graciousness of a bygone era."

Quickly scanning the rest of the clippings, Liza discovered that all of them celebrated the success of Warren Manors. Extensive renovation went into each new Manor, to say nothing of the time and money devoted to the interior design. Warren International had gone far out on a limb, making massive cash commitments so that multiple estates could be worked on simultaneously and finished in record time. "So far," read another story, "the company has been able to complete three such manors without any sacrifice of quality. Had the restorations been completed at a far more leisurely pace, this would have been a notable accomplishment. As it is, one can only marvel at the dedication that could produce such excellence."

Liza was stunned. But nothing had prepared her for the statement that followed. At a garden party, Claire told the newspaper that she "really had little to do with the whole thing. It was truly my daughter Page who conceived and executed the entire plan. The reporters continually try to give me the credit and I continually tell them I cannot accept it. This is Page Warren's triumph."

The article concluded with the fact that Warren International had increased its overall revenues eleven percent, an astounding figure given the huge initial investment into the Manors.

Liza dropped the clippings on the floor and closed her eyes to think. Claire and Page were having so much success so fast, and Liza hadn't even been aware of it. Those bitches, trotting all around the countryside, playing the grande-dame routine, and amassing money right and left—not one cent of which did they plan to share with Liza. Well, as of today, she was no longer the ignorant fool. A smile spread across her face and she lay serenely still for a few minutes. Everything was coming together. She reached out for the telephone on the night table and dialed. Cradling the receiver between her ear and shoulder, she sat up and rummaged around the table's small drawer until she located her passport.

"Get me Steve," she commanded into the receiver when a voice finally answered. "It's Liza Carlisle." These damn travel agents were such a pain. Steve came on the line in a matter of seconds; Bennett was one of the agency's best clients. "I want a first-class ticket on the next flight to London," Liza instructed. "No, one way only. I'll pick it up at the airport. Call me back with the flight and time."

Hanging up, Liza hurried over to her closet and pulled out her largest suitcase. The closet had originally been another bedroom, which had been converted to accommodate her enormous wardrobe. Special automated revolving racks had been installed, similar to those of a professional dry cleaner. Beige silk lined the walls and there were dozens of shelves holding Liza's endless supply of shoes and handbags. Any noise she might make in the brightly lit closet was muffled by the plush off-white carpeting. Her face a study in intensity, Liza pressed the control buttons that set the metal poles in motion. She felt a gentle breeze against her naked skin as the clothing was briskly pulled around and around.

The choice of what to take couldn't be rushed; her decisions had to be just right. Stepping forward, she felt something soft under her foot and looked down. The leopard tights were crumpled on the floor where she had hurriedly torn them off an hour ago, anxious to get into a cool tub. Two dozen identical pairs lay neatly folded in her dresser drawer. Liza knew her leopard tights would be staying behind. This particular trip required a new look, an altogether different image. Her ivory linen suit was a good place to start, a bit more conservative than her usual outfits. And where were those very simple leather pumps? Pulling down several shoeboxes from the extra storage racks overhead, she began to laugh.

"Hey, Mom," she said softly, "little Liza's coming for a visit."

Chapter Ten

By the time Page walked out onto Tottenham Court Road, she was exhausted. Shopping used to be fun, she thought to herself as she searched in vain for an empty cab. Now it was endless work, trudging from the fancy foods of Harrod's to the paintings at Thomas Agnew & Son, pricing, ordering, comparing. She supposed that most people would have been thrilled to be able to spend well over four thousand pounds in one day without a second thought, but that had long ago stopped impressing her. And the fact that it was a Thursday was no help. To the rest of the world, that meant the weekend was almost here. Since Warren Manors had become a reality, weekends had ceased to exist for Page. It seemed as if she did only three things: paperwork, shopping, and traveling. All for the greater glory of Warren International.

Giving up on the idea of a taxi, Page headed for the nearest underground station on Goodge Street. I have absolutely no right to complain, she mused, stopping at a traffic light. Hers was a wonderful life. Still, when she first proposed the idea of Camden Manor, she'd had no idea how many details would have to be attended to every single day. Page now chose the sites, interviewed the hosts, oversaw the renovations, and spearheaded the publicity campaigns. There were now three—soon to be four—Warren Manor houses gracing the British countryside. It gave her a tremendous sense of accomplishment, but right now she felt as if she would trade it all in for twenty minutes in a hot bath.

Caught up in her thoughts, it wasn't until the light changed that Page noticed the young man sitting at the wheel of a dark gray Peugeot and staring at her. Handsome, she thought. And familiar. All at once she remembered. An actor. The one who played Cassius. Insufferable. Rude. And pulling up right in front of her.

"It's Miss Warren, isn't it?"

Damn it. This was the last thing she needed today. How long ago had it been since she'd met him originally? Six months, maybe longer. She remembered their meeting all too well.

As if to make up for what she was thinking, she put out her hand and, in her most pleasant tone of voice, said, "Yes. Page Warren. And you're Simon Roberts."

He had been watching her from the comfort of his air-conditioned car. Despite her obvious fatigue on such a muggy day, she looked beautiful. Although their meeting had been several months before, Simon remembered her quite well. Challenging. Cheeky. Not quite what she appeared to be. He found he was glad to see her. Judging by her cool greeting, the feeling didn't seem to be mutual, but his mood was much too good for him to be put off by whatever it was she was thinking behind that well-raised exterior.

"Can I give you a lift?" he asked, looking sympathetically at the heavy bags she was carrying.

"Oh, no. Thank you very much. I'm just on my way to the underground." Page was reluctant to extend this encounter. She recalled with unusual clarity the antagonism she had felt when they first met.

"Page." Simon's voice was soft. "It's unbelievably hot, you're carrying too much, and all of London is in the underground right now." He pointed to his watch, which read five-fifteen.

Page didn't want to talk to anyone at this moment, especially not this man, but finally the heat and her exhaustion convinced her, the deciding vote cast by the cool air conditioning she could feel escaping through his open window. "All right, then, thank you. I appreciate it."

Simon got out of his car, depositing her parcels on the backseat and holding the door for her. "We may run into a bit of traffic, I'm afraid, but it should be more comfortable than the train."

Page was so glad to be seated and cool, the thought of traffic didn't bother her in the least. "I live on Albion Street, if it's not too far out of your way."

"No, that's fine."

Simon's reply sounded sincere. Intrigued, she looked more closely at him. He was handsome, with his dark curly hair already showing the smallest hints of gray. Casually dressed in a khaki summer suit, with a plaid shirt and knitted tie, he appeared remarkably benign for a man she remembered as contemptuous and reserved. Page was caught totally off-guard as she realized how attractive he was.

Simon turned to her. "The cars are barely moving. I hope this doesn't make you late for something important."

"No," she answered briefly. Aware of how rude she must seem, she added, "I have quite a bit more work to do tonight, but I'll have time later."

Simon glanced over at her as she spoke, looking frankly at her slender, graceful body. Uneasy at his scrutiny, Page turned the subject away from herself. "What have you been doing since I saw you last?"

"Auditioning, mainly. A couple of spots on the BBC. Actually, I've just come from a meeting that could change my life." The excitement shone in his eyes.

"A meeting about what?" Page asked, fascinated despite herself.

"Carl Meyer is casting *Birds of Passage,* and I'm up for the part of Jonathan."

"That's quite an opportunity," Page said. Carl Meyer was acknowledged on both sides of the Atlantic as one of the finest young directors to come along in years. *Birds of Passage* was a bona-fide literary masterpiece, which had unexpectedly become a bestseller as well.

"The part isn't mine yet. I feel superstitious even talking about it. You know, actors never get a role once they say it out loud to another person. It's a law." His humor did not hide a nagging belief in this show-business maxim.

"I bet you'll get it. You're awfully good." Page couldn't believe she was so eager to give him the satisfaction of her praise, but the man sitting with her today seemed completely unrelated to the person she had met that night with Chris.

"Please don't say that. My not saying anything is Rule One. *Your* not saying anything is almost as important to the capricious thespian gods who hold my fate in their hands." Simon laughed at himself, then continued in an intense voice. "You know, I'd give anything to work with Carl Meyer. I feel about movies the way your friend Chris feels about the stage. The range of emotions, the character building you can do in the intimacy of a camera lens is magical. And Jonathan is such an extraordinary man." He spoke of the character as if he really existed.

Page had read the book shortly before her work on Camden Manor had begun, and liked it. Indeed, the actor who played Jonathan could become a major star. She realized how perfect Simon would be for the part and said as much to him.

"Perfect? Thank you, but when anything seems perfect, I get suspicious."

"Why?" Page asked. "Have you had such disappointment in your life?"

"The usual, I suppose." The actor's face was studiously noncommittal.

"I don't believe you mean that." Page's curiosity was aroused. Up to this moment he had been so accessible. Why would he retreat like that? She decided to pursue the subject. "What were you thinking of just now?"

Simon looked hard at her. Finally, he decided to give her a real answer, not simply put her off as he had done so many times before to so many women. "Actually, I was thinking about my mother. She died suddenly when I was a small boy."

Simon was only seven years old and life had seemed just right. Big house, nice dad, great mom, dog, friends, the works. He had been sleeping outside on the warm July evening, joyfully enclosed in a tent behind his house, his best friend Ron asleep next to him, when the siren woke them up. It took a couple of minutes for both boys to come fully awake and to slip out of the tent around to the front yard to see what was happening. He would never forget the dread, how slowly it came, how thoroughly it covered him from head to toe, when he realized that it was his mother lying, motionless, on a stretcher, his father helplessly awash in tears. The little boy had grown to be a wary teenager. When he was sixteen, at a teacher's urging, he had reluctantly auditioned for a school play, and, to his initial chagrin, got the part. Playing Henry Higgins in *Pygmalion,* he made a remarkable discovery: he felt entirely safe when he could be someone else. He often thought that his choice of profession had more to do with that feeling than with talent, although luckily, he had that as well.

"Do you ever trust anyone?" There was no hostility in Page's tone.

Simon thought a moment, and again decided to respond with more than just a glib answer. "I fell in love once. I imagine that constitutes trusting someone."

"Forgive me—I'm prying."

"That's all right. I don't mind." Simon hesitated, then went on. "I don't think I ever trusted anyone after Mom's death until I met Sarah Hughes."

Page immediately recognized the name of the respected actress. "We were doing *Romeo and Juliet* at a small theater run as an actors' cooperative. Far from the lofty West End, I assure you. Perhaps it was the idealism of the place or the passion of the characters we were playing. Whatever it was, I allowed myself to fall in love with her, no holding back. And she loved me the same way."

"What happened?" Page almost hesitated to ask.

"One day, she didn't love me anymore. She never planned to hurt me. To stop loving me. It just happened. After the production was over, Sarah went to Cornwall to do Maggie in *Cat on a Hot Tin Roof*. She fell in love with Brick—William Harper. It wasn't cruel or thoughtless. It just was."

Page knew, as all England knew, that Sarah Hughes and William Harper were still married, the parents of several children, said by the press to be ecstatically in love. Often acting together, they were one of the country's most famous couples.

Poor Simon, Page thought. "Thank you for telling me that. It explains a lot. You know, when we were first introduced, I thought you were indifferent. I didn't have any idea how much you might need to protect yourself."

Simon looked at Page and smiled briefly. "I think I was getting to be a little too good at protecting myself. You know, remembering Sarah doesn't hurt anymore. For years now, I've made my disappointment my guide, and perhaps it's time to stop. I guess I've become rather hardened."

In fact, Simon had become unerring in picking out the liars and the users who were in huge supply on the London stage. To the others, the people who were genuinely kind, truly talented, he was cordial. Never rude but never warm. Only onstage did he unleash the feelings he kept under such strict control. He sometimes wondered if his talent would be as strong if he allowed his passion to emerge in real life. He needed to close himself off, so his acting could have real anguish, real longing behind it. Was this true, he wondered, or was it something he needed to tell himself to get through the lonely days and nights?

Simon was almost always alone when he

wasn't performing. Even at parties, in conversation with fellow actors, he seemed a thousand miles away. Safe in his isolation. People found him intimidating, but his talent and good looks made him a draw. So there were plenty of invitations. Sometimes he would go—that is, if someone else's plans happened to coincide with his urge for a beer. He would join a group, sit down in a pub for exactly as long as it took to drink two pints of bitter, then get up and go home. Women often found his brooding presence fascinating. Once in a while, he would leave with one of them. They would always go to her place, so he could make an exit whenever he chose. He tried to be fair on these occasions. He never promised anything, never said he'd call when he had no intention of doing so. And he was an excellent lover. He knew he was cheating these women of passion, so he made sure to make up for it in consideration and skill. Some women came to appreciate his honesty. If no one was allowed to really touch him or love him, at least there was no cruelty beneath the cool surface.

He regarded Page. She seemed to understand everything he said, yet she hadn't made a big deal of it. She was unusual, this girl. Simon thought back to the night *Julius Caesar* opened. "I had you all wrong," he said.

At this, Page smiled. "You're not the only one."

Simon pulled the car up in front of the Warren house and reached across the front seat to take Page's hand before she could open the car door. "I have a rehearsal tonight, but how about dinner tomorrow?"

Page responded shyly. "Yes, I'd like that very much."

What was it about this man? Either he made her furious or he left her feeling like a breathless child.

After Simon dropped her at the house, Page was much too excited to finish the work she'd planned to do. She hardly spoke a word to Claire at dinner. All she could think about was her date with Simon the following night. Trying unsuccessfully to fall asleep, she kept seeing his blue eyes in her mind.

She was still in a haze when she reached her office Friday morning. Seated at her desk, her thoughts kept jumping from the promise of the night before to the anticipation of that evening. Only after a phone conversation with the newest Manor host did she finally begin to concentrate on the stack of memos and correspondence crowding her desk.

Chapter Eleven

Liza Carlisle turned right on Duke Street and stopped directly in front of Warren International. She paused to admire the six-story building's architectural beauty. Erected in the 1840s, the design indicated that it had once been a private mansion on the grandest of scales.

How long Liza had waited to see this up close. Perhaps I'll turn it back into a private home, she thought, smiling, as she gazed up at the tall windows and intricate ornamentation. She wouldn't mind living here. As a matter of fact, it would do quite nicely. With a laugh, she went through the wrought-iron gate and ran up the marble steps to the front door.

Liza had refrained from making her first appearance until today, although she had arrived in London the previous morning. She didn't want jet lag to dull her wits, and, besides, she thought she might as well take a few hours for herself before the game began. From Heathrow Airport on Thursday morning, she had gone straight to the Savoy Hotel and checked into a suite overlooking the Thames. A brief nap was followed by a shower and a tall gin and tonic. Then she was off for some shopping, fitting in stops in Mayfair, Knightsbridge, and Kensington. The hours sped by as Liza came upon one thing after another that seemed made just for her. This was the kind of shopping she liked; the best of everything, the right kind of service. It was after seven that night when she returned to the hotel with her purchases.

By nine o'clock, she was down at the hotel bar relaxing over a dry martini. When the attractive Brazilian man sitting next to her paid for her drink, she was more than happy to strike up a conversation in return. Over dinner, he kept her amused with his stories about traveling on the Amazon River, making Liza promise she would visit him in Rio during Carnivale. She wouldn't permit him to stay the night; as soon as they'd finished in bed, she sent him home so she would be sure to get a solid eight hours' sleep.

Friday morning, Liza woke up, refreshed and ready for anything. She slipped into a cashmere sweater dress of the palest pink, smiling with satisfaction at her reflection in the mirror. London's mild September was a welcome relief from the steamy New York weather she'd left behind, and, filled with anticipation, she enjoyed every minute of the walk to her mother's office.

As she pulled open the heavy wooden doors of Warren headquarters, Liza noted the high-arched ceiling, magnificent gleaming wood floors and marble staircase. A small iron cage elevator was to her left. This must be the first elevator ever made, she thought, amused, as she closed the rickety gate behind her. The top floor would probably be the one she wanted. She pressed the button marked six and waited, tapping her foot impatiently during the slow ascent. The muffled sounds of voices, ringing telephones and clacking keyboards rose and faded as she passed each floor.

At the end of the sixth-floor hallway, Liza was greeted by a young red-haired woman typing at a Queen Anne desk.

"Good morning. May I help you?"

Liza leaned over to savor the aroma of a large

arrangement of irises. "I'm here to see Claire Warren."

"Do you have an appointment with Mrs. Warren?"

"No, but I feel certain she'll want to know I'm here." Liza smiled broadly.

"I'm terribly sorry, but Mrs. Warren doesn't see anyone without an appointment." The woman's response was polite but firm.

"Just tell her it's Liza Carlisle. I can assure you that if you don't, you will find yourself out of a job in no time flat." Liza's tone remained pleasant if her words did not.

The secretary hesitated. She seemed about to say something, then apparently thought better of it. Instead, she picked up the telephone and dialed an extension. "There's a woman here to see you, Mrs. Warren. I told her an appointment was required, but she insists. Her name is Liza Carlisle." There was a pause. The secretary swiveled her chair in the direction of one of the two large oak office doors behind her. "Mrs. Warren? Are you there, Mrs. Warren?" she said into the telephone.

Liza swiftly crossed to the door she now knew was Claire's and entered the office.

From behind her desk, Claire looked up, saying nothing as she stared at the woman before her. She slowly replaced the telephone receiver. It couldn't be; it was impossible.

"Hello, Mother," Liza said, breaking into her most dazzling smile.

Claire caught her breath. The eyes, the face, the smile. Dear God.

"*Liza, oh, Liza,*" she cried out. "Is it really you?"

Claire flew across the room and embraced Liza as if she would never be parted from her again.

"It's so wonderful to have found you," Liza said with great feeling, as she held her mother tightly.

Weeping with joy, Claire tenderly took Liza's face in her two hands, drinking in the sight of her daughter.

"My baby," she whispered.

Just then, there was a quick knock and the door to Claire's office was opened. Page stood there, flipping through a sheaf of papers, obviously looking for something.

"Wilson's said they would send over an updated proposal for that landscaping, but I never got it," she said without raising her eyes. "They didn't send it to you by any chance, did they?" She looked up and took a quick step back, surprised by the scene before her. "Oh, excuse me. I didn't know you had... I...forgive me."

"It's all right, darling," Claire said through her tears, smiling. "Come in, come in. I have the most incredible news."

Bewildered, Page observed the woman to whom Claire was clinging. Claire always kept her emotions in check; she had often told Page that she believed private matters were best kept that way. Page had never seen her mother out of control like this, crying at the office. What could this woman have said to her? Who was she? Page watched her take a seat on the couch and casually cross her legs. There was something familiar about her.

"Page, sweetheart, I'm afraid you're about to have something of a shock. You see, this is Liza Carlisle. She—"

"Liza Carlisle! Of course, I knew I recognized you!" Smiling brightly, Page walked forward to shake her hand. "How lovely to see you."

"Hello, Page," Lisa said quietly.

Astonishment was plainly visible on Claire's face. "You two *know* each other?"

"Of course we do, Mother," answered Page, sitting down excitedly next to Liza on the couch. "We were at Beaumatin together for a little while. Not too long, actually, was it, Liza?"

Liza directed her response to Claire. "One semester, as a matter of fact."

"Right, just the one term," Page went on hurriedly, eager to finish her story so she could catch up with her old schoolmate. "Anyway, Liza was so nice to me. In fact, I really looked up to her. How terrific, Liza, your visiting here."

Claire spoke slowly. "Wait, I don't understand. You two were at the same school at the same time?"

"Yes, Mother, I've explained that," Page said a little impatiently. Why was her mother acting so peculiar?

Claire's expression was full of pain as the meaning of the words set in. "Oh, Liza, you were right there!"

"I certainly was," Liza answered with a half-smile.

"So now you've come to visit," Page forged ahead, trying to get to the bottom of all this.

Claire jumped back into the conversation quickly. "No, no, I hope she's not just visiting. You've come to stay with us, Liza, please say you have."

"Oh, yes. All I want now is to be with the two of you." Liza rose and went over to kiss Claire on the cheek.

"Let me tell Susan to have your things sent over right away—you're moving in with us," Claire said. "Where are you staying?"

"The Savoy."

"Fine. I'll be right back." Claire exited, leaving her two daughters alone in her office.

"Now I'm the one who doesn't seem to be following," Page said haltingly. "Do you know my mother? Oh—is it that you're planning to come to work for Warren International?"

Liza leaned back against Claire's desk, supporting her weight on her hands and crossing her ankles in front of her. She smiled, but there was a frightening intensity in her glittering gaze that hadn't been there a moment before. With a short laugh, she mimicked Page's questioning tone. "No, I'm not *planning to work for Warren International*. Warren International is going to work for *me*."

Before the stunned Page had a chance to reply, Claire re-entered the room. "Everything's taken care of, Liza. So let's get you settled in.

I'm going to do whatever I can to convince you to live with us permanently."

"Oh, yes. I want to live with you and be with you, and, if you'll have me, work with you. We should be together always from now on." Liza took her mother's hand.

Page couldn't believe what she was hearing. Was this the same woman who had just delivered those verbal darts? Her words to Claire sounded like sugar. For that matter, could it be the same Liza Carlisle from boarding school who was so sophisticated, always getting into trouble? Oh yes, it was coming back. She was only there one term because she was expelled. *That* Liza had been wild and tough. How demure she was now. How innocent and fragile. Why, she'd practically batted her eyelashes at Claire.

"Mother..." Page didn't know what to say, what to ask.

Claire turned to her, but it was clear her mind wasn't on her younger daughter. "Oh, yes, dear. You see, well, it's rather difficult to explain, but Liza is your sister. She..." Claire faltered, trying to find the words. "She wasn't able to be with us all these years. I'll tell you—I'll tell you everything later."

Page stared at her mother. "What on earth are you saying? How could Liza be my sister?"

"It's such a long, complicated story, Page." Claire was obviously reluctant to go into the details just then. "You see, you and she were actually born in America. I was married to someone else, the man who was your father. Then I got separated from Liza."

Page's face went white with shock. "I don't believe this. You're saying that Dad wasn't—who was he? How could you have kept this from me all these years? *Why* did you?"

"Oh, Page, honey, I—we never wanted to hurt you. But sweetheart, it's not at all simple, and we should sit down and talk about it tonight. The three of us. I promise all your questions will be answered."

Claire put an arm around Liza's shoulders as they walked toward the door, Page apparently forgotten. Claire's words spilled out in a happy rush. "Now, come and tell me everything. Oh, it's incredible—I can't tell you what it means to have you back. We have so much to talk about."

The door closed behind them and Page was left alone in silence. She felt unable to move. Her *sister*. Why hadn't Page known about her? What the hell was happening? And those eyes. What was it Page had seen in those eyes?

Page felt a cold fear. Icy cold.

Page wandered from one end of the house to the other, unable to sit still for more than a moment. She'd felt unnerved since Liza had arrived that afternoon, and of course she'd had to cancel her date with Simon. He'd been confused but understanding, and they'd rescheduled for a couple of nights later.

Dinner with her sister and mother hadn't made it any easier. Her *sister*! Even the sound of the word made her uncomfortable. How could her mother have been keeping such a secret all these years? She'd been dying to talk to Claire privately, to ask all the questions that kept running through her head, but there hadn't been even a second. Her mother was so focused on Liza, she hardly even heard Page when she'd asked a timid question or two.

Not that Page even knew where to begin. She could barely get past the fact that John Warren wasn't really her father, let alone the question of why she'd never even been told about Bennett Carlisle. Her mind was ablaze with confusion. Not just confusion, she acknowledged, as she once again tried to sit quietly on the tufted couch in the library. In fact, she felt fear. There was something frightening about the way Liza spoke to Page as opposed to the tone she used with Claire. Something unnatural about the way she just appeared, out of nowhere. Like a vulture, Page thought, immediately chiding herself for being so unkind.

Well, unkind or not, she had to talk to her mother. She just had to. But Claire had been upstairs with Liza since dinner. She could hear their voices, chirping away. Her mother had half-heartedly asked Page to join them, but she knew that all Claire really cared about was catching up with Liza. And that was fine. Well, she amended, not exactly fine. But understandable under the circumstances.

Yet she needed to have a few minutes with

Claire. She had to understand. Not realizing she was doing it, she stood up yet again, walking slowly now through the living room, all the way back to the large kitchen. She looked up at the square clock above the sink. It was past ten. Surely Liza would have jet lag. Certainly her mother would come downstairs for her accustomed cup of tea soon.

But it was past one when Claire emerged from the back stairs. Page had almost given up on her.

"Oh, Mother," she breathed, when she heard the footsteps on the wooden steps.

Claire looked at her younger daughter in surprise. "What are you still doing up, darling?"

"How could I go to sleep?" she asked, her voice trembling. "There's so much we have to talk about."

"Oh, honey," Claire said tiredly, "it's way too late for a conversation now. Besides, I have plans to show Liza a hundred places tomorrow, starting early. We can talk later on tomorrow, okay?" She smiled almost dismissively.

"No, we can't talk later on tomorrow," Page cried. "We can't wait another minute."

Claire peered at her daughter, alarmed. "Page, what is the matter with you? You're screaming like a banshee."

Page breathed deeply, trying to control the emotion that was welling up inside her chest. "I'm sorry, Mother, I don't mean to be rude. I'm just in shock here. I mean, all this is, well, shocking."

Claire poured plain tap water into a glass

and took a seat reluctantly at the kitchen table. "Honey, I really will be happy to tell you everything, but it's overwhelming for me, and I'm exhausted."

"I realize it's 'overwhelming' for you, Mother, but at least you knew you *had* a daughter named Liza. I never even knew who my father was. In fact, I still don't know." Her voice rose as she went on. "I don't know if he loved me or not, or what he does, or what he looks like."

Her mother frowned. "I don't really want to go into the subject of your father right now." She held up a hand to stem the objections she could read on her daughter's face. "I know you're entitled to understand, and I'm happy to tell you." She hesitated. "Well, actually happy is perhaps too strong a word. Your father—that is, your birth father, Bennett Carlisle—is a complicated man. I can't really say how much he loved you or how much he missed you. I'm sorry to be cruel, but I don't know that he is capable of loving anyone."

Page reddened. "Of course, you never really gave me much of a chance to find out, did you?"

Claire looked at her daughter, her fatigue plain. "Page, I don't know that I can ever explain what happened adequately enough. It was so long ago, and I was so miserable." Her voice grew beseeching. "And John loved you completely. You *were* his daughter, as far as he was concerned. No father could have loved you more."

"But how could you not even have told me about him? Or about Liza? Didn't you think I would care? Don't you think I might have been less lonely if I had only known?" Page couldn't help the tears from running down her cheeks.

Claire shook her head from side to side. "It sounds so simple, but it wasn't. Honestly. You can't understand the threat I lived under. The threat that I might have lost you as well. I couldn't risk it."

"Sure, maybe, until I was eighteen. But I'm in my twenties. Why couldn't you have at least told me before I went to Columbia. I could have met him. I could have gone to see Liza. She was like a sister to me in Switzerland—why, she could have been a real sister. All those days I was miserable and out of place in New York, I could have had people who cared about me, who might even have loved me!"

"Oh, Page." The exhaustion on Claire's face was unmistakable now. "Maybe I can't ever make you understand. I don't know."

"Try, Mother, please. I just don't get it, not any of it."

Claire drank from her water glass. "Sweetheart, I'm sorry. Really, I am."

They both looked up at the sound of Liza, calling from her room. "Mom, you have to come here. I just found the most wonderful picture of us!"

Page watched her mother's face break into a smile. She saw her hesitate, knowing that her mother was trying not to leave her stranded, but also knowing that the pull from upstairs was just too strong.

Claire stood up. "Page, I'm sorry, honey. We'll hash this out tomorrow, I promise. But I have to go up now. I have to go to sleep."

Page didn't answer. She didn't say what she was thinking: no, Mother, you have to go to Liza.

Chapter Twelve

Frightened or thrilled? Page couldn't decide which she felt as she sat in front of her mirror, layering her hair into a French braid. Tonight it seemed impossible to arrange one hank over the other in exactly the right order, although it was a relief to concentrate on the intricate mechanical task, one that would keep her from thinking too much. Still, she couldn't stop mulling over the last couple of days, no matter how busy her hands were. First, a man she barely knew—and barely liked—turned up, making her feel a kind of excitement that was totally new to her. Then, Liza. Page longed to be happy about both of them.

Instead, she felt confused. She put the finishing touches on the braid and contemplated the jars and tubes of makeup set out on the table before her. After all, she'd always wanted a sister. Now, she had one.

As for Simon, his warmth had been a real

surprise. Page felt as if the two of them could have sat in his car and talked forever. There was no denying the attraction. She kept wanting to reach over and touch him even though they were virtual strangers.

Why am I so frightened? she wondered. The man coming to pick me up in half an hour is the same man who made me feel so comfortable. How can I remember that and still be scared to death?

And why am I fooling around with cosmetics I don't have any intention of putting on, when I should be downstairs with Mom and Liza? As if on cue, Page heard her mother's voice calling her.

"Page, darling, please hurry. I'd like us all to have some time together before you go out."

"Coming, Mother." Page applied a light lip gloss to her mouth and a touch of pink blush on each cheek. She looked at her image in the mirror critically, finally adding a dark gray mascara to bring out her eyes. Then she stood up and walked over to the large mahogany wardrobe in the corner, checking her entire outfit in the full-length mirror lining the inside right-hand door. The ivory wraparound silk blouse, with its sides overlapping in a V just above her breasts, its only fastening a loose tie at the waist, set off the pale beauty of her skin, while the black skirt of the same thin material hugged her slender hips, then swirled around at the knee. It was an ensemble that was childlike in its simplicity, but looked somehow seductive on Page. Her jewelry, too, was simple: a tiny, antique gold locket around her neck and a narrow bracelet made up entirely of small pearls, setting off the slight tan she had picked up over the summer. She had no wish to dress up, knowing how casual most actors were when they weren't onstage, but she needed to feel pretty tonight.

Liza was alone in the drawing room when Page finally went downstairs.

"Where's Mother?" Page asked in a voice that came out more timidly than she intended.

"She's just getting us drinks. She'll be back in a minute. You seem all dressed up. Not for me, I trust." Page was struck by the sharpness in Liza's tone.

"I'm going out with a friend." Page didn't feel like elaborating.

"A boyfriend?" Liza paid no attention to Page's reluctance.

"A man...a friend. His name is Simon."

"Well, I hope your romantic technique has improved since the last date you told me about."

Page flushed at Liza's reminder of what had been one of the worst nights of her life. She still felt embarrassed when she thought about the things that boy had said to her outside the dance at Beaumatin. In fact, she had never been entirely at ease with a man since, except Chris, but he was her best friend. Her mother routinely encouraged her to date more, meet new people. Somehow she was too busy. Page knew she wasn't as comfortable in social situations as most of her friends, but she had always preferred not to dwell on why that might be. Now, with Simon due to arrive in twenty minutes, she wished she understood it all a little better.

Liza scrutinized Page from head to toe, narrowing her eyes as she appeared to assess each garment. "Is the Alice in Wonderland look popular in England right now?" The malice was evident as she shot the question at Page.

Page tried to ignore it, but found she couldn't. Damn, she thought. I wanted to look elegant and understated, not like a ten-year-old. A few minutes before, she had felt uneasy; now she was petrified.

Liza saw her comment register. She knew the implication would hit home with her baby sister. Well, she deserves it, the spoiled little princess, Liza thought peevishly. I bet the guy is a big jerk. As she saw her mother walk in, carrying a silver tray with three glasses of white wine on it, Liza adjusted her expression and turned to Page, an engaging smile on her face.

As Claire entered, she saw her daughters deeply immersed in an intimate conversation. How wonderful, she mused. She had been stunned to discover that the two had been friendly in Switzerland. She felt the warm glow of happiness as she looked at them. Liza looked so right here. Page was a little pale, but perhaps she was nervous about her date tonight.

There were tears in her eyes as Claire put the tray down on the coffee table, and handed each of her daughters a glass. "Let's make a toast to the future. To our future together."

She raised her glass to her lips and was followed first by Liza, then a moment later by Page. Claire sat down so she could see both girls clearly. "Liza, Page, I wish I could make everything up to both of you. I still can't believe we're all here in this house finally. You can't know how I've longed for this."

Page realized how true this was. Her mother must have been thinking about Liza all those times she seemed so far away. "Mother, I understand everything you said—at least, I think I understand—but I'm still confused. Why didn't you talk to Liza or at least write to her?"

At Page's words, Liza tensed in her seat.

"Oh, honey, I did," Claire answered. "You don't remember your father, but his threats were real. If I had communicated with Liza before her eighteenth birthday, he would have taken you back to America like a shot and I would have lost both of you. But I did write as soon as I could. As soon as you got to Vassar." Claire looked at Liza as she said this, trying to measure how much of the girl's bitterness might remain.

Liza appeared to have no idea what her mother was talking about. "You wrote to me?"

"Of course," Claire said, "in September of your freshman year. I felt it would be safe then."

"I never got a letter." Visibly shaken, Liza was obviously telling the truth.

"But you wrote back to me. That telegram."

"What telegram? I didn't send you any telegram." A shrewd look came over Liza's face. "I bet Bennett intercepted the letter." Claire and Liza nodded to each other in perfect understanding.

Page felt mystified. Was her real father such a monster, or was Liza playing some kind of game? Page had no idea which was true, but she felt more baffled than ever.

The sound of the doorbell interrupted the three women. Page stood up, nervously smoothing her skirt and checking for errant strands of dark blond hair. She walked toward the front of the house. Mrs. Walker, the housekeeper, had opened the door for Simon, and he was waiting at the foot of the huge curved staircase that graced the entryway. Page was struck by how at ease he seemed, handsome and cool in a casual beige linen suit. Relief washed over her. Somehow his lanky frame and handsome, sculptured face seemed more familiar than her mother and sister did tonight.

"Hello, Page," Simon greeted her. "You look terrific."

"Thank you," she replied quietly.

The hushed spell was broken by Liza, who appeared suddenly, two glasses of wine in her hand, an inviting smile on her face. She walked right past Page and placed one of the wineglasses in Simon's hand. "Mother insists you come and join us for a few minutes. I'm Liza Carlisle, Page's sister."

Without waiting for a response, Liza took Simon's other hand and led him toward the drawing room.

Following close behind them, Page recalled how she'd envied Liza's charm and nonchalant beauty at school. She was always so stylish and outgoing. I must still seem childish next to her, Page thought, her confidence ebbing with every step. But when Liza introduced Simon to Claire, he reached back for Page's hand and continued to hold it as he and Page sat down on the couch.

"Simon Roberts..." Claire murmured. "Why does your name sound so familiar?"

"Simon is an actor, Mother," Liza answered the question. "I've read about him. He's been written up in *The New York Times* and *Variety*, you know." She turned to Simon. "They say you're the best young actor in England."

"Hardly," he said, looking embarrassed but pleased. "Are you in theater? It sounds as if you follow it closely."

"Well, not exactly. Actually, I produce videos," Liza answered in a modest tone of voice.

"But, darling, how fabulous!" Claire's enthusiasm was immediate. "How creative and exciting that must be. You always had flair," Claire added, beaming at her older daughter, "even when you were tiny. You used to make up little stories and paint beautiful pictures. And you were so smart. All your preschool teachers commented on it. Every one of them!"

Page watched as Liza grinned back at her mother. Again, their connection made her feel totally left out. Only the warmth of Simon's hand on hers kept her from the uncertainty and sadness she hadn't been able to shake all afternoon. What kind of person am I, she thought, resenting my own sister? She saw Claire beaming. How can I begrudge pleasure to the one person I love the most? Mother has never been so excited, and here I am feeling sorry for myself.

Simon noticed how quiet Page had become since they joined her family. While he didn't understand it, he sensed that she was unhappy. "Our dinner reservation is in fifteen minutes. Perhaps we should be going, Page," he suggested politely.

Liza hugged Page warmly as the couple stood to walk out of the room. "I'm so glad to be home with you, sis," she said impulsively, making Claire glow with approval.

"Me too," Page answered, hugging her back and trying to mean it.

Page and Simon were sitting on floor pillows in one of the tiny private chambers at the Japanese restaurant, Hatsunan, surrounded by high walls made of a heavy paper that separated them completely from other diners. A large platter of assorted sushi lay between them on the wide dining table, which was only about ten inches off the ground.

Simon was mixing wasabi into a shallow dish of soy sauce without taking his eyes from Page. "I don't like noisy restaurants much. I hope you don't mind."

"No," Page agreed. "That's fine. Surprising maybe," she added enigmatically.

"What do you mean?" he asked, intrigued by her comment.

"I thought an actor would enjoy being recognized."

"I'm not above the feeling, believe me, but tonight I wasn't looking for recognition. I was looking for you." Simon said this matter-of-factly, but the words caused Page to blush. Simon decided to bring the conversation to a more natural level.

"So how is the hotel business?" he asked, placing a layer of ginger on top of his tekka-maki before picking it up with chopsticks and dipping it into the dish of soy sauce.

"It's wonderful," Page answered, glad to be back on familiar terrain. "That day we ran into each other was especially rough, but I really love what I do."

"You invented that inn thing, didn't you?" Simon's respect was plain. "Clever. Does your sister work with you?"

Page stiffened at the question, answering briefly. "No. Liza just arrived here. That's why I had to cancel our date the other day.... It's a little hard to explain."

Simon observed her reaction and tactfully guided the conversation back to Page herself. "So what do you do every day? Start when you get out of bed."

Page smiled, as he meant her to do. "I brush my teeth. Fascinating, yes?"

"No fair," he said more seriously. "I want to know what you really do. I went on and on about myself."

Page began to talk about her work shyly, but warmed as she described her first visit to Chipping Camden and the subsequent success of the Warren Manors. As she spoke, Simon thought about how beautiful she was. Where he had originally seen her as icy, he now appreciated the delicacy of her features, the expressiveness of her blue eyes.

Page described the difficulties of the first Manor house and found herself telling Simon how she had planned the initial trip to the Cotswolds, dragging Claire along without telling her where they were going. She realized as she spoke that she had never told anyone else about that afternoon. In fact, she hardly ever let herself think about how impulsive her actions had been, how ashamed she'd been driving home in the silent car. Yet it felt good to tell Simon. He wasn't laughing at her. On the contrary, his comments betrayed a sensitivity that left her feeling much better about the whole thing.

She was growing more relaxed with him. "You asked before about my sister, Liza. Believe it or not, I just met her a couple of days ago."

Simon was confused. "I don't follow you."

"Liza was raised by my father in the United States. Until recently, I didn't even know I had a sister." In a tiny voice, Page told Simon about Liza's sudden appearance and how confused she felt. "You know, the funny thing is, I did know Liza before. We were together at boarding school, but neither of us had any idea we were related. I really adored her. She was like an older sister." Page caught the irony of her words only after she said them.

"When are you going to meet your father?" Simon asked.

Page was stunned by the question. "I never even thought about that. I don't know how I feel about it. He doesn't sound like a very nice man from what my mother said. I don't remember him. I wish I did. It might make all this a little easier to deal with. Right now, I'm not even sure who I am. I'm not really Page Warren and John Warren wasn't really my father and nothing is really as it seems to be." Page made no attempt to hide her pain. She felt close to Simon, as if she had known him forever.

He appreciated her trust. Her natural reserve was similar to his, so her opening up this way made her even more attractive. He wanted to reassure her, to make everything all right. He reached his hand to her face, tracing a path down her cheek, to the hollow of her throat.

Page fell silent as she tried to overcome her nervousness. She had never really enjoyed this kind of attention. But Simon was different, and she felt herself responding to his touch. Without realizing she was about to speak, she heard herself say, "Simon, I'm frightened."

He moved his fingers upward, pushing back the little tendrils of hair that had escaped to frame her face. "I would never hurt you, Page. I would never let anyone hurt you." The vulnerable woman sitting here beside him made Simon feel protective. Her honesty stirred him and he was glad they were alone in the tiny room. He no longer wanted to contain his feelings. He reached out for her, one hand embracing the back of her neck, the other trailing a leisurely path along the inside of her arm. Sliding next to her on the shiny floor, he leaned over and began to trace the outline of her mouth with his tongue. Page felt her fear begin to dissolve and it was she who finally kissed him, her arms circling his neck.

Sensing her pleasure build, Simon cushioned her upper body with his arm and eased her down gently until her head rested on one of the silk floor pillows. As his other hand moved down the softness of her skirt, outlining the curve of her hip, the firmness of her thigh, his lips once again pressed into hers, more demanding, more urgent this time.

Page was overcome by pleasure. She wanted this man. Her hands explored his muscled back through his shirt, then his upper arms as he moved downward. She couldn't believe the taunting pleasure as his lips moved against her naked skin in the V of her blouse, making her long for him to go further. Feeling her desire, he lifted his hand and slid one side of the filmy garment off her shoulder, lowering his mouth to her breast, his body now on top of hers. Easing his hands under her skirt, he began to move up her inner thigh, slowly, so slowly.

Page moaned, giving herself up to him, meeting his passion with her own urgent need. She felt his hardness at her body's center. Again he understood and increased the pressure of his body on hers, as if even through layers of silk and linen, they could satisfy each other's yearnings.

At the same instant, they both heard voices from just outside the room and sat up hurriedly. Page rearranged her blouse while Simon straightened his jacket and shirt, moving back to his original position near her on the cushions. As the waiter came in to retrieve the sushi platter and empty wineglasses, they remained quiet, their high color and quickened breath the only evidence of what had been going on seconds before. After the waiter left, they looked at each other for a long moment, saying nothing. Suddenly, Page burst out laughing, an uncontrolled, sustained ring of happiness and abandon, of foolishness and fulfillment.

If he could choose one sound to listen to forever, that would be it, Simon thought as he put his arms around her once again.

Chapter Thirteen

Bennett Carlisle looked out his office window. He always enjoyed this view of downtown, the panoramic expanse of New York's oldest buildings. Taking a deep breath, he exhaled with satisfaction. Nothing and no one could touch him way up here.

Reluctantly, he turned and sat down behind his desk, its shining black marble surface disturbed only by a sleek telephone. Across the room stood a glass conference table imported from Italy. It was surrounded by wide, rich-looking leather chairs, similar to, but not quite as impressive as the one behind Bennett's desk.

There were no decorations, no personal touches in the room. That was the way Bennett liked it. Formal, expensive. Should any of the firm's clients come in for a meeting, they were ushered into the large conference room down the hall, where antique furnishings and tea served in bone china with sterling silver accessories lent the proceedings a more personal air. When it came time for Bennett to negotiate deals or meet with those whom he perceived as his opponents, this was the place in which he preferred to do his work. Intimidation on his own turf. A powerful tool.

Today, however, Bennett was reflecting on a problem outside of his office. He loathed wasting business hours on personal matters, but in this case some sort of action was clearly called for on his part.

It was a minor annoyance, really. As he was leaving the apartment that morning, his housekeeper had approached him.

"Excuse me, Mr. Carlisle," she had said tentatively, "but there's something I thought you might want to know."

It was a rare occasion on which Bennett was late to the office, and he didn't plan this day to be one of them. "What is it, Mary? I'm in a hurry."

"It's Miss Carlisle. I know she doesn't always come home at night, but I'm getting a little worried about her."

Now what, Bennett wondered impatiently. "And...?" he prodded the woman.

"Well, I cleaned up her room about four days ago. She'd gotten dressed to go somewhere, I could see that. But there were a lot of clothes out, more than usual. And she hasn't been back or called me with instructions for getting clothes ready for next week, like she usually does..." Mary's voice trailed off. She didn't like upsetting Mr. Carlisle, and she knew any problems concerning his daughter were likely to make him mad.

"Four days isn't that long," Bennett snapped. "What do you want me to do about it?"

"Sir, it's just that if anything bad happened to her, maybe we should call the police or something. She usually does call me if she's not coming home. She's never gone this long without some word."

Bennett didn't believe for a minute that anything had befallen Liza. He knew she was perfectly capable of taking care of herself. She was no doubt off on one of her idiotic jaunts to Greece or Cannes or some such place.

But he had to do something, he reflected now, drumming his fingers on the desktop. A maid had told him his daughter had been missing for several days. If by some remote chance something really had happened to her, he would have quite a time explaining to the police why he'd never reported her missing. Telling them that his slutty daughter commonly stayed out for days at a time certainly wasn't going to help his business reputation. By not reporting it, he would appear to be an uncaring father—or worse. No, he'd better find her himself before the situation got out of hand.

Disgusted by having to take up even a moment with this nonsense, Bennett jabbed at his intercom button and told Jane to come in to his office. She appeared, pad in hand, almost instantly it seemed.

"Jane, you've known Liza since she was a child," he said in a friendly tone. "I believe you may be familiar with some of the places she likes to go, the people she likes to see. We keep missing each other in the house, and I need to speak with her. For some reason, I can't seem to remember where she went off to. Could you possibly track her down for me?"

Puzzled, Jane responded. "Of course, sir." She left and returned to her desk, thinking how odd it was for her employer to make such a request. In all the years she'd worked for him, he'd never asked her to become involved in any way in his personal life, much less his relationship with Liza. That is, if they had a relationship, she thought, recalling the stilted interactions and Liza's snide remarks she had witnessed over the years. She shook her head. Missing each other at home, he'd said. Hardly. He obviously had no idea where his daughter was.

It didn't take long before Jane returned to Bennett's office. She waited until he completed a telephone conversation, then approached his desk.

"Where is she?" Bennett demanded brusquely.

"She's in London, Mr. Carlisle. She often uses our travel agent to book her trips, so I gave them a call to see if they knew anything. Sure enough, Liza booked a first-class seat to Heathrow four days ago. One way. And she did use it. They couldn't tell me any more than that."

Dismissing his secretary, Bennett sat back in his chair. Of course. She went to London. To Claire. That's why she bought a one-way ticket, and didn't even tell the maid where she was going or when she would be back.

He'd been halfway expecting it. The little ingrate. She was cut from the same cloth as her mother. Claire had left the girl bleeding, possibly dying, to disappear with some man, to indulge her own selfish desires at the expense of the entire family. He, on the other hand, had provided Liza with the best of everything—when he thought of the schools, the trips, the cloth-

193

ing, all the money he'd spent on her over the years. For what? So she could run off to her mother, complain about what a terrible father he had been, forget the fact that he was the one who had stayed with her, he was the one who devoted his life to raising her. It was incredible, unbelievable. Damn her!

And why now, at this particular moment? Maybe it was the threat of being deprived of her allowance. Ah, yes, he thought. That must have done it. The bitch, too lazy to stand on her own two feet. Now she would go and try to suck her mother dry. Well, let her. They deserved each other. Wait until Claire saw what a brat her precious little Liza had grown up to be. Claire was in for quite a surprise. Fine. The child she was so desperate to get back could be a millstone around *her* neck for a change. But Liza had better realize that she burned her bridges as far as he was concerned. There would be no coming back. He would wash his hands of her the same way he had with her mother.

Bennett thought for a few minutes. Then, he picked up the telephone and dialed. A receptionist quickly put him through to his lawyer's direct line.

"Richard Payson here," a deep voice answered the phone.

"Hello, Dick. It's Bennett Carlisle. I want to make a change in my will."

"Well, no time for small talk today," his lawyer said with a chuckle. "Okay, Bennett, what is it you want to do?"

"Instead of leaving my money to my daughter Liza, I've decided to leave it all to my alma mater. I want everything to go to Harvard, with the provision that part of it be used to erect a new library wing in my name."

There was a shocked silence on the other end of the line. "Bennett, are you serious? Have you and Liza had a fight?" He paused for a moment. "Besides, there is a generous bequest to Harvard as the will stands now." He waited a moment, as if expecting Bennett to respond, but heard nothing. "Please, I would be remiss if I didn't advise you to take some time and think over such a drastic change."

Bennett smiled. "There's nothing to think about, Dick. Harvard will make good use of the money, and it's certainly a worthy cause."

"But...but...hold on," the other man was practically stumbling over his words. "Why would you want to do such a thing? You're talking about cutting your own child out of your will altogether. Just like that! With a snap of your fingers, altering the allocation of millions of dollars. This is a will, mind you, that you yourself drew up and have left largely unchanged for nearly twenty years."

Bennett was quiet for a few seconds. "You know, Dick, you're right. Liza certainly should get something. Put in a provision that she receive, let me see...make it five hundred dollars a month for life." How infuriated that would make her, a bigger insult than if he'd left her nothing. Five hundred dollars. She would be beside herself.

"Bennett, please, reconsider. Let's get together over lunch and talk about this."

"Just do it," Bennett said, and quickly replaced the receiver.

The events of the morning had left him restless. He reached inside his jacket and pulled out a small gray address book, flipping through its pages as he searched for a name that would pique his interest. Here was one. Rosemary Farmingham. He barely knew her, had only met her once, but there was something about her he found exciting. She was thirty-five or so, very attractive, married to an overweight divorce lawyer worth several million. He picked up the telephone and dialed.

"Hello." Rosemary's voice was light, expectant somehow, as she answered.

"Rosemary. Good morning, this is Bennett Carlisle."

The delight was evident in her voice. "Why, Bennett, what a lovely surprise! I have to admit I was wondering if you were going to call. I was getting worried you were just pulling my leg, taking advantage of a woman who might have had one drink too many and was unable to resist flirting with you."

"How could I not call?" Bennett despised these little verbal games, but knew perfectly well that they were necessary. He lowered his voice to suggest intimacy. "A beautiful mysterious woman runs her hand up the inside of my leg at a party. What could be more tantalizing than that?"

Rosemary laughed. "You're too wicked for your own good."

"The question is, am I wicked enough to persuade you to meet me at The Plaza in an hour? There's a suite reserved with a cold bottle of Dom Perignon on order."

"Bennett, it's only ten-thirty. You must have quite a thirst to extend such an invitation this early in the morning," Rosemary answered teasingly, clearly enjoying herself. "I'm not sure. I'll have to think about this. I *am* a married woman, you know."

"Ever since we met, I haven't been able to stop imagining what it would be like to take off your clothes—very slowly, one piece at a time—and kiss you all over. Kiss you and lick you until you explode."

"Mmmm, you are persuasive. Tell me more."

Bennett leaned back in his chair. Bulls-eye.

At eleven-thirty precisely, Bennett was standing in the middle of the suite he had reserved after finishing his conversation with Rosemary. Pouring some club soda into a champagne flute—he never drank alcohol during the business day—he sat down on the couch, annoyed at being kept waiting. But that, too, was part of the game. Rosemary couldn't arrive before he did. That wasn't how things went. He was almost surprised when he heard her knocking on the door less than five minutes later.

"How beautiful you are," Bennett said with a genuinely admiring look as he clasped Rosemary's hand and gently ushered her inside. His eyes quickly took in the luxurious, long dark hair that framed her face, the high heels emphasizing her long legs beneath a tight-fitting white skirt, the swell of her breasts under the matching suit jacket, worn without a blouse. The jacket was kept closed with a wide belt and a large sapphire pin placed low enough to hint at her generous cleavage. "You're even more beautiful than I remembered from the party the other night."

"You, however, are exactly as I recall you," Rosemary said, putting down her purse and running her eyes appreciatively up and down Bennett's frame. "Tall, well built, divinely attractive."

Bennett poured her some champagne and picked up his own glass. "Why don't we share this inside? I don't want to wait another minute. Later on, we can order up some lunch and talk."

"You don't waste any time, do you?" Rosemary laughed.

He found her laugh oddly irritating. But he pushed his irritation aside and followed her into the bedroom. Walking at a leisurely pace, she removed the belt and the pin that held her jacket closed. She slipped the jacket off as Bennett came up behind her and unzipped her skirt, sliding it down over her hips and letting it fall to the floor. Underneath, she was wearing only a white garter belt and sheer stockings.

Stepping clear of her skirt, she began to unhook the garter belt.

"Leave that on," Bennett ordered her hoarsely. "The shoes, too."

She smiled. "Fine. Now you."

Loosening Bennett's tie, she pulled it over his head without bothering to unknot it. He kicked off his shoes, hurriedly disposing of the rest of his clothing with her help. They lay down on the bed together. Bennett caressed her breasts, softly at first, then more roughly. She moaned with pleasure, stroking his hard penis, and brought her mouth up to his. Her full mouth was giving and moist against his. She ran her tongue around his lips, trying to ease them apart. Bennett pulled back his head and began to suck on her nipple, holding her breast, while moving his other hand down her stomach. With a quick motion, he thrust two fingers inside her. She wasn't wet yet, and cried out involuntarily at the painful intrusion.

Embarrassed, hoping she hadn't spoiled things between them, Rosemary whispered, "I'm sorry, that hurt me just a little bit."

Hurt, Bennett thought bitterly. You women are the ones who do all the hurting. He tried to concentrate on her, but all he was really aware of was the rage welling up inside him. His breathing was coming faster now, as he rubbed her breast even harder. At the same time, he was struggling to insert a third and fourth finger into her.

"Bennett," she whispered a little louder, "please, you're hurting me."

He must have heard her this time, for he took both hands away and leaned back on his knees, looking down at her.

"Let's try again," she said, her voice wavering a bit as she saw the anger in his eyes. "I'm sorry, I guess I wasn't ready."

Without speaking, Bennett quickly put one hand on her shoulder and the other under her buttocks, turning her over so she lay on her stomach. He knew he should stop but he couldn't. He knelt above her, his arm coming around her lower waist to jerk her midsection up so she was on all fours. She was stunned by the roughness of his actions. Feeling his stiff penis pressing against her anus, she went rigid.

"No, I don't want to," she cried out. "Stop it! I don't want that."

She was relieved to feel him pull away from her, only to find his penis immediately replaced by probing fingers as he attempted to make room for himself to enter. Again, he pushed against her, grunting as he fought her tightened muscles. As she struggled to get away from him, he brought her wrists together behind her head and held them there with one hand. With the other, he maintained his grip on her waist, keeping her in position. It was difficult for her to breathe, her face nearly buried in the pillow. He was far too strong for her to break free.

Wrenching her head up, she yelled, "Stop it, goddamn it, you're hurting me!"

With a final push, he succeeded in entering

her, as she screamed out in pain. He thrust over and over, gasping as he reached around and grabbed onto her breasts. Then, with a long groan and shudder, he came.

The only sound in the room was Rosemary's soft crying as she crouched, unmoving, her face to the wall. Bennett released her and stood, quickly picking up his clothing from the floor and starting to dress. Struggling to get her tears under control, Rosemary took several deep breaths before she turned to him.

"You bastard." Her voice was filled with venom. "Don't think you're going to get away with this."

Bennett, zipping his pants, regarded her with only mild interest. "Really? What exactly do you plan on doing about it?"

She glared at him. She would call the police, that's what she'd do. And tell them what? That she had met a man in a hotel in the middle of the afternoon? Her husband was powerful enough to ruin Bennett Carlisle. But that's not who her husband would punish. She bit her lip. Bennett was right. The only way she could expose him was to expose herself, to admit that she went to a hotel expressly to cheat on her husband. She got up, staying as far from Bennett as she could, and yanked the blanket from the bed, wrapping it around herself. Her hair was tangled, and she knew her eye makeup must be smeared from crying. She rubbed the skin beneath her eyes, trying to clean off some of the mascara, and ran her fingers through her hair, as if fixing her appearance could somehow help her regain her dignity. Yet she could see it didn't matter; Bennett, sitting on the far edge of the bed and lacing up his shoes, appeared to have forgotten she was even in the room.

Putting on his jacket, he turned to her once more. "Thank you for a charming interlude in a busy day," he said, as graciously as if he were dropping her off after a date. "It was a supreme pleasure."

Part of him knew he had crossed into dangerous territory with this woman, a member of his own social circle. But he was damned if he would let her see his concern.

Rosemary narrowed her eyes. "You go straight to hell, you son of a bitch."

Bennett paused. There was something pleasantly familiar about her, about her hair and coloring—he'd felt it all along, but didn't know why. Now, as she stared at him, her eyes smoldering with rage and frustration, it was coming to him. Oh, Christ—she looks like Liza.

He spun on his heel, hurrying through the suite, and slammed the door behind him.

Chapter Fourteen

She just couldn't get away from this rotten weather, Liza thought as she stepped into the garden behind the Warren home. During her first week in London, every day had been sunny and brisk. But it had suddenly turned humid. This was the third straight day of it, an oppressive closeness. In hopes of staying cool, she was wearing a light cotton blouse knotted at the waist, the shortest shorts she could find, and open-toed sandals.

Liza stood just outside the back door and shaded her eyes to get a better look at the opposite side of the garden. It wasn't a far distance. The garden was actually a small plot of greenery and blooming flowers, generous for a home situated in the center of London, but small by comparison with the grounds often surrounding large suburban houses in America. Three narrow paths criss-crossed through it and a wicker table with two chairs stood off to one side in the shade of a tall tree. Meticulously cared for, the area radiated peace and calm.

Past the rows of bright flowers and manicured shrubbery, Liza could see Page and Chris kneeling down. Their heads nearly touched as they hammered nails into the large piece of unpainted wood between them. Page wore a yellow sundress, while Chris was in jeans; he had removed his shirt and perspiration glistened on his back.

"Aren't they just the cutest?" Liza muttered sarcastically under her breath. It wasn't enough that the two of them saw each other practically every day when Chris drove Page in the Bentley. Here he was on a Sunday morning, his day off. Page's little consort, her sidekick, Liza thought irritably. Didn't he have anything else to do? Didn't he have a girl-friend? After all, he wasn't bad looking. On the other hand, who wanted a poor, struggling actor who was really just a chauffeur? Not I, that's for sure, she said to herself as she started down the path.

Page and Chris both looked up as she approached, and she waved, smiling.

"Hey, folks, what's going on out here?" Liza asked cheerfully. Although Chris was inconspicuous about it, she was gratified to note that his gaze took in her long legs, her bare midriff, her breasts against the flimsy cotton shirt. Well, at least we know he likes girls, she thought with an inward laugh.

"Good morning, Liza," Page answered in a pleasant voice. "We're making a bookcase for a production that some friends are putting on next week. They didn't have the budget for props, so we volunteered to build this. Everyone is making something."

"I can't imagine why you'd want to hammer away like this on such a miserable hot day," Liza said. "With all the hotel furniture this family owns, why don't you use something real? There are beautiful old pieces you could have shipped in, rather than slapping together two-by-fours."

Chris stiffened. "We'll make do with our two-by-fours, thank you," he said.

Liza shrugged. "Just trying to help. Anyway, that's not what I came out here for. Chris, my mother and I would like to go to the office and then to a few hotels. We'd appreciate it if you would drive us. I know you have some spare uniforms here, so you can change."

Annoyed, Page broke in. "Liza, surely you're aware that Chris doesn't work for us on Sundays, not even when we're out of town at one of the Manors. Surely, you can take a taxi to wherever you're going."

"I know, Page, I know." Liza made her voice regretful. "I hate to ask him. It's not for me. Actually, it's that Mother is so anxious that I learn the business. She doesn't want to waste a minute, especially considering how much time we've lost in the past."

Chris stood up, brushing himself off. "It's okay, Page. Your mother's been damn good to me and if she wants a favor here and there, it's no big deal." He faced Liza. "I'll bring the car around to the front of the house in about ten minutes. Will that be satisfactory?"

How he dotes on Page, Liza thought, watching him smile at her sister as he put on his shirt. Page must eat it up. Perhaps it was time Chris started doting on someone else.

"We'll be ready." Liza flashed him a big smile, reaching up to take a small twig out of his hair. "You're the best, Chris. I knew you wouldn't mind." She spun around and walked back to the house.

Chris and Page looked at each other. "She's something else, isn't she?" Chris said.

Page sighed. "Something else. I guess you could put it that way."

A little over an hour later, Claire and Liza emerged to enter the waiting Bentley. Claire wore a linen suit, and Liza had discarded her shirt and shorts for a beige silk dress. Chris put down the script he was reading in the car's front seat and got out to open the door for them.

Claire looked surprised to see him.

"How nice of you to drive us on your day off, Christopher," she said as she entered the car. "It wasn't necessary, really, although it's very thoughtful."

Chris forced a smile. Claire had known nothing about this. Well, he wasn't going to let Liza get to him. Once she had settled in next to her mother, he closed the car door gently and hurried into the driver's seat.

"At your service, ladies," he said, a shade too brightly.

Looking into the rear-view mirror, his eyes met Liza's. She winked. Chris turned away. Better be careful with this one, he thought.

At Warren headquarters, Claire told Chris they would be finished in a couple of hours. She and Liza went upstairs. Once inside her office, Claire headed straight for a closet, rummaging around. She emerged with a large set of rolled-up papers, bound by rubber bands, which she opened out and spread across her desk.

"These are the plans for the first Warren Hotel that John and I built together," she told Liza proudly. "It's the one in Paris. We worked with some wonderfully talented people, and the plans are still a priceless example of how to build a good hotel. Vision, imagination, practicality, economy—everything came together here. After you've had a chance to study these, Liza, we can discuss what makes them good, why they translated into what was the company's most successful operation."

Liza examined the pages carefully. "May I take them back to the house, Mother? I'd like to spend tonight going over them."

Claire was delighted. "Of course, darling. I hadn't meant to push you, and I know I tend to get carried away with the business." She hugged Liza. "If you only knew how much pleasure it gives me to have you here, to see you every day. What a joy, to have you share such a strong interest in the business."

Share, my ass, Liza thought. Your precious little Page is the only one you share anything with. She averted her face so Claire couldn't tell what she was thinking. How are you going to share all those years, Mother, when you were off with your honey, old John sweetheart, and you didn't give a damn about me? Yes, we'll share some things, all right, but it's not going to be this business.

Liza turned back to Claire. "A cup of tea, Mother?"

Claire was bent over the blueprints and notes before her, reliving the excitement and challenge of her first Warren project. The only question, Liza mused as she observed her mother, was how long it would take. For starters, how long until she could drive a wedge between Claire and Page that would sever their relationship for good? Liza knew she had to be absolutely sure the damage was irreparable, that there was no chance Page and her mother would reconcile. The two of them together could stand up to the rest of Liza's plan; each one alone could not.

There were still some details to be worked out, some obstacles remaining. But Liza was confident she was on track, and with Page out of the way, she could proceed. It was simple, so elegant really, she thought, leaning over Claire's shoulder and pretending to examine the blueprints.

"Tell me about the way you decide on a site for a new hotel, Mother, and how you finance it," Liza said aloud. "I'd be interested to know about that."

The two women sat down on the couch together. Claire eagerly took Liza through the basics of determining where a hotel should be located, obtaining an independent feasibility study, and what steps followed the study's findings. She felt she had barely gotten started when Liza gently reminded her that they had planned to visit some of the other hotels in town that afternoon, so they should be leaving.

By six that evening, Chris had driven the two of them to five of the best hotels in London. At each one, Claire and Liza had taken a walk through the lobby, with Claire quietly pointing out such details as the ambiance, the grooming of the staff, and the speed with which guests were being checked in and out.

Next, they went to each hotel's bar and ordered a drink. Claire fired off a list of what Liza should be observing: the pricing of drinks, the bar's furnishings and level of cleanliness, the length of time it took before the waiter brought their drinks. Were they serving any amenities such as hors d'oeuvres? Did a customer have to wave to get a second drink or did the waiter promptly appear as soon as the customer had finished the first one? Discreetly, Liza scribbled notes.

Claire was warmer than usual in her thanks to Chris when he dropped them off at home, understanding that they had appropriated most of his day off. As he held the car door open, she made a mental note to arrange for him to receive double-time pay for the day. She stood, waiting for Liza to gather up her things in the backseat.

"You know, darling, I'm absolutely exhausted," she said after a moment. "I think I'll go right upstairs for a nice bath."

"You've had a long day, Mother. Go on in, and I'll see you at dinner," Liza answered.

Chris watched as Mrs. Walker opened the front door to admit Claire. He was startled to find that Liza had gotten out of the car and was standing right beside him. She took a step forward, so close that he could feel her breasts lightly brush against him.

"You were wonderful to take such good care of us all day, Chris," she said warmly. "It really meant a lot to me to have that time with Mother. Thank you very much. And of course, I'll ask her if it's all right to give you extra compensation for your time."

How could she still look so fresh in this heat, as if she just stepped out of a shower? he wondered. His own shirt was sticking to his back. Her skin looked so smooth, her lips so full and soft. Chris realized he was getting an erection. He stepped back, mortified. God, I'm like some horny teenager, he admonished himself angrily.

Liza was watching him, a friendly smile on her face. He had to say something. "No problem," he managed to get out.

"You know, it's so nice to have another American here, someone I can talk to without feeling as if I ought to apologize for my Yankee accent," she said. "I've been lonely for someone from home."

She'd never struck Chris as the type who got lonely for anything. Maybe he was wrong about that. "Sure, Liza. I'm around if you want to talk."

"And what if I want to do more than talk?" she asked, so quietly that for a moment he thought he'd misunderstood. She didn't wait for an answer. "See you tomorrow," she said, and headed for the house.

Well, I'll be damned, he thought. He was unable to keep himself from staring at her firm, high behind moving against the thin silk of her dress as she walked. What was her game?

During the next week, Chris was completely bewildered by Liza's treatment of him. He never knew what her mood would be when she entered the car. Sometimes, he seemed to be invisible, receiving only a distant nod when he held the door open. He was certain, then, that he had completely misread her earlier flirtatiousness. At other times, she was friendly, initiating conversations about American cars and baseball teams. Back at the Warren house, she came out to talk with him if she saw that he was waiting to have dinner with Page and Simon, as he often did.

The only thing that was clear to Chris was how much more beautiful Liza appeared each day. It was increasingly difficult to deny his intense attraction to her. He found himself thinking about her, about all that glorious hair, her long legs, that small waist. She had so much class, yet she was so damned sexy at the same time. He was going crazy wanting her, thinking she was responding to him, only to decide she barely noticed his existence.

Still, all his instincts told him not to trust Liza. He knew that Page was having problems adjusting to her arrival. Not wanting to pry, he had refrained from asking Page about it directly. They'd known each other a long time, and if she wanted to unburden herself to him, she knew she could. So far, she'd said practically nothing to him about her sister. But there was something wrong—he sensed it—and his loyalty to Page made him doubly cautious.

On Monday of the following week, Chris drove Claire and Liza to a series of auctions, idly keeping one ear on their discussion about whether they should replace the manager of their hotel in Copenhagen. Eventually, Claire told Chris to drop her at the office; Liza would continue to an appointment at the London Warren. Although Liza had said little to Chris all morning, once Claire left them, she spent the rest of the drive soliciting his opinions about some of the newest plays opening in the West End. When they stopped in front of the London Warren, Liza quickly let herself out of the car. Before going inside, she turned suddenly to speak with him through his open window.

"My meeting should take about a half hour. Why don't you park the car and go into the hotel dining room for some lunch? Have something terrific, and, of course, charge it to my account."

Chris was taken aback by Liza's suggestion. He resented the implication that he was the lowly help being treated to a high-class meal.

"I don't need a free lunch, thank you," he replied.

"Oh, no, Chris, please don't feel that way. I would never want to insult you." She was instantly contrite. "I just hate to think of you sitting out here all the time being bored. You must be hungry—it's nearly two o'clock. Please, I'd consider it a favor."

Chris was suspicious, but he'd had enough fish and chips on his lunch breaks to last anyone a lifetime. He didn't know that Liza cut her appointment short to be certain she got downstairs before he had finished and gone back to the car. She stood in the entrance to the dining room, ignoring the maitre d', who had recognized her immediately and rushed over. Watching Chris finish a club sandwich, she smiled and waved to catch his attention. It's almost too easy, she thought, as he smiled back and gestured for her to join him.

Slowly, Liza crossed the room. She wore a red crepe de chine blouse with a pencil-thin charcoal gray skirt, touches of silver jewelry at her ears, throat, and wrists. Chris watched her walk, watched the smooth way she slid into the chair opposite him. He heard the rustle of her stockings as she crossed her legs.

She leaned forward. "You know, I get the feeling you don't like me," she said earnestly.

Chris was startled. He hesitated before responding. "I've never given you any reason to have that impression," he said finally.

"But I'm right, aren't I?" She looked into his eyes.

"No, not at all."

Liza sighed. "I know that I'm the interloper here, just barging in and disrupting everyone's lives. But, Chris, you have a family, don't you?"

"Yes, of course. My parents, back in Detroit."

"That's more than I've had," Liza said. "I've been looking for my mother my entire life, wondering all these years if I'd ever see her again. I was all alone, no mother, no sister—only memories of them. You can understand that trying to pick up the pieces of a family at this stage isn't the easiest thing. There's bound to be friction until we get everything sorted out."

Chris was surprised by the depth of feeling evident in her words. She's really had a lousy life, he thought.

Liza signaled for the check. "What do you say we forget about business for today and you take me on a tour of the English country-side? Not as our driver, but as a friend. I'd love that. We'll pick up some wine and just enjoy what's left of the day."

Chris couldn't remember when he'd had such a glorious, carefree afternoon as those hours spent driving with Liza by his side. She was bursting with energy, talking, laughing, teasing—delighted by everything around them and forcing Chris to see it all anew, to marvel at the beauty as he had when he'd first come to England. He'd been so caught up in his acting, he realized, he hadn't had time to relax or clown around the way they were doing today. Here and there, they stopped and got out of the car, first to share a blueberry tart in a small country village, then to enjoy spectacular views of the rolling hills.

It was nearly five o'clock when Liza suggested they stop to drink the wine they'd purchased before setting out. Chris pulled the car off the road to a small clearing in a field of flowers.

He fetched a blanket from the car's trunk and followed Liza, who had left her shoes in the car and was making her way in stockinged feet on a path leading farther into the field. She carried the Bordeaux, as well a corkscrew and two wine glasses she'd brought along with it. At her signal, Chris spread out the blanket and they sat down on it, enjoying the sense of being hidden from the rest of the world as the day drew to a close.

They finished the wine, talking about nothing much, just looking at one another, quiet and comfortable. The sun was dropping quickly, and long, low fingers of orange and yellow shot out across the sky.

Liza lay back, looking upward. She's so incredibly beautiful, Chris thought, desperately wanting to touch her, aching from the effort of controlling himself. He had no idea what her response would be but he had to believe she might never be as approachable as at this minute. But what about Page? He couldn't pretend that Page would be pleased about his becoming involved with Liza.

"Why are you frowning?" Liza interrupted his thoughts with her quiet question. She propped herself up on one arm and gently touched his face. Before he knew what was happening, they were kissing, softly, ever so softly. Liza curled her fingers around the back of his neck, rubbing gently, as Chris tentatively stroked her hair. Growing more confident, he ran his fingers along her arm, and brought his hand to caress her magnificent breasts. Their tongues mingled now with urgency.

They lay on their sides. Liza raised her leg to drape it around Chris's hip and pull him closer. A moan escaped from him as he ran his hand along her leg, feeling it so firm yet silky. He discovered she was wearing real stockings, with a lace garter belt. His fingers played along the soft flesh above the stocking tops.

Liza eased him backward and bent over him, languidly kissing his face and neck. As she opened the buttons of his white shirt with one hand, she brought his hand up to her mouth and softly sucked on his fingers, one by one. His shirt open, she brought her mouth to his nipple and ran her tongue delicately around it. Her hands found his zipper.

Chris was groaning louder now, in an exquisite agony. He had to find release, yet wished it would go on forever. Roughly, he pulled Liza on top of him, sliding his fingers in and out of her wetness. She was breathing fast and hard now and reached down, hastily pushing aside the narrow strip of lace panty that separated her from him.

"Do it, hurry!" she gasped, using her other hand to find Chris's swollen penis. Guiding him inside her, she cried out in pleasure. They found their rhythm, nothing slow and gentle about them now as they moved together frantically. Chris pulled Liza down to him, rolled them both over so he was above her and thrust, hard, harder as the two of them climaxed together.

The next two weeks were the happiest Chris had had since coming to London. Even if he couldn't be with Liza during the days or every single night, she made it well worth the wait as soon as they were alone together again. If he was driving her with Claire or Page, they kept things neutral, other than the shared glances in the rear-view mirror. But when they met at night, usually not until she was done with business at seven or eight, they would head straight for his apartment to make love. After that, Liza would insist on taking Chris out to dinner; she wanted him to eat at London's best restaurants, and although she always promised to let him pay, somehow the check never materialized at the table. After dinner, they'd hit all the late-night clubs, and it seemed Liza was intent on dancing with Chris at every one. By two or three in the morning, they would find their way back to Chris's apartment to make love once more.

Chris didn't understand how Liza managed to look perfect every morning, while he was bleary-eyed from so many late nights. But he couldn't wait to do it again. She was the most fun, the most daring—the most everything. He couldn't get enough of her, was practically light-headed from being in a constant state of desire.

It was difficult for him to conceal his disappointment when Liza told him that she

217

and her mother were taking a tour of all the Warren Hotels outside London. Claire had decided it was time for Liza to see the rest of the company's operations firsthand. Just as she had once taken Page on a trip to meet the management in each hotel and learn about how the company was run, Claire had scheduled three weeks that would provide Liza with the maximum exposure to the business.

Chris knew he was being selfish, wishing Liza would refuse to go. He had to restrain himself from asking her to stay behind. Besides, he had been neglecting his friendship with Page, not to mention his hustling for acting jobs. Of course, Page was always with Simon these days, so she wasn't exactly pining over the loss of his company. Nonetheless, he felt bad about how little he had seen her—and, of course, that he had never told her anything about himself and Liza. He realized he had been right to keep silent about it when he saw how her spirits lifted as soon as Liza and Claire had gone. In one way, her obvious relief irritated him. Why couldn't she get along with Liza? What was the big deal? Liza was a handful, but she was so exciting to be around. He knew he was losing control of his emotions, but he didn't care. He was in love and hated keeping it a secret. Why couldn't Page and Simon and he and Liza all go out together? Not that he really wanted to share Liza with anybody else.

Page seemed delighted when Chris asked her to meet him the following Sunday afternoon at the National Gallery. Chris arrived first, and as he watched Page walk toward him, he realized how long it had been since he'd even taken a good close look at her. She looked sensational, her hair gleaming, her skin radiant.

"Hi, Chris. I hope you haven't been waiting long." Page kissed him on the cheek, taking his hand as they ran up the steps to the museum's entrance.

He couldn't get over how wonderful she looked. "Page, you're absolutely glowing. Is it love? Don't tell me you're pregnant?"

A faint blush colored her cheeks, as she shook her head with a laugh. "You're awful! No, I'm not pregnant. But I definitely am in love. I can't begin to tell you what it's like. Simon is just amazing."

"Page, I'm so happy for you. It's great that you found someone who's actually nice enough to deserve you."

They headed inside, pausing here and there among the paintings. They stopped in front of Gainsborough's *Blueboy*. Chris wondered if she might be more receptive now to the news about his romance with Liza. Page was so happy with Simon, maybe she had softened toward her sister.

It was worth a try. "Listen, I want to say something about Liza—"

The expression on Page's face made Chris stop in mid-sentence. "Why do we have to talk about Liza?" she said angrily.

"I just thought—"

"What did you just think? Liza's been

nothing but trouble since the moment she got here. I'm thrilled that she's away for a few weeks. I know that sounds terrible, but it's the damn truth."

Chris had no idea that Page felt so strongly. "Liza's not so bad," he said. "She's smart, she's funny..."

"And she's not to be trusted." Page finished his sentence. "Chris, please," she continued, more softly now. "It's been such a long time since we've gotten together. Can't we just be us, like before Liza came here?"

Chris saw that he wasn't going to get any further today with Page on this subject. When Liza got back from her trip, he decided, they would straighten it all out.

The three weeks without Liza were interminable to Chris. But after she returned, other than driving her and Claire back from the airport, he couldn't get to see her at all for two days. She was sequestered in the Warren office, one meeting after another, apparently trying to catch up on the work that must have piled up on her desk. She hadn't called for him in the car either. She must have been taking taxis.

Finally, on Thursday night, Chris went directly to the Warren house on Albion Street. He found Liza in the drawing room with Page and Simon, who were on their way to see a movie that a friend of Simon's had produced.

"Chris, hello, come in." Page jumped up to hug him as he entered. Simon also rose and the two men shook hands.

"How's it going, Simon?"

"Couldn't be better. It's great to see you. When can we get together?"

"Right, let's do it next week," Chris answered, thinking perhaps this would be the occasion for him and Liza to fill in Simon and Page on their situation. He turned to Liza. She stood, a smile on her face, but made no move to come to him.

"Oh, Chris, we have to run. I'm so sorry," Page said. "We'll give you a call about next week. Good night, Liza."

"Have a great evening." Liza spoke with apparent warmth. "Remember, Page, you were going to advise me on where to get a haircut tomorrow."

"Yes, fine," Page said. She had no idea what Liza was talking about. The subject of haircuts had never even come up between them.

"Thanks," Liza said. "Lovely to see you again, Simon."

Simon gave her a quick wave and a grin as they left. Chris was finally alone with Liza.

"God, I've missed you," he said, hurrying over to her. Liza poured herself a glass of red wine from a decanter on the mantelpiece. She swirled the red liquid in her glass, studying it.

"Liza?" Chris put his arms around her.

She pulled back and looked at him coldly. Chris reached for her free hand, but she snatched it away.

"What's going on here? I thought we loved each other?" Chris's expression hardened.

Liza fixed her gaze on him. "I can't imagine whatever gave you the idea I loved you," she said in a flat voice. "You're our chauffeur."

Chris recoiled as if he had been slapped. "I can't be hearing this," he said, shaking his head.

"Don't tell me you actually thought we were going to be involved in some kind of ongoing thing?" Liza's tone rose slightly to indicate disbelief that Chris could ever have entertained such a notion. "We both had some fun. That was all. Grow up."

Chris was paralyzed. Liza sat down calmly and sipped her wine.

"You bitch," he whispered finally. "How could I have been so stupid?"

"I can't help what you are, now can I?" Liza responded, picking up a magazine from the table by her side. She rested it in her lap and began to read.

Chris whirled around and left the house. Hearing him slam the door behind him, Liza smiled, never taking her eyes from the words in front of her.

"Liza, darling, here you are." Claire had come downstairs and entered the drawing room. "Did I hear someone leaving?"

"Yes, Mother. Page and Chris went out."

"Together? I thought Page was with Simon tonight. Well, it doesn't matter," Claire answered her own question, her mind on other things. "I was hoping we might spend some time tonight on the budget projections. Putting it together is a fairly long process and we'd best get a head start."

Liza stood to join her mother. "Why don't we talk about it over dinner, start thrashing out the major points? It's just the two of us here tonight, so we can move into the library later and work undisturbed."

Claire linked her arm through Liza's. They began walking toward the dining room. "Wonderful. You know, I'm overwhelmed by how quickly you pick things up, how much you've learned in such a short time."

"It's easy, with a teacher like you," Liza said, turning around to pull the drawing room doors shut behind them.

Chapter Fifteen

Page opened and shut her attaché case for the fifth time since Simon had left her waiting in the leather chair ten minutes before. What am I so nervous about, she wondered, thinking of something she had forgotten to take from the office, checking inside her briefcase and finding it already there. She stood up and began to walk around the lobby of Brown's Hotel, admiring the tasteful furnishings. A painting of two riders reminded her of the Manor she was working on in Sussex. Had she taken the estimate for bathroom fixtures? She rummaged through her papers one more time. They were right there. What's the matter with me, she thought.

Simon is the one who's auditioning, not me. She looked at her watch. He should be down in another few minutes. Everything couldn't be better, she mused as she sat down once more, crossing her right leg over her left, then uncrossing them.

Catching her reflection in a large mirror across the room, Page was embarrassed by how clearly her anxiety showed. Okay, what was this about? She forced herself to think calmly. Simon? No. She was happier than she ever imagined she could be. Work? The seventh Manor house was exactly as impossible and would work out exactly as well as the first six. No it wasn't her love life and it wasn't her work life. What was left?

Page knew the answer, but could hardly bear to voice it, even to herself. Family. Her mother and her sister. As the image of Liza flashed in her mind, Page's lips tightened. Ah, the mystery solved. I'm a veritable Sherlock Holmes, Page thought, her sarcasm directed at her own feeling of helplessness. More pictures rushed into her mind: Liza standing in Claire's office for the first time; Liza and her mother leaving for their tour of the Warren hotels; Liza and Chris laughing together as he washed the Bentley; Liza and Simon busily comparing off-Broadway shows. Liza, Liza, Liza.

I am sick of her, Page admitted to herself, staring straight into her own eyes in the mirror. After one defiant moment, she started to feel guilty. She remembered her mother's description of Liza, lying on the playground in Wisconsin, bleeding, hurt, all alone. Page was chastened by the thought of how her sister must have suffered over the years. Still...it was difficult to feel any sympathy for someone who so obviously knew how to take care of herself. And just how to take care of me, Page reflected darkly. Maybe I'm nuts, but I just can't see whatever it is that other people love in Liza. They all find her so charming. Sure, she's charming to everyone but me. Mother loves her. Simon thinks she's fun. Even Chris has come around. Could I be so wrong about her? Page considered all the times Liza had been mean to her, then, in the next moment, ever so nice to someone else. Am I crazy, or is everyone else blind?

When Liza and Claire first returned from their trip through Europe, Page had gone with Chris to Heathrow to pick them up, glad to have her mother and her sister back. The entire way home in the car, Claire raved about Liza's grasp of details, her flawless French, her ease with every level of Warren staff from the foreign managers to the maids. Claire had decided to unpack and rest for a couple of hours, while Liza went to the office with Page. In the car, the sisters talked about the little touches that made the Warren hotels so different from one another. Each had a distinct national flavor, so the visitor who spent Thursday night in the Paris Warren knew he was in a different country when he slept in the Brussels Warren on Friday.

"How is Pierre Furie?" Page had asked.

The Belgian managing director had been wonderful to her when she had taken the same trip with her mother a couple of years before.

Liza waited a moment before she answered. "He's well enough. I'm surprised you'd be concerned under the circumstances."

"Under what circumstances?" Page couldn't imagine what Liza meant.

"Oh, nothing." Liza was obviously thinking of something specific, but unwilling to say it.

Page was getting more and more curious. "Why are you so hesitant? Pierre was so nice to me in Brussels. We really became friends."

Liza looked cynical at these words. "Sure, Page. Friends, that's just what Pierre said. Friends."

"Liza, what are you talking about? What did Pierre tell you?"

Liza refused to say one more word on the subject. Which left Page completely unsettled. She had no idea what Liza had on her mind, yet even now, a full month later, she felt uncomfortable every time Pierre's name came up.

In fact, Liza provided her with plenty to feel unnerved about. She again uncrossed and recrossed her legs, trying to find a comfortable position. Was there even one moment of real pleasure with Liza? One conversation that even resembled the closeness they had shared at school? No, everything Liza did seemed pointed and strange. I don't care how much everyone else likes her, something is wrong, Page concluded.

She could never get to see her mother alone anymore as Liza always seemed to be in Claire's office. Every time a problem came up with one of the Manors that needed her mother's attention, Page would come to Claire, and there her sister would be. Claire was delighted to have her girls together, but to Page it felt like two against one. And Liza never hesitated to offer her opinions. Not that she was stupid, Page added to be fair. Liza was sharp, which somehow made her presence even more annoying. It used to be fun to hash out problems with Claire, go over the alternatives, come up with creative solutions. Now it was all played out in front of Liza. Page missed the easy communication with her mother, the intimate exchange of ideas that had deepened their respect for each other. That had been fun, damn it. Nothing at work had been fun since Liza arrived.

At first Page had blamed herself. Maybe she was the one with the problem. It wasn't easy having to share her mother after all these years. But Page was certain it was more than that. Finally, Liza had gone too far. Two days before, Page had visited the Sussex Manor and found some very unpleasant surprises: couches she had never ordered, wallpaper she had never seen, landscaping she knew nothing about. When she chided Lady Hawthorne, the original owner, about the changes, she was shocked by the answer.

"Oh, I didn't pick out any of that. Your sister Liza was here two weeks ago. Doesn't she have a good eye? I just love the blue chintz on the sofa. Periwinkle, Liza called it. I'm surprised she didn't mention it to you. Why don't you talk to Henry if you have any questions? They did it together."

Page was stunned, but still managed to ask, "Who's Henry?"

"Why, the manager Liza hired, of course," Lady Hawthorne had answered, clearly puzzled by Page's ignorance.

Page was furious when she got back to London and confronted Liza in her new office at Warren headquarters. "How dare you interfere in my work!" she exploded.

"Don't be ridiculous," Liza had snapped back, her voice dry and cold as it always was when they were alone. "Mother gave me carte blanche to do whatever I thought best. The Manors are not *yours*. They are *Warren's*. There are two of us now, and I have just as much right to make decisions as you do."

Outraged, Page decided to go to Claire. She took a moment to cool off before making her way to her mother's office. As usual, Liza was already ensconced in one corner, a model of serenity by the time Page entered. Page told her mother everything—the furniture, the hiring, the gardening, the fact that Liza never mentioned any of it, either before or after. She railed while Liza stayed completely unruffled, not saying a word. Claire had looked from Liza to Page, the former seated demurely, eyes cast down, the latter hysterical, pacing wildly. She turned to her younger daughter and spoke carefully, as if she were talking to an invalid. Perhaps Page was working too hard; maybe she needed a few days away. It was important for Liza to learn every part of the Warren empire. After all, she was a third of it now. And finally, the coup de grace, Claire had walked over to Page and put a hand on her daughter's shoulder as she said almost pityingly, "Try not to be jealous of your sister, dear. After all, you've had so much all this time. Can't you share it just a little?"

It's so unfair, Page raged within herself, reliving the conversation over and over again as she waited for Simon. She thinks I'm either a spoiled, selfish brat or a lunatic. This isn't jealousy, and I'll be damned if I'm going crazy.

As if proving her mother right, Page stood up once more and started pacing around the lobby, her eyes ablaze. When Simon spotted her, he was too excited to notice her agitation.

"It's down to three of us," he whispered, as if the acting gods might punish him if he were overheard. "I can't believe it. I might really get this." Carl Meyer had come to London just the night before, asking Simon to meet him in his room at Brown's and read the part of Jonathan once more. "He said he would let us know tomorrow. Definitely tomorrow."

Page took in Simon's excitement and said, smiling, "I don't know if you're going to last until tomorrow."

Simon was not offended. "I'm not sure myself. But, of course, you've developed quite a knack for taking my mind off things. Perhaps we could go home, and you could think of something that would get me through the night." He took her hand and they walked out of the hotel to a waiting cab.

They rode down Shaftesbury Avenue to Simon's flat on Bedford Place. Page rested her head in the hollow of his neck, his steady pulse, his warm skin finally beginning to relax her. This is one corner of my life Liza can't touch, Page thought. She could hardly believe she was the same woman who had begun dating Simon two months before. From a frightened, inexperienced girl, she had grown into a passionate, spontaneous woman. Simon seemed to know instinctively how to ease her fears, how to arouse her. Her reserve, her isolation melted away when they were together.

Simon felt it too. The rightness of them. They seemed like two parts of a whole. They'd seen each other almost every day since they'd re-met, and his feelings seemed to have no upper limit. Having Page in his life made everything easier for Simon. Even the frustration of waiting to hear from Carl Meyer was not so terrible with Page at his side. In fact, Simon realized, leaving her to film in the United States would be murder if he got the part. Don't count your chickens, he chided himself as the cab drew up in front of the unprepossessing building he'd lived in since he first came to London.

Simon's flat on the ground floor was noisy and small, but to Page it seemed enchanted.

Although her mother's townhouse was far more elegant, this had become the place she felt most like herself. Only two people were allowed, she and Simon. No one else could enter their private sanctuary. Nominally, Page still lived on Albion Street; now this was home to her. As she walked into the flat, she put everything else—Liza, her mother, her job—out of her mind completely. Page took her coat off and carried it into the bedroom where the apartment's one closet was located, while Simon went directly to his telephone answering machine and played back the one message waiting for him.

"It's Chris, honey. He says he'll meet us at Bengal Palace at eight o'clock," he reported to Page as he joined her in his room. "Let's see, that's about two hours from now." He put his arms around her and suddenly, without warning, picked her up and deposited her on the bed. "We're going to play statues."

"What do you mean?" Page was suspicious and aroused at the same time.

"Now, let's see..." Simon was circling the bed, looking devilish. "Okay, here goes. Find a comfortable position."

Page moved so her head rested easily on the pillow, with her arms folded in front of her and her legs primly together, covered by her skirt.

"Are you sure you want to leave your hands like that?" Simon's voice teased her.

"That depends on what the rules of this game are," was Page's tart reply.

"There are only two rules," he answered in

a professional voice. "Rule number one, you have to stay completely still. Rule number two, I get to do whatever I want."

"That's no fair," she cried, placing her hands down on the bed and starting to pull herself up.

Simon held her as she was. "Don't worry," he said. "I'll make it fair."

Page lay back down and Simon released his hold. He surveyed her up and down, his eyes finally coming to rest on her feet. "Not too comfortable with those on," he murmured, pulling off one shoe, then the other. "Or these," he added, exploring under her skirt until his hand came to the waistband of her pantyhose.

Page reached down to help him, but again he stopped her. "No moving. No moving at all." His voice was serious, making her shiver with anticipation. He finished what he was doing and then returned to a standing position. Page lay quietly, waiting for his next move. He finally sat down on the bed next to her and wordlessly began undoing the buttons of her sweater. Letting the sides of the garment fall open, he placed his hands on the sides of her neck, then warmed her shoulders and her breasts as his fingers traveled down to her waist. He didn't linger on any part of her body, but continued his trip, unzipping the back of her skirt and pulling it slowly off her body.

Now almost nude, Page began to respond to his touch as his hands moved languorously over her firm stomach and around to the backs of her thighs. Page began to fit herself to his touch.

"No, you have to stay completely still," he whispered, as he bent his head down, sliding his lips over her hip bones down to her center, his tongue taking in her essence, deeper and deeper, as his hands held her fast.

Page shuddered with pleasure, no longer able to remain motionless as waves of ecstasy broke within her. Simon placed one hand on her mound, meeting the rising tide of his tongue's work with a firm pressure that caused her to scream in fulfillment.

"Please," she gasped, "come inside me. I need you inside me."

Simon removed his own clothes quickly and entered her, finally allowing their bodies to join.

As they lay in each other's arms afterward, Page felt calm and joyous. She reflected on her anxiety earlier that day and thought of saying something about it to Simon. He had helped her with so many things; maybe he could ease her worries about Liza. No, she decided, lazily stroking his chest. I don't want anything to interfere today. Not in this place, not right now. Besides, she thought uncomfortably, Liza was always so charming to Simon. He might dismiss her fears the way her mother did. The very notion made her put her arms around Simon and draw him close, hiding the tears that began to sting her eyes.

Chris was sitting by himself at Bengal Palace, staring into a glass of red wine, when Page and Simon arrived.

"You two look cheerful," he said, noting the high color on both their faces.

"You don't," Simon replied truthfully. "What's going on?"

"The usual. Making rounds, making rounds, and making rounds. They don't seem to be beating the bushes for guys from Detroit this week on the London stage. I can't imagine why not. Besides, who could compete in the happiness sweepstakes with you two?" Despite his words, Chris's tone was cheerful. "You know, I consider myself totally responsible for your happiness. In fact, I think you owe me ten percent."

"You'll have to make up your mind, Chris." Simon narrowed his eyes as he spoke. "Are you Dear Abby or William Morris?"

Simon had always been at his most relaxed with Chris, which was a great source of pleasure to Page. Sitting down to dinner with her favorite two men made her feel thoroughly at peace for the first time in days. But she, too, had noticed Chris's expression when they first walked in, and it worried her.

"I thought you were bringing a date tonight," she said.

"Late cancellation," was his terse reply. He changed the subject quickly. "I hear Carl

Meyer's in town, Simon. Is there something I should know?"

"Not yet. Actually, I think I'll go make a call." Simon checked to be sure he had his answering machine beeper before he left the table. "Excuse me, folks. I promise I'll only do this once tonight."

"Sure." Page and Chris replied at the same moment, amused disbelief on both their faces.

"Is he calling Carl Meyer?" Chris asked Page once Simon was gone.

"I would answer, but you know how superstitious he is. I'm afraid if he doesn't get the role, it'll be my fault. You're all crazy, you know, you actors." Page was only half teasing.

"And what if he does get it, Page? What will you do, go with him?"

Page's chagrin at his question was clear. "I can't. I wish I could, but there's too much to do. Besides, if I left now, there might not be a job for me when I got back. Or a mother." Page caught the surprised look on Chris's face. "Sorry. I forgot. That subject is out of bounds." Page remembered she had once mentioned her distrust of her sister and Chris had sprung to Liza's defense. But this time, he was quiet.

Page was sorry she had brought it up again and said so. "You look unhappy enough tonight. I didn't mean to lay my troubles on you." Chris still didn't say anything. There really did seem to be something very much the matter with him. "What's going on?" she asked, placing her hand on his arm and forcing him to look at her.

"Well, maybe it's the same thing that's the matter with you," he finally responded. "The lovely Liza." His tone was bitter.

Page stared at him. "What do you mean?"

"I really have to get this out, and I'm afraid you're the only one I feel like telling it to." Chris looked hard at Page. "I wish I had listened the last time you talked about Liza. You were right. Maybe even more right than you know." Page was watching him closely, not knowing what he was about to say, but fearing every word.

"Liza and I were involved. That is, *I* thought we were involved. I was dead wrong."

Page's face was a blank as she tried to take in his words. "Involved. Involved how?"

"Involved like sleeping together. Involved like I was falling in love with her. You know, when Liza first got here, I didn't trust her at all. But then, well, she was so pretty and so much fun, and she really went out of her way with me." Page knew how true that was. It had nearly killed her to see Liza joking with Chris seconds after hurling some deadly remark at Page.

"What happened? What went wrong?"

"Damned if I know. A week ago, she dropped me flat. She stopped even talking to me. When I asked her what was going on, she told me to grow up. *Grow up.* A direct quote." The sting of the remark still showed as he repeated her words.

"But, Page, that's not the worst of it. Thinking back, I don't believe she ever gave a shit about me. She was just playing with me. What I can't figure out is, why."

But Page thought she knew why. In fact, she was absolutely sure. Liza had done it to hurt her younger sister. Seducing Chris and then trampling all over him was a way of getting to Page. God knows what Liza got out of it, but Page knew she was right. She didn't want to say all this out loud to Chris. It seemed grandiose, almost paranoid.

She was saved from having to speak by Simon's arrival back at the table. As Simon sat down, Chris composed himself and smiled at his friend. "So, Simon. What's the story?"

Simon beamed back at him as he threw his arms around Page. "No," he said. "Not Simon. Call me Jonathan."

Chapter Sixteen

One ear cocked, Liza paused outside Page's bedroom on her way down the hall. The heavy oak door muffled her sister's voice, but her words were still audible.

"—be with you too, sweetheart," Page was saying sadly. "But you know I just can't walk away from the Manors, it's too busy a time."

There was silence for a moment. That would be Simon begging on the other end of the line, Liza thought cynically, telling Page how lonely he was for her.

Then she heard Page speak again. "It's been terrible for me as well. If there were any possible way, I'd be on the next plane. I promise I'll get over there as soon as I can."

Liza didn't wait to hear the rest of the conversation. She knew Page and Simon spoke every day, and it always went the same way. Apparently, Page felt some obligation to oversee the opening of the newest Manor before she could join Simon in the States. If he were mine, I'd have taken off with him the first day—screw the business, Liza said to herself disgustedly. You don't leave a gorgeous guy like Simon alone on a Hollywood movie set. She started down the stairs.

"Is my taxi here yet, Mrs. Walker?" Liza asked as the housekeeper emerged from the drawing room carrying a sterling tea service.

"Any minute, Miss Carlisle," the older woman responded.

Liza surveyed her luggage, packed and standing by the front door, as she retrieved a black leather raincoat from the hall closet. Draping the coat around her shoulders, she crossed over to the drawing room where she knew she would find her mother.

Claire looked up from the papers she held in her lap as her daughter entered.

"I'm going now, Mother." Liza bent down to kiss Claire on the cheek.

"I'll miss you so much. I've gotten so used to having you here." Claire smiled regretfully as she took her daughter's hand. "Couldn't the business you have to attend to be dealt with over the telephone?"

"It'll only be a few weeks. But I really have to take care of some things. You know, a person can't move overseas just like that—" Liza snapped her fingers. "—with no loose ends."

"Well, have a wonderful time in New York, darling." Claire brightened as an idea occurred to her. "Maybe we could travel there together one day, you and I. Oh, I'd love that. I've avoided New York for so many years. It was too painful, knowing you were there and not being able to see you."

Through the window Liza could see a taxi pull up in front of the house. "Have to run. Take care, Mother," she said, turning to go.

Claire looked out at the waiting car. "Liza, why on earth isn't Chris driving you to Heathrow? Why should you need a taxi?"

Because I don't want Chris poking around in what I'm doing, Liza silently retorted. Aloud, she said, "Actually, he's running a few errands for me, dropping off some papers that need delivering. It's no bother, really."

Before the conversation could progress any further, Liza gave a quick wave and hurried off. "I love you, darling," Claire called out after her. From inside the drawing room, she watched her daughter gracefully slide into the taxi's backseat while the driver loaded her suitcases into the trunk. How barren it would seem without Liza. Claire caught herself, remembering that, of course, Page was still there. But Liza's return had filled such a huge hole in her life, had assuaged two decades of guilt. She sighed and turned back to the work at hand.

The flight was delayed, and it was nearly midnight in New York when the plane touched down at Kennedy. Liza had made sure a limousine driver would wait for her, no matter how long it took, so she was able to hurry past the crowd of people looking for taxis and enjoy the ride into Manhattan. It seemed like years since she left, she mused, delightedly drinking in the sight of the city skyline. Naturally, there was no question of going back to Bennett's apartment. A reservation had been made in her name at the Plaza Athenee on East Sixty-fourth Street. She checked in and went to bed, immediately falling into a deep sleep.

The next morning, Liza got up at five-thirty and dressed slowly, carefully. It was important that she look her best for the next couple of days. By seven o'clock, bundled up in sable against the sharp November wind, she was on her way down Park Avenue to the Regency Hotel.

When Liza entered the hotel's dining room, Eleanor Martin was already seated, a lone young woman surrounded by a sea of men in dark business suits. She waved Liza over, hugging and kissing her warmly on both cheeks before they settled back in their chairs. Liza noted that Eleanor had changed neither

her pageboy nor her taste for tweedy suits since their days together at Vassar. It wasn't that she was bad-looking, thought Liza, appraising her former classmate, but she certainly could use a lot of help.

"Hello, Poochie, it's been absolutely ages," Eleanor said in her small, high voice, squeezing Liza's hand and beaming at her across the table.

It was all Liza could do to keep from wincing. She had nearly forgotten how annoying Eleanor's high-pitched voice and little-girl mannerisms could be. Plenty of the other girls at Vassar had been bothered by these traits, but, given that Eleanor was one of the richest young women in America, most had chosen to overlook them.

Liza smiled broadly. "You look fabulous, Eleanor. Truly great. Have you done something new with your hair? It's sensational."

Eleanor patted her pageboy. "Do you really think so? No, it's the same style, but I'm going to a new hairdresser, and his cut is a lot better. I've also lost a couple of pounds. Maybe that's it."

"Well, whatever you're doing, keep it up." Liza picked up her menu. "Shall we hurry and order, so we can get down to some real talk?"

"Oh, yes, I want to hear everything about everybody. I'm up on my own crowd, of course, but you always knew the really interesting girls at school. I want every detail. First, you. Where have you been keeping yourself? It was so terrific to hear from you last week. Gee, it must be a year since we got together."

Liza briefly explained that she had moved to London and was working in the hotel business. Before Eleanor could question her further, she expertly steered the conversation around to what had occurred in the lives of their fellow Vassar graduates. Most of what she told Eleanor was made up on the spot, since there were only a few girls besides Eleanor whom Liza had chosen to keep up with after leaving college. She had no great affection for any of her fellow Vassar graduates; those she did see or talk to were simply the ones she had determined might be useful to her in the future. Eleanor, of course, knew nothing of this, so was delighted to have Liza fill her in on what she believed to be the alumnae gossip. In return, she was only too glad to share the latest of her friends' love lives. Liza affected interest, although she tuned out most of what was being said. When the waiter brought their coffee, she casually raised the subject of Eleanor herself.

"Tell me now, what you have been up to? Are you having a grand time, single and on the loose in New York?"

Eleanor's face fell slightly. "Well, it's true that I keep incredibly busy. Or, maybe I should say, Mommy and Daddy keep me incredibly busy. But it's not easy to find somebody nice to go out with and they're suspicious of every man who shows any interest in me. They've always been that way."

That was an accurate description, Liza knew. Originally quite poor, Eleanor's father had made his fortune in shipping. As soon as he became a member of the monied class, he had decided that everyone else was a gold digger, simply waiting for an opportunity to steal his wealth. He had every expectation that his daughter would somehow be used as a means of wresting his money away from him, or, at the very least, would herself be duped into giving up the considerable millions he had put into her name. Knowing how naïve Eleanor was, Liza didn't blame him for his fears on that account.

Liza looked sympathetic. "It's hard for lots of women to find a nice guy, Eleanor, not only you. But you know things are much easier in London."

"They are?"

"For some reason, there seem to be lots of great single men there. I know so many—I wish you'd come over so I could introduce you to a few."

"That would be super. I'd love it," Eleanor responded, clapping her hands together happily. "It's always fun being around you. I could fly over next month if you think it would be a good idea. Ooh, how terrific."

Liza smiled in agreement. "You know—" She trailed off thoughtfully, tapping her spoon on the tablecloth.

"What is it?" Eleanor asked anxiously.

Liza leaned forward in her chair. "You've always been a good friend to me, Eleanor. I'm going to let you in on something." She lowered her voice. "It's a business thing. We've never done any business together, but I trust you and I want you to be able to take advantage of this."

Eleanor bit her thumbnail, waiting.

"You see, I have a very high position in this company, Warren International. They have twenty-five top-quality hotels all over Europe—none here—and six smaller places, what we call Warren Manors. The company is run by a woman, and she's done a good job, really built it up. But she has these problems—drinking, some married boyfriend who won't leave his wife, that sort of stuff. In the past couple of years, she's completely lost interest in the business. She's letting it go to pieces. The company is still in perfect shape, but only because I've practically killed myself trying to cover for her, and continually backtrack over her work to fix her mistakes."

"How awful," Eleanor said.

"It is. I guess I should say it *was*. You see, despite my covering for her, the board found out about how she was screwing up. They're ready to get rid of her. It's a relief, actually, even though I was very fond of her. She's just someone who shouldn't be working anymore."

"My dad has people like that, people he says will be better off out of the pressure cooker," Eleanor said comfortingly, wanting to appear as if she could empathize with these problems of management.

"That's right," Liza nodded. "Anyway, as you know, there are always leaks in business, so some of her problems are known around town. What this all means is that when word gets out there's going to be new management, the stock is going to take off. We'll be doing great things and everyone will want to be in on it. And—" Liza's quiet tone dropped down to a whisper, "I think they're going to choose me to replace her."

"Oh, how exciting for you," Eleanor cried.

Liza leaned back. "It means more to me than you can possibly imagine. So what I was thinking was that you could be part of this. It would be so much fun for us. You'd come in as a stockholder and have free run of all our hotels. I know you can stay anywhere you want now, but that's not the same as being the owner, trust me. You'd have your own suite in every Warren hotel—London, Paris, Zurich, anyplace you wanted—and you could use them as bases around the world. We could travel around together and you could really have some independence."

Liza took a sip of water. She knew it wouldn't be difficult to make good on her promise of hotel suites if she were forced to. But she was just as certain that she wouldn't be. Eleanor lived with her parents, and despite her constant talk about how she was going to move out and have nothing to do with them, Liza knew she would never leave them voluntarily. She was too used to being sheltered, too fearful of stepping outside the shadow

245

of their protection. Even the plan for Eleanor to fly to London and spend some time with Liza would never be followed through; somehow, Eleanor would keep putting it off. Liza was also well aware that Eleanor had never made a business decision in her life. She was completely innocent about how corporations operated. Liza pressed on.

"It's the soundest investment in the world, Ell, and can only make you money. Your dad will be incredibly impressed. And I'll be so happy to have a friend involved in the company. Truthfully, I'd also breathe a lot more easily knowing I had your support on the board, a pal I could definitely depend on to stand behind me. You know how rough business can get. So, it's a rational move for you, although, to be perfectly honest, it could take a bit of money if you really want to see a good return."

Eleanor's uncertainty was plain. She was eager to join, but was afraid of what her father might say. Squarely facing her fear of looking foolish, Eleanor plunged ahead with a nervous question.

"How much money would it take?"

Liza was well prepared with her answer, having given it a great deal of thought in the previous few days. She knew the figure had to be low enough for Eleanor to commit without her father having to find out.

"We could start with three million." She nearly held her breath, waiting to find out if she had called it right.

The look of pure relief that appeared on Eleanor's face told Liza all she needed to know.

By eleven o'clock that night, Liza was back in her hotel room, ready to collapse with exhaustion. She hadn't stopped running all day—first the breakfast with Eleanor, then lunch with Susie Dickerson, followed by tea with Henry Taft, and dinner with Bobby Hilliard. Tomorrow it would be more of the same, another day of nonstop appointments.

Settling into a steaming bubblebath, Liza permitted herself to relax completely for the first time that day. Just as she'd anticipated, it wasn't going to be easy. No one had been as effortless a sell as Eleanor. Henry Taft had turned her down flat, claiming he was overextended as it was—disappointing, but also not entirely unexpected. An ex-lover of Liza's with plenty of money, Henry was nearly fifty, and highly conservative when it came to investing his money. Not that Liza believed the reason he gave for his unwillingness to invest in Warren stock. She knew full well that he just didn't have the confidence in her ability to run a corporation. That's what happens when you play the frivolous mistress, Liza thought grimly, turning on the hot-water spigot with her toes. Why is it that men think if a woman is good in bed she can't be good at anything else?

No matter. Bobby Hilliard, an old pal from

the club scene, had come through for her. Since their early days of hanging out, he'd become a tremendously successful—and rich—singer and songwriter. He had responded immediately to the picture Liza painted of getting the owner's red-carpet treatment at hotels around the world, throwing all the parties he wanted at the expense of Warren International. He was used to traveling anyway. Being able to stay in what would be his own luxurious playground appealed immensely to him, as did Liza's suggestion of what a kick it would be for the two of them to control this straitlaced corporation. No problem, was Bobby's response. He was in for three million.

Susie Dickerson was still on the fence. Susie was another Vassar graduate, but, unlike Eleanor, she had chosen to work after college rather than relying on her family's vast wealth to give her days meaning. Susie was an antiques dealer, and frequently traveled to Europe on buying trips. Liza had presented her with a more sophisticated argument for getting involved: the stock was a good investment; there would be tax advantages; Susie could quickly broaden her network of contacts into the international antiques market by affiliating herself with Warren International. Susie wanted a week to research the firm. Let her, Liza thought. Knowing that Susie was too smart with her money to invest without checking things out first, Liza had told her that Claire and she were mother and daughter, until recently living apart as a result of her parents' divorce. In this version of the story, Claire wanted to retire, though she was keeping it a secret until the time was right for a formal announcement. Liza presented herself as the logical choice to succeed her mother, with Susie deriving the many benefits of being so closely allied with the new president. By the time Susie caught on to the fact that Claire was actually being forced out of the business, it wouldn't make much difference. Claire meant nothing to her personally; as a businesswoman with an investment to protect, she would still be likely to throw her support behind Liza.

In a leisurely manner, Liza dried herself off and rubbed cream all over. Then she got into bed, grateful for the softness of the cool sheets beneath her naked body. More of the same, starting first thing in the morning, she thought. If the next round of meetings didn't get her to her goal of thirty-five million, she had some backups for the following day, and, if need be, the day after that. She turned off the light and was asleep almost at once.

It was another three days before Liza could leave the city. By Friday night, she was settled into a first-class airline seat, sipping Scotch on her way to Los Angeles. Stretching her long legs out before her, she swirled the golden liquor around in her glass and frowned. She had gotten firm commitments for twenty million dollars, leaving her fifteen million dollars short. A number of her friends were uncertain, or needed time to look into the idea. Well, hell, she told herself, twenty million isn't exactly chicken feed. Not many people could come up with that kind of money in three days. But she needed thirty-five million to make it a lock. She had gone over the figures dozens of times. With that much stock in the hands of her supporters, she could stage a proxy fight, force Claire out for good, and take over as head of Warren International. Without another fifteen million to bring the total up, she didn't feel she could count on being the one selected to replace Claire. It was easy to pinpoint the other executives in the company who would jump to challenge her for the job. Where could she get the rest of the money?

Well, she would work it out, she just knew it. This would simply require several more trips to New York. No doubt some of her prospects from this visit would decide in her favor. In the meantime, she had some other Warren business to attend to, something that was a lot more fun. She could hardly wait for the flight to be over.

Simon let himself out of the limousine before the driver had a chance to come around and open the door for him.

"Thanks so much," he said, speaking through the half-open front window. "Three hours ought to do it. If you could pick me up around ten, it would be much appreciated."

The studio had placed the limo and driver at his disposal for the entire filming of *Birds of Passage,* but it made him miserably uncomfortable. Whenever he emerged from the car, everyone passing by stopped to check if he was somebody famous. After a month and a half in Los Angeles, he could see how star-crazy the people here were. At home, he and Page rarely used her family's Bentley, and even when they did, Londoners never exhibited the same naked curiosity.

At least there was no one to stare at him out here. He turned to face the house as the limousine pulled away. Peaceful, right on the beach, with lots of glass and a wide deck that extended all the way around. In the fading glow of dusk, the bright lights within exuded a warm, inviting feeling. Liza must have some fancy friends, Simon couldn't help thinking. He didn't know much about L.A., but he knew that beachfront property in Malibu screamed money. Oh, what a snob we're becoming, he reprimanded himself as he walked up to the front door and rang the bell.

He was unprepared for the Liza that greeted him. He was used to seeing her in sophisticated suits and dresses, sleek in her high heels and generally wearing too much makeup for his taste. This woman looked like someone else entirely. Her long hair was pulled back into a tight, high ponytail, her face completely free of makeup. Barefoot, she wore jeans and a plain white T-shirt. She looked fresh and clean, even vulnerable. Simon was taken aback.

"Hello, Simon, come in." Liza spoke warmly,

smiling and taking him by the hand. "It's so nice of you to keep me company tonight."

As she led him inside to a spacious living room, Liza decided that California was definitely agreeing with Simon. With a lightweight brown leather bomber's jacket slung over his shoulder, wearing casual khaki pants and a white shirt with the sleeves rolled up, he looked healthy and relaxed. Not that there had ever been any question that he was attractive, she thought, catching his pleased expression as he noted the blazing fireplace. Her hunch had been right; it was a perfect touch.

"Seemed a bit cold tonight, and I thought a fire might be nice. Please take off your shoes and relax. Let me fix you a drink. Gin and tonic, isn't it?" she asked.

"Yes, right, thanks." Simon sat down on the white couch, stretching his legs out before him as he watched Liza's slender form move across the room to the bar.

Her back to him as she mixed their drinks, she spoke lightly. "You looked surprised when you came in. Why was that, if you don't mind my asking?"

Simon laughed, embarrassed. "Did it show that much? I'm sorry, you'd think an actor would have better control over his expressions. It's just that I've never seen this side of you. You're always so..."

"So..." Liza turned to look at him quizzically.

"So—I don't know, sophisticated. In control."

"You think I'm in control? Thanks for the compliment. I'm flattered." Liza sat down on the couch beside him, tucking her feet up under her as she handed him a drink. She placed her own on the coffee table nearby. "At the moment, I'm just kind of on my own and very happy that you agreed to come by. It can get lonely here."

"I *was* a little surprised when you called me for dinner. Not that I wasn't delighted, of course. But I imagined you would have lots of friends here." Simon took a sip of his drink. It was strong, but he didn't have to drive home tonight. He enjoyed its warmth, thinking what a relief it was to be able to relax with someone he knew from home. "What about the people who own this house?"

Liza was leaning across the table, putting some brie on a cracker for him. "Father's friends, really. An older couple. I happened to call them about visiting just as they were leaving for Majorca, and they were nice enough to offer me the use of the house while I'm in town. I don't have any friends here myself. This isn't my kind of place; I never come to L.A. unless I have to."

"Somehow I assumed this was a vacation for you."

"Oh, no." Liza laughed. "I have some business left over from my days in producing. There are a few people who want me to produce a special for them. It's a big job, and even though I have no intention of leaving Warren right now to do it, I felt I owed it to them to tell them so in person. At least I can give them some input on the project. We go back a long way." Liza wondered if Simon was buying all this. She stood up to refresh his drink.

Simon followed Liza across the room so he could enjoy the view of the ocean through the plate-glass doors. "How *is* the business back home? How is Page?" he asked.

Lisa suppressed a smile. She'd guessed Simon wouldn't last five minutes before he got around to the subject of Page. In fact, it had taken him a good ten until he brought up her sister's name. She had to hand it to him, he had excellent manners.

She turned, moving in closer. Her eyes took on a faraway, sad look for the briefest moment. "Page is fine, of course, just fine." Then, her cheerfulness sounding only a touch forced, she said, "You know, I'm famished. Are you ready for dinner?" She slid her arm around Simon's waist and leaned in to him as they walked toward the dining room. "It's so wonderful to see you. You're always hurrying off somewhere at home. Who would have thought that becoming a major movie star would mean you had more time to sit and talk? Well, you probably don't even know how much I always enjoy your company."

Again, Simon felt somehow thrown off balance. Liza was always friendly to him, but tonight she was different somehow, her defenses down, more intimate than she'd ever been. He returned her gesture, casually putting his arm around her waist. "Believe me, I'm starved for intelligent conversation."

By the glow of candlelight, they shared two bottles of red wine over dinner, first arguing animatedly about a show they'd both seen in London, then laughing together over the strange and ridiculous customs of Hollywood living. Simon told her about rehearsals, how difficult it was for him being the outsider on the set. He might be the lead in the movie, but he was still an unknown with few contacts in Hollywood. A Brit who knew nothing about how the movie business was run.

As Liza cleared the dinner dishes from the table, Simon leaned back in his chair, clasping his hands behind his head. "The duck was delicious. I didn't know you could cook like that."

Liza grinned. "Thank you, but the truth is I ordered it in earlier this afternoon. Why work to achieve mediocrity when perfection is available in take-out?"

Simon threw his head back and laughed. "Truer words were never spoken."

By the time they finished their coffee, it was nearly eleven. Simon knew his driver would be waiting patiently in front of the house and figured it was time to leave, but Liza urged him to stay a while longer. He hesitated for a moment, yet didn't protest when she brought out two brandy glasses and a bottle of Courvoisier.

"I don't know when I've had a better time," she said, as they settled back down on the living-room couch.

"The pleasure has been all mine, I assure you," Simon responded sincerely. "I've missed having someone to talk to. I'm pretty isolated here. Especially without Page or Chris, there's no one at all to ring up or have a coffee with." At the mention of Chris's name, Liza winced slightly and closed her eyes. Her discomfort didn't escape Simon's notice. "Did I say something wrong?" he asked, confused.

"It still hurts a little bit," Liza responded, looking down.

"I don't understand. Is Chris all right?"

Sarcasm was evident in her voice. "Oh, yes, Chris is terrific, just great." She shook her head. "Forgive me, I don't mean to sound bitter. But I really thought we had something wonderful."

This was the first Simon had heard of any personal relationship between Chris and Liza. He waited, unsure what to say.

"You know we were lovers," Liza continued. Simon's face registered his surprise at this information. "But, Simon, I thought you knew all about it."

"No, I didn't."

"Then you don't know why we split up? You don't know..." Liza's face went ashen as she stopped in mid-sentence.

"Don't know what? I'm sorry it didn't work out. You two seem like a perfect fit, now that I think about it."

"Oh, Simon, why am I the one who has to tell you this?" She took a deep breath. "The reason Chris and I split up was because I found out he was sleeping with—with someone else." Her next words were very quiet. "He was sleeping with Page."

Simon looked at her, uncomprehending. "What? Sleeping with Page? No, no, they never dated, they were always just friends. I'm certain of it. If they'd been lovers, I'm sure Page would have told me."

"No, Simon, I'm not talking about the past. I don't mean they used to be lovers. I mean they *are* lovers. Now. For the past few weeks— since just before you left, and certainly since you've been gone." The ache of talking about it was written across Liza's face.

Simon stared at her but said nothing. Then he walked over to the fireplace and gazed at the dying embers. Finally, he turned back to her. "You're absolutely certain?" he asked in a flat voice.

"How can you ask me that?" Liza sounded anguished. "I loved Chris and it's over now because of this. I thought you must have known, that you didn't mind if Page was with you both."

Simon exploded with rage and pain. "Are you out of you mind?! My God!" Seeing Liza's eyes fill with tears, he struggled to regain control of himself. "I'm sorry, I didn't mean—"

"Oh, Simon, I'm the one who's sorry," she interrupted. "Sorry I had to tell you. Sorry it happened. I can't believe how much it hurts. All I think about is how I could have been so stupid. Anyone can see how close the two of them are." Liza was crying freely now, trying to wipe her tears away. "How could I have ever thought there was room for me in Chris's heart? Page and he are—well, you know, you've seen them together."

It was true. Chris and Page had always had a special relationship. But he had believed, without the shadow of a doubt, that they were friends and nothing more. Was it possible Page could be that duplicitous, tell him she loved him and run to Chris's bed without a second thought? A groan escaped him. The pain of it was all too familiar. It was as if he were being transported back in time, back to his early theater days, to the moment Sarah Hughes had told him she no longer loved him, that she was leaving him for William Harper. That had been the last time he'd permitted himself to care for a woman. Until Page. Now here it was, happening all over again. The sensation was hot, burning his insides.

Liza looked at him sadly. "Everyone knows, Simon. It's no secret."

"No," he said quietly. "No. Why would you lie to me about this?"

She walked over to the telephone. "Here, I'll show you."

Carefully, her back to him, she dialed a number in London. Once the connection was made, she handed the receiver to him. She watched his face crumble as he heard the answering machine's message. Of course, she knew exactly what he was hearing. After all, she had recorded it herself, doing it over and over until she was sure it sounded exactly like Page's voice.

Hello. Chris and I aren't home right now. Please leave us a message so we can call you back the minute we get in.

Simon hung up the phone. His entire relationship with Page flashed through his mind. How quickly he'd fallen in love with her, how easy it had been to trust her after so many years of trusting no one. Page, he thought wildly, Page, how could you do this to me?

Fury rose above his pain. She didn't love him; she never loved him. Simon was suddenly sure of it. And Chris, his best friend! He envisioned the two of them, naked in bed together, Chris's face just above Page's. Simon felt like he was suffocating.

He was jolted back to his surroundings as Liza came toward him. Her tear-stained face looked so fragile and soft. "Please, Simon..." She practically fell against him, burying her face in his chest. He encircled her in his arms, fighting back the violence of his feelings.

When Liza raised her face to his, it took no more than a few seconds before their lips met. They kissed deeply, passionately. Simon couldn't think, couldn't speak. Barely knowing what he was doing, he tore off Liza's jeans and yanked the T-shirt over her head. They dropped down to the soft beige carpet, gasping with the intensity of their hunger as they both struggled to free Simon of his shirt and pants. He roughly released Liza's hair from its constricting band with one hand, while, with the other, he hurriedly pulled down her white bikini panties.

Intertwined, they rolled over and over, their hands roaming everywhere, their mouths and tongues urgently seeking. Finally, from her position on top of him, Liza rolled off to lie on her back, panting. Simon moved above her and found his way inside. He slid into her easily, she was so warm and wet. Liza reached down, putting her hand between their bodies so she could stroke his testicles each time their rhythmic movements separated them. As their motions became more frantic, she put both arms around him and brought her legs up high, wrapping them around his back.

Simon suddenly pulled away and turned Liza over on her stomach, entering her from behind. They thrust against one another, perspiration glistening on their bodies, both of them grunting with the force of their lovemaking. Her back arching, Liza shuddered again and again. It wasn't until her orgasm had completely subsided that Simon let himself go, shaking as he climaxed.

They collapsed, Liza on her stomach, Simon still inside her with his face buried in her neck. Several minutes passed before their breathing was quiet again. He picked his head up and gently smoothed the damp hair from Liza's neck.

"I don't know what got into me," he whispered. "It wasn't right. Please forgive me."

Liza answered in an equally soft voice.

"No, no, Simon, it was beautiful. You're a wonderful man."

He dropped his head back down. Liza could almost feel his guilt setting in now that the passion of his fury had subsided. He would get over that. She wriggled comfortably beneath the weight of his long, muscular body. My, she thought, when they said revenge is sweet, they didn't know the half of it.

"No, no, I know it's sold out. I don't want to *buy* tickets. I have tickets waiting at the box office. Jesus, do you speak English? What *time* is the performance?"

From where he stood in the bathroom, Simon heard Liza's irritated tone ring through the house. He paused in the middle of shaving, regarding his half-lathered face in the mirror as he listened.

"Well, thank you very much," Liza spat out sarcastically. "It only took ten minutes on hold for me to get this tricky piece of information. Eight o'clock. Fine." She hung up the telephone. "Idiot," she muttered to no one in particular.

Slowly, Simon rinsed his razor under the running water and brought it again to his cheek. In the three weeks since they'd become lovers, Liza had treated him like a king, there was no question about it. She got up with him at five a.m. to fix him breakfast before he left for the set, and was waiting when she got back late at night. A gourmet meal—ordered in—would be set out for the two of them. Then a shared hot bath and massage by Liza usually preceded their lovemaking, after which he would pass out, completely exhausted from the blur of events his days had become. Having picked up a suitcase's worth of clothes, he had barely returned to the apartment he was renting, instead spending what little free time he had with Liza at the Malibu house. Days seemed to be slipping out from under him without his noticing.

It was only in the past week that Simon had been able to steal a few nights off so that he and Liza could get out of the house for dinner or a movie. That was when he had started noticing it. With him, Liza was the soul of sweetness, accommodating and delightful. But with other people, she was arrogant, unthinking, rude. He thought back to the other night, how embarrassed he'd been by the way she'd haughtily swept past the waiting crowd outside a nightclub, pressing a hundred-dollar bill into the palm of the doorman to ensure their admission. Her manner toward storekeepers, waiters, delivery people—anyone she considered beneath her—appalled him. Here it was again on the telephone just now; maybe she had been kept waiting on the line, but was that any reason for her to snap so rudely at whoever was on the other end? How different she was from Page. Nothing could induce Page to speak to people like that.

Damn, why did Page have to pop up again?

Simon thought angrily. He hurried to finish, carelessly splashing some water onto his face. Right, great, he reminded himself, she was polite to ticket sellers while she was screwing her lover's best friend. He grabbed a towel and dried his face as he walked out into the bedroom.

Liza was zipping up a black and red minidress as she stepped into black high heels.

"Almost ready, lover?" she asked, smiling.

It was clear that Liza didn't have any of Simon's reservations about traveling in the limousine. They were dropped off at the Ahmanson Center and reached their seats only seconds before the concert began. Simon was grateful to have a night out, now that time had become such a precious commodity. He closed his eyes, relishing the sweetness of the music until intermission arrived.

"Let me buy you a glass of champagne," Simon suggested, steering Liza over to the bar.

"Love it. Won't you have one too?"

"No, I think not. I don't want to find myself feeling it tomorrow. But I'll watch you drink it, how's that?" he grinned, signaling to the bartender.

Liza didn't have a chance to move away in time. The bartender, leaning over to hand her the glass, spilled the champagne down the length of her sleeve.

"Damn it, you moron," she cried out angrily, grabbing a napkin and dabbing at her arm. Several other patrons turned to see what the commotion was about. She looked at the young man, who was red-faced, stammering apologies. "If serving drinks is too difficult for you, perhaps you'd be better off in a gas station or somewhere else less challenging than this."

Simon broke in, his tone placating. "Liza, it was only an accident. He didn't mean to do it. Please, I'll get you another dress." He was mortified by her display of temper and couldn't have felt more sympathetic toward the hapless bartender. Being the object of Liza's wrath was clearly a position to be avoided if possible.

Her anger fled as quickly as it had come. Liza smiled at him. "Oh, you're right. Please excuse me. I don't know why it should bother me so much. Of course, I'll be fine. The dress is unimportant." She dropped the napkin she'd been using and took Simon's hand. Back in their seats, she snuggled up against him for the second half of the program. But he could no longer enjoy the music.

Liza was especially sweet and considerate for the rest of the evening. When they returned home, she barely let him remove his jacket before she was kissing him, easing off the rest of his clothes, eager to make love. He obliged her, but he found his heart wasn't in it. Afterward, she slept, while Simon lay awake next to her in the wide bed, staring at the shadows on the ceiling. The room was bright, illuminated by a nearly full moon.

He turned to look at Liza. She was sleeping on her stomach, her face turned away from him, with the sheet kicked off to one side. The moonlight played on her naked body. He watched her, admiring the delicacy of her curves, the small of her back sloping in, the inviting lines of her thighs and legs. So beautiful. It was Page's body. Of course, how could he not have noticed it before? Tentatively, unable to resist, Simon reached out and ran a finger along her shoulder blade. Her skin was so soft, just like Page's. How he ached for Page. Ached to spend even one night with her sleeping curled up in his arms. He could never forgive her for betraying him like that, but nor could he pretend that he wasn't longing for her.

He looked out the window at the small waves quietly lapping at the shore. Liza wasn't the one he wanted. She had been there beside him when he was blinded by anger and jealousy, had stepped in to help him through those first difficult weeks. He was grateful to her for that. But he was fooling both her and himself if he continued to act as if they could ever have any meaning for one another. She was a substitute for him. The bodies might be similar, but Liza and Page were as different as any two people could be. It was Page who had hurt him, Page he loved, Page he would never have again.

In the morning, Simon waited until they had both showered and dressed before he asked Liza if they could talk seriously for a few minutes. She sat on the edge of the bed, watching him expectantly. He paced, trying to formulate his words, and finally stopped to face her.

"You've done so much for me, Liza," he began. "I'll always appreciate you for that."

Liza frowned. He could tell she knew what was coming.

"It's hard for me to say this, but I think we both know it's the truth. We're not right for each other. We barely knew one another before we became this couple—it's as if we just fell into it."

"Simon, I care for you. And I think we're wonderful together." She spoke lightly, as if dismissing his words.

He looked pained. "I don't want to hurt you. But surely you know, surely you can see it. I'm still in love with Page. In time, I'll get over it, but right now, I have nothing to give you—or any woman. To let you believe otherwise would be a lie."

Liza's voice rose, a note of panic creeping in. "Don't say that. You've given me a lot. And I don't need anything from you. I'm happy to do the giving if that's what you want."

"Please understand." Simon sat down beside her and took her hand. "Even if there were no Page to contend with, we're nothing alike. You're a beautiful, intelligent woman, and any man would kill to have the affection and attention you've given me. But we're not meant to be together."

She snatched her hand away from him and jumped up, her eyes blazing. "How dare you patronize me! I don't need your pitying little speeches, telling me some other nice man will come along and love me. You conceited son of a bitch! Sniveling after a woman who threw you over for a low-class chauffeur posing as your friend. And you're feeling sorry for *me*? You're the one who's pathetic. You bet your ass I can snap my fingers and have someone here to replace you in two seconds. You're too stupid to understand what you could have had with me. Fine, moon over my sister. The two of you are a perfect match."

Crossing to the closet, she began tearing Simon's clothes from their hangers, throwing them on the floor. "Get the hell out of my house and out of my sight," she yelled. "You disgust me."

Simon ran to her side. "Liza, please." He tried to take her in his arms.

"Get out!" She shoved him away.

The force of her anger shocked both of them into silence. They stared at one another. When she spoke again, her tone was icy. "I mean it. Leave. Right now."

"All right, if that's what you want, I'll go. I'm sorry it's ending this way." Simon's eyes were full of regret as he left the bedroom.

Liza heard him walk through the living room. As the front door clicked shut behind him, she sank down on the pile of his clothes. At least she hadn't begged him to stay. How did things get so out of control? A fling with Simon was just part of her plan; she wasn't supposed to fall in love with him. But she had. Liza curled up into a ball on the floor and cried.

Chapter Seventeen

This is Simon Roberts. I can't come to the phone right now. Please leave a message at the tone.

Page hung up, her frustration apparent in the crumpled ball she held in her hand, minutes before a delicate paper angel. Three weeks, she agonized, three weeks and not a word. Where was he? Why didn't he return her calls?

She looked around the living room. In the corner was a fourteen-foot Christmas tree, ornaments twinkling in the sunlight that streamed through the snow-frosted windows, scores of brightly wrapped gifts underneath. It was like a scene out of a fairy tale, but there was none of the childlike joy on Page's face that should have accompanied it. Just a sense of dread she couldn't avoid.

Carrying still more presents to the tree, Claire walked by her daughter. "What's the matter, dear?"

Page felt she couldn't answer without bursting into tears, so she said nothing. Looking at the silent girl, Claire was uncomfortably reminded of the days Page had spent alone as a child, playing that one damned note over and over on the piano.

"Please, Page, at least talk to me. Nothing is so bad that you can't tell me," Claire implored.

Page fought back the tears as she made

herself respond. "It's Simon, Mother. I've been trying to reach him for a while and I can't seem to get through."

"But darling, you know what they say about making movies. He probably leaves for the set at the crack of dawn and comes home late at night, exhausted. And the time difference between here and California is making it worse. I'm sure you'll hear from him this weekend. You'll see, the phone will ring on Friday. After all, even movie stars must be off on Christmas Eve." Claire's words didn't seem to be reassuring Page. "Don't be so down, honey. I'm just sure I'm right."

Page hadn't wanted to voice her fears, even to her mother, but if she didn't talk to somebody, she was afraid she might scream. "Mother, you really don't understand. I haven't heard from him in nearly a month. Not a day. Not a few days. Three *weeks*. I've left dozens of messages. He hasn't returned even one. I've tried him at the studio, but he never comes to the phone." Page's face was white. "I don't know what's going on."

Claire was surprised. She hadn't noticed anything was wrong. Of course, she thought guiltily, she'd been so busy shopping for gifts and getting ready for Liza's homecoming from New York. The thought of her other daughter filled her with excitement, which served to add an edge of anger to her guilt. Why couldn't Page be happy now that Liza was back? Claire realized that those words would only inflame Page if she said them aloud. Page was so touchy about her sister. Claire brought her attention back to the matter at hand. Three weeks really was a long time.

"How were things when he left for California?" Claire questioned.

"Perfect." Page felt anguished as she recalled their parting, their passionate farewell before Simon left for Heathrow. When he first got to Los Angeles, there were frantic phone calls, his voice filled with longing. Then nothing. As if Simon had been a dream.

Claire was moved by her daughter's misery, but she felt helpless. "Everything will work out. I didn't get to know Simon all that well, but he seemed to love you very much. You have to trust in that."

She moved to embrace Page, but her daughter seemed frozen, untouchable. Oh, God, it really was like when she was a little girl. "Honey, I'm sorry, but I don't know exactly what to say. Now, why don't you finish up that tree? Your sister should be home in a few minutes and we can all have dinner."

"Yes, Mother," Page answered dully.

"It feels like months since she's been away rather than weeks. I can't wait to have you two here with me again." Claire's face lit up with joy, making Page feel even worse.

Page returned to the tree, carefully placing ornaments on each of the large branches. The miniature wooden horse from their trip to Brighton when she was six. The blown-glass snowflake her father had brought her from Hungary. No, she thought, sighing, not her father.

John Warren. She hated thinking about all that. No matter how many times Claire had explained why they never told her the truth, Page couldn't help wishing they'd handled things differently. A father she didn't know. A sister she didn't like.

And now she seemed to be losing Simon. She could find a way to deal with everything else if only he would call. She looked at the telephone, willing it to ring, but the only sound she heard was the front door opening.

"Mom, I'm home." Liza's voice rang out.

Page heard her mother hurrying to the door, heard the excitement in her voice as she welcomed her daughter back. She couldn't face it just yet, Page thought to herself, the warmth in Liza's voice, sounding strained and phony to Page's ear. After several minutes of "thrilled to be home" and "how much I missed you," she was relieved to hear her sister going upstairs.

Suddenly, Claire was standing by her side. "Aren't you going to greet your sister?" It was not a question, and Page didn't have the strength to argue. Wordlessly, she made her way upstairs.

Her knock on her sister's door was greeted by a friendly "Come on in," followed by a cooler "hello" as Liza saw who it was.

"Hi," Page offered, attempting a smile.

"Yes, hello," responded Liza, who quickly turned around and continued unbuttoning her blouse.

Page had no idea what to say next, nor

could she think of a graceful way to leave. Finally, she came up with "Mother is very happy to have you home for Christmas," and started to turn toward the door.

Liza whirled around and smiled, her voice stopping Page in her tracks. "And how about you, little sister? Are you happy to have me home, too?"

Taking in the catlike smile and the gleam of satisfaction in Liza's dark eyes, Page's discomfort was so great that she didn't respond to the question. She stood, as if waiting for something to happen.

A gloating look came over Liza's face, followed by a mask of pity. "I'm sorry about Simon. Really I am."

"What are you talking about?" Page shuddered involuntarily.

"Sometimes these things happen. I certainly never meant to hurt you." Liza's eyes were pure ice.

"Hurt me?" Echoing the words, Page felt rooted to the spot.

"Surely Simon told you." Liza looked her sister straight in the eye. "We're together now. I'm sorry. I was sure he had called you or written. I never meant you to find out this way."

Page looked at Liza in horror. It explained everything. It even felt inevitable. She had known from the first moment Liza arrived that the worst had come with her. The familiar feeling of dread she'd lived with when she was a little girl slowly spread throughout her body once again. Her tears, once they started, were unstoppable. She slumped into a chair, weeping.

Liza stood above her grieving sister as Claire hurried into the room.

"Liza, Page, what's happening here?" Claire was horrified by the scene in front of her.

Page's only response was muffled sobs. Liza looked at her mother with an air of diffidence. She rubbed her hands over her eyes, as if she, too, were on the edge of tears.

"Liza, what's this about?"

"Mother, I've done something awful." Liza's voice was softly imploring. "I never meant it to happen, but we just couldn't stop ourselves." She hesitated a moment, then continued in the same quiet tone. "Simon and I fell in love. We never wanted to hurt Page. It just...happened."

Claire was shocked. She looked to her younger daughter, who was suffering openly, then to her older daughter, obviously ashamed. "How did this happen, Liza? How could you do this to your sister?"

Liza grabbed her mother's hands as she passionately made her case. "I had to go to Los Angeles and I ran into Simon. We had dinner, we spent some time together... Oh, Mother, it was wonderful and terrible..." Agony was in her voice. "We died over what this would mean to Page. Honestly. But there was nothing we could do." She paused. "Surely you remember what it's like to be so in love that nothing else seems to have any meaning?"

Page raised her head, a stricken expression on her ravaged face. She knew that her sister was referring to Claire's passion for John Warren, and she couldn't believe even Liza would be that cunning. But Claire's expression was softening. She did indeed remember the way it had been with John. If it hadn't been for that, none of this would be happening now.

"Liza, I know you didn't mean any harm, but you can't be planning to continue with this." Claire's eyes were begging Liza to make everything all right.

"Oh, Mother." Liza sat down on the bed, her head in her hands, her voice almost a sob. "I don't want to make you unhappy. I don't want to make anyone unhappy."

Page sat watching the scene. She couldn't believe what she was hearing. Her mother was swallowing all of it. The fake tears. The rhinestone torment. Page's crying had stopped and was gradually being replaced by a sense of invisible walls descending around her, cutting her off from the other two. She tried one last time to break through to her mother, tried to get past her feelings of loneliness, of betrayal.

"Mother." Page's voice was an anguished whisper. "Surely you see what's happening. Don't you know what she's doing?"

Claire was torn. Liza, vivacious, bright Liza. Claire understood how upset Page must be, but certainly the girl couldn't think her sister

274

would do this on purpose. She said as much to Page, who rushed out of the room.

Claire didn't see her younger daughter leave the house late that night. She only knew what Page wrote in her note:

Dear Mother,
I'm sorry, but I can't stay here right now. I'll be with my father.
                                                    —Page

Chapter Eighteen

"Oh, Bennett. This apartment is a dream, just absolutely beautiful." The woman's light, high voice lifted gracefully across the vast foyer to the living room, where the polished wooden floors seemed to radiate her enthusiasm. Page was jolted awake by the sound. Sitting on the velvet sofa, the room now almost fully dark, it took her a moment to remember where she was. Her father's apartment. Fifth Avenue. New York City. She heard a man's voice acknowledge the woman's compliment, then the rushed footsteps from the back of the apartment.

"Mr. Carlisle, sir." It was the young maid who had let Page in. "There's a woman here who says she's your daughter. She's in the living room. I hope it's all right. I didn't know what to do, so I—"

Bennett cut her off impatiently. "So Liza has come home," was all he said. Whatever he thought about the return of his daughter, he wasn't choosing to share with the maid or his companion.

"It's not Liza, sir." The maid sounded nervous, unsure of what his response would be. "It's someone claiming to be your daughter. But her name is Page Warren."

Page realized that she should move, go to where the voices were, introduce herself. After all, that's why she had come, wasn't it, to meet her father. Yet she was silent, rooted to the spot. It was as if the chair she sat in had invisible arms, holding her fast, as if invisible hands covered her mouth, not allowing a word to escape.

She heard the man's forceful steps coming toward her, watched as he switched on the lights, making her blink in the sudden glare. He stood, appraising her. The maid and the other woman, swathed in mink, hovered in the doorway, observing the tableau.

"Why, Bennett, I've never see you so discombobulated before." The wealthy-looking woman was chuckling, again her voice like soothing bubbles. She walked over to Page's chair, taking in the young woman's exhausted appearance. The smudges under her eyes as if she had been crying. "I'm Perdita Lowes, a friend of your father's. So you're Bennett's daughter. Page, right?" Her warmth was infectious and Page found herself able to stand at last, even to meet the woman's outstretched hand with her own.

"It's not Page, it's Meredith." Bennett moved closer to her, looking appreciatively at her blond hair and finely drawn features. "I knew at least one of my daughters would have to look like my side of the family." He took her into his arms for a few seconds, patting her uncertainly on the back before releasing her. "I'm glad you've finally come. I've been waiting a long, long time."

"I'm completely confused." Perdita's pleasant voice once again cut through the awkwardness between father and daughter.

Page finally spoke. "I'm not expected," she began to explain to the woman, quickly realizing she had no idea how to say any of it. "I arrived early this afternoon and I'm afraid I was so tired I fell asleep in the chair. I'm sorry, I didn't mean to interrupt your evening."

"Don't be ridiculous, Meredith. Obviously, I'm the one interrupting. Bennett—" Perdita turned to him. "You and your daughter no doubt have things to discuss. I'm going home. We can do this another time." She moved purposely toward the doorway, but Bennett stopped her.

"Thank you, Pedita. Perhaps Meredith and I should have some time alone. But let me just get those profiles for you. They're right in my study. I won't be a minute. Mary, get my daughter a drink, won't you?" He walked out, the maid following closely behind him.

Perdita turned around, her curiosity unabashed. "Meredith...Page—which one are you?"

"Both, I guess. I was called Meredith originally, but I've been known as Page for years."

"Why do you and your father seem like strangers?" Perdita continued to probe, although her delight in unraveling the mystery made her intrusiveness somehow disarming.

"My mother and my father separated when I was just two years old, and I haven't seen him since. So, yes, I guess we are strangers of a sort."

"I had heard about your mother leaving Bennett. Not from him, of course. I've never met anyone who plays it so close to the vest. My husband and I had been told he was devastated by her leaving. Your father is a tough customer, but really a sweetie underneath. I can't imagine why any woman would hurt him like that. And to take his child away...well! It's no wonder he's so reluctant to commit himself again."

This picture of Bennett shocked Page. She had never considered her father as a victim, abjectly wounded. Once Claire had opened up the subject of Bennett, the vision of her father that emerged was hardly the man this woman was conjuring up. Yet Pedita seemed like quite a straightforward person. Genuinely nice, in fact. Page took in the plump figure, the expensive rings on chubby hands that moved gracefully whenever she talked. Page

278

was still angry at her mother, but she had no intention of going into details in front of this stranger, no matter how kind she seemed.

"I'm not really too clear on what happened in the past, or for that matter, what is happening right now." Page groped for a change in subject. "Is your husband coming tonight as well? I thought at first that you were my father's date this evening."

"Well, I am, after a fashion." Again Perdita's answer came with a warm grin. "Actually, your father has been a friend for years. Of my husband's and of mine. Herbert died eight months ago, and Bennett is taking care of some business for me. He's arranging the sale of Herbert's business. That's what he went to get, some materials he wanted me to see from a number of companies that are interested in buying it. He thinks I ought to take an interest, but I'm afraid I don't understand a word. I'll take the stuff with me, but the decisions are all going to be Bennett's. And I'm sure he knows it, the old dear." Perdita gave Page a piercing look. "Your father seems cool, but when the chips are down, he's really there for you. I know. I learned it the hard way. Since Herbert's death, he's come through like nobody else. I'd have been lost without him. For years, Herbert and he sat on the same boards and we danced at the same parties, but I never knew how much depth he had. Why, until today, I'd never even been in his home. Yet he's the one person I couldn't do without right now."

Bennett had left the room to find the papers for Perdita, but that wasn't the only reason. He hated to be surprised. His success, his fortune had been based on careful planning, on attention to detail. But these damned women! His wife, Liza, Meredith— it was as if they all conspired to undo the fabric of his well-ordered life, and always at a moment's notice. He felt unnerved, and for a moment loathed his younger daughter for making him feel that way. Taking a deep breath, he forced himself to calm down. Anger would accomplish nothing. There must be something to be gained from her sudden intrusion, just as both Claire's and Liza's departures had left him both richer and happier once the initial rude shock had worn off. After a few seconds' thought, he began to smile. Perhaps Page's arrival wouldn't increase his fortune, but it could certainly provide some amusement.

Bennett's return to the living room, a sheaf of corporate catalogs in his hand, stopped Perdita's heartfelt speech, but he'd overhead some of it on his way in. He caught the look of surprise on his daughter's face as she listened to his praises being sung.

"Here you are, Perdita. I urge you to look at these companies carefully. I think one of them might make you a very wealthy woman." Bennett spoke with some irony, since it was clear that she was already well off, and not at all embarrassed to display the fact.

"Your gift to me is freedom, Bennett, not

wealth, as you well know. Much more important than money, I assure you," was Perdita's affectionate response.

Bennett's reply was terse. "Only to the few who have enough of it." He smiled, taking any possible sting out of his words.

Page watched their interaction with great interest. She'd had only Claire's description of Bennett, and how off the mark her mother had been! Her father was charming and down to earth. Yes, he looked formal, in his expensively tailored clothes amid these beautiful surroundings. But he was quite kind, and biggest surprise of all, funny. She also liked his choice of friends. Perdita was so American, with her jewels and furs and unabashed riches. Page could imagine her mother finding Perdita slightly vulgar, but the woman was delightful with her casual intimacy and frank curiosity. Even her plumpness was enticing, making her seem real and accessible. Page hoped she would see more of Perdita during her stay in New York. Perhaps her father's interest in the woman was about more than business. Wouldn't that be nice?

Bennett noted his daughter's approving look at Perdita. Well, he thought, why waste a resource, any resource.

"Perdita, you must join us for dinner one night this week. Wednesday, perhaps?"

The woman looked at Page. "Would you mind sharing your father for one night?"

"I'd love it!" Page's response was immediate.

Perdita picked up the catalogs and walked

toward the front door. "Now that I know I'll see you again, it's definitely time to leave."

Bennett and Page stepped back into the apartment after seeing Perdita into the elevator. They stood in the foyer, both uncertain about what to say, what to do now that they were alone.

Bennett broke the ice. "Meredith, which would you like better, dinner or bed? You must be starving and exhausted."

"Actually, I'm both." Page was grateful for her father's consideration.

"I know what we'll do. I'll have just a small dinner prepared for the two of us here, right now. Then you'll go off to bed. We'll leave the fancy restaurants for after you've gotten some rest. How does that sound?" Bennett unbuttoned his jacket and loosened his tie as he led her to a small room at the back of the apartment, where a comfortable couch faced a television and an elaborate video and sound system. Chocolate-brown carpeting and hunting sketches made the den cozy.

"This is wonderful," Page said as she relaxed on a padded leather chair.

"Do you mind my calling you Meredith? It must seem strange after all these years."

"Actually, I'd prefer Page. I don't remember anything about being Meredith. I'm sorry, but I don't even remember you. I was raised to think that John Warren was my father. I hope that doesn't hurt you too much."

"Page," he enunciated the name with care, "don't you worry about any of that. You just sit here while I tell the staff we're staying in." Bennett gave her a warm smile as he walked out of the room. Five minutes later he was back, carrying a tray replete with cans of soda and beer.

"I don't know what you like," he said a bit sadly, depositing the tray on a coffee table. "Some food is on its way. Now, what will you have? Coke, beer, ginger ale? Some wine, perhaps?" He indicated a wine rack discreetly hidden in one corner of the room.

"Just a soda, thank you. Anything stronger and I'm afraid I might fall asleep again right here." Page had more to say, but she hesitated, trying to decide how much to tell and how to tell it. Finally, the words began again. "I'm sorry for the inconvenience I'm causing. It can't be easy to have me fall out of the sky like this. I should have phoned or written, but things just sort of happened."

Knowing his daughter Liza, Bennett could imagine what kind of things could just sort of happen. There certainly couldn't have been much love lost between them if Page had acted so impulsively. He bet she left Claire and Liza with as little notice as she arrived here, he thought. As casually as possible, he asked, "How is Liza these days? I haven't heard a word from her since she left."

Page's look at the mention of her sister's name was enough to confirm Bennett's suspicions, but the answer to his question was studiedly noncommittal. "She's fine," Page said evenly, no enthusiasm but no open disparagement in her tone.

"You know, Liza and I were not on the best of terms when she left here. Frankly, I've been quite disappointed in her behavior." Bennett's voice conveyed a sense of intimacy, of reluctance at betraying one daughter to another.

Page wasn't eager to open the subject up, but she admitted that she had also had her difficulties with Liza. "I don't feel comfortable going into details," Page added, "given how strange this whole situation is and how little we really know each other. But I guess Mother and Liza and I are at a bit of a crossroads."

Bennett reached over and took her hands. "No," he said earnestly, "we don't really know each other, do we? By the end of your stay, I hope that's changed. You can't imagine how I've missed you, how terrible it's been for me, losing a daughter. When your mother left, I thought you were gone forever. Now we can do it over again, do it right."

For a moment, Bennett was taken aback as he realized that he actually was glad to see her, was pleased that the beautiful young woman was his daughter. It was strangely moving, her coming to him for help. He liked the fact that she needed him.

Page's inability to match this man to the person who'd been described to her was obvious, causing Bennett satisfaction that showed nowhere on his face. He continued to talk affectionately as a tray of sandwiches was brought in by the maid. "We're keeping it simple tonight. You're exhausted and I think you should go to bed immediately after we finish eating. Then, starting tomorrow, we'll do New York with a vengeance."

His promise was not empty. For the next ten days, Bennett and Page were chauffeured to practically every famous restaurant in the city. From Le Cirque to The Four Seasons to Lutece, they saw the city as only the wealthiest and most knowledgeable could. From her years at college, Page knew another New York, a city of West Side pizza joints and small student apartments, of impromptu parties and off-off Broadway plays. Her father's New York was sophisticated and expensive. Now Page traveled only by limousine, sat fourth row center at the most sought-after plays, dined with the city's power brokers. Bennett invited her to come to his office, where Page was stunned by the costly elegance of Carlisle and Poole. Her father explained a little about what he did every day, the deal-making, the financial evaluations. When he was talking about the business, Page could see just a little of her sister's sharpness, her quick, analytical mind reflected in their father. But Bennett displayed none of the mendacity, none of the hidden meanness that so characterized Liza. The time spent with her father provided Page with a welcome distraction from the problems she'd left behind. She found she could avoid thinking about how angry she was at her mother and her sister in the crush of such a hectic schedule. At night, however, as she lay in bed trying to fall asleep, she was unable to escape thoughts of Simon. Why had it all gone wrong? She wondered if she would ever know.

As the days passed, Page was pleased to find she felt closer and closer to Bennett. At dinner with Perdita Lowes, she observed his lighter side. He displayed humor and charm, rich additions to his patrician bearing. She could understand how others, her mother even, might have missed the real Bennett under his custom-made suits and impeccable manners. To Page, he was a perfect combination of discretion and warmth. He never pressed her about why she had left England, never seemed to be anything but pleased at her finally coming home to him. He spoke little of Claire, although it was clear in his manner that she had caused him extraordinary pain, pain so great he could never bring himself to remarry. Page continued to hope that his relationship with Perdita would grow into something more than a friendship, for the older woman's brashness was, just as Page had thought, a cover for great kindness and vitality.

As he watched his daughter enjoy her days, Bennett had mixed emotions. As young women went, Page was fine. And he gloried in his continuing ability to shake the version of his character that his wife and older daughter had obviously worked so hard to establish. But despite his initial pleasure at seeing her, he was bored. Even with Liza in the house, he had been free to do whatever the hell he wanted. He hadn't spent any time with her and she hadn't expected him to. This whole episode was beginning to be more trouble than it could possibly be worth. The solution came to him at dinner one night, as he and Page sat over gravlax and vodka at Café des Artistes.

"Page," he said, carefully looking around as if to make sure no other patrons could hear them, "I don't know precisely why you chose to come to me when you did, but I suspect there was more to it than mere curiosity. I sense some alienation between you and Liza, even possibly between you and your mother."

She tried to answer as tactfully as she could. "Yes, it's true. Liza and I had some trouble— I'd rather not go into the details—and Mother took her side. She wouldn't even listen to what I had to say. I'm still angry about it. In fact, I haven't even called home since I got here." As she spoke, the memories crowded in, and she became more emotional. "Mother really hurt me, just as I now know she once hurt you. Right now, I don't really care if I see either her or Liza ever again."

Bennett watched tears forming in Page's eyes. He'd had no idea he was opening up something so explosive. Playing the devoted dad for a couple of weeks to annoy Claire was a pleasant diversion; having Page with him permanently was a different matter entirely. He kept a sympathetic face while he quickly weighed his options. In a matter of seconds, his course was clear.

"Page, darling," he confided mournfully, "I know how much that kind of betrayal hurts. After all, I've been through it." His head hung for just a moment before he continued to speak. "But it's not good, this staying away. You need to face your mother. I never did, and I'm still suffering for it. You *must.* I can't let you enslave yourself to unresolved anger that will be yours forever. It will stand in the way of every relationship you have. No matter how much your stay has meant to me, I would be less than a father if I didn't urge you to return, to fight the battle that must be fought."

"I love you, Daddy!" Page exclaimed, using a word she had avoided since she'd arrived. Then, overcome, she buried her face in her hands, trying to muffle her uncontrollable crying.

I hope no one knows who we are, Bennett thought, looking with distaste at the public display as he signaled the waiter for the check.

The next day, Bennett dropped Page off at Kennedy Airport for the flight to London before going to his office. Waiting for him back on his desk were two dozen red roses. A note was enclosed.

Dad, you'll never know what this time has meant to me. I love you.
                                        —*Page*

Bennett looked at the flowers with aversion. All wrong, he thought, frowning. The wash of

288

red was so at odds with the rest of the room, the stark beauty he had paid such a fortune to achieve. He grabbed the roses with both hands and threw them in the black porcelain waste-basket, careful to place them top down, so none of the red would show. Then he tore up the card, showering its pieces over the flowers, and carefully pushed the wastebasket under his desk where his eye would not accidentally fall on it.

"Mother, you were entirely wrong about him," Page announced, not for the first time in the five days since her return to England.

Claire and both her daughters were on their way to dinner with the members of Warren International's board of directors. Liza sat qui-etly looking out the window of the Bentley while her mother and sister began the argument that was by now predictable.

"Page, I'm sorry if you don't believe me," Claire said, exasperated by her daughter's stubbornness, "but your father is not the man you're describing. And I'm not the ogre you seem to think I am. I have no intention of giving you a minute-by-minute account of our dif-ficulties, but, believe me, Bennett was not, and, I assure you, *is* not, some kind of wounded animal. Whatever his reasons for being so kind to you, he is a cold and selfish and brutal man, and he hasn't missed me—or very likely, you—for a minute!"

"You haven't seen him for over twenty

years. How would you know?" Page shot back. "Let's just drop it. I have a father now, and I'm glad. What might have been...well, I'll never know, and I'll have to live with that." Page turned to look out the other window, leaving Claire silently fuming.

Liza had no desire to interfere in their exchange. At first, when Page had come home with tales of intimate dinners and confidential talks, Liza was seized with jealousy. How dare Bennett give of himself to Page, Liza railed in the privacy of her room. But soon enough, she realized there had to be an angle, and she knew just what it must have been. She could imagine Bennett's glee when he saw that Page offered him an opportunity to strike out at Claire so effectively. And he was right, Liza thought, giving her father points for acuity. Claire and Page were at each other all the time now. Page was furious at her mother's abandonment of poor Bennett—Liza chuckled out loud every time this phrase came out of her sister's mouth—and Claire was continually frustrated and annoyed by her younger daughter's naïve assessment of the man whose cruelty had practically ruined all their lives.

Well, fine, Liza thought as the three women sat silently near the end of the drive. Bennett's mischief would fit in perfectly with her own plans. Let Claire and Page stay angry. In fact, she thought, a smile maliciously creeping onto her face, they had no idea just how angry they were about to get.

Chapter Nineteen

Be careful what you wish for...the phrase had begun to haunt Simon since the shooting of *Birds of Passage* had ended three weeks before. America might not find out about the hot new British star until the movie opened six months down the road, but Hollywood certainly knew. Simon Roberts was no longer a person; he had become a property. HOT IN LA-LA LAND had been the headline in *Variety* weeks before the film even wrapped. He felt hot all right, he thought bitterly, pacing around his small room at the Chateau Marmont, so famous for the writers and actors who'd lived there. Hot. Hot as in uncomfortable, hot as in overexposed to blinding light, hot as in could be dropped like a hot potato at a moment's notice.

This was one city that lived up to its reputation. He'd heard about the phonies, the slick manipulators, the showy cars, the perfect bodies and minus IQs. Astonishing, he thought, every word was true. He had come here wanting only to do good work. And it was good, damned good. But in this town, good work translated into fawning sycophants who thought your talent might somehow rub off on them, or, worse yet, superagents who wouldn't have touched you a year ago, who now wouldn't leave you alone no matter how many times you said no. And friends, all those friends. People you'd never even met who suddenly insisted you come for lunch, for parties, for weekends, as if you were best buddies.

Hollywood was really a tiny town, he decided. Once the dailies of *Birds of Passage* were shown to a few studio insiders, the word was out and Simon Roberts was in. America had discovered Olivier and James Dean rolled into one. Seeing this assessment of himself in a gossip column one day made him laugh out loud. God, these people were crazy. He'd gone to several parties where total strangers who couldn't possibly have seen his work would come up to him to tell him how great he was. A few of the men who pulled this stunt were themselves famous actors. Jesus, how pathetic. Was that going to be him in a few years? he wondered.

Simon was desperate to get away from all of it, but he couldn't leave. "You've gotta play ball while the iron's hot," his agent had insisted, cheerfully mixing metaphors. Simon knew he was right. Richie Forrest was a decent guy, and he knew his business. Simon would do better to stay on the coast while negotiations started for his next project. Based on only the rumor of greatness, his price had already gone through the roof. His fee for the first movie was a pittance compared to the offers Richie was fielding. Simon wasn't even sure he wanted there to be another movie. He'd felt plenty isolated at times in England, but that seemed like nothing compared to how lonely he was here.

Page had spoiled him, he admitted to himself, his face dark as he looked at the perfectly blue pool just outside his room. The romance had lasted such a short time, but it had taken away his edge. Now he needed that edge all over again. How seductive the relationship had been. Cozy and passionate at the same time. Stepping out of his self-made prison had proved to be easy with her. Finding his way back in was much harder.

He walked away from the window, annoyed by the shining brightness of the boringly perfect California day. His thoughts kept returning to Page. He'd loved her so much. Damn, he still loved her. But he could never forgive her for lying about Chris. No, he admitted to himself, it wasn't just that they had been dishonest about their "friendship." He just couldn't bear that she had been sleeping with someone else, anyone else. That she had moved in with him practically the moment Simon left town! That it was Chris only made it worse. How could they have thought they could pull it off? According to Liza, everyone had known but him. All that pal nonsense, how could he have swallowed it! And all those messages Page left on his machine—did she hope to string him along so that she could carry on with both of them when Simon returned to London? Liza was hardly a model of sweetness and light, but at least she had set him straight so he could stop being such a public fool. He was in so much emotional pain, he had considered calling one of his and Page's friends, but it was just too humiliating.

The hell of it was that he still missed Page. He'd never forgive her—the betrayal went too deep—but he was scared he'd never get over her, either. Well, maybe he'd actually have a good time tonight at the party Carl Meyer was giving. At least there'd be people that he actually knew, cast and crew from *Birds of Passage*. He could have a few drinks with colleagues who liked him instead of hiding in a corner from strangers who loved him.

What to do till the party started? That was his constant problem. Too much time, too little to do. No wonder American movie stars got into so much trouble. But drugs were not his solution, nor had he joined in the Hollywood jock crowd. Playing tennis and talking about free weights just wasn't his style. He walked over to the side of his bed where a bunch of books and scripts were stacked. No scripts right now, he thought, already sick of the terrible material that had started coming to him practically the day he'd arrived. He needed something good, something that would remind him of why he became an actor in the first place. He picked up a collection of American plays, turned to *Death of a Salesman,* and stretched out on the bed.

The party was not going well. Most of the actors and technicians from *Birds of Passage* were out of town, already at work on other projects. The guests overflowing onto Carl Meyer's enormous terrace seemed a curious mix of his socialite wife's fancy friends and the usual crowd of actors and agents on the make. Then again, Simon thought, at least he'd learned how to deal with these people. First, he was approached by a man in his seventies dressed like a butler on *Masterpiece Theatre,* who claimed to have loved Simon's work in every play he'd ever done on the British stage, then went on to praise him in three parts he had never even played. Seeing Simon remain unimpressed, he took a monocle out of his waistcoat pocket, placed it in one eye, and left to try out his act on the American guests. From what Simon was able to observe, the man's luck improved immediately. Americans were so impressed by Brits, he thought, not for the first time. Tonight, at least five different women, each a young actress who thought he could help her, had complimented him on his accent. They spoke as if being English automatically made him smarter, more sophisticated...and being as smart and sophisticated as he was, perhaps he could introduce them to director X or producer Y, or maybe there was a spot in his next picture, and, oh yes, they knew how rich his career on the stage had been back home and they just loved "drama and Shakespeare and stuff," as the last young woman had so elegantly phrased it.

Disgusted, Simon decided it was time to go home. He apologized to his host for his early exit, and was amused when Carl winked at him, whispering, "Monstrous, isn't it? If I could leave, I would be out the door with you."

Simon had no idea where his car was. Valet service was the order of the night, and he couldn't even guess where on the large grounds the parking team had left his rented Volvo. The valet currently on duty was a redheaded girl who looked about twenty. The freckles dusting her pretty face, and the yellow and purple polka-dot socks that jutted out from under her black uniform pants set her off from the crowd he'd just left.

As he handed her his ticket, she observed, "You must have had a slam-bang time at this turkey farm to be leaving so early."

Simon smiled at her, amused both by her use of the English language and by her sheer nerve. "Is it that obvious?"

The girl smiled back. "Sure it is. But don't let it worry you. These parties are for only two kinds of people, the users and the bruisers, and you don't look like either one."

Simon was intrigued by her. "Define your terms. In fact, let me walk with you to wherever you've hidden the Porsche."

"It's not a Porsche. I'd guess, oh, say a Peugeot," was the girl's smart-aleck response as they set out together across the grounds.

Simon chuckled. "Actually, I have a rented car, but if we were home, you'd be on the money. How do you do it?"

"Well, I grew up in Hollywood, and I've been working my way through college by doing these parking gigs. You get to know what Los Angeles is all about, namely people and their cars. And, of course, their tans, their figures, their ranking on party lists, and, in some cases, coming up with their next month's rent. A lot of the BMW's you see here"—she waved at the crush of imported German vehicles parked everywhere on the lawn—"contain men and women who couldn't afford the price of a cheeseburger."

"So which are they, users or bruisers?" Simon wanted to know.

'Oh, I think of them as bruisers in training. At parties like these, they practice up on their basic skills, so when their luck changes a little, they can put all they've learned right into action. Flirt a little, hurt a little."

"My God," Simon cried, "have you made this up in parking lots all over Beverly Hills, or were you born cynical?"

"I was born adorable; the rest I had to learn."

Simon laughed. "It's too bad you're working. I'm sorry we can't go out for a drink."

"I'm off in twenty minutes, so, if you mean it, my name's Sharon." She walked toward the Volvo without hesitation, not even bothering to check the number on the ticket, and handed the keys to Simon.

"And what's your name if I don't mean it?" Simon asked with a grin.

Sharon was twenty-three, older than Simon had first thought, taking her time about getting through UCLA. California-raised, she seemed to have few ambitions. But she was clever and sharp, wicked when it came to the movie scene. She knew the territory better than he did, and her imitations of the rich and famous were hilarious. Best of all, she'd obviously never heard of him, which pleased Simon immensely. This girl was no grasping starlet; she was just fun. Besides which, she was great-looking. Like a bratty young version of Nicole Kidman, Simon thought admiringly.

He'd followed her in his car so she could drop hers off at home before they went on for a drink. But, once inside her house, a small cottage in West Hollywood, they found themselves having so much fun, they never left. Simon let her do all the talking. He had no desire to reveal himself as a rising star, nor did he wish to interrupt her barbed and uncanny insights into her hometown. When they ended up in bed, he was glad, although her aggressiveness came as a surprise.

Sharon didn't wait for cues. From the moment he touched her, she was on the move, her hands roaming all over his body, her tongue taking in every corner of his mouth, then descending to his penis, where she worked with practiced skill. Finally, she moved her body over his, riding him hard until they both climaxed.

He was excited by her unapologetic force, but something held him back. First sexual encounters were generally more reserved, more exploring than this. He had enjoyed her, but found himself quiet when they finished.

"That was great," Sharon said, sliding her hand across his chest as she lay beside him. "You're as good in the sack as you are onstage."

Simon caught her hand and held it. "How did you know I was an actor?" He turned to face her, letting her hand go and pulling away.

"Of course I know who you are. Did you think I was an idiot?" Sharon wasn't the least apologetic.

"I don't know," Simon mumbled uncomfortably. "You never said anything."

"I read the papers along with everyone else in this town. I'd have to be deaf, dumb, and blind not to know who you are. Every actress in town knows you, for Christ's sake."

"Actress? I thought you were a college student." Simon was sitting up now, reaching down to the floor to retrieve his pants.

"I am a student. A drama student at UCLA. I never said I wasn't. Actually, I worked Carl Meyer's party so I'd get to meet him, show him who I am."

"And when you didn't get to do that, you picked me up instead. You thought maybe I'd introduce you to Carl." Simon was now fully dressed, his face expressionless.

"What's so terrible about that? That's how things are done here. I never pretended anything else." Unembarrassed by her nakedness, Sharon stood to face him. "Listen, Simon. Hollywood is give and take. I gave and you were plenty willing to take. So don't go all self-righteous on me now."

Simon felt disgusted. She was right. That was Hollywood, and that was beginning to be him. Standing at the foot of her bed, he made a decision. Staying in California could only mean more scenes like this one. He didn't care how many movie offers his agent could conjure up, this just wasn't for him. He felt dirty in this town and he was sick of it.

Back at his room, he dialed Richie Forrest's number.

"Sorry to call so late. I'm on the eight o'clock flight to New York tomorrow morning."

"Why? Are you going back to London?" Richie asked groggily.

"No," Simon replied, visions of Page and Chris going through his mind. "New York. I'll find something there. A play. Maybe off-Broadway, something small like the old days, before I became Simon Roberts."

Chapter Twenty

Nancy Drummond put down her cup of coffee and picked up the pile of mail lying on her desk. She sorted through the envelopes, separating out the invitations. As society editor for *The Empire*, she received well over fifty party invitations every week. In the past three days alone, she had covered a dozen openings, galas, and benefits. They had all begun to feel the same to her.

She hesitated at a small cream-colored envelope. Her name and address had been written by hand, but there was no clue who the letter was from. Putting down the rest of her mail, she slit open the envelope.

Dear Ms. Drummond:
Assuming you will be attending Neville Ford's party on Valentine's Day, I have a suggestion for you. Become acquainted with Page Warren of Warren International. She has a story to tell, if you're enough of a reporter to get it out of her.

There was no signature. Fascinating, Nancy thought, trying to recall what she knew about Page Warren. Let's see now, Warren International was run by a woman, but the name Page didn't ring a bell. It was Carol. No, Claire. Claire Warren. She had two daughters, and one of them was an American who had recently popped up out of nowhere. But that wasn't Page. So what story would Page have? Was there some problem with the business?

Nancy checked her desk calendar. There it was, Friday, Neville Ford, eight o'clock. She reached for a pencil and crossed out the two other events she'd been planning to cover that night. An anonymous note. What could be a more intriguing beginning for a story? She picked up her coffee and took a sip, already composing the opening paragraph in her head.

By ten o'clock on the night of February 14,
Neville Ford's Belgravia townhouse was
mobbed. As one of London's premier fashion
designers, he attracted the city's wealthiest and
most stylish, all of whom had risen to the
occasion of this party. The crowd sparkled with
sequined gowns and dazzling jewels.

Conspicuous consumption was definitely the
order of the day, Nancy thought as she surveyed the scene. Exotic flowers graced tables
practically groaning under the weight of artfully arranged imported delicacies. Gold and
silver hearts and colorful neon cupids hung from
the walls and ceilings, tongue-in-cheek but
extremely expensive.

Checking to see what the fashion story was
for the evening, Nancy scrutinized the female
guests. So much money and so little imagination. Virtually all of them were wearing
black. The cost of any one of their dresses would
support a small Third World nation, she said
to herself sarcastically. Heading for the bar,
she reached out to take a heart-shaped canape
from a passing waiter. She'd been there only
an hour, but had already picked up two juicy
pieces of gossip for tomorrow's column: one
concerning the royal family, the other a
rumored affair between one of Neville's assis-
tants and a member of Parliament, both men.
Probably neither bit of information was entirely
true, but she would run them anyway.

She was unlikely to come up with anything else here tonight. Yet she was held by the promise of the anonymous note. She'd been waiting all evening for Page Warren to appear, but so far, nothing. Maybe this was a fool's errand, she thought to herself. Well, wait just a minute. There Page was, coming in right now with two other women. Nancy threaded her way through the crowd, moving closer to the front entrance. She also recognized Claire Warren. From the research she had done two days before, she identified the third woman as Page's sister, Liza Carlisle.

The reporter appraised the group. They were an impressive-looking trio. The sister, Liza, bore a strong resemblance to the mother, both of them tall and striking, with similar faces. But while Claire seemed restrained, almost haughty in her demeanor, Liza jumped into the party with both feet. She immediately dropped her velvet cloak into the arms of a waiting butler, revealing a strapless red dress, and plunged into the crowd. Page, Nancy noted, hung back with her mother. More fragile-looking than the other two, Page had a gentler aspect. Perhaps she was shy. Nancy observed their host rush over to embrace Claire and her daughter. They must be worth plenty, she mused. Neville reserved his hugs only for the A-list.

Nancy watched, waiting for the right opportunity. Finally, her patience paid off. While Claire was busy talking with a couple in one corner, Page made her way alone to the bar.

Nancy followed quickly to find a spot next to the young woman amid the crush of guests clamoring for the bartender's attention.

"Dreadful, isn't it?" Nancy said off-handedly.

"It certainly is," Page answered, jostled forward by the slightly drunk man behind her.

Nancy looked at her. "Actually, you know, there's another bar right upstairs that no one seems to have discovered. I think I'll try that. Want to come?"

"Why not? It can't be any worse than this."

The bar in the second-floor library was quiet and uncrowded.

"What a relief," Nancy said, smiling at the bartender and ordering a white wine spritzer, her usual party drink when she was working.

"That sounds good. I'll have the same," Page chimed in.

Nancy picked up her drink. "Have you ever been here before? It's really quite a house."

"No, I never have. Actually, I've never met Neville Ford before tonight. Mother's been wearing his clothes for years, and they often socialize. This is the first time I've come with her to one of his parties."

They took their drinks and wandered out into the hallway, stopping to admire the original Bonnard on the wall.

"My name is Nancy." The reporter smiled warmly.

Page extended her hand. "I'm Page Warren. Nice to meet you. Are you a close friend of our host?"

"Just casual acquaintances, really," Nancy replied. "In fact, I know very few people here. I hate big parties like this. I find them intimidating."

"I know just what you mean. No matter how many I go to, I never feel quite comfortable."

"Do you think everybody in the room secretly feels that way?" Nancy asked conspiratorially.

Page laughed. "If so, they do a hell of a job covering it up."

Nancy laughed back. "Why don't we sit in those big chairs downstairs near the fire and have a normal human conversation. We'll look like the two most comfortable people at this shindig."

From where Liza was standing near the grand piano, she could see her sister coming down the main staircase, talking easily with a slightly older, dark-haired woman. Liza leaned over to the tall young man who'd been flirting with her for the past twenty minutes.

"Who's the brunette on the steps?" she asked casually.

He looked over. "Oh, that's Nancy Drummond, a writer for that rag *The Empire*. She's always at these things."

Liza smiled. She knew no reporter could resist that note.

"Offer them ten percent over the normal discount if they agree to book all six of their conventions with us next year."

"Fine, Mother," Liza said. "I'll call Jack Knox tomorrow when he gets back from Brussels."

Liza and Page were seated in Claire's office for their daily wrap-up session. It was after seven. Page closed her leather notebook.

"I'm sorry, but I'm going to have to run now. I'm meeting Nancy at eight for dinner."

Claire looked up. "You've been spending a lot of time with her in the past few weeks."

"Yes, she's very nice. We're getting to be good friends."

"That's lovely, Page. What's she like?" Claire asked.

"Smart, funny. She's a writer, working on a novel."

Liza interrupted. "I don't know. There's something odd about her."

Page looked at her sister, irritated. "You have no reason to say that. You only met her once and that was for no more than a minute."

"Sorry. You don't have to jump all over me." Liza shrugged. She knew her objection would make Page rush to the woman's defense. "I can see my usefulness is over for today. Mother, I'll see you at home for dinner. I've got some calls to make before I leave."

Liza and Page both walked out of Claire's office. Page stopped to retrieve her coat and briefcase and rang for the elevator. Liza headed directly for her own office, shutting the door tightly behind her. She opened her desk drawer, digging until she found the piece of paper hidden toward the back. On it was a telephone number. She dialed overseas and waited.

"Mason-Cahill, good afternoon."

"Paul Cahill, please. Liza Carlisle in London calling." She glanced at her watch. It would be about one o'clock in New York now.

"One moment, please."

Liza tapped her foot impatiently until she heard the deep male voice on the other end.

"Paul Cahill here."

"Paul, lovely to talk to you. This is Liza Carlisle."

"Have we met?" Paul Cahill's voice was polite but guarded.

Liza shifted slightly in her chair. "No, but I'm a great admirer of your organization."

Mason-Cahill was the largest hotel chain in the United States. Their hotels were clean and efficient. They were also standardized, sterile, and completely impersonal—the exact opposite of everything Warren International strove for.

"Well, thank you, Miss Carlisle. Are you in the business?"

"As a matter of fact I am. I work with my mother, Claire Warren."

Paul Cahill's voice was infused with a sudden respect. "Of course. I've frequently stayed in your hotels on business trips. They're magnificently run. How can I help you?"

"I read about your interest in expanding overseas, and I had a thought." Liza paused. "I don't know if you're interested in acquiring hotels or you're restricting yourself to building. But I wondered if the Warren chain might interest you."

"Are you telling me your hotels are on the market?"

"No, not exactly. But I suspect that if the proposal were right, it's something we might consider."

Paul Cahill's excitement was palpable over the phone line. "I'll call your mother immediately."

"Speaking frankly, I think you should know that's not the best way to approach this." Liza chose her next words carefully. "Mother might be resistant—after all, she helped to create the entire chain. But my sister, Page Warren, and I are a little more forward-looking, and we can see the possibilities in some kind of arrangement between our two companies."

"Why don't I fly over there? I can get away on Wednesday. The three of us can have lunch together."

"Again, Paul, just between us, I think it would be best if you approached my sister on your own, as if this were your idea."

There was a moment's hesitation. "Why is that?"

"She's been working with my mother for many years, and even though I'm confident she'll be receptive, she might be a little skittish if she knew I'd acted so aggressively."

"I understand. These matters have to be handled delicately. I know the business has been in your family a long time. I'll call her in the morning and try to set up a meeting. Does that sound all right?"

"Excellent," Liza replied. "I'm sure we'll be able to meet face to face soon after. I really look forward to it."

Paul Cahill spoke warmly. "Thanks so much for thinking of us. You won't regret it."

"That looks great," Page said, taking the tall glass of vodka and tonic Nancy was offering. "It's been a long day."

She sat down, appreciating the soft cushions of the couch, and kicked off her shoes. "It's so nice of you to make dinner," Page continued, smiling. "I'm too exhausted at night to even contemplate cooking."

"No trouble at all. Besides, writing at home all day, I'm happy to have the activity to distract me. And, of course, it's always great to have your company." Nancy watched Page take a long swallow of her drink. "I just put the chicken in the oven. I hope you're not starving. It may be a while."

"That's fine," Page said. She was in no hurry.

"Let me freshen that for you." Nancy took Page's glass and re-emerged from the kitchen a moment later, two drinks plus a full pitcher on the tray she carried. She handed Page a glass, keeping the other for herself, as she sat down. "Now, tell me how things have been going."

"Oh, fine. We're negotiating with a wonderful designer for the addition to the Zurich Warren. I think it'll really make a difference."

"Gee," Nancy said thoughtfully, "how do decisions like that get made? With your mother and your sister and you, how do you decide who does what?"

"Well, we all sort of do everything. The Manors were my project in the beginning, but now I pretty much share them with Liza."

"You mean it was your idea? Does it bother you, having to share it?"

Page hadn't eaten all day and was starting to feel the drinks. "No, it doesn't really bother me. Well, maybe a little."

Nancy leaned forward to pick up the pitcher and refill Page's glass. "I know I only met Liza briefly, but the two of you seem so different."

Page was silent.

"I hope you don't mind my saying this, but she comes across as rather, I don't know, highhanded," Nancy continued.

"She's had a tough time, I guess," Page answered reluctantly, torn between wanting to confide in her friend and the instinctive feeling that she should defend her sister. It would be nice to let go with someone, she thought, to be able to stop acting as if everything were wonderful.

Nancy moved closer to Page on the couch. "You know, Page, I get the sense you're holding something back. I don't want to pry, but I feel like we've become pretty good friends. If something were bothering you, I'd be glad to listen."

Page took another sip of her drink. "Liza and I don't always see eye to eye. And Mother tends to favor her a bit. Maybe because she feels guilty."

"Guilty?" Nancy asked quietly.

"Because of what happened when we were children." Page leaned back and closed her eyes. "It's not something I generally talk about."

"Was it so horrible? Were you beaten?"

Page looked over at her, shocked. "Oh, no, nothing like that. I'm talking about Mother raising me and leaving Liza behind in the States."

Nancy was quick to seize on her words. "Leaving Liza behind? Where was this?"

"Oh, we lived in Madison, Wisconsin. Really, I'd prefer not to talk about it, if you don't mind."

Nancy made a mental note. Liza's last name was Carlisle. The city was Madison, Wisconsin. This had to be it. With a little digging, these two facts would undoubtedly lead her to the story. She'd get on the phone first thing in the morning she thought, silently savoring a moment of victory.

She stood up. "Why don't we have dinner now?"

Page smiled at her. "Terrific."

Page walked briskly toward Chez Michel. What do these people want with me? she

311

wondered. Paul Cahill had called just that morning, telling her he would be in London only for the day and asking if they could get together for lunch. She tried to find out what the purpose of the meeting was, but he couldn't be persuaded to say any more than that over the phone. Mason-Cahill was an important American hotel chain. Page couldn't imagine what their interest in her could be, but she wasn't about to refuse a luncheon invitation from the head of the firm.

She entered through the restaurant's heavy glass doors and was led to a table near the window where three men were seated. They all stood as she approached. The tallest of the group stepped forward.

"I'm Paul Cahill, Ms. Warren. These are my associates. We're delighted you were able to join us on such short notice."

Page shook hands with the men as they introduced themselves by name. Paul Cahill pulled out a chair for her and she sat down.

Because her back was to the restaurant's entrance, Page didn't see her mother and Liza enter fifteen minutes later.

"Liza, I hope this restaurant is as good as you tell me it is," Claire said. "I hate taking this much time out of the workday."

Liza was prepared with her response. "I promise you, Mother, the chef is so wonderful, we're definitely going to want to consider him for the London Warren."

Glancing around the room furtively, Liza was gratified to see Page dining at the corner table. Thank goodness Page was so fastidious about writing down every appointment; it had been a simple matter for Liza to find out what time and where the lunch would take place. This was going to work out just the way she planned it.

"Why, Mother, look who's over there." Liza affected surprise.

Claire followed Liza's gaze. "Oh, how nice, there's Page. Let's say hello."

"Just a minute, Mother." Liza put out a hand to stop Claire. "Do you know who that is with her?"

"No, I have no idea. Why?"

"I recognize the gray-haired man from the States. That's Paul Cahill of Mason-Cahill Hotels. You know they're planning to expand into Europe. I wonder what they're talking about with Page."

"I'd like to know why she didn't mention this to me," Claire said, annoyance in her voice. "They're very big business."

Liza sounded protective. "We've been out of the office all morning."

"Please, don't tell me a man like Paul Cahill called her up five minutes ago and asked her to have a bite," Claire retorted. "She must have known about this for weeks. Do you think they could be offering her a job? Would Page consider leaving us?"

Looking uncomfortable, Liza said nothing.

"Wait a minute. You know something about this, don't you? I can see it all over your face," Claire said.

"Well, maybe I shouldn't say anything, but I've had a couple of conversations with Page, and I get the feeling she wouldn't mind leaving the hotel business altogether."

"What are you talking about?" Claire asked sharply.

"Mason-Cahill is a big chain. They have a lot of money. Maybe they're interested in buying us out."

"If that were true, why wouldn't they be talking to me? I'd tell them right away I would never consider selling."

Liza hesitated. "Maybe they know that. Maybe they hope Page could influence you somehow."

Claire stared at Page and the men surrounding her. She could see that the four were deep in conversation. "I can't believe this. It's outrageous. How could Page do such a thing to me?" Her eyes blazed with anger. "I'm sorry, Liza, we won't be having lunch today."

As Claire stormed out of the restaurant, Liza followed. She took a last look in her sister's direction. Page had never even noticed they were there.

When Page returned to Warren headquarters an hour later, her secretary informed her that Claire wished to see her immediately.

"How could you do it?" her mother demanded, enraged, as soon as Page walked through the door.

Page was mystified. "How could I do what?"

314

Claire slapped her hand down, hard, on the top of her desk. "Don't play games with me," she shouted. "I saw you having lunch with those Americans. I know what you were doing. You were selling me out."

"This is incredible," Page said in disbelief. "How could you think that?"

"You have lunch with a hotel chain expanding in Europe and you keep it a secret from me. What the hell else could we think?"

"*We?* Who do you mean?" Page asked.

"Liza, of course. We went to Chez Michel to have lunch. So your efforts to keep it a secret failed."

"Oh, Liza, of course." Page echoed her mother's words cynically.

"Never mind your petty grievances with your sister now. I want an explanation."

"Mother, I never kept anything secret. Paul Cahill called me this morning and insisted we have lunch. You weren't here. And, yes, he did talk to me about wanting to buy, but I turned him down flat. I knew you wouldn't be the least bit interested."

"But *you* were interested," Claire snapped back.

"Where are you getting this from?" Page was now angry herself.

The door to Claire's office opened. Liza entered. She was holding a copy of *The Empire*, folded open in her hand. She wore an agonized expression.

"Mother, you'd better take a look at this," Liza said, holding out the paper to Claire.

"Can't you see this isn't the time?" her mother said sharply.

Liza persisted. "It's important, Mother. I wouldn't bother you otherwise."

Impatiently, Claire held the paper in front of her and scanned it. There was silence as she read. Then she looked up.

Page had never seen her mother look so furious. "What is it?" she asked, almost frightened.

Claire's voice, raised in anger moments before, was now deathly quiet as she passed the newspaper to Page. "I hope you're happy now."

Page glanced at the headline. HOTEL MAGNATE: ABANDONING MOTHER, UNWED WIFE, by Nancy Drummond. Page felt her stomach lurch. *Nancy Drummond.* She ran her eyes down the length of the article. How did Nancy ever find out? It was all there, the whole thing. Liza bleeding in the playground, deserted by her mother; John and Claire posing as a married couple while she was actually married to someone else. Everything was presented in the most damaging light, making Claire seem a heartless monster. Oh, God, Page thought, what have I done?

"Do you have anything to say, Page?" Claire asked.

Page struggled to find words. "I didn't know... I'm so sorry."

"You're so sorry," Claire practically spat out the words. "Sorry for trying to sell my business out from under me? Sorry for destroying my reputation, for exposing the intimate details of my life—distorted—for the whole world to see? I don't know why, Page, but you've betrayed me. I can't trust you anymore."

"Mother, I obviously misjudged Nancy. But I didn't tell her any of this. I never tried to hurt you. And I would never do anything to hurt the business."

Claire exploded. "You expect me to believe that?"

"I certainly do." Page's temper flared again. "I'm sick and tired of defending myself against lies. Sick and tired of your lack of trust. Sick and tired of battling the two of you."

Standing off to one side, Liza watched as Page actually began to tremble in her anger. Pain and embarrassment were both clearly visible on her face. I've really done it, Liza thought, stunned by just how successful her plan to destroy their relationship had been. Despite the fact that she herself had brought about the scene unfolding before her, she couldn't help feeling sorry for Page. When Liza had envisioned driving a wedge between her mother and her sister, she had assumed she would enjoy every minute of it. But this was far from pleasurable. Perhaps she had gone too far. Suddenly, she was unable to recall why it had been so important that Page be punished. Not exactly sure what she was going to say, Liza took a step forward.

"Page—"

Page spun around to glare at her. "I don't know how and I don't know why, but this is all your doing. You've made my life miserable since the minute you arrived. Why did you ever come? Why couldn't you just *leave us alone*?"

Page's outburst stopped Liza cold. Of course, she thought, annoyed at herself for her momentary weakness, that's what this is all about. I was cut out of their lives, and my darling little sister would have loved it if I'd never been born.

Page walked to the door, opened it, and turned back to face them one last time. "Someone will pick up my things. I'll be at my father's."

Chapter Twenty-one

Page looked up at the black enamel clock. Like everything else at Carlisle and Poole, it was attractive to the eye and perfectly correct. It was six o'clock already, she realized, surprised at how many hours she'd spent poring over the financial details of Lowes Corner, the chic department store Perdita Lowes had inherited from her husband, Herbert. In the three months since Page had been working with her father, she'd been exposed to American business in its grandest form, but her growing friendship with Perdita made this assignment particularly pleasurable.

Bennett had decided that the best way for

Page to begin her career in banking was to learn everything there was to know about corporations, how they were financed, evaluated, and structured. So, for the first two months after her arrival, she'd been ensconced in the company library, analyzing past transactions, mostly mergers her father had arranged. For the next month, under the careful supervision of Lee Fielding, one of Bennett's smartest young associates, she'd begun researching businesses Bennett was thinking of negotiating for. Her job was to look into the break-up value of companies, exactly how much money individual parts of corporations would be worth if sold separately.

Lee had coached her in the use of spread sheets; she would feed one new number into the computer and, as if by magic, thousands of corporate statistics were adjusted in seconds. She'd had some experience with this in the hotel business, but mid-size electronics companies, national newspaper chains, sports franchises, all of them made economic sense to her now. She had finally begun to speak knowledgeably about annual reports, land value, the comprehensive 10-K forms American corporations filed annually with the Securities and Exchange Commission. She'd even begun to enjoy it.

Page was proud of her growing understanding of multinational corporate data. Still, despite the fact that Lowes Corner was small in comparison, it was Page's most exciting project so far. Representing Perdita,

Bennett was actively trying to find a buyer for it. Page and Lee were busy researching its value, and this time, she and Lee were more coworkers than teacher and student.

Perdita Lowes was ready to sell the department store, which had been considered a retail jewel while three generations had run it as a family business. But Herbert and Perdita had no children to succeed him, and he had been sick for five years before he died. He was unable to enforce the level of quality and service that had made the store one of the most respected in New York. Lower sales, and, perhaps even more deadly, a decline in reputation followed quickly after news of Herbert's cancer leaked to the gossip-hungry fashion press.

The Corner, as the family always called it, was a department store that felt like a boutique. For sixty years, its employees had upheld traditional, personalized care for the city's wealthy gentry, but had also managed to appeal to younger, trendier buyers. The older customers had remained, but the new crowd was whimsical. Word of Herbert Lowes's illness had taken some of the cachet from The Corner; his eventual death dealt it a second serious blow. Perdita had no intention of personally resurrecting the fortunes of The Corner. With her profit from its sale, away from what had been the center of her happily married life, she would begin to live again.

Page and Lee analyzed the store to come up with a fair market price. They had spent the day immersed in balance sheets, income statements, and cash flow analyses and felt almost ready to guess how much the business might go for. When they first started, each had picked a number almost blind, and written it on a piece of paper, agreeing that whoever came closer to the final sale price would win dinner.

"You'd better hope I lose," Lee had cracked. "If I don't, you're buying dinner for seven. And my kids have very expensive taste." He and his wife, Sally, had an old-fashioned relationship, which seemed to Page ideal for both of them. Lee had the unusual capacity to combine fierce, unhidden ambition with a good sense of humor and a total dedication to his family. In Sally, he had found a wife whose foremost desire was to make him comfortable when he got home from a hard day's work. With five children all under the age of eight, their household was noisy and messy, but love practically bounced off the walls. Page had been invited for dinner many times and had grown close to both Lee and Sally. Visiting with them sometimes made her lonesome for England and her mother, but Page had no intention of giving in to her momentary homesickness.

Lee and Page had vowed to finish their work that night, no matter how long it took. Looking at the time made her realize that it could go well into the night. She was caught yawning as Lee walked into the library carrying a stack of magazines.

"Stay awake, imperial daughter. I found

some old interviews with Herbert Lowes. You never know what we might learn."

Page groaned. "Slave driver."

"Yes, the father tortures the servant, the servant takes it out on the child. Exactly as it ought to be." Lee's eyes gleamed behind his tortoise-shell glasses.

Page turned to him as he placed the stack on the table and pulled a chair up beside her. "You tease about Dad a lot, but some of the people here really seem scared to death of him."

"Well," Lee replied, "he's a very smart guy."

Page was aware of how neatly his answer side-stepped her observation. She had noticed how timid some of her coworkers at Carlisle and Poole seemed in front of Bennett. More than timid, she admitted to herself, actually frightened. How interesting that Lee, who didn't seem at all intimidated by Bennett and was never at a loss for an opinion—even Lee would cut off the subject practically as soon as she brought it up.

No time to dwell on that tonight. "Okay, let's dig into Herbert Lowes." She thumbed through the pile of magazines, finally pulling out a copy of *Forbes* dated December 1992. "Christmas. The perfect time to interview a retailer."

Lee grinned in response. "Let's see," he said, rifling through the remaining issues, "perhaps I'll find a *Playboy* interview."

"Fat chance," Page responded. "According to Perdita, that's the last place you'd find him. I had dinner with her last Tuesday, and all she talked about was their life together. It sounded like heaven."

"Well, if you'd given Stephen Grant half a chance, you might be happily married, too." Lee shook his head as he spoke.

Page thought back to the perfectly nice young man Lee and Sally had fixed her up with the week before. She never should have agreed to a blind date. She'd known she wasn't ready to meet anyone, but there was no way to explain to Lee how thoroughly frozen she'd felt that night. When Stephen had dropped her in front of her door, she'd practically run inside. No more blind dates. No more dates, period.

"I'm sorry, Lee. He was fine, really he was. We just weren't meant to be."

"Page, how in the world do you know if something's 'meant to be' in the course of one dinner?"

"How long did it take you to fall in love with Sally?" Page looked as innocent as possible, given that Sally had told her the details of their courtship the last time she'd visited.

Lee couldn't keep a grin off his face. "Fifteen minutes. Right between the artichoke and the bisque. But I didn't actually propose until way after the peach melba." He eyed Page with suspicion. "You knew this already, or you never would have asked, right?"

Page didn't have to acknowledge a thing, since at that moment Bennett's secretary stuck her head in the doorway. "Page, there's a man waiting outside your office," Jane said.

"He wouldn't give his name. Claimed to be an old friend."

"Perhaps it's your Prince Charming, come to spirit you away on his steed." Lee couldn't resist a final dig.

Page looked dubious. "If it is, I'll buy your whole family dinner for a month." Putting down the magazine, she stood and started toward the door. "If the prince and I don't immediately depart for Buckingham Palace, I'll be back in two minutes."

Jane had no intention of leaving Bennett's daughter alone with a stranger in what was by now a nearly empty building, so she accompanied Page on the way back. Besides, the man who waited for Page looked none too respectable.

"Perhaps I should try to get his name again," Jane suggested, just before making the final turn in the hallway to Page's office.

"It'll be fine," Page reassured her, rounding the corner.

"Fine! That's an understatement." Chris's voice greeted her even before she caught sight of him.

She practically flew to where he stood. "What are you doing here?" The words were muffled by their huge bear hug.

"I'm here to say hello, and then good-bye," he answered, holding her at arm's length. "You look fabulous. High finance must agree with you."

"Never mind how I look. What do you mean hello and good-bye?"

"Hello, I'm back in New York. For the duration, I think," Chris replied. "And good-bye, I promised I'd drive a friend of mine to the airport. I have to pick him up in twenty minutes."

"But you can't come and just leave like this." Page was indignant.

"Yes, I can. But tomorrow night, I'll take you away from these overpriced digs and remind you of your roots. That is, if you're free."

"You're not going to make me eat in the Columbia cafeteria, are you?" Page raised an eyebrow in distaste.

Chris grimaced. "Not if *I'm* eating with you."

Page suddenly realized that Jane had been standing beside them and started to introduce her to Chris, but before she could get the words out, Bennett appeared in the corridor.

"Jane, I was looking for..." He stopped talking at the sight of the unlikely trio in front of him.

"Father," Page said, "this is my friend Chris Layton. Chris, this is my father, Bennett Carlisle, and Jane Fellows."

Jane extended her hand politely, but Bennett merely nodded. His eyes traveled down Chris's body, from his unruly dark hair to his T-shirt and blue jeans.

Bennett turned back to Jane. "I need you in the office," he said curtly.

As Bennett and his secretary walked away,

Chris watched them from behind. Page was mute with embarrassment.

"Makes your mother feel like a tropical breeze, doesn't he?"

Page remained silent, which made Chris uneasy. When he'd had trouble with Claire, Page had found it almost funny. She'd obviously been sure enough of him and her mother not to worry about their relationship with each other, seeming to know instinctively it would work out in time. He wondered why she was so ill at ease with her father.

Chris deftly switched back to the subject they'd been discussing before Bennett arrived. "Tomorrow night, Page. For old times' sake, let's meet in front of Juilliard. I promise it won't be our final destination, but it would be fun to visit the neighborhood. I told the guy I'm meeting tonight that I'd do a couple of things for him tomorrow that involve driving to Connecticut, but I should be able to get there by six-thirty."

"That's fine, Chris," Page responded. "I'm going to be here late tonight; it would be a pleasure to leave tomorrow after a regulation eight hours for a change." She looked affectionately at him. "You know, once in a while, I think about home, but now that you're here, I realize you're the only thing I've really missed."

"Maybe." His tone was noncommittal. "We'll talk about that tomorrow." He picked up a gray sweatshirt from one of the chairs and started to walk toward the elevator bank.

"Six-thirty. Juilliard steps." He took one more look at the elegantly understated surroundings. "Dress down, okay?"

Page laughed as she watched him leave. She was still smiling when she joined Lee in the library.

"So it *was* the prince," he said, observing her closely.

"No, even better. Someone who doesn't disappear when you turn the last page of the fairy tale."

Her bitterness surprised Lee. As friendly as they had become, Page never said much about herself. "Do you want to talk about it?" he asked.

"Nope." The expression sounded unexpectedly grand in her British accent. She looked at Lee gratefully. "But it's nice to know I could if I wanted to. Now, back to Herbert Lowes."

Chris and Page were sharing a plate of Buffalo chicken wings on the terrace of The Saloon, an outdoor café around the corner from Juilliard. She was watching the June sun, almost gone behind Lincoln Center, just across the street. Chris was staring at her, taking in every inch of her crisp pink linen suit and open-toed high-heeled sandals.

"You look different. Better. What's the story?"

She glared back at him. "How did I used to look? Haggard? Dingy?"

"Stop digging. You know that's not what I mean. You always look beautiful. You just look more content than I had expected. Older."

"Older! How can you say that to a woman!"

"It's a compliment. You look more self-confident, more adult. Before you left home, I thought you might never climb out of yourself. I was worried about you. So was Claire."

"Since when are you such a fan of my mother's?"

"She came through for me when I needed someone. And I really needed someone, believe me."

"What happened, Chris? Why are you back here?"

Chris watched the cars speeding down Broadway. For the first time since they'd been seated, his eyes were not meeting hers. "It's tough to talk about, even with you." He paused for a moment. "Embarrassing." Once again he stopped.

Page waited quietly. Finally, the story poured out. "Remember my nerves the opening night of *Julius Caesar*? Well, it happened again. You know the one-act I was doing in that workshop production when you came back from New York the first time? I never told you, but I could barely climb onstage each night. I shook through the entire run, but I made it to the end."

Chris looked directly at Page. "The next time, I wasn't so lucky. Martin Purcell, the guy who cast me in *Julius Caesar*, did another experimental Shakespeare. *Hamlet*. He decided to use me again. Only this time he gave me a real part. Laertes! He said I was born for it." He shook his head, self-disgust written all over his face. "He should have been right, too. That's what really kills me. First performance, there was Hamlet, center stage, and no one could find Laertes. I was hiding out behind the theater. There was no understudy; Purcell had to go on himself. The story was all over the place by nine o'clock that night."

"Oh, Chris. I'm so sorry." Page picked up his hand and held it.

"It wasn't even everybody talking about it that did me in. It was my own self-hatred. I just didn't want to be alive. That's where your mother came in."

Page withdrew her hand. "What did she have to do with it?"

"Well, I was practically suicidal, and your mother knew it. When I went to pick her up the next morning and take her to the office, she took one look at me, pulled me into the house, and talked to me for hours." Chris's eyes forced Page to listen to him. "If it weren't for Claire, I think I really would have gone over the edge. She made me face myself, and I'm much better off for it. Once I made the decision to leave the theater, all I felt was relief."

"Chris, I don't want to talk about my mother. Just tell me what you mean by facing yourself. And what are you doing in New York?"

"I'm not exactly sure what I'll be doing, but it won't be acting. Sometimes, fear is a way of hiding. But, sometimes, it's a way of letting yourself in on something. And the message for me is damn clear. I saw acting as a way out of what I came from, but it isn't the right way. Nothing that feels that bad can be good. I can't be meant to go through that kind of torture every time I do my job. You said it yourself the night of *Julius Caesar*, and you were on the nose."

Page scrutinized his face. To her surprise, Chris didn't look particularly unhappy at this acknowledgment. "So what are you planning to do?" she asked.

"I'm not sure. I only got back a few days ago. For the moment, I'm driving. Like the old days." He grinned at Page. "The car isn't as impressive as the Bentley, but the pay is good."

"What do you mean, you're driving?" Page was confused.

"Well, I've been staying with Peter Jeffries, one of my old friends from Juilliard, and he keeps coming up with trips for me. To the airport, to Connecticut, to New Jersey. Everyone is so busy in this city, and no one can count on catching a cab, so I've been taking his Chevy, sometimes with him in it, sometimes not. I'm beginning to think there's a real business in this. Limousine service for people without limousines. I understand there are a number of successful car services here."

"That's not such a bad idea." Page was intrigued. "If you need some capital, I do have some money of my own. It might be a pretty good investment."

"Thanks, kiddo. Maybe I'll just take you up on that one of these days. Now, what about you? I meant it when I said you looked older. And I don't mean wrinkled. I mean more sure of yourself."

Page hardly knew where to start; so much had changed in the last few months. "Well, I'm fine. My father is amazing. I mean, he's involved in the kind of deals that end up on the front page of the *Times* every other week. I've met oil magnates and railroad owners."

"How boring," Chris responded.

"Don't be mean. I'm enjoying what I'm doing. I'm not that fond of the part where you have to go out every night of the week to keep up your contacts, but the basic work is really exciting."

"Why do you have to go out every night?" Chris asked.

"My father's company is hugely successful, and a lot of that comes from socializing, linking up with businesspeople and politicians, being around when deals are just in the beginning stages. Bennett brings the right people together—people who want to buy with people who want to sell. His instincts are amazing. Last month, he arranged a merger worth hundreds of millions of dollars that started with a round of golf in Dallas. He was playing with a man who headed up an educational publishing company and wanted to retire. So my father introduced him to the CEO of a rubber-importing outfit in Pittsburgh whom he'd met at a party a couple of years ago.

Sure enough, the importing company was hungering for a more accessible public image, one that would attract investors. Books turned out to be perfect." Page gestured out across the busy Broadway intersection to the crowds of people milling around Lincoln Center's bubbling fountain. "There are so many millions of people here. But these enormous financial transactions make the whole world seem small, even conquerable."

Chris took another bite of his food, boredom at the financial details warring with anger at Page's avoidance of any real intimacy. "Okay, your father's Midas, and you're Attila the Hun."

"You don't have to be cruel."

"I'm not trying to be." Chris's tone softened. "Listen, you're my best friend. I'm glad you like what you're doing. I even believe it— you look too good to be miserable—but it can't all be quite so perfect. You haven't spoken to your mother in months. You have to feel something."

Page stared out at the traffic, defiantly refusing to speak.

Chris was relentless. "And Simon. I bet you haven't spoken to him either."

Now her pain became apparent. "That's over. I hate it, but it's the truth." Page faced Chris squarely. "Listen. I'm not trying to hide from you or pretend that everything's fine. I loved Simon. Maybe I'll always love him. And, yes, I miss my damned mother, too. But I'm actually all right." Her eyes blazed as she spoke. "I'm growing up. I no longer die at the sound of a cross word. I can miss my mother, and miss Simon, and *go on*! And that's just what I'm doing."

"I'm sorry, Page." Chris was contrite. "I didn't mean to push you so hard. Really, I'm proud of you. Maybe you needed to get out." He smiled gently. "Maybe we both needed to get out." Chris lifted his wineglass. "Let's order a main course and I'll leave you alone."

Page finally relaxed in her chair. "What happened to our famous privacy?"

"Maybe that's changed too. It's probably time. Friends are supposed to invade once in a while."

Her eyes glowed menacingly. "I can't wait to start. Now, let's see. Any women on the horizon?"

"Jesus, I've only been back a week. Besides, right now, I couldn't afford a woman. Although Peter's sister was part of the package I took to Connecticut this morning. Pretty cute."

"So ask her out." Page was enjoying this act of interference.

"I've created a Frankenstein. Leave me alone."

"Friends are supposed to invade once in a while." Page's tone mocked his earlier remark.

Chris decided to shoot back. "Speaking of invasions, how about your father, Mr. Warmth? What's the scoop on him?"

"He's taught me an incredible amount. He's great at what he does."

"And?" Chris knew he was pushing, but he refused to stop.

Page waited a few moments before she answered. "And... I don't know. In the office, I spend most of my time with Lee—you'll meet him and his wife soon. They're great. My father's been nice to me, but I don't really know him very well. I hardly ever see him. I saw more of him when I was here for just a couple of weeks last time. If I didn't hate Liza, I might actually feel sorry for her, growing up in such a cool environment."

At Liza's name, Chris stiffened. "She would have had to grow up in a penitentiary to explain away her personality."

Page was thoughtful. "It's nice to be at a distance. So many miles away, so busy with work. She means nothing to me. She's a blank."

"Bitchiest blankety-blank-blank who ever lived," was Chris's surprisingly cheerful assessment.

Feeling a rush of tenderness for him, Page lifted a chicken wing, as if in a toast. "To us. To nosey friendships, to Peter's sister, to high finance and limousine entrepreneurs. To the future."

Chris lifted a wing and touched it to hers, a broad smile on his face.

Chapter Twenty-two

The air-conditioned elevator was a relief after the steaming heat of New York's streets in August. Even so, Liza grew increasingly uncomfortable as she rode up to her father's apartment. She had called the housekeeper earlier to make certain neither Bennett nor Page would be there when she arrived, but she'd been delayed over drinks with Susie Dickerson, and it was already a quarter after five. Certainly, she would have to say the delay had been worth it; after nearly six months of cajoling, Susie had finally agreed to invest several million in Warren International stock, bringing the collective total of funds from Liza's group of investors near the thirty million mark. Not that the people involved even realized they constituted a group. Legal requirements stated that a group purchasing stock in one company was obligated to report that purchase. Technically, they were guilty of collusion. But only Liza was aware of the group; each individual knew nothing of the others in her plan.

She had to laugh. To think she'd gone from a jobless dilettante to someone who could maneuver this. But it turned out when she really wanted something, she knew how to apply herself. She wished there was someone other than herself who would be proud of her. Right now, however, she needed to be more concerned with the vastly unpleasant possibility of running into her father or her sister, who she knew had been living here with Bennett since the spring.

The housekeeper, Mary, came out of the kitchen as she heard Liza letting herself in the front door. Returning the woman's greeting with a nod and a wave, Liza hurried to her bedroom; she didn't want to spend a minute more than she had to in this apartment. She passed the guest bedroom, and, glancing in, noticed Page's belongings carefully laid out around the room. Settled in for the long haul, Liza noted.

Her own bedroom was clean and neat, but clearly uninhabited. She headed directly to the black desk near the window and unlocked the bottom drawer. Sighing, she began sorting through the papers within it. This was a chore she had put off for months. She was hoping she might come up with some surprise, something that would enable her to invest some of her own money into Warren stock. Or, at least, something she could bring back to her new accountant in London to generate some serious cash.

Soon she had everything spread out in front of her: bankbooks, some certificates of deposit, and an insurance policy Claire had taken out when Liza was born. Damn it, she thought. Nothing here was worth very much, maybe seventy-five thousand altogether. It wasn't nearly enough. How could she have drifted along for so many years without bothering to look after the funds—such as they were—that were in her name? If she'd only paid attention, she might have turned these documents into a real portfolio. Her father was a multimillionaire. How had she wound up with so little? Well, she had to admit Claire had taught her a few things. It was as if she'd become a different person, she mused, remembering how just a year before she would run through thousands of dollars, heedless of where it went or where the next supply of funds would come from. She was far shrewder about spending and investing money now. Now that she had a purpose, a clear goal.

Nothing to be done about it, she thought. If only there were a chance she would get lucky when she went to meet Connor Pinchon tomorrow. Pinchon was an incredibly wealthy entrepreneur who had started out in real estate. She had prevailed upon a friend of hers in New York to arrange this meeting, assuring Steve that it would be worth Pinchon's time to see her. But she would have only a few minutes to charm this man before he dismissed her. She hoped she was up to it.

Gathering up her papers, she slipped them into a large envelope and hurried out to the entranceway. She was about to reach for the doorknob when she saw it turn, heard the key in the lock. Liza froze. Would it be her father or her sister? She wasn't sure which was worse.

The door swung open and Bennett stood before her. It was nearly ninety degrees outside, but he looked fresh and cool. His only response to the sight of his daughter was to raise one eyebrow sardonically. "Back so soon?" he asked.

A vague fear rose up in Liza as she took an uncertain step back. "I had to get a few things. I'm leaving right now."

"Nonsense," Bennett said with a thin smile as he stepped across the threshold. "Stay and talk a bit."

What was he up to now? "We don't have anything to say," Liza snapped, angry at herself for being afraid and nearly losing her composure.

Bennett shook his head regretfully. "Sad, but true. Now, on the other hand, your sister Page and I have a great deal to say. She's been working with me, you know. Has a tremendous future with the firm. A charming young lady in every way."

Bennett had taken Page to work at Carlisle and Poole? Stunned, Liza said nothing.

"We've built up quite a relationship in the time she's been here," he continued, picking up the mail on the hall table and casually sorting through it. "She's bright, very attractive, has an excellent sense of humor. Page grew up—well, I'd have to say virtually perfect. Just the kind of daughter any father would be proud of."

Liza knew Bennett was doing this deliberately. He had to be. Singing *anyone's* praises this way was totally out of character for him, no matter how taken he might be with them. But that didn't stop the sharp rush of pain Liza felt. Page had gotten him to take her into the business. There had never even been a hint that Liza might work with Bennett in all the years she was growing up with him. A sense of humor? Page? *Virtually perfect?* There wasn't one thing Liza had ever said or done that he considered right, or even acceptable. Damn him. With a great exertion of will, she calmed herself.

"It's lovely to hear the two of you have hit it off so well," she said sarcastically. "I hope you're very happy together."

Bennett's eyes met hers, as he dropped the pile of mail back onto the hall table. "If I'd had any idea how different it could be, what it was like to raise a *real* daughter, I would have made arrangements to swap with your mother years ago." He smiled and paused before continuing. "I take it I can assume you won't be needing anything else from me in the future."

Liza was glad to reply. "Goddamn right I won't."

"Good," Bennett said calmly. "Then you won't mind that I've made a slight change in my will. You see, you're out of it. I've left everything to Page."

Liza had no way of knowing that what he was saying was untrue. Bennett had cut her out of his will, that was so, but he had left everything to Harvard, not to Page. Telling Liza this little lie was, he thought, a brilliant stroke. As he watched her face crumple, he was completely satisfied.

He walked past Liza and started down the

hallway. "Mary," he called out, "what's for dinner?"

Chapter Twenty-three

"Chris, it's incredibly nice of you to do this yourself."

Joanna Jeffries's feathery voice affected Chris the same way every time he drove her. One part of him wanted to tear her clothes off; the other felt completely protective, as if he would kill any guy who was thinking what he was thinking.

From his bland response, she could never have known the struggle going on in his mind. "It's okay, Jo, I have to keep my hand in. I get restless when I'm chained to my desk." Chris steered the navy blue stretch limousine, with its distinctive COACH 1 license plate, into the parking lot of the Short Hills mall.

"You could at least charge me your regular rate. You can't possibly be making a profit on this."

"Hey, you're my oldest customer. Without you and your brother, there would be no Stagecoach. I'd still be in jeans and a T-shirt, looking for a job."

"You *are* in jeans and a T-shirt," Joanna laughed as she walked around to the back of the limousine and began removing an assortment of cartons.

"Let me do that," Chris said, lifting Joanna completely off her feet and depositing her to one side, as he took over the job of getting the boxes out of the large trunk.

"I hate it when you treat me like a toy," Joanna cried indignantly.

Chris eyed her tiny frame and spiky hairdo, as he continued unloading. "I like that. The Joanna doll. It walks, it talks, it weighs eighty-eight pounds."

She punched him lightly on the shoulder. Just a hair over five foot two, she hated to be reminded of her diminutive stature.

"Small but mighty, the queen of the unnecessary jewelry business pummels her staff into submission." Chris finished removing the boxes and closed the trunk with a thud, as if punctuating his remarks.

Joanna began to gather several of the cartons in her arms, preparing to carry them into the mall. "What does that make you, king of the road?"

"You've got that right," he replied smugly.

The growth of the Stagecoach Car Company was enormously satisfying to Chris. From random trips for Joanna's brother, Peter, the first week he'd gotten back to the States, Chris had gotten the idea for the taxi and limousine business. Peter Jeffries was dutifully working his way up in one of New York's biggest talent agencies. The company's clients provided an endless supply of script deliveries between the city and the wealthier sections of Connecticut, New Jersey, and Long Island, plus personal chauffeuring to theaters, clubs, or any-where else they might happen to get noticed.

Within three months, Chris had bought two used limousines and was regularly trans-porting the rich and famous around, or per-forming their errands while they were otherwise engaged. Business was growing every day.

It was actually Page who had paid for the first limo, insisting that it was a good invest-ment. She'd also helped him with the business and financial details of establishing a company and hiring two other drivers. Attracting clients was proving to be easy. In addition to the people he'd already met through his work for Peter, Chris had his own theatrical con-tacts from Juilliard and London. Stagecoach was fast becoming known among actors and musicians, creative people whose special problems he was in a perfect position to understand. Chris was gaining a reputation as the guy who could handle crazy hours, drunken stars, and demanding fans. In this city, his Detroit street smarts and tough exterior were a plus, marking him as cool, a bit of a celebrity in his own right.

And he was enjoying every minute of it. For once in his life, money wasn't a constant problem. For the first time in years, he was free from worrying about acting, and he reveled in it. Finally, being the real Chris Layton was more fun than playing the part of somebody else. In fact, the only thing that got under his skin these days was Joanna Jeffries, Peter's younger sister. Brash and independent, she looked like a punk rocker, but both her brain and body were like steel.

Chris really admired Joanna, with her quirky talent and uncanny business sense. She had begun by fashioning bracelets and pins out of a glittery tin that cost almost nothing to buy. After a few years, her downtown fashion statement made a splash in offbeat SoHo boutiques. When the style caught on with suburban women, her success was assured. These delivery trips to malls had begun with one store in White Plains. Now, Stagecoach routinely ran at least four calls a week for Joanna, from southern New Jersey to Boston and beyond.

"One of these days, you're going to have to hire someone to deliver this stuff for you, Jo. You're getting too big to do all this yourself."

Joanna and Chris were walking toward the mall's entrance, weighed down with boxes, so her words were slightly muted by the packages in front of her face. "Speak for yourself. Since when does the president of Stagecoach drive with his own two hands?"

"Since one of his drivers got the flu and called in sick."

Joanna wondered if that were true. Chris often drove her himself. She only wished it meant he found her attractive. She'd wanted him since she first met him, when he was staying with her brother, before he moved into the loft in TriBeCa, all the way downtown. But romance seemed to be the last thing on his mind. He never stopped reminding her that she was

Peter's younger sister. He treated her as if she were fourteen, Joanna mused irritably. Trailing a few steps behind him, she looked at the back of his head longingly. One of these days, she swore to herself, she was going to make him look at her. *Really* look at her.

Chris stood by silently as the buyer for Forbes, a small, exclusive women's shop on the second rung of the mall, checked through the boxes. He loved watching Joanna in action, an astonishing mix, he thought, of Moon Unit Zappa and a used-car saleswoman. The manager at Forbes was like dozens of others he had seen in the past few months: starchy, a fake almost-but-not-quite British accent, totally bowled over by Peter's baby sister. By the time Joanna had finished with these people, they thought they were lucky to pay only eight dollars apiece for pins that cost about forty cents to make.

Chris wasted no time in teasing her about this on their way back through the parking lot. "What are you going to do when America gets tired of cheap tin? Used pennies, maybe?"

"Used human parts," she responded, glancing menacingly at his arm as they arrived at the car.

Chris opened the front door for her. Before closing it, he leaned in and said laughingly, "When you grow up, it's going to be much harder to put this stuff over on people."

Joanna made no reply as he got in on his side. She was too furious to speak. How dare he treat her like an infant, she thought. Chris directed several remarks to her as he drove through the wealthy suburban neighborhoods, but she refused to say a word. In fact, she was feeling angrier with every block.

Finally, she came to a decision. As he drove at a leisurely pace down the residential street that would take them to the highway, Joanna leaned over and pulled the key out of the ignition. Chris was startled but managed to stop the car without an accident.

"What the hell do you think you're doing?" he yelled as he turned and grabbed the key back.

Without saying a word, she put both hands around his neck and kissed him, holding on as he tried to pull away in surprise. Finally, he extricated himself from her embrace, breathing heavily as he held her at arm's length. He was speechless.

But Joanna had plenty to say, and she held nothing back. "I am not a baby. I am not a teeny-bopper. I am not a Valley girl. I am a fully grown, twenty-two-year-old woman. *I'm an entrepreneur, for Christ's sake!*"

For a few seconds, they stared at each other, then burst out laughing. But Joanna wasn't finished. "Listen," she said urgently, but quietly, "I'm in love with you and I'd like to know if you feel the same way, 'cause if you don't, I promise I'll never bring this up again, honest. I just need to know what's really going on here."

Chris couldn't believe what he was hearing. I'm the biggest idiot who ever lived, he thought. There's a child in this car, all right, but it's me. He leaned over and kissed her, deeply and passionately, ignoring the car honking impatiently behind them and the group of children who had gathered by the side of the limo and were pointing and giggling furiously.

Chris had been so busy running back and forth between the Stagecoach office and Joanna, he'd completely missed the ads for *Uncivilized Acts*. Only when he saw a feature piece in the *Times* did the name Simon Roberts jump to his attention.

Excitedly, Chris drew Joanna's attention to it as they lay in bed one Sunday morning, both coaxing just a few more minutes together before they had to go to work. "Look at this, honey. Simon's in a play opening tomorrow night at the Cherry Lane. But there's a preview tonight. Let's go. You'll love Simon."

"He's the one Page used to go out with, right?" Joanna asked.

"Yeah. We haven't spoken to each other since they broke up. I guess he felt awkward about it. Maybe he thought I'd be mad at him or something."

"Are you?" She honestly wondered. When Chris had told her the story of Simon's abrupt switch to Page's older sister, Joanna herself had felt angry at Simon, and she'd never even met him. And since Joanna had become involved with Chris, Page had become an important friend to her, too. As different as

346

Page and Joanna seemed, they'd taken an instant liking to each other.

Chris thought about Joanna's question. "No, I'm not mad. I'm still mystified, though. I tried to get in touch with him, but he never returned my calls. I've never seen anyone so in love with a woman as Simon was with Page."

"Except you with me, of course," Joanna corrected him.

"No," he said, a smile playing on his lips. "I think of you kind of like a daughter—no, a favorite niece—"

"Oh, shut up," Joanna interrupted, climbing on top of him.

The preview at the Cherry Lane was completely sold out, as Chris discovered to his chagrin when he called for tickets. Only with the help of one of his regular clients—a Tony Award-winning British actor who owed Chris a favor for keeping a recent alcoholic exploit off the front pages—was Chris able to get a pair of house seats at the tiny Greenwich Village theater.

"Boy, his publicity's really paid off," Chris commented to Joanna, as they found their seats amid the crowd. Simon's movie hadn't even opened yet, but the New York papers already referred to him as a star. It was a recurring theme in the *Times*, the *Post*, and *New York* magazine, all of which Joanna had brought to Chris's attention over an early dinner.

Joanna grumbled about it. "How do they

347

know how good he is when he hasn't even done anything yet?"

But Chris knew they were right. "Wait till you see him onstage. He's the best."

As they waited for the curtain to rise, she ran her hand down Chris's arm. "This must be hard for you, sitting in the audience instead of being up there yourself."

"No," he answered, taking her hand and holding it. "It's not hard at all." With a sudden intake of breath, he looked toward the stage and added, "Being up there. That would be hard."

Uncivilized Acts ran one and a half hours without any intermission. The story of two brothers and a sister who came together after a fifteen-year feud was by an unknown playwright, with two unknown actors featured along with Simon. As the curtain came down, the entire audience rose to its feet. All three actors were applauded, with Simon cheered wildly.

"What did I tell you?" Chris whispered to Joanna, who was clapping as enthusiastically as everyone else.

There were six curtain calls plus two for the playwright before the house had quieted down.

"Let's go backstage," Chris suggested. "Maybe he's free for a drink."

The dressing area was quiet. Celebrities and well-wishers were more likely to show up after the play had actually opened. They found Simon standing alone, taking off his makeup.

"You were incredible!" Chris's words startled the actor, who hadn't seen the couple walk in. "Simon, this is Joanna Jeffries."

Simon looked taken aback, but put his hand out to Joanna politely. "How do you do?" he said in clipped tones.

"You were stupendous up there!" Chris exclaimed.

"I'm nowhere near the actor you are," Simon responded in a tone too cold for his words to be interpreted as a compliment.

Joanna couldn't imagine what was going on, but clearly her presence was not appropriate. What a shame if impending fame had already turned this guy into a jerk, she thought. "Excuse me, Chris. I'm going to look for the ladies' room. I'll meet you outside. No rush."

Chris watched her walk away, then turned back to Simon's blue-eyed glare. There was an uncomfortable silence while Chris tried to figure out what was going on. "You *were* terrific tonight," he said, searching Simon's face for any sign of their former friendship.

Again Simon's tone was pure ice. "I'm sure you're terrfic at night as well."

"Have we had a fight I don't know about?" Chris finally asked.

"You see," Simon replied, "you are a wonderful actor. Look at the innocence on that face."

Chris was bewildered. "Simon, what in the world are you talking about?"

"Oh, cut the crap." Simon wheeled around in anger, refusing to look at Chris a moment longer. "I know all about it. Judging from the girl with you, I gather it didn't work out. Or do you and Page simply take vacations separately? Friends for a while, lovers for a while. Too terribly modern, isn't it?"

Chris was beginning to catch on. "You think Page and I had an affair? Are you crazy?"

"I'm merely well informed." Simon's expression was one of disgust. "Don't bother to lie. Liza told me all about it."

Chris almost laughed as the light dawned, but the impulse was quickly replaced by sadness. "You poor bastard. So that's what happened. I never understood what you did to Page."

"What *I* did to Page!" Furiously, he turned back to Chris. "Love. Friendship. You two have a strange understanding of those words."

Chris shook his head. "You've been taken, pal, and taken by an expert. It's the only excuse I can find for what a fool you've been."

Simon's hostile expression remained unchanged.

"Didn't you ever listen when Page talked about her sister?"

"She never said a word about Liza." Simon's response was slow, unwilling.

"Maybe you were just too self-centered to hear it." Now Chris was getting angry. "Listen. Liza is the most manipulative liar ever born. What'd she do, follow you out to California and tell you we were together?"

"She was in California on business and she had no reason to lie to me." Simon's voice was hard as a rock.

Chris couldn't contain a rueful laugh. "You dumb sucker. She had every reason. Her whole life has been dedicated to ruining Page's, and it seems she's been even more successful than I realized. Liza managed to separate her from both her mother and her boyfriend. What a talent that girl has."

"What do you mean, separate Page from her mother?" Simon asked.

"Page has been living with her father here in New York for months. Liza, Little Miss Sincerity, arranged things so Page and Claire aren't even speaking to each other. Page is out of the country, out of the business—" Chris narrowed his eyes at Simon as he finished his sentence—"and out of the life of the only man she ever cared about."

"Why should I believe you?" Simon was listening intently to every word.

"Oh, Simon. Think about this a minute. You know me. You know Page. You spent too much time with us to be taken in this way." Chris's eyes bored into Simon. "Come on, man. Do you really think it was coincidence that Liza came to California, that she spread that manure about me and Page, that she ended up in your bed?"

Simon had the grace to look sheepish at the mention of his brief affair with Liza, as Chris continued.

"Did you ever see Liza do any actual business there, or was her business taking you away from Page?" Chris could see Simon running the questions through his mind. "You must have watched Liza in action. Who's the liar? Come on, you tell me."

Simon reached for a chair, sitting down heavily. He looked back up at Chris. "You said Page was in New York, with her father?"

"Get dressed. You're coming with Joanna and me. I'll tell you everything over the drink you definitely need." Chris placed his hand on Simon's shoulder, and the gesture was accepted.

"Chris, I need time to think about this, time alone to sift it through my brain, or what's left of it."

Chris's tone was firm. "No, I'm sorry, but that just won't do. You'll have to sulk on your own time. I've finally found a woman who means something to me and I want you to know her. You're coming out with us. Now. No excuses."

Simon had to acknowledge how much he wanted to go. He needed to find out about Page. He needed company. And, slowly, he was becoming aware of how wonderful it felt to be with Chris again. His friend. His *only* friend in this city. His thoughts were clearing. Page and Chris. The whole thing was a total fabrication. It meant Page might still be free. Suddenly, he felt as light as air.

"Chris, why don't you go find Joanna and wait outside for me? I'll be there in two minutes." Simon stood up and began to pull his costume off. "Don't leave without me."

Chapter Twenty-four

Page tapped her foot impatiently. Bennett was already fifteen minutes late for their three o'clock meeting. He had agreed to make time for her when she'd called his secretary and insisted, but he obviously hadn't felt it necessary to alter anything he might have previously scheduled for the day. Perhaps he had a sense of how unpleasant this meeting was going to be, she thought, as she drummed her fingers on the arm of the chair outside his office, too nervous to wait at her own desk.

She wasn't sure when she'd first become suspicious. Bennett had arranged the sale of Lowes Corner for thirty-five million dollars, making Perdita Lowes perfectly happy. After all, while the store had had prestige at one time, its reputation had declined. Combined with the fact that its location had become less fashionable in the past ten years, it could have sold for considerably less. Page had guessed the business would go for twenty-five million dollars, while Lee had placed the number at thirty. True to their bet, Page had taken Lee's entire family to dinner. With five boisterous children in tow, and Lee and Sally in a loud, celebratory mood, Page wasn't sure that La Grenouille would ever treat her quite the same way again.

That night, Page had invited Bennett and Perdita to join them, and, although she suspected her father's acceptance came more from Perdita's prodding than from actual enthusiasm, she was pleased to have him there, and greeted him as the man of the hour. When Lee proposed a toast to his success, Page joined in heartily. Over the meal, Perdita announced that she would be leaving for California the following week, graciously thanking them for helping her to start a new life with no financial worries. Page's only disappointment on that occasion was the lack of romance between her father and Perdita, having secretly harbored the hope that they might be in love with each other, not just friends involved in a business deal. But that night, Page gave up on her fantasy and enjoyed the moment for the financial triumph it was.

Just three months later, the situation looked quite different. Abbott Brothers, the outfit that had purchased Lowes Corner through Bennett, had resold the store to one of New York's major real-estate moguls at an astounding profit. Ninety days after Abbott paid thirty-five million to Perdita, Roland Realty paid eighty million to Abbott. The sale was featured on the front pages of the *Times* and the *Wall Street Journal*, a fascinating but by no means unique story in the annals of New York City empire-building.

It seemed that for the past year, Roland had quietly been buying every square foot of the block that Lowes Corner occupied. When they found themselves with all the buildings but that one, it made the land under the store skyrocket in value. Page had been surprised by her father's reaction to the second sale; she would have expected him to be upset. After all, Bennett was a perfectionist in business, a man who drove himself as hard as he drove others. She thought he'd focus on the additional forty-five million dollars he hadn't made for Perdita, rather than the thirty-five million he had, and the enormous difference in Carlisle and Poole's commission. But when she saw him at the office the day the story broke, he never even brought the subject up. When she referred to it, his only comment was a cheerful "How nice for the Abbott brothers."

Page found this so unlike her father, she mentioned it to Lee. It was on seeing his reaction that she really began to worry. There was no smile behind Lee's horn-rimmed glasses as he closed the door to his office before replying. His words were indirect but his message was clear. She should stop asking questions. What was it he knew, she'd asked him, refusing to let him off the hook. His response was serious and emphatic. He *knew* only two things: her father was his employer and he had a wife and five children to feed.

Instead of being put off by those words, Page had decided to pursue the matter. If Lee's instincts were enough to make him so frightened, there must be a real story behind this, and she was determined to find out what it was. Her first step was to consider collusion between Roland Realty and her father, but a few questions to Bennett's secretary made that possibility seem unlikely. According to Jane, they were sworn enemies, having gone to battle over a deal ten years before. Bennett's private comments about Kenneth Roland had been numerous and caustic, as had Roland's public comments been about him.

It took a week for Page to decide what to do next. She began to examine Abbott Brothers, the company that made the windfall, flying to Albany to do research at the Department of State. There she found something unexpected. Abbott was not an old family-owned merchandising outfit from Kansas City, as Bennett had causally mentioned when they'd made their bid for Lowes Corner. In fact, studying the incorporation agreement, she found out that not one of the officers was even named Abbott. Abbott Brothers was actually a holding company, a wholly owned subsidiary of the Park Corporation of Wilmington, Delaware.

One phone call to Delaware later, Page had her answer. That state also required companies to file incorporation agreements. According to the company's documentation, the president of the Park Corporation was Edith Michaels. Page knew exactly who that was; it couldn't possibly be a coincidence. During her months at Carlisle and Poole, she'd had several occasions to talk to Dick Payson, Bennett's lawyer. His secretary was remarkably businesslike whenever she answered the phone. "Edith Michaels," she would pronounce crisply. "Who may I say is calling?"

Now, Page watched her father's secretary

patiently typing a stack of letters. She wondered if Jane Fellows's name appeared on any interlocking directorates. Jane seemed so honest, but, then again, so did Edith Michaels. Had Page believed her father to be a completely honest man? She admitted the truth to herself silently: if she had, she would never have begun her search.

Page almost wished she hadn't done her work so well. It was easier to act the way Lee did, play it safe, keep the questions to yourself. After all, what would she do now, inform the authorities? No, she could never send her father to jail. But at the very least, she had to confront him. She glanced at her watch. Three-thirty. She decided to go back to her office and begin cleaning out her drawers. She doubted there was anything Bennett could say that would persuade her to continue working for him, and she wanted to be out that very night.

It was already four o'clock when Jane buzzed Page to say Bennett had returned and was ready to see her. She caught a quick glimpse of herself as she passed a mirror in the corridor on the way to his office, surprised to see how composed she looked. Pondering this, she realized it wasn't so surprising after all. She was no longer a person easily reduced to hysterical tears. Not by her sister, not by her mother, and, most assuredly, not by Bennett.

Her father didn't even pretend to smile as she entered his huge office. He'd been annoyed by her peremptory demand for a meeting, and saw no reason to hide it.

"What is it, Page? I'm extremely busy today."

She refused to let him rattle her. Taking her time, she said simply, "Abbott Brothers is a front for the Park Corporation. The Park Corporation is a front for you. You have just made forty-five million dollars. Congratulations."

"What are you talking about?" Bennett's face was white with rage, but he was trying to sound calm.

"It's absolutely illegal, but that's not the worst part." Page walked around her father's desk and stood directly in front of him, forcing him to meet her eyes. "The really terrible thing is that you did it to Perdita, a friend who adores you."

Bennett chose not to respond.

Page decided to pursue her curiosity about the one angle of the plan she hadn't figured out. "Tell me something. How did you know about Roland's plan to build on that block?"

Bennett ignored the question and asked one of his own. "What are you intending to do with this information?"

"I guess you'll just have to wait and find out," was Page's response as she turned around and walked out of the room.

Bennett didn't even see the light on his phone indicating that Jane wanted him to pick up. Would Page make this public? Or even tell Perdita? He thought about it for a few moments. Never, he decided. She was too nice for her own good. He was glad he hadn't answered her question. He thought with pleasure of the moment when Leo Erwin, the poor man's real-estate broker, had tried to drum up capital for a half-baked development project by bragging to him of his recent sales to Roland. That idiot sold two adjoining buildings next to Lowes Corner under a pledge of secrecy, yet he was too stupid to realize that Ken Roland, the real-estate czar of New York, would be acquiring the whole block. Once Bennett had started watching the properties, he saw it immediately.

So his little daughter had turned out to be a crackerjack investigator. It wouldn't make any difference. He knew Page. She would keep it to herself. Maybe her brains would enable her to make a living as a private detective. The thought made him chuckle.

Entering the dark living room, Page flicked on the light switch and settled herself in on Chris's couch. Building a business certainly hadn't left him any time for interior decorating, she thought, looking around the almost empty loft. It was nearly midnight but sleep eluded her. She picked up a copy of *The New Yorker*. Perhaps the cartoons would entertain her for a few minutes, she thought, idly turning the pages. Her attention span wasn't even the length of a caption, she chided herself, smoothing her white cotton nightgown over her knees. She threw down the magazine in disgust and settled for staring into space, her activity of choice since arriving at Chris's two days before.

Page had come to Chris's directly after packing up her things and vacating both her office at Carlisle and Poole, and her bedroom at Bennett's apartment. Chris had listened intently as she told him the whole story, including her brief, sad conversation with Lee before she'd walked out the door, both knowing their friendship was over. Chris had been wonderful, even sympathizing with her intention not to make Bennett's activities public. Then, clearly wishing he could wait for a more appropriate moment, Chris had told her about his meeting with Simon the night before. Overwhelmed by her afternoon with Bennett, Page found she could barely take it in. She understood more now, but she didn't see how she could get over the fact that he was so quick to believe that she would do that to him, and that he hadn't even attempted to talk to her about it.

Chris tried his best. "One thing at a time. At least Bennett's out of your life. This is home for as long as you want. Stay forever."

His words were heartfelt, but there was no way she would inflict herself on him any longer than necessary. He'd insisted on staying with her the night she got there, but once she convinced him she was basically all right, he moved a week's worth of clothing into Joanna's apartment. He knew Page well enough to understand that she needed a couple of days alone. Page was grateful to him, but now she was just about ready to start looking for her own apartment. And a job, she said to herself firmly. She wondered how long it would take to find one. No more spoiled little princess with a job in Mommy's business or Daddy's business ready for her at a moment's notice. Chris wanted her to come into Stagecoach with him. She'd helped him build it, and he claimed she could make a place for herself there. At one moment, she thought it was a good idea; the next, it sounded like a terrible mistake.

She was startled out of her reverie by the sound of trash cans being knocked over in the alley behind Chris's building. "Oh, stop obsessing about everything." Page giggled as she realized she'd said the words out loud. It made her feel better. Her thoughts took a more optimistic turn. There were plenty of jobs she could do and places she could live.

Almost twelve-thirty, and she wasn't the least bit tired. At least she could earn her keep while she was there, she thought, getting up and going to the broom closet. Judging by the dust that was raised every time she lifted something, she was sure the apartment hadn't been cleaned in at least a month. She lifted the cumbersome vacuum cleaner out of the closet, vowing to cover every inch of the loft.

She was thinking of how good it felt to get something done when the ring of the phone cut through the machine's noise. Turning off the motor, she reached for the receiver.

"Hello," she said, slightly out of breath but cheerful.

"Hello…Joanna? Is that you? It's Simon. Is Chris around?"

Simon. Page was dumbstruck. Feeling the confidence drain out of her body, she managed to keep her voice cold and clear.

"No. This is not Joanna, and Chris is not at home."

"Page, oh God, Page, is that you?"

His eagerness was all that Page had wished to hear so many months before. Now, she steeled herself to the sound of his voice, cutting off even the possibility of a conversation. "You can reach Chris at Joanna's apartment or tomorrow at Stagecoach," she said crisply, and put down the phone before Simon had a chance to speak.

The telephone rang again almost before she had taken a breath, but she made no move to answer it. Nor did she stir when it rang again five minutes later. But this time, when the ringing finally stopped, she took the receiver off the hook. Slowly, she walked over to the small, uncomfortable couch and sat down, bruised by emotions more intense, more painful than any she'd had since leaving England. She remained there, unmoving, unaware of the minutes passing. Deep in her pain, she never even heard Chris's key in the lock, didn't know he was in the room until he stood in front of her.

"Page, what the hell happened? I've been trying to call you for an hour."

She looked up and saw his worried expression, the perspiration on his face indicating how he must have rushed to make sure she was all right.

Chris pulled up a chair facing her. "What is it? You were fine when I spoke to you this morning."

"Simon called."

"Oh, I see. What did he say?"

"He didn't say anything. He was looking for you." Page realized her words left a lot out. "Well, he tried to say something, but I...I just didn't want to talk to him."

Chris couldn't keep the excitement out of his voice. "Why shouldn't you talk to him? You love him."

"Chris, please stop bullying me." There was an edge of desperation in her tone. "I can't afford to be thrown back into that. You know, since he called, I've just been sitting here like a child. Damn it, I'm not a child anymore. I don't want someone to have that power over me."

Chris spoke as gently as he could. "Page, when you're in love, that comes with the territory. You just have to trust him and go with it. If you never let your guard down, you might as well be dead."

"I can't let anyone hurt me like that again." The tears Page was holding back could be heard in her voice.

Chris was unyielding. "If you refuse to speak to him, someone *will* be hurting you again. And I don't mean Simon. I mean Liza. Do you really intend to let her get away with that?"

Page thought about what Chris was saying.

She was almost ready to consider his point of view, but the sound of the doorbell frightened her composure away.

"Don't answer it, Chris. It might be him," she pleaded.

"Sorry, Page, but I'm a better friend than that." Chris took a long look at her and got up. "Who's there?" he called out loudly enough to be heard in the corridor.

Simon's voice came back immediately. "It's me."

Chris made his way to the front door and opened it. "Hi, I'm just leaving," he said with a trace of a smile and walked straight out of the apartment.

Too unnerved to remain seated, Page had risen at the sound of Simon's voice. As he came inside, he saw her right away, a beautiful statue, frozen in space. Silently, they stared at each other, an invisible line of attraction pulling them like a magnet.

Simon went to her. He raised his hand and traced first her face, then her shoulders, her breasts, her hips, as if he needed to reclaim every part of her. Page's fears were swept aside as she gave in to the deep longing unleashed by his caress. He kissed her fiercely, finally pulling her down to the floor, and urgently pushing their clothing aside. When he entered her, they both cried out, each caught in a hunger that had to be fed immediately.

He penetrated deeply over and over again, as Page raised herself to meet his passion with her own. Their coupling was a short, hard storm, and when it abated, she saw her raw emotion reflected in the intensity of his blue eyes.

Gasping for breath, Simon rolled her on top of him and ran his hands gently up and down the length of her back. He held her head away from him, drinking in her face; then, slowly, he brought her close, cradling her in his arms as if he would never let go.

When he awoke the next morning, he was still holding her. Sometime in the night, they had moved to the bed, to make love again slowly, achingly aware of how much they meant to each other. Not once had he lost contact with her skin. Nor could he keep from touching her now, although he didn't really want to wake her. He ran his fingers down her neck, over the top of her breasts. As he explored her body, she opened her eyes slowly, watching him as if he were a part of a dream. His hand went lower, over her firm stomach, lower still, until he began to stroke her inside, rhythmically, deeper and deeper until her breath grew shallow and she moaned with pleasure. His hands remembered everything, bringing her to wave after wave of ecstacy.

At the height of her passion, an image fought its way into Page's mind. She saw Simon as he was right now, but with him was Liza. Abruptly, she pulled back.

"Page, what's the matter? Did I hurt you?" Simon was stunned by her movement.

"I don't know," she answered, crashing

back to reality, suddenly needing to know. "Liza lied about me and Chris. But how about you? Did she lie about you, too?"

"Page, I always loved you. I was just so hurt." He couldn't be less than truthful, but he was desperate to make her understand. "I'm sorry I was such a fool," he said, reaching for her once again.

Page drew away completely. "How could you have believed her? You knew what she was like. You knew how much I loved you."

"But when I heard your message machine..." he faltered. " 'When Chris and I get home...' You sounded so happy."

"What message machine?" Page's brow furrowed.

"Liza called Chris's apartment in London. I heard it myself. It was your voice."

"I never left any message like that. And I never lived with Chris. It may have been somebody's voice, but it wasn't mine."

"Oh, Christ. *Liza,*" he said in disgust.

"How could you have fallen for all that?"

Simon said nothing. Then he spoke again, urgently. "You don't understand how cut off I felt in California. I *wanted* you to come with me, and you refused. How was I to know Liza was lying?"

Page was furious. She sat up on the bed and pulled a shirt on. "Am I supposed to worry about your fidelity every time we're apart? Does going away imply you can cheat on me any time you want, and classify it under insecurity?"

Now Simon was angry as well. "Listen,

Page, I was stupid, but you could at least try to hear my side. I had no idea Liza was lying. Be fair. You hardly ever talked about your sister. I didn't know what she was really like. If Chris had come to you and told you I'd been sleeping with someone, wouldn't you believe it? Jesus, Liza told you that she and I were involved, and *you* swallowed it whole."

"But that was the truth, wasn't it?" Page snapped.

"At the time, yes. But what's important is that you believed her. Why wouldn't I have believed what she said about you?"

Page waited a long time before she answered. When she spoke, her voice was still tight with controlled rage. "I don't know, Simon. Maybe you're right. Maybe Liza was convincing and maybe you were lonely," she said. "But I just can't do this. It hurts too much. Please leave. Now."

"Page, you can't mean that?"

His voice was anguished, but she wouldn't be swayed. "I'm going into the kitchen. When I come out, I don't want to find you here." She turned and left the room.

By the time Simon was dressed, his shock had turned to anger. Walking out of the apartment, he slammed the front door hard.

Chapter Twenty-five

The October afternoon had been cold and windy, with threatening skies, the weather London was famous for. Only five minutes before, the storm had finally broken. Rain pelted the townhouse's windows as Claire lay on her bed, staring at the piece of paper in her hand. Yesterday, she had instructed her secretary to track down the telephone number written upon it, but now she couldn't seem to bring herself to make the call. It hadn't been difficult to locate Page at Chris's New York apartment; she'd left his address and telephone number with Bennett's housekeeper when she moved out. Claire could only speculate what must have transpired between her daughter and Bennett. First, there had been that honeymoon period during which Page had been so enamored of him. Now, this abrupt departure from his home and company, apparently in anger. What had he done to Page?

Page was a grown woman and was well able to take care of herself. Claire sighed, hoping this was really true, that Page was prepared for the realities of life outside the insulated world of Warren International. Maybe I shielded her too completely from the pain of my mistakes, Claire thought. It was a worry she had nursed over the years. Page was so fragile, such an innocent. Claire caught herself up sharply. But what about the treachery of leaking the family's private history to that smarmy reporter? And the incident with that American hotel chain? All of it inevitably led back to Page's animosity toward her sister.

A draft swept through the bedroom, and Claire reached for a woolen fringed throw that lay at the foot of her bed, wrapping it around her shoulders. It was unusual for her to be home in the afternoon, but after a morning of wall-to-wall meetings, she found she was exhausted. Leaving the office at three-thirty wasn't really a criminal offense, she'd told herself. Her company could undoubtedly survive if she took a few hours off. In fact, she *was* tired, but she also wanted to be home, alone, to make this call.

She didn't know quite what she was going to say, wasn't even sure how she felt about things. Admittedly, in the first weeks after Page had left London, it was actually a relief to be freed from worrying about what problem her younger daughter was going to come up with next. Perhaps it was wrong for any mother to admit to a feeling like that, Claire thought with a frown, but she couldn't pretend otherwise. Page had betrayed her, could have cost her the company, had tried to come between Claire and Liza at every turn, despite knowing full well how much it meant to Claire to have Liza finally in England.

However, once Claire's initial fury at Page had worn off, these past months without her had been awful. She missed Page terribly, was at a loss both at home and in the office without having her to talk with. Thank God

Liza had been there. But being estranged this way from Page was an unbearable situation; there had never been anything other than minor disagreements between them over the years.

No one knew better than Claire how proud she was, how much difficulty she had apologizing or asking for help. But she would just have to overcome that; it was time for her to make an attempt to set things right with her child. Resolutely, she sat up and dialed the telephone. She was surprised to find how nervous she felt, her heart pounding as she listened to the static of the overseas call going through. It was ringing. Two, three, four times.

"Hi, this is Christopher. You can leave a message for me or Page after the beep. We'll get right back to you."

Claire hadn't anticipated an answering machine, though, of course, it made perfect sense. It was about eleven o'clock in New York, and Page was probably out for the day. Should she hang up? She cleared her throat.

"Page, it's Mother. I don't know if you want to talk to me, but I'm here when you're ready. I'll be waiting for your call."

Claire hung up. She had made the first move. If Page didn't respond, at least Claire knew she had done what she could. Maybe now she could stop lying awake at night, tossing and turning as she worried about her younger daughter. It was all becoming too much. Claire closed her eyes and dozed, comforted by the steady beat of the rain.

In New York, Page stood in Chris's apartment, dripping, wrapped in a towel, staring at the telephone. She had heard it ringing while she was in the shower and debated getting out to answer it. The answering machine clicked on just as she grabbed a towel and hurried into the living room, tracking water behind her. About to pick up the receiver, she froze at the sound of her mother's voice.

How like her, thought Page. Not "I'm sorry, I love you, let's make up." No, just a message stating that the queen would be receiving when her subject requested an audience. Well, she was free to wait for Page to call. It wasn't going to happen. Why did Claire have to be so distant, so formal? It was as if she had given all her warmth and passion to John Warren long ago and had none left for her children. No, make that for *one* of her children, Page thought bitterly. Her mother didn't seem to have any problems showering Liza with affection. Even before Liza had come into the picture, Page had had to make every extra effort to get her mother to show any real approval beyond a few meager words of praise. With Liza around, it was just that much worse. But why go over all that again? It was time Page got on with her own life, and stopped waiting for Claire to become the mother she would never be.

The answering machine's light rapidly

blinked on and off, signaling that there was a message. Reaching out, Page turned the machine off altogether, and went back to finish her shower.

It was nearly ten a.m. several days later when Liza knocked on Claire's office door and opened it slightly.

"Are you ready, Mother? It's time."

"Come in, sweetheart. How lovely you look. What a beautiful suit," Claire said, admiring her daughter in the black skirt and jacket with black satin lapels. "Ready for the meeting?"

"All set. I was up late last night going over my notes again," Liza answered.

"You're incredible. You know, I have great admiration for how hard you work. I was the same way—couldn't get enough of the business." For a moment, Claire looked far away. Then she gathered up her papers. "Shall we go?"

The two women walked down the hall together. Every month, the top Warren management met to examine the company's standing, discussing everything from profit and loss statements to the guests' comments and criticisms. These meetings were crucial to the ongoing success of Warren International.

For the first several months, Liza had been permitted only to sit in and listen. Then, little by little, she had handled smaller projects, bringing up various proposals or sharing her research findings on suggestions that had come up in prior discussions. Today was the first time she would be solely responsible for running the meeting from start to finish. Claire would, of course, be present, but she wanted Liza to have the experience of chairing the meeting.

Seated around a long oak table were the men and women who, along with Claire and Liza, made up Warren's top management team. They were talking quietly as they partook of the fruit, scones, tea, and coffee that had been set out. The men stood as Claire and Liza entered. Claire moved around the room, shaking hands and exchanging friendly greetings, until she came to her seat—typically at the head of the table, but today, one chair over to the right of that position. Liza sat in the spot usually occupied by her mother.

There was Joseph Wiggins, the general manager, and Noel Kent, Warren's chief operating officer, both of whom were close friends of Claire's, as they had been of John's in the past. Arthur Stevenson was the chief financial officer. Dorothy Bourke had been in charge of the London Warren, the company's flagship hotel, for the past fourteen years, and as a major stockholder in the firm, she, too, was always included in the meetings. The only one missing, Claire thought as she surveyed the faces in the room, was Page. But Claire didn't expect anyone to mention it. After her curt dismissal of several initial inquiries about Page, no further questions were raised. Everyone knew better than to press the president and CEO on what was obviously a sore point.

The five other people in the room looked at Liza with varying degrees of expectancy and skepticism. She sipped from a glass of water and began.

"This has been an outstanding year for Warren International. We've been averaging an occupancy rate between eighty and eight-one percent in our hotels, eighty-eight percent in the Manors. It's hard to ask for anything more. But we're going to ask for more, of course. We always ask for more. That's the only way we'll stay on top of the business. I have some suggestions that I believe you'll find of interest, ideas targeted to increasing our primary customers, the business traveler and the frequent leisure traveler. But first, let's take a look at the past month."

Liza was confident and at ease as she guided the meeting, reviewing gross operating profit and analyzing their cash-flow position. Next came the guests' comments. In each Warren hotel, guests were provided with cards soliciting their opinions on such topics as the cleanliness of the room and the speed with which they could check in or out. Liza read these cards aloud, mediating a discussion of the praise and criticism the hotels had received in the last few weeks.

It was nearly eleven-thirty before Liza turned the meeting to the area of project capital expenditures. "I have some other thoughts now," she began, picking up a sheaf of papers. "Number one, we should spend the money to remodel the entire kitchen in the Zurich Warren. Number two, we should think about a few new computer software programs that could be extremely helpful for our reservations system; I've done some research on this and I'll give you all the facts. Number three, it seems to me it's time we instituted limousine service to and from the Warrens located within a reasonable distance from an airport. Why don't we talk about that right now? We're hardly the first to come up with the idea, and it's a fairly sizable investment, but I believe it to be absolutely necessary. Let me tell you why."

As she reviewed the statistics she had prepared the previous week, Liza was surprised to realize how much she was enjoying herself. It occurred to her that, without even noticing, she had acquired a sense of purpose, even beyond that of getting even with Claire and Page. She had learned the hotel business, really understood it now, and damned if it didn't turn out she was good at it. Getting up in the mornings, she was eager to get to the office, glad to tackle the challenges of her daily responsibilities.

Liza turned her gaze to her mother. Claire was businesslike and professional as always, jotting down notes quietly. But when she looked at Liza directly, she couldn't hide her expression of utter pride in her daughter. There was so much love in Claire's eyes that it was impossible not to see it. For a brief moment, Liza faltered in her speech. Through everything, through all the lies and deceptions of the past year, Claire still refused to believe that Liza could do anything to harm her. She trusted Liza and loved her as no one else ever had. That was the simple and pure truth.

Shaken, Liza quickly finished up and brought the meeting to an end. Claire stayed to talk informally with the rest of the team as they all helped themselves to some more coffee. But Liza, claiming an appointment, hurried out of the room.

Chapter Twenty-six

"Page, Larry from the Stanley Hotel is on line two." Her secretary's voice rang out across the busy office.

"I'm talking to Nora Tate in Milan. See if you can find out whether the answer is yes or no while I still have her on the phone," Page whispered loudly, holding her hand over the receiver so Nora wouldn't overhear her remarks to Marilyn.

A moment later, Marilyn's voice was jubilant as she bellowed the good news. "It's a go!"

"What's a go?" It was Nora Tate's question to Page.

Page chuckled. "I knew Marilyn's voice was loud enough to be heard over the Atlantic Ocean."

"Very funny, but was that about me?" Nora was not a woman to let her questions go unanswered.

"Yes, Nora," Page answered patiently. The opera singer was one of Page's favorite clients, but as she constantly had to remind herself, a diva was a diva. "Your hotel is set. You'll be at the Stanley."

"At whose expense?" Nora wanted to know.

Page didn't bother to hide the satisfaction in her voice. "Theirs, of course."

"My dear, you're a genius." Nora's genuine admiration was quickly replaced by another worry. "And someone will be waiting for me at Kennedy, right?"

"Just as they always are," Page responded soothingly.

"It'll be one of the big limos, right?"

"With a bar, with a handsome driver, with dark, dark windows you can hide behind or look out of, depending on your mood."

"Sweetie..." Nora's voice had taken on a childish, whining tone. "Would you mind reading me the *Opera News* article again? There was so much static on the line, I missed some of it before."

Page kept her temper in check as she looked at her watch and realized that another ten minutes would completely blow her chance for lunch with Joanna. She had absolutely sworn not to cancel this time, no matter what came up. "Nora, I'll put Marilyn on the line. She'll be happy to do it. I'm afraid I have to run out for a few minutes."

"Oh, okay." Nora's lack of enthusiasm was apparent, but Page took her acceptance at face value. Nora would get over it.

Page had been surprised at the demanding attitudes of Stagecoach's clients when she'd first come into the business. But she soon realized that those demands were a direct reflection of the terrible anxiety the performers who made up the bulk of her client list felt every moment of their lives. She forced herself to remember this as she continued her conversation with Nora.

"We'll set up some of the interviews at the Stanley, so their hotel will be mentioned in the papers. Do try and say something nice about them on television, so they continue to foot the bill, okay?" Page knew how impossible it was to get Nora to do anything she didn't want to, but she hoped the message had gotten through.

She thought about this as she walked to Joe Allen's to meet Joanna. Nora was a shrewd woman, who carefully watched every dime, and knew what good manners were, even if she didn't always choose to use them. Unlike some of Page's other famous clients, she might even deign to thank Marilyn for wasting ten valuable minutes reading to her over the phone.

"They're all babies," Chris had warned Page when she'd joined him in the business.

"Put yourself in their places," Page had replied perceptively. "Imagine you were given everything you ever asked for, and many things you didn't ask for, all the time, by everyone. What do you think you'd be like after a few years? I'd certainly be a beast."

"Instead of the greatest beast-handler of all time," Chris had responded appreciatively.

The whole thing had been quite an experience, Page thought. Even before she started working there officially, Page had helped Chris to find a number of corporate accounts. They made an excellent complement to his celebrity clientele. But she hadn't really intended to work with Chris permanently. She'd planned to finally do something on her own.

Her fight with Simon put an end to that plan. The day after their brief reunion, Chris had found her in tears back at the loft. He insisted she help out at Stagecoach for a few days. With *Birds of Passage* due to open in only three weeks, Simon's picture would soon be plastered all over the city. Chris knew Page had to stay busy, be among people, not hide out and dwell on her unhappiness. That was how it began, but her position at the limousine company changed rapidly as Page immersed herself in the work. Almost by accident, she found herself expanding the scope of the business. It started when one of Chris's most famous actor clients called to say he was coming in from California and mentioned in passing that he needed a place to stay. With time on her hands, Page offered to make a reservation for him at the Paragon on Fifth Avenue in the Sixties.

On the phone with the night manager, who happened to take the call, Page had a sudden thought. From her years of working in the hotel business, she knew how much a hotel could benefit from a famous resident. Spontaneously, she made a suggestion to the man on the other end of the line: if *her* movie star referred to *his* hotel in television interviews, might they lower his room rate?

The hotel manager was more enthusiastic than that. Free publicity was priceless. Get him to talk about us, he said, and we'll put him up free for a week.

Chris's client was impressed when she passed this information along. It turned out the hotel was impressed as well, as she found out the next morning when the owner of the Paragon called. Did she have any other celebrities on tap, any other ideas for tie-ins that would bring the Paragon to the public's attention as the chic place to stay in New York? She thought about all the famous actors who routinely used Chris's services, the downtown design types with whom Joanna was in contact, the rich and well-known business people she herself had come to know while working with her father. How about a party? she said. If they supplied the room and the food, she might be able to come up with a fairly good group of people. Would that do the hotel any good?

The huge party at the Paragon one month later made a bigger splash than even Page had anticipated, with the glittering mix of artists, actors, designers, and businessmen making the pages not just of the *Times* and the *Daily News*, but *People* magazine and *Entertainment Weekly*. The hotel asked her to consider taking over their entire public-relations operation. Page was frank about her inexperience, but they were willing to risk it, limiting payment to actual mentions in the media.

Soon, other celebrities and other hotels began calling her. She discovered with pleasure that everything she'd learned from Warren International and Carlisle and Poole could come together. Within a few months, her innate skill at handling difficult people, and Chris's list of actors and musicians, by now quite extensive, had enabled her to expand Stagecoach into a full-scale public relations concern.

Chris oversaw the travel section, while Page took care of the publicity and business functions. By mid-winter, they had built a client list that included actors from England and America, opera singers, hotels, and travel agencies, plus a number of corporate accounts.

Page was adept at combining her instincts with common sense. Before Nora Tate had called her, Page had never handled a singer, but the problem the soprano presented them with was one Page knew she could solve. Although Nora was coddled and applauded at home in England, her performances at the Metropolitan Opera went largely unnoticed by American audiences. Armed with enthusiastic reviews from overseas, Page arranged for a whirlwind publicity cycle to coincide with Nora's next trip to the States. By night, she was Violetta; by day, she was meeting with magazine writers, appearing on local television talk shows and classical radio stations, having lunch with the Opera Guild, signing CDs at music stores, visiting students at the High School for Performing Arts. Not only did it all make news, but her bows after each performance were now accompanied by the untamed cheers of fans who transformed singers into stars.

Public relations was a business that appeared infinitely more glamorous than it really was, Page discovered. For every successful event, hundreds of calls had to be made, setting up, double-checking, confirming. Page now had four people on her staff, yet the work never stopped. But, despite occasional complaint sessions with Chris when they would find themselves still working at midnight, Page knew she was relieved to have the endless details take up her time and her mind.

The thoughts from which her hard work protected her would come, unbidden, at three or four in the morning. Out of a deep sleep, she would suddenly awaken, realizing she'd been dreaming of Simon holding her, making love to her. Being confided in by clients, as she often was, made it no easier; these creative artists spoke intimately of their insecurity, their profound loneliness echoing so many of Simon's words in the past. Deep in the night, images of him appeared. In her mind, he would be alone in California, vulnerable to Liza's lies, which, as Page well knew, played to his deepest fear.

During the days, Page refused to think about her problems. Her life consisted of business and snatches of time with Chris and Joanna. There's nothing wrong with that, she said to herself as she walked down the steps leading to the restaurant.

Joe Allen's on Forty-sixth Street was a popular hangout for actors performing on Broadway and at the string of off-Broadway theaters all the way west. Joanna was already waiting at an isolated table way in the back, which Page decided must mean she had something to talk about. She *was* particularly insistent about this lunch, Page recalled as she created a path through the crowded tables.

Joanna rose to greet her friend with a kiss on the cheek, revealing blue jeans beneath a bulky green sweater. One large earring, a feathered peacock formed in multicolored tin, accented the dozens of silver bracelets she wore on both wrists.

"This better be a design day. Somehow, I can't imagine that outfit playing in Scarsdale or Darien," Page remarked as she scrutinized the ensemble.

"I should send *you* out on those trips," Joanna tossed back, eyeing Page's conservative gray wool dress critically. They enjoyed teasing each other, but not so secretly, Page admired Joanna's originality, while Joanna always thought Page looked gorgeous, as if she'd just stepped out of *WWD*. People often looked at them curiously, wondering what the expensive-looking uptown type was doing with the spiky SoHo cherub. Page and Joanna had no cause to wonder; their friendship had deepened to the point where Chris no longer had to act as the bond between them.

"So what's up?" Page's tone was anything but casual.

Joanna's response was ingenuous. "Who says anything's up?"

"I do, and I know I'm right," Page replied.

"You're not *always* right, you know." Joanna couldn't help smiling as she continued. "You happen to be this time, but not always."

"So?" Page probed. "Are you going to tell me or would you like me to take three guesses?"

"One guess."

"You're getting married!"

The shrieks that came from both women caused a moment of silence in the room, as many of the other patrons craned their necks to see what the commotion was about. Joanna waited until the natural hum of conversation picked up around them before going into the details. She and Chris had decided the day before, and were intending to waste no time.

"We're both so busy, we just want to do it right away," Joanna explained.

"That's not very romantic," Page commented.

Joanna laughed. "If you think *that's* not romantic, wait until you hear *where* the ceremony's taking place."

"I can't even imagine. Obviously if I said a church, it would be too simple."

"Not my style. We're being married by a friend of my mother's who's a judge."

Page nodded. "So it's to be City Hall."

Joanna shook her head. "No...not exactly. Actually, it'll be in the Criminal Courts Building, Friday at noon."

"In a holding cell, perhaps?" Page suggested sarcastically.

"In Judge Wallace's perfectly respectable office on the seventh floor. As my maid of honor, you are expected at eleven forty-five."

"Oh, Jo, I'd be delighted. Who else is coming? I assume it's a small group."

"Definitely. Just the bride and groom, you, my brother, my parents, and Chris's best man..." Her smile evaporated as she went on. "Simon Roberts."

Page sat perfectly still. Simon, she thought, of course. Chris's best friend. "I'm sorry, Joanna. I just can't do it, I can't possibly come."

"No, that's not true." Joanna had rehearsed this part with Chris many times, so the words came easily. "You *can* if you want to, hard as it may be. And you're going to because *I* want you there. Listen, Page, Chris and I are your best friends. No matter how informally we may choose to be doing it, we are planning to marry only one time, and it's just as important to us as it is to the debutantes who plant their names in the paper. We want the people we love around us, and, I'm sorry, but that includes you and Simon. You don't have to say a word to each other, but you do have to show up."

Page sighed. "I'll try my best."

"Your best is likely to be very good, since I'm going to be sleeping over at your house Thursday night and going down to the judge's chambers with you Friday morning. Chris maintains certain superstitions, and our not seeing each other the night before the wedding happens to be one of them." Joanna's smile was rueful.

Page managed a slight smile in return. "What sentimentality from a man planning to get married in the Criminal Courts Building."

Friday morning started out clear and bright, as Page well knew, having stayed awake all night. She and Joanna went out for breakfast, and watched the sky turn cloudy as they sat in the window booth of the coffee shop near Page's Gramercy Park apartment.

"Looks like rain," Joanna said. "A perfect omen."

Page wondered if she'd heard wrong. "Excuse me?" she questioned.

Joanna grinned. "If Chris can go with his superstitions, I can go with mine. They just happen to be a little more creative."

"What, for example?" Page inquired.

"Like anything that begins too auspiciously can't possibly work out. Sun turning to rain— now that's perfect weather for a wedding."

Joanna looked radiant this morning, just as brides were meant to, and Page had no intention of dampening her friend's spirits. But she couldn't help voicing her thought. "Simon and I had an inauspicious beginning. There goes your theory."

"Not necessarily." Joanna spoke earnestly. "If I can wear a beige cashmere dress and pearl earrings at my one and only wedding ceremony, you can think about pulling certain of your decisions out of their cement blocks."

Betraying her lack of sleep, Page's answer sounded testy. "It wasn't *my* decision. It wasn't *my* anything."

Joanna was unfazed. "Exactly who was sitting in for you that night?"

"Hey, Jo, it's your wedding day. Let's not get into this. You obviously don't understand, and I'm not in the mood to explain it."

"You're wrong. I do understand. Far better than you do, by the way." Joanna looked hard at Page, as if trying to see into her mind. "Or maybe I don't. Maybe you're right. Maybe you never loved him very much to begin with."

Page knew exactly what her friend was up to, and she wasn't about to be goaded. "Come on. Let's get you home. The car will be there in an hour, and that bridal look of purity takes longer to achieve than you might think."

By the time the limousine pulled up in front of the Criminal Courts Building, rain was pouring down in sheets. Running inside together under a huge black umbrella provided by the Stagecoach driver, Page somehow got completely soaked, while Joanna stayed fresh, as if by magic. The bride-to-be simply shook her head, her short spikes of hair springing back to attention. Page looked down at her navy-blue woolen suit. The elegant velvet collar had been pulled askew by her coat and the long skirt had trailed into a small puddle, leaving the edge of her hem dripping onto her stockings. Her hair, carefully arranged in a sweeping chignon that morning, had been destroyed by the strong wind.

Joanna laughed out loud at the sight. "You used to be the most elegant woman I knew." She indicated the throng of rough-looking characters milling around the lobby, undoubtedly awaiting court appearances. "It must be nice to belong."

"I can see the headline now," Page threatened. "Bride Slain by Maid of Honor."

"Let me make it up to you," Joanna responded, reaching into her handbag. She pulled out a package of pantyhose she'd brought along and handed it to Page. "My mother's last words of advice yesterday were 'Take an extra pair.' At the time, I wasn't too touched, but it looks as if she had a point."

Page looked doubtfully at the difference in their height. "Do you really think they'll fit?"

"They certainly beat what you're currently wearing," Joanna said. "Come on, take these and make yourself beautiful. I'll go upstairs and find Chris and my family. Don't forget, the judge is on seven."

Page asked a policeman standing nearby where to find a restroom, and made her way to the back of the lobby following his instructions. The institutional ladies' room was empty, and Page was able to change her stockings and straighten out her clothing with little trouble. Her hair was another matter. There was no way to resurrect the fashionable look she'd achieved before, so she removed the hairpins completely, brushing the long, dark blond strands straight down her back. She added a touch of color to her lips, took a last glance in the mirror, and returned to the lobby.

Standing in front of the elevator bank, she heard several people approach behind her.

"You're Jonathan, right, from that movie?" a heavily accented voice was asking.

"Oh, I know that's you, I just know it," came its female accompaniment.

Page stiffened. It had to be Simon. She could imagine how rudely he was about to behave, accosted by strangers who had exactly the kind of New York accent he'd ridiculed so accurately when they first met. But when she heard him answer, his words were kind.

"Thank you so much. How nice to be recognized."

"You were great!" the man added magnanimously. "I'm Frank Stillman and this is my wife, Jean. We're here to testify. How about you?"

"I'm Simon Roberts. I'm here to watch my best friend get married."

Page was shocked. He spoke so warmly. Was this the same person who'd spent a lifetime hiding from people? How gracious he sounded, how happy for Chris. Had he changed that much? Their last meeting had been so brief, so charged, could she have missed what he had become in the storm of their passion?

The conversation went on politely behind her, as questions continued to whirl about in her head. After all, she thought, she wasn't the same. Could the frightened little girl she used to be have helped to create a company practically out of thin air?

No, she realized. I've grown up, and evidently so has Simon. We're new people, adults, who make new decisions every day. She turned around, realizing she was making the most important decision of her life.

"Hello, Simon," she said.

Completely startled, Simon stared at her, not moving for a moment. He answered quietly. "Hello, Page."

She held out her hand. "It's good to see you."

Simon looked deep into her eyes. Then, smiling, he took her hand and pressed it gently against the side of his face.

Chapter Twenty-seven

Lee Fielding tried one more time to find a comfortable position, smoothing the sheet, plumping his feather pillow to exactly the right height. He'd been having trouble sleeping for months, and tonight was no exception. Damn it, he thought, looking at the clock on the bedtable—4:00 A.M. He eased his body out of bed as quietly as he could so he wouldn't disturb his wife.

I must be crazy, he thought, closing the door and walking toward the living room where he planted himself in his chair, the one his children religiously maintained as "Daddy's." I have everything I ever wanted—shit, I have everything *anyone* ever wanted—and all I do is pace in the middle of the night.

Lee looked around the room, noting the pieces of his life represented there. Pictures of his children lined one wall, every one of them a knockout, he'd always believed. A wedding photo of him and Sally stood on top of the Steinway baby grand in the corner, the marriage if anything even happier now. The piano was the newest addition to the room, a material representation of the unexpected bonus he'd been given months before.

Observing it now reminded him of Page Warren. Of the work they'd done together on the Lowes project, and the bonus he'd received as a result. With that thought, his anxiety deepened. The day Page left Carlisle and

Poole, his troubles had begun. She'd gone without a word, without a good-bye. He couldn't understand it.

Let's get a little more honest here, he said to himself sarcastically. He knew exactly why Page had said nothing. He'd made it clear that if anything was wrong, if anything improper was going on at Carlisle and Poole, he didn't want to know about it, and she was friend enough to respect his wishes. And he was more than happy to go along.

He shifted uncomfortably in his chair. No, he thought. Not just to go along. To be handsomely rewarded for his silence. To be paid off, clear and simple.

Lee stood up, his discomfort at this acknowledgment forcing him to pace around the room. But no amount of walking, no amount of hiding was possible tonight. The whole scenario crowded his mind, erasing even the remotest possibility of sleep.

At first, he'd had no idea why Page had left Carlisle and Poole. Her exit was so quick, so complete, that her secretary didn't even know where to send her personal things, leaving a large box with Lee on the assumption surely he, at least, would hear from Page. But she hadn't called. He knew he could find her if he really tried. In fact, he was not at all surprised when a client told him about her partnership with Chris in Stagecoach a couple of months later. But their positions were clear. Whatever made Page leave would be dangerous for Lee to know. A man with five children in private school had no room for moral stands.

Ironic, he thought, still stalking around his living room. He'd known nothing then about Bennett's sale of Lowes Corner. No, he thought grimly, *sales*. The first one to the dummy corporation, the second for twice the price. Lee had never even considered that there might have been funny business going on. At the time, it seemed as if Bennett had done Perdita Lowes a great service. After all, the sale to Abbott Brothers went for a much higher price than Lee had thought it would.

As for the subsequent sale of the properly to Roland, well, real estate in New York was like that. Buildings became hot properties overnight, and that seemed to be that. Lee had honestly not given it a thought.

It was Bennett himself who changed that. From the moment Page left, he seemed to eye Lee warily, as if measuring him for something he might know. Lee figured he was imagining this at first. Bennett Carlisle was not in the habit of looking too deeply at his staff. Just as long as you did your job, did your job perfectly that is, Bennett couldn't have cared less what was going on in anyone else's head. But the strange glances continued. Then, out of nowhere, a raise. Then a promotion. Then a large office. And all the time watching Lee carefully. Watching me for what? Lee had wondered at the time, squashing any possible answer before he found something out he wouldn't want to know.

But Bennett broke his own cover. Lee had been checking into a real estate proposal in lower Manhattan and had used the sale of Lowes Corner as part of his research. Stopping by Lee's office one day, Bennett's eye had fallen on the Lowes file. His expression turned black for a moment, and he was obviously holding himself in check when he lightly touched the file with one hand, clasping his other hand hard on Lee's shoulder.

"Loyalty is rewarded at Carlisle and Poole," Bennett had said quietly. He released his grip almost immediately, adding in a more relaxed voice, "You are very important to me, Lee, and your work is excellent. Don't think I don't appreciate how much you do for me, how much you've always done."

Lee looked out his windows at the New York skyline, almost turning light now. God, how he wished Bennett had never said anything. The moment the words were out, Lee knew what must have been on Bennett's mind all those months. There had to have been something wrong with the Lowes transaction, that big sale just months after Perdita had made her money. The idea made him sick.

More than sick, he thought. A collaborator in fraud. Lee could no longer hide behind his ignorance. When he got back to his office that afternoon, he'd opened the carton Page's secretary had left. And there it all was. Abbott, the Park Corporation, the names, the numbers. Page had done her homework very thoroughly. Despite his unease, he was proud of his former protégée.

I taught her well, he reflected, finally sitting back down on the chair, the room almost fully light now. Lost in his reverie, he jumped at the sound of a door closing as Sally entered the room, worry etched in her face.

"Lee, honey. What in the world is going on? You've barely been in bed all night." Sally's voice wavered, so unlike her usual confident tone.

"It's nothing, baby. I just have a lot on my plate today, and I wanted a couple of hours to clear some stuff up."

Suddenly tears began to spill down Sally's face, and her voice broke completely. "It's not just today, and you know it. It's months now." She knelt on the carpet in front of him, her agonized eyes boring into his. "You're having an affair. Just be honest about it. I can't bear this anymore. I'd rather just know, please, just tell me…" Sobbing, she couldn't continue to speak.

Lee was stunned. "Affair? Me?" He took her face in his hands. "Honey, I'm the happiest man who ever lived. You mean everything to me. You always have. Don't you know that?"

"You haven't been happy in ages! You brood around the house, you don't sleep. If it's not another woman, what is it? I know we don't have money problems since I pay the bills."

He took in her tear-stained face, her slender

hands still trembling in his. Of course he had to tell her. She was his wife. His other self, he'd always thought. And slowly he poured out the whole story.

Sally was silent as he went through the days from Page's departure to the opening of the carton. But Lee could see the rage building in her eyes as he described Bennett's financial scheme, his extraordinary secret profits.

"What are you going to do about it?" she asked when he was finished.

"I don't know," he answered as honestly as he could. "Up to now, all I could think about was you and the kids, the mortgage, the schools..-

. the *safety*."

He looked at Sally. She was back to herself again, strong, positive, supportive, most of all clear. He saw the answer in her eyes. "I guess we both know what I'm going to do," he said, smiling for the first time at the pure relief flooding his veins.

Lee reached for the phone on the coffee table and dialed a long-distance number. Forcefully now, he spoke into the receiver. "In Washington, please, I'd like the number for the Securities and Exchange Commission."

Chapter Twenty-eight

The late morning sunlight filtered into the dining room. Taking a sip from her coffee cup, Liza scanned the front page of the *London Times*, then turned to the business sections and began to read closely. I'll be on these pages soon myself, she thought with a smile. I wonder what headline they'll use. LIZA CARLISLE NAMED TO HEAD WARREN INTERNATIONAL. Or maybe DAUGHTER TOPPLES MOTHER IN HOTEL EMPIRE. That was more likely.

Mrs. Walker entered the dining room. "There's a telephone call for you, Miss Carlisle."

It was Bobby Hilliard, calling from Brussels. "Hey, Liza, how's it going?"

"Bobby, how great to hear from you." Liza wasn't in the mood to talk with him right now, but she had to be nice. After all, he'd bought all that Warren stock.

"Baby, when's that stuff going to happen that you kept talking about? The band and I are here at the Warren, but they're sure not treating me like I own the place. You said you'd be taking over and I could count on a good time."

Liza spoke reassuringly. "These things have to be done with care. Nothing moves that fast. You don't put a CD out overnight, right? But it won't be too much longer now, I promise."

They talked for a few minutes more before

Liza was able to get off the phone. Damn, she thought. Just what she needed, her stockholders breathing down her neck.

She walked back into the dining room and sat down. At least what she'd told Bobby was true. She was almost ready to make her move. It had taken her nearly six months to cement her relationships with most of Warren's directors, wooing each of them until she was certain she could count on their support when she went up against Claire. The process had been longer than she'd expected. Her campaign required endless dinners and weekend visits with them, all of which had to be done without her mother's knowledge. Ingratiating herself with these people wasn't the problem; it was taking time away from the demands of her job that had proven to be so difficult. She'd been working nonstop, developing another Manor near Oxford and researching the prospects for expanding Warren Hotels into Canada. There was still one more board member she had to work on before she had all twelve in her pocket. Two more dinners with Horace Parnham ought to do it, she decided.

Liza looked up to see her mother coming down the stairs.

"Good morning, darling," Claire said quietly, tightening the sash of her pale blue robe and sitting down at the table.

"I don't think I've ever seen you sleep this late," Liza said, glancing at her watch. "It's nearly eleven-thirty. You were really tired, weren't you?"

"We've been planning this trip for such a long time. I'm so sorry, but I don't think I'm up to it." Claire poured herself a cup of coffee from the sterling silver pot on the warming tray in front of her.

"That's all right, you're allowed to be sick once in a while. Paris will be there when your cold is gone," Liza replied brightly.

"I know, but I wanted to spend a few days alone with you, relaxing, doing some shopping"—Claire coughed and took a sip of water—"just enjoying some time together. We have so little of it."

Over a month before, Claire had suggested the two of them go to Paris for a few days. Their schedules were so busy, this was the first weekend both of them could arrange to take off. Liza had found the idea boring, but she managed to act suitably enthusiastic. Now, hearing her mother was too sick to go, she felt inwardly relieved. Her weekend would be free.

Claire reached for the cream, and Liza noticed a large bruise on the inside of her forearm. "What's that, Mother?"

"What?" Claire turned to her.

"On your arm. Did you hit yourself on something?"

Claire examined the bruise. "I guess I must have."

Liza looked carefully at her. Claire was pale, with deep circles under her eyes, despite the many hours she'd slept. "Maybe you should see a doctor. You don't seem well."

"Oh, it's nothing." Claire took a piece of toast and broke off a corner. She coughed again. "Well, my throat *is* dry, and I suspect I might have a fever. Maybe Dr. Gibson can give me an antibiotic or something. I'll give him a call right now."

Clive Gibson was an old friend of Claire's. Although he didn't normally keep Saturday hours, he was willing to see her at one o'clock that afternoon. Only moments after her mother had left for the doctor's office, Liza was on the telephone with Horace Parnham, making a date for dinner that night.

Claire returned an hour later.

"What happened?" Liza asked.

Her mother smiled tiredly. "Nothing much. He did some tests and said to get back into bed. I'm sure I'll be better by Monday."

But Claire wasn't better on Monday. Liza went into her mother's bedroom before leaving for the office and found Claire lying in bed, talking on the telephone. She waved Liza inside as she finished her conversation.

"Thank you, Clive. I want to discuss this with my daughter. I'll get right back to you." Hanging up, she rubbed her eyes and then gazed out the window as if unaware that anyone else was in the room.

Liza waited expectantly, but Claire didn't speak. "Mother, what is it? What did the doctor say?"

Slowly, Claire turned and focused on her daughter. "Sweetheart, we have to talk about something."

Liza sat down in a chair next to the bed. She watched Claire pull herself up to a sitting position; her mother seemed to be struggling.

"What's the matter?" Liza leaned forward.

"Dr. Gibson wants to do some more tests. I have to go into the hospital today."

Liza stared at her mother. Something really *was* wrong.

"While I'm gone, I'll be counting on you to take care of the business." Claire took Liza's hand. In the meantime, perhaps you would come with me while I check in. It would mean a lot to me."

Liza responded immediately. "Of course. Let me pack some things for you right now and call the office."

Claire smiled. "Thank you, darling."

"Excuse me."

Liza pressed up against the tiled wall, making room for a man in a wheelchair to pass in the narrow hospital corridor. Her mother had already been here two days, and Dr. Gibson had yet to tell Liza anything about Claire's condition. He had just stopped by again, this time bringing a second doctor. The two had been inside the room with Claire for over twenty minutes, the curtain draped for privacy around her bed. Liza paced impatiently back and forth just outside the door. Her head was pounding from the close air and antiseptic smell.

The physicians emerged from Claire's room and stopped to talk to Liza.

"Liza, this is Jules Stone," Dr. Gibson said. "He's a hematologist, a blood specialist. I asked him to step in on your mother's case."

"Why?" Liza turned to Dr. Stone, a pale man in his early forties. "What's the problem?"

His voice was soft. "Your mother has acute leukemia. I won't pretend that the prognosis is a good one, but we're doing all we can."

"What the hell does that mean?" Liza demanded.

He paused. "Why don't we sit down?"

The three of them walked down the hall to the visitors' lounge, where they pulled three chairs close together in the corner.

"In our bone marrow," Dr. Stone said, "we make white cells to fight infection, red cells to carry oxygen and platelets to help clot. Acute leukemia is a disease in which there's an unchecked proliferation of abnormal white blood cells. This crowds out the normal white cells, as well as the red cells and platelets, and limits the production of new, healthy cells. The onset of this type of leukemia tends to be sudden, and it runs its course very quickly."

Liza interrupted. "Runs its course? You're telling me it's fatal?"

Dr. Gibson frowned. "Well, there are courses of treatment that can help. We're starting your mother on chemotherapy immediately."

"That has terrible side effects, doesn't it?"

"It varies with the individual," said Dr. Stone. "But there's really no alternative here,

402

if you want your mother to have a chance. If she doesn't have the chemo, I guarantee you she won't live a month—if that long."

Liza felt as if she had been struck. "My God, I had no idea..." She took a deep breath. The doctors waited quietly. "Does my mother know?"

"Yes," Dr. Gibson replied. "We've discussed all this. She's agreed to the treatment."

Liza tried to collect her thoughts. "Is there anything else we could be doing? Aren't there operations? I read somewhere about this."

Dr. Stone gave her a sharp look. "You're talking about a bone marrow transplant. Yes, that can be done, but you have to have a donor who matches. And assuming you could find a donor, your mother is still not a perfect candidate."

Liza ignored his last comment. "But if we could find the right donor, it could be done in her case?"

"Finding that donor isn't a simple matter. A sister or brother would be the best match because they come from the same parents, meaning the same gene pool. Your mother was an only child."

"What about me?"

"A daughter is less likely to be suitable. We'd have to test you."

Dr. Gibson stood up. "This is not a decision to be made hastily. First, we have to see how your mother does on the chemo. Then we'll talk about bone marrow transplants. In the meantime, we'd better have you tested tomorrow so we don't waste any time."

Liza nodded her agreement.

"Fine. We can arrange it, but I'm not making any promises." Dr. Stone extended his hand. "I'm sorry the news wasn't better."

Dr. Gibson shook Liza's hand as well. "I imagine we'll be speaking in the near future."

Mrs. Walker had long since cleaned up after dinner and gone to bed. The house seemed cavernous tonight to Liza as she walked from room to room, unable to settle in any one spot. She kept going over the conversation she'd had with Claire's doctors that afternoon. A month. Her mother could be dead in a month.

All those plans, Liza thought. All the time I put into getting rid of her and taking away the company. And now she may die.

She wandered into the drawing room and looked out the window as she'd watched her mother do so often. It's funny, she reflected, this is much more of a revenge than anything I could have planned. So how come I'm not getting any satisfaction from it? She thought back over the year and a half since she'd come to stay in England, the countless hours she'd spent with Claire, traveling, working, talking. So many images came back to her: her mother's look of joy when Liza had first arrived in her office; the quiet sadness on Claire's face whenever Liza made plans to be away for any extended length of time; the pure pride Claire exhibited that day Liza had run the monthly Warren meeting.

Liza poured herself a glass of brandy. Up until now, the whole thing had seemed like a game. Suddenly, a picture of herself as a teenager flashed through her mind. She was back in Bennett's apartment with Ellen, watching as the housekeeper ironed, chiding her for some undone chore. She remembered how she felt when Ellen died. With a jolt, she realized it was only here in England that there was someone she really mattered to. Claire was the one person left who loved her. If her mother died, there would be nobody.

Overwhelmed, Liza sat down on the couch. Instead of trying to destroy her, she thought, I should have been trying to make up for the time we lost. Now I may end up with everything I wanted—and I'll be alone again.

It was a long time before Liza went to bed that night.

At the hospital the next morning, Liza was tested for her suitability as a bone marrow donor. When they'd finished drawing her blood samples, she headed straight for Claire's room. It was dim, despite the brightness of the day outside. Her mother seemed to be asleep, but she opened her eyes as soon as Liza approached the bed.

"Hello, Mother," Liza said, taking Claire's hand.

"Hello, darling."

Was her mother's voice even weaker than yesterday or was Liza only imagining it? "How are you feeling?"

"Did you speak with the doctor? Did he explain everything?" Claire asked anxiously.

"Yes." Liza crossed the room and pulled the blinds open. "Don't worry, we're going to do whatever it takes and make you well."

Her mother's smile was doubtful.

Liza pulled a chair over to the bedside. "Mother, don't you want me to call Page?"

Claire's response was immediate. "No. I've tried to patch things up with Page. She's made it clear she doesn't want any part of me."

"But this is serious. She'd want to know."

"Page would feel she has to come. I refuse to manipulate her that way."

"Mother, please consider what you're doing."

Claire closed her eyes. She remained silent for several minutes. Finally, she spoke.

"You know, Liza, many years ago I made a choice. Maybe it was the wrong choice. Certainly, I paid a price for it, and I seem to keep on paying. It's funny. I had Page, but I couldn't have you. Now, it's just the reverse. I seem doomed to share my life with only one daughter at a time." She adjusted the pillow behind her head, and took a slow, deep breath. "Now, sweetheart, if you wouldn't mind, I think I'd like to rest for a while."

Liza leaned over and kissed her mother's cool cheek. "I'll be back later when you feel up to having company again."

Leaving the room, Liza went to the visitors' lounge. She leafed through several magazines, but took in none of what was on the pages before her, her mind racing. Periodically, she would go back in and check on her mother, who continued to sleep. That afternoon, the doctors began the chemotherapy.

For the next three days, Liza spent all her time at the hospital with Claire, still waiting for the test results on her suitability as a transplant donor. Early Monday evening when Liza stepped into the corridor to stretch her legs, she spotted Dr. Stone reading a patient's chart near the nurse's station. She walked over immediately.

"Any word yet?" she asked.

"I was just coming to find you. The results came back late this afternoon." His eyes were sympathetic. "I'm sorry, Miss Carlisle; they indicate that you aren't a compatible donor for your mother. That rules out the transplant."

"Not necessarily," Liza replied. She looked around. "Is there a phone I can use on this floor?"

Simon rummaged through the bureau drawer. He was supposed to be at the Four Seasons at twelve-thirty, and it was already twenty past. Where were those damn keys? Page was always telling him to put them in one place, but he could never break the habit of dropping them haphazardly whenever he came into their apartment.

He was on his way to meet an interviewer who was notoriously tough, who loved exposing every little foible of the stars he wrote about. He'll probably take it out of my hide, Simon thought as he raced into the kitchen, scanning the surfaces. Still no keys. These extra few minutes would undoubtedly translate into a description of him as arrogant and conceited.

The telephone rang. Simon cursed under his breath. Christ, I'll never get out of here. He grabbed it.

"Yes?"

There was a crackling sound, and then silence for a moment.

"Is Page Warren there?"

"No, she's not." Simon spotted his keys on the counter next to the refrigerator and gratefully shoved them in his pocket. "Can I take a message for her?"

"Who am I speaking to?"

He wondered why he hadn't recognized the voice right away. "Liza? It's Simon." He frowned, his tone becoming sarcastic. "What can we do for you *this* time?"

"I need to talk to Page. It's urgent."

As Liza explained Claire's condition, Simon's expression turned to one of concern. He listened quietly while she discussed the possibility of a transplant.

"My blood's been tested, and I'm not a candidate," she concluded. "But Page might be."

He didn't respond immediately. "You know, Liza," he said finally, "I can't speak for Page, but there's something I want to say to you. You're asking a great deal from her. Not that she won't do it—I have no doubt she'll be on the first plane back. But you owe her something."

He waited. Liza said nothing.

"You deliberately hurt Page and her mother in every way you could. You've poisoned Claire's life and her relationship with Page. You tried to destroy Page's relationship with me, and you made it impossible for her to remain in London. Now you want her to walk back into it. Before you put Page through the hell of this illness, you need to make things right. To begin with, Claire should know the truth."

Liza's voice was unsteady, but she made no promises. "Please, Simon, just tell her."

She hung up.

It took Simon less than five minutes to cancel his interview and head for Page's office. She looked up in surprise when she saw him.

"I thought you were being skewered at the Four Seasons today."

Simon closed the door behind him. Curious, she waited for him to speak.

He didn't know how to tell her. There seemed to be no other way than to come right out with it. "Page, Liza just called. She says your mother is very sick. She's in the hospital with leukemia, and they need you."

Page appeared momentarily stunned, but the look on her face quickly became skeptical.

"Liza doesn't know when to stop, does she? It's incredible. Leukemia—could she have come up with anything more cruel?"

"You don't believe her?"

"Why should I?" Page was angry. "My mother was completely healthy. And Liza's never told the truth about anything in her life. I have no intention of being fooled by her again. I only wonder what she really wants."

Simon looked hard at her. "Liza said acute leukemia. Apparently, that comes on fast. And," he said, his tone measured, "it's over fast as well."

She stared at him.

"Page. What if she's telling the truth this time?"

Chapter Twenty-nine

It was winter in Madison. The large house, normally so well heated, was icy cold. Claire pulled her thin cardigan sweater close around her. There was no time to go back for warmer clothes: she had to get away. She reached out to open the front door, then froze.

"Claire. Come here."

She heard Bennett's voice, his footsteps on the staircase. Jumping back, terrified, she ran into the living room and hid behind an Oriental screen.

"I know you're here." Louder now, more insistent. "I know you're here!"

With a start, Claire woke up. Slowly, her eyes focused on the green walls, the metal railing of her hospital bed, the many vases of bright flowers around the room. She felt disoriented, confused. It took a few moments before she realized she'd been dreaming. How strange, she thought as she tried to calm herself. Over twenty years and I've never dreamed about Bennett before.

Feeling weak and nauseated from the chemotherapy, she turned her head toward the window. Perhaps a little sunshine would distract her. She didn't hear the door open, nor did she see Liza step into the room.

Liza stood, silent, unobserved. How thin and frail her mother was. She hadn't noticed how quickly Claire was losing weight. The alabaster skin had lost its luster, and her beautiful silver hair was thinning. The woman Liza had hated for so long was a controlling, invincible figure. The person before her now was only human—sick, vulnerable, visibly afraid.

Simon's words on the telephone yesterday echoed in Liza's mind. He was right, she admitted to herself. I *did* poison my mother's life. And for what? Was she ever the enemy I imagined? Liza felt consumed by a sense of loss.

Suddenly aware of her daughter's presence, Claire turned to her and smiled. Liza found herself coming to a decision. She couldn't make her mother better, but she could do what Simon had urged. She could try to repair the damage before it was too late.

"Hello, darling." Claire's voice was faint.

Liza approached the bed. "Mother, I have to tell you some things that are important for you to know."

"Is something wrong?" Claire noted her serious expression.

"How can I explain?" Liza began. "When I first came to England, I saw things differently from the way I do now. I made some choices I regret."

Claire looked confused, but waited for her daughter to go on. Liza chose her next words carefully.

"I wasn't honest with you when I told you about Simon and me. It wasn't an accident. We weren't swept away by some grand passion. I went to California specifically to see him, to get him to fall in love with me, to make him break up with Page."

Claire stared at her in disbelief. "What are you talking about?"

Liza pressed on. "I also wanted to hurt the business. The reporter who wrote that story about you in *The Empire*—that was my doing. I led her to Page. And I brought those American hotel developers here to make you think that Page was selling you out. It was no coincidence that you saw them in the restaurant that day."

"What on earth are you saying?" Claire asked incredulously. "You deliberately came between Page and Simon?" She gripped the railing on her bed and pulled herself up to a sitting position. The rest of Liza's words were starting to sink in. "You could have ruined my business. Why would you do that?"

Liza looked directly at her. "I hated you for leaving me. I hated Page for having you. I hated the way you loved each other."

"You've felt this way all the time you've been here?"

"I've felt this way all my life."

"Dear God," Claire breathed, falling back against the pillows. "I had no idea."

Liza could see her mother going over it all, fitting the pieces together. Claire's face slowly hardened in anger.

"How could you have tried to hurt me like this? To hurt Page?"

"I'm sorry, Mother."

Claire didn't even hear Liza's words. Her fury was growing. "You were so loving, so devoted. And all the time you were just making a fool of me. I should have known it was too good to be true."

"You have to try and understand." Watching her mother's eyes blaze, Liza couldn't stop herself from getting angry. "It wasn't that simple."

"You came here to destroy me." Claire enunciated each word slowly. "How could you have done it?"

Liza's words were an explosion. "No, Mother. How could *you* have done it! *How could you have left me?*"

The two women were shocked into silence.

Liza turned and left, letting the door swing shut behind her. Claire, stricken by her daughter's words, felt tears stinging her eyes. She was grateful when the door was pushed open again a few moments later; she and Liza would have another chance to talk things out.

"Hello, Mother." It was Page.

Claire caught her breath. "Oh, my baby," she cried, her tears spilling over.

Page tried to keep her face composed. She couldn't believe what she was seeing. Her mother looked twenty-five years older than the last time she'd seen her. It was obvious Liza had been telling the truth, although Page hadn't believed it until this moment. Claire was gravely ill.

"Mother, how are you?" Page asked, sitting down on the edge of the bed.

"I'm so happy you're here." As weak as she was, Claire's smile radiated joy.

"Of course I'm here. Did you think I wouldn't come?"

"I wouldn't have blamed you if you hadn't." Claire reached up to stroke Page's long hair. "Sweetheart, I'm so sorry. I didn't see what was happening right in front of me. Liza's just explained it to me—about the reporter, about Simon. It was my fault. All if it. Forgive me, honey. I love you."

Whatever bitterness Page had felt toward her mother melted. Putting her arms around Claire, Page was flooded with love and relief. She had waited such a long time.

Chapter Thirty

It looks just like blood, Claire thought, as she watched the liquid dripping slowly from the inverted plastic sack into the intravenous line that ran directly into a vein in her neck. She'd assumed bone marrow would look important, as if its appearance would somehow reflect its life-saving potential. And the process itself was painless, nothing more than being hooked up to an I.V. line for a couple of hours.

Dr. Stone had explained that Page's blood typing showed she was a single haplotype match—acceptable as a bone marrow donor for Claire, although not the ideal double haplotype match. Both he and Dr. Gibson held out little hope for the success of the transplant, but Page and Liza insisted they explore every possible means of treatment. Page was more than willing to undergo her part of the operation, being put under general anesthesia and having her bone marrow extracted—harvested, as the doctors called it.

Claire had been less enthusiastic about the procedure. She was aware that her chances were slim, and was reluctant to have Page go through the pain and possible side effects of the extraction. But her daughters seemed united in their determination that the doctors give it a try. It was about the only thing they *were* united in, she thought. In the past three weeks, Page and Liza had barely exchanged a word with one another, and they were careful never to let their visits with Claire overlap.

She coughed, and closed her eyes tiredly, letting her mind wander. How much both of them have changed, she reflected. Liza's caring was genuine now, such a contrast to the past sweetness that now seemed so obviously false. After their bitter confrontation that day, Claire had spent a sleepless night imagining what the past twenty-five years had been like for Liza. Left by her mother without explanation, having Bennett as her only parent, finding out that her younger sister was living happily under Claire's loving protection. And never having the slightest clue that her mother desperately wanted her. No one to love, no one to love her back. Of course Liza had grown up wanting revenge. Could she have turned out any other way?

When Liza had come back to the hospital the following afternoon, Claire was greatly relieved. They talked quietly, reviewing business decisions that needed to be made during Claire's absence from the office. Neither one of them referred to the accusations of the day before.

When Liza got up to leave, she turned to Claire, and said softly, "Mother, we can't undo the past. I love you. You did what you had to do. I did what I had to. It's not important anymore."

How precious her time with Liza had become since then, Claire reflected, feeling a momentary twinge where the I.V. needle met her skin. She turned her head slightly, alleviating the pressure. Her thoughts moved to Page. Her younger daughter had become so sophisticated and self-assured, all traces gone now of the insecure girl she once was.

There's so much of me in my daughters, she thought. Her bold, passionate side, which had driven her to leave her marriage and give up her life in Madison, was plainly visible in Liza. Page's transformation echoed her own from a timid young woman to an ambitious, successful executive. She was so proud of both of them. But would they ever be able to share their lives with one another, she wondered, to understand how much stronger they would be together?

The plastic sack was almost empty now. For the first time since she'd heard Dr. Gibson say the word *leukemia* out loud, Claire permitted herself to feel hope.

Liza and Page sat next to each other uneasily. Claire knew they resented being made to show up in the same room at the same time, but she had insisted. She felt it was crucial that she speak to them together. In the week following the transplant, she had felt surprisingly well, even regaining some of the strength her illness had so rapidly drained from her. Then, she was frightened when she lost the feeling of well-being just as quickly as it had come. She had grown steadily weaker until even talking had become an effort. Some days were better than others. Today, merely staying awake was a battle. The doctors had mumbled something about infection, but she found herself too tired to question them. Maybe it was the new drugs they had put her on.

There was one thing that had to be done, however, no matter how difficult it was for her to concentrate. Claire looked at her daughters, sitting there in stony silence.

She forced herself to smile. "I wish I could tell you that if I had my life to live over again, I'd know exactly what to do," she said slowly. Liza and Page leaned forward, straining to hear her. "Was there some way I could have kept both of you from being hurt? The truth is, I still don't have the answers." She found herself out of breath. Neither daughter spoke as they waited for her to continue.

"No amount of saying I'm sorry will make any difference now. But the future is up to you. I want you to know that my will divides everything evenly between the two of you." She looked at Liza. "It always has."

Tears stung Liza's eyes. "Please, Mother, there's no need to talk about this. You're going to be fine."

Claire felt herself sinking, drifting off into sleep. She summoned all her will to remain alert. "You have a choice," she whispered. "You can go your separate ways, angry, not speaking, perpetuating my mistakes. Or you can make your peace with the past."

There was a pause. "When you were little girls..." Her voice was barely audible, her eyes half-closed …playing together all day long…you were so close…you don't know what it does to a mother to see her children the way you are now—hurting each other."

Page broke in tearfully, unable to bear the sight of Claire struggling so desperately. "Mother, you should sleep now."

But Claire couldn't give in to her exhaustion until she'd finished. "All I want before I die is to see the two of you together again…sisters."

Liza and Page waited. Their mother was quiet, appearing to be asleep. Suddenly, she opened her eyes. She seemed to be looking right through them.

"Mommy," Claire said, "you look so pretty. Are you going out tonight?"

Liza gasped. She and Page turned to one another, horror on both their faces.

Claire went on, smiling. "Promise to wake me up when you come home, okay?"

Page buried her face in her hands, as Liza went over to the bed and gently touched Claire's arm. She started to speak. But there was nothing to say.

Page and Liza sat with Claire in silence for nearly an hour. It was only when her breathing became shallow that they spoke.

"I think we'd better get someone," Page whispered.

Liza hurried out of the room, stopping the first nurse she saw. "We need Dr. Gibson right away," she said, alarm in her voice.

It took ten minutes to locate Dr. Gibson, and

another five before he was able to get there. After a quick look at Claire, he instructed Page and Liza to wait for him outside. From where they stood in the lounge, they could see nurses rushing in and out.

Moving closer to the doorway, Page saw Dr. Stone coming down the corridor, still pulling off his trenchcoat as he hurried into Claire's room. Page turned to Liza, who had come to stand next to her, as she, too, saw the hematologist arrive.

"It's bad, isn't it?" Page said, frightened.

"Yes," Liza nodded. "I think it must be."

The door to Claire's room finally opened, and Dr. Gibson stepped into the hallway. Watching how slowly he closed the door behind him, they each instinctively hesitated, not wanting to hear the words.

He saw them, and almost imperceptibly squared his shoulders before walking over.

His voice was soft. "I'm sorry."

Chapter Thirty-one

Page was reaching for her cup of tea, a pile of papers balanced in her lap, when Liza entered the study and sat down. The two acknowledged each other with a nod, but exchanged no words. Liza picked up one of the many files on the large oak desk and began reading through it.

Distracted by her sister's arrival, Page rubbed her eyes tiredly and looked around her. Claire's study was a small room, warm and inviting, artfully decorated in rich, red tones. Bookcases and antique wooden filing cabinets lined the walls. While their mother had been alive, neither daughter had spent much time here. Claire had always seemed to prefer it that way, keeping this room as a sort of sanctuary for herself. Now her daughters faced the task of dismantling it, sorting through the many drawers, cabinets, and files—the accumulation of an entire life's work. They agreed that it was best to deal with it all as quickly as possible, although Page had initially hesitated about having Liza involved, wondering if she would use the opportunity to cause further trouble, somehow taking advantage of whatever they might learn in the course of going through the papers. But she realized that she was out of Liza's reach now. There was no longer anything her sister could do to hurt her. There had even been that odd shared moment of satisfaction the day before when Liza had handed Page the *International Herald Tribune*. There, marked by Liza in red, was news of their father's indictment for conspiracy and fraud. The two had exchanged a nod of understanding, but said nothing. There wasn't anything to say.

Page studied Liza, bent over the desk, absorbed in her task, her long, dark hair falling loose and nearly covering her face. As it turned out, far from exhibiting the deviousness

Page had come to expect, Liza had proven to be absolutely straightforward in handling this job. She had worked steadily, sorting and labeling. Most of what they came across concerned the business, but there were also papers relating to Claire's personal life. It was only when Liza uncovered these reminders, the private notes and mementos, that Page saw her falter. Liza would cry quietly, seemingly unaware of Page's presence, unable to continue for a few minutes.

Page, too, had cried often in these past two days as she struggled with her mother's death. She found some comfort in the knowledge that she and Claire had reconciled before it was too late. She also had the memories of a lifetime together to bring her some solace. But Liza's tears were of a different kind. Her stricken face spoke of some greater remorse; her weeping was full of an anguish that pierced even Page's heart. As wary as ever of her sister, Page nonetheless had to admit that no one could pretend such grief. And she knew Liza's sorrow came from a different source altogether than hers did. Mourning for what might have been, Page realized, must be the cruelest of punishments.

Liza, glancing at her watch, put the papers aside and turned to her sister.

"I'd better get going. There are still some decisions to be made for the funeral. Let me find out the details, and we can go over it tonight."

"Everything you've chosen so far has been perfect," replied Page truthfully. She paused, wondering if she should add what was on her mind or if she was opening herself up to trouble. Well, it was only fair to admit it. "You know, Liza, I realize you've been handling most of the funeral arrangements, and then making sure I agree with your decisions. I want to tell you I appreciate it. You've taken the hard part off my shoulders, yet still managed to include me."

Liza smiled. "Thank you for saying that."

"So don't let me hold things up. Just let me know what to expect. If I have a serious problem with anything, I'll tell you." Page twisted in her chair, trying to relieve the tension in her back from sitting for so many hours. "Meanwhile, I'm going over to the hospital. They called this morning and said we have to collect Mother's belongings."

Liza winced. "Thanks. I think I'd have a tough time with that."

They left the house together. Liza preferred to walk and started down the street alone. Page followed her retreating figure with her eyes, as Mr. James, the chauffeur Claire had hired to replace Chris after he left for New York, opened the Bentley's door for her. She got in, feeling very small and alone in the large car. Observing the older man seated in front, it was impossible to keep from envisioning Chris there, craning his neck to joke with her or give her a hard time about something. How much she and Chris had gone through since those days. Everything was different now, she reflected. Everything.

In front of the hospital, Page ran into Dr. Gibson. She thanked him for all he had done to help Claire.

He shook his head regretfully. "I was very fond of your mother. It just wasn't within our power to save her."

"I know that," Page replied politely. "Everyone did what they could." There was nothing left to say but the usual platitudes.

He smiled. "You know, your mother was very lucky to have two such devoted daughters. I heard how you came to London right away, and, of course, your willingness to undergo the transplant.... And Liza was wonderful."

Startled, Page only nodded, as if in agreement. Other than when it was unavoidable, Liza had made sure never to be around when Page was visiting, so she had no idea how much time her sister had spent with Claire.

"She was incredible," he continued. "Before you arrived, she was on duty twenty-four hours a day—well, until we threw her out. Never left your mother for a minute. She was relentless, trying to find out how we could improve the treatment, pursuing that transplant. If I had a child, I'd want her to do the same for me. I sometimes felt she kept Claire going through the sheer force of her will. Please give her my condolences."

A surprised Page told him she would be glad to pass on the message. They shook hands, and she headed inside.

Liza strolled along the Thames on Cheyne Walk, relieved to be finished with her appointment and out in the open air. She was finding it hard to concentrate, to make even the simplest decisions. Not that she should find the planning of the funeral so difficult, she chided herself. Her months at Warren International had taught her how to juggle far more details at once than this required. A tear slid down her cheek. Not again, she thought. She must have cried enough in the last two days to last a lifetime.

She sat down on a low bench facing out over the river, enveloped in her grief. Why did my mother have to be dying before I could let her love me? Liza asked herself for the hundredth time. But, as always, no answer came.

She closed her eyes, remembering once again the day she first arrived at Warren headquarters, coming face to face with her mother and sister. She could see the joy on Claire's face when she realized it was actually her long-lost daughter standing before her. Page had been so stunned, finding out that her old boarding-school classmate was actually her older sister, back to settle the score. Liza had gotten great pleasure out of Page's confusion that day.

God, I was so damn smart, Liza thought bitterly. Why hadn't she been smart enough to realize that little Meredith couldn't have begun to understand what was going on in those years after their mother left Madison? Page had grown up as a stranger to her—not an enemy trying to do her out of anything. She had never even known that she had a sister. How could she possibly have pieced together the picture from her point of view?

Liza recalled how she used to imagine Page relishing her victory over her abandoned sister. It was painfully obvious now that Page was incapable of such an emotion, that she could never derive satisfaction by cheating someone else out of what was theirs. The type of deceit that required just wasn't a part of Page's makeup. Perhaps Claire and John had instilled that honesty in her, anxious to make up for their own guilty secrets. Or perhaps it had always been her nature. Liza almost smiled, thinking of the contrast between her sister and herself. Hard to believe they were sisters when you looked at it that way, she mused. But they were. She bit her lower lip. Page was the only family she had now who meant anything to her. And after this was over, she'd never see her again.

Liza got up and continued to walk.

Page and Liza didn't cross paths again until the following day, when they met in their mother's office at Warren headquarters just before one o'clock. They had an appointment with Claire's personal lawyer, Frederick Wynn, and Arthur Stevenson, Warren

426

International's chief financial officer. Claire's life and her work were almost synonymous, so the purpose of today's meeting was to go over the details of her estate as they related to the business.

The two men hadn't arrived yet. Restless, Page began walking slowly around the room, unable to stop herself from looking over Claire's belongings and letting the flood of memories in. It was sad, yet somehow comforting, to be there among her mother's things, untouched since she had first gotten sick nearly two months before. Page stopped as she came to the antique partner's desk, Claire's prized possession.

"Liza," she began tentatively, "I know we haven't dealt with actually dividing Mother's things, but I would very much like to have this desk. Mother and John shared it, and that has a special significance to me. It would mean a lot if I could take it back to share with Chris at our office."

Expecting Liza would resist her as a matter of course, Page halfheartedly waited for the response. But Liza merely nodded. "Of course, Page, that's fine. We can ship it to New York right away."

"Well, I'll try to make it up to you when we go over the rest of her things," Page said. "I know this is a valuable piece, and you're entitled to—"

Liza waved her hand to dismiss the notion. "Don't worry about that. Please take the desk. You and Chris enjoy it."

Page said little else until the meeting began, thrown off balance by her sister's newfound generosity. Far more amazing to her, however, was what came next. Arthur Stevenson provided both of them with financial statements and extensive backup information providing a complete analysis of Warren International's financial situation. Having been away for so long, Page asked a great many questions until she was brought completely up-to-date. The conclusion was inescapable.

Putting aside Claire's own decisions and investments, Liza herself had done a superlative job. She had overseen the completion of a new Warren Hotel in Edinburgh, as well as the refurbishing of the Paris Warren. There was the conversion of two estates into new Warren Manors as well. She had also taken charge of purchasing a site for a new hotel in Amsterdam. Examining the feasibility studies and the financing arrangements, Page saw it was an excellent move, carefully planned and executed. Every area with which Liza had become involved was running smoothly and profitably. Whatever Liza may have had in mind when she came to England, she had wound up a sharp businesswoman with a firm grasp on the hotel industry.

There was no need for Liza to review the documents; she was completely familiar with them. Instead, she sat quietly, watching Page question the two men about what had gone on in her absence. It seemed like an eternity had passed since Page had been in those offices, talking about the company, analyzing the problems, hashing out solutions. Page's eyes flashed brightly as she was involuntarily caught up in the old excitement. It was partly her great love for Warren International that had made her such an easy target, Liza mused. How shocked Page had been that Claire could even suspect her of selling out to those American hotel developers. And with good reason. If anyone other than Liza had suggested that Page was betraying the company, Claire would have fired them on the spot, knowing such a thing was impossible.

No longer listening to the conversation going on around her, Liza crossed over to look out the window. Yes, she had maneuvered things so that Page would walk away from the business, Liza thought. But the simple truth was that she had stolen it from her. Their mother had trained Page, groomed her for years, to take over Warren International. That's how it was meant to be.

When Liza knocked on her bedroom door later that evening, Page was on the telephone. Still talking, she opened the door and gestured for Liza to come in, surprised to see her. Page couldn't remember the last time Liza had come up to talk with her. Even during these last few days, most of their conversations had taken place in the more formal atmosphere of the living room or in Claire's study. Neutral territory, Page had thought. It was strange to see Liza, wearing a robe, sitting on Page's bed, one leg tucked up under her, as she waited for Page to finish her conversation.

"No, don't worry about me, I'll be fine. Talk to you tomorrow." Hanging up, Page ran her hands through her hair. "That was Chris."

"Is he coming for the funeral?"

"He wants to, but I told him they need him there, running the business. We can't both be gone at the same time. Besides, there's nothing he can do here, really."

"And Simon?" This was the first time either one of them had brought up his name. Page looked sharply at Liza, but read nothing in her face.

"No, he can't come. He's doing a new play on Broadway, and it's impossible for him to leave right now. It just opened two nights ago, as a matter of fact."

"I'm glad for him," Liza said simply. "But that's a shame for you."

"I'll be all right." Page was taken aback by Liza's apparently genuine concern.

"Well," Liza changed the subject, "that's not actually what I came in here to talk about." With one finger, she began tracing the paisley design of the quilt on the bed. Page waited.

"I want to discuss the business." Suddenly, she looked up. "I've enjoyed it tremendously. It gave me a challenge, a purpose, a lot of excitement. But we don't have to act as if there's any question which one of us is supposed to be Mother's successor. She wanted you to run Warren International, obviously, from the minute you left college and got into it with her."

A pain shot through Page at the memory of returning from New York to join her mother after John's death. That had been such a bittersweet time for Claire and her. She hurriedly pushed it out of her mind.

"What I'm trying to say," Liza went on, "is that it's time for you to come home to London and take over the business. And it's time for me to go back to New York and do whatever it is I'm going to do. Maybe I'll travel for a while until I decide what that is. But I should be leaving. And you should be stepping in."

"You're just going to bow out gracefully?" Page made no effort to hide her skepticism. "Despite what you may believe, Liza, I'm not a fool. I know you've been approached by the board about taking over. So you've got what you always wanted. Besides, it's very easy for you to pretend you can just hand Warren over to me."

"Come on, Page," Liza replied. "You did so much for the company. You even created a new division, and those Manors have made a fortune. Plus, you've had all this success with your own company in New York." She saw Page raise an eyebrow. "Did you think we hadn't heard about it over here? The point is, we both know the board would be happy to have you instead of me if I said no to the job."

"You'd say no, just like that? After everything you did to get to this point?"

Liza nodded. "Yes, I would. If I knew you were coming back to it."

Page searched Liza's face, but could find nothing to indicate that the offer was anything but real. Still, still...had her sister found one last way to hurt her? Liza knew how much the business meant to Page. Before she could stop herself, Page thought of all she had put into Warren International, of all she could still do with it. Excitement flooded her. Oh, to take it over, she thought, to really run it.

She stood up. "I'll let you know what I decide."

The minister's voice was deep and resonant. "In my father's house are many mansions. If it were not so, I would have told you. I go to prepare a place for you."

A bright sun shone above them, the day even warmer than usual for early May. Page, in a trim black suit, her eyes hidden behind dark sunglasses, looked up from the mahogany coffin to scan the sea of faces around her. So many people had come. Earlier that morning, hundreds of friends, acquaintances, and business associates had crowded the church for the service. And well over fifty people had come out to the cemetery. They stood there, hushed, listening to the minister's words. Her mother's life had been so full, so complicated, Page mused. It was such an odd combination of joy and sadness, public accomplishment mixed with private turmoil.

Page felt her knees tremble slightly. These past five days had been exhausting, and she'd barely slept at all the night before. The strain of keeping herself in control today was taking its toll. But she was determined not to break down.

She turned to look at the large headstone next to them, reading what was etched into it. *John Warren—Beloved Husband and Father.* He might not have been her biological father, but he was her real father, she saw that now, and as good a father as anyone could ever hope to have. If only she could see him again, talk to him once more. Forcing herself to turn away, she looked back down to the gleaming coffin with its brass handles. In a few minutes it would be over. She realized that her mother would be gone then in a way that was somehow more final than her actual dying.

"Yea, though I walk through the valley of the shadow of death, I will fear no evil. For thou art with me..."

Not knowing why, Page suddenly became aware of the birds chirping in the nearby trees. She gazed across the open grave at Liza. Her sister's skin appeared almost translucent against her black dress as she stood, unconsciously tugging at the white lace handkerchief she held. Their eyes met.

The faintest image flashed before Page. A little girl with a dark ponytail, wearing a navy sailor dress and clutching a large teddy bear. It was so distant a picture, gone almost as quickly as it had come. But Page knew what it was. Liza, her big sister, back when the two of them were children in the old house in Madison. How many other memories of their years together were locked away somewhere in her mind?

"...earth to earth, ashes to ashes, dust to dust; in sure and certain hope of the Resurrection unto eternal life." With the minister's concluding words, the coffin was slowly lowered into the ground. People began to leave, some stopping to murmur words of condolence before heading off to the rows of limousines that would drive them back into town. From where each of them stood, the two sisters watched the cars pulling away, until only the limousine that would take them back to the house remained. They were alone in the complete quiet.

Slowly, Liza walked around the gravesite to stand next to Page. "Have you made your decision?"

Page weighed her words carefully. "I've given this a great deal of thought. You know how I feel about the company. But the truth is, I also love my own company back in the States. That's something I helped build, and it means just as much to me in a different way. And..." She hesitated, then spoke softly. "Simon and I are getting married."

"Oh. Congratulations," Liza said.

"Thank you." Page acknowledged her sister's words with a nod. "We had planned to stay in New York, where I have my work and he has the theater."

"So you won't come back?"

"I have a whole life there now, Liza. And it's time I stopped walking in Mother's shadow. I *can't* come back. I don't want to. But you—you're a different story. You love the business just as much as I do. And there's no question that you're good at it. I'm telling you the truth—I hope you'll stay and take it over."

Liza looked at Page, but said nothing. Then, she turned away, staring off into the distance. "Do you think Mother would have been pleased with the funeral?"

"Yes," Page answered. "You did a good job."

There was a pause. Liza spoke again. "I guess we'll be saying good-bye soon."

Page took off her sunglasses and slowly folded them. "You know, Mother's birthday is about three months from now. I was thinking about coming back for it." They turned to face one another as Page continued. "It might be nice to spend some time here on that day. Perhaps you'd meet me, and we could visit her together."

"I'd like that," Liza said quietly.

The two of them exchanged a smile. Then they turned and walked toward the waiting car.